The Arkansas Regulators

Transatlantic Perspectives

Series Editors: Christoph Irmscher, Indiana University Bloomington, and Christof Mauch, Ludwig-Maximilians-Universität, München

While standard historical accounts are still structured around nation states, *Transatlantic Perspectives* provides a framework for the discussion of topics and issues such as knowledge transfer, migration, and mutual influence in politics, society, education, film, and literature. Committed to the presentation of European views on America as well as American views on Europe, *Transatlantic Perspectives* offers room for the publication of both primary texts and critical analyses. While the series puts the Atlantic World at center stage, it also aims to take global developments into account.

The Arkansas Regulators

Friedrich Gerstäcker

Translated and edited by
Charles Adams and Christoph Irmscher

berghahn
NEW YORK · OXFORD
www.berghahnbooks.com

Published in 2019 by
Berghahn Books
www.berghahnbooks.com

English-language edition
© 2019 Charles Adams and Christoph Irmscher

Originally published as
Die Regulatoren in Arkansas in 1846

Library of Congress Cataloging-in-Publication Data

Names: Gerstäcker, Friedrich, 1816–1872, author. | Adams, Charles Hansford, 1954–
translator, editor. | Irmscher, Christoph, translator, editor.
Title: The Arkansas Regulators / by Friedrich Gerstacker ; translated and edited by
Charles Adams and Christoph Irmscher.
Other titles: Regulatoren in Arkansas. English
Description: English-language edition. | New York: Berghahn Books, 2019. | Series:
Transatlantic Perspectives; volume 5 | Includes bibliographical references.
Identifiers: LCCN 2018049619 (print) | LCCN 2018054156 (ebook) | ISBN
9781789201383 (ebook) | ISBN 9781789201376 (hardback: alk. paper) | ISBN
9781789202120 (pbk.: alk. paper)
Subjects: LCSH: Pioneers—Arkansas—Fiction.
Classification: LCC PT1885.G7 (ebook) | LCC PT1885.G7 R413 2019 (print) |
DDC 833/.7—dc23
LC record available at https://lccn.loc.gov/2018049619

British Library Cataloguing in Publication Data

A catalogue record for this book is available from the British Library.

ISBN 978-1-78920-137-6 hardback
ISBN 978-1-78920-212-0 paperback
ISBN 978-1-78920-138-3 ebook

To Lauren and Rhonda

Figure 0.1. From *Les Brigands des prairies*, a partial French translation of *The Regulators*, by Bénédict-Henry Révoil, illustrated by E. Coppin. *Journal illustré des voyages et des voyageurs* (October 1858). The full translation appeared in 1874. Image courtesy of the translators.

Contents

Illustrations

Figures

Map

Acknowledgments

The Arkansas Regulators is the product of a friendship that began several decades ago in Bonn, Germany, a friendship that survived and flourished as we moved to, and lived in, different places across United States. The project first took shape in Fayetteville, Arkansas, and it was completed in Tampa, Florida, where Friedrich Gerstäcker never traveled, although we think he would have liked the Spanish moss and the mangroves and would have laid a longing eye on the alligators.

The translators want to thank their spouses, Rhonda Adams and Lauren Bernofsky, for their support and forbearance. This volume is dedicated to them, with all our love. We wish to express our appreciation for the dedicated team at Berghahn Books. Christof Mauch, our series editor, and Chris Chappell, senior editor at Berghahn Books, were models of editorial patience. Soyolmaa Lkhagvadorj, Elizabeth Martinez, and Ann DeVita shepherded our manuscript through the production process with care and professionalism. Two anonymous readers offered suggestions, which we gratefully incorporated. Thanks are due also to Tom Paradise for creating an outstanding map for this book and to the staff at Special Collections at the University of Arkansas, Fayetteville for their assistance. We are especially indebted to Zach Downey of the Lilly Library, Indiana University Bloomington, who prepared our images for publication and provided the cover photograph. Nathan Schmidt read through the entire manuscript, saving us from several embarrassments. Finally, Indiana University Bloomington and the University of South Florida provided welcome resources for travel. A grant-in-aid from the Vice Provost for Research at Indiana University Bloomington allowed us to include the illustrations.

Friedrich Gerstäcker was a passionate if not overly fastidious translator himself (more about that later in our introduction). Although we have not taken the same liberties with his text that he cheerfully took with the works of others, we like to think that he would have applauded our effort to make one of the most remarkable German-American adventure novels accessible to English-speaking readers.

Charles Adams and Christoph Irmscher
Tampa, Florida, and Bloomington, Indiana
November 2018

A Note about the Text

Die Regulatoren in Arkansas was originally written for the publisher Otto Wigand in Leipzig, who published the novel in three volumes in 1846. Wigand's publishing house was taken over by Hermann Costenoble, who re-published *Regulatoren* in a stereotyped edition in 1853, with new, stereotyped editions to follow from 1858 onward. In 1872, Costenoble began publishing Gerstäcker's *Collected Works* (*Gesammelte Schriften: Volks- und Familienausgabe*, in more than forty volumes!). For new editions of *Regulatoren*, Gerstäcker made slight edits, ranging from stylistic changes to historical updates. For example, the reference to the "wild" reputation of Texas in the preface to the first edition in 1873 yields to a more topical reference to California. The text used for this translation is, indeed, the 1873 version, the last one authorized by Gerstäcker himself. It was published as volume 7 of the *Gesammelte Schriften*. All later editions of the novel in German are unreliable. For an exhaustive comparison of earlier versions, see David Stäge and Thomas Ostwald, *Vergleichslesung "Regulatoren in Arkansas," Beiträge zur Friedrich-Gerstäcker-Forschung Nr. 8* (Braunschweig: Friedrich-Gerstäcker-Gesellschaft, 2011).

Gerstäcker's place names are often slightly inaccurate. In our translation, intended for a modern reader who wants to rediscover Gerstäcker, we have silently corrected his spellings, listing the original ones in our notes. This is also how place names appear in the original map included as the frontispiece of this volume. Gerstäcker sprinkles his German text with American phrases, from exclamations such as "good bye" to specific terms such as "circuit rider" or "state's evidence." Since the original effect of these insertions cannot be reproduced in an English translation, we document the first occurrence of each of these phrases in the endnotes. Subsequent occurrences of the same English phrase in Gerstäcker's original text are not indicated. The notes offer historical, biographical, and geographical contexts and explanations but are, of course, not meant to be exhaustive.

In his novel, Gerstäcker uses punctuation, italics, and sometimes unconventional grammar to replicate the rhythm and flow of conversation. We have followed him closely in this by, for example, retaining lowercase letters where correct usage would demand capital letters or by preserving commas where they are not required by modern standards. Most conspicuously, we have imitated, as much as possible, his idiosyncratic preference for dashes, rather than periods, in his renderings of exchanges between characters.

Abbreviations

FG   Friedrich Gerstäcker

RA   Friedrich Gerstäcker, *Die Regulatoren in Arkansas: Aus dem Waldleben Amerikas – erste Abteilung,* ed. Thomas Ostwald and Wolfgang Hochbruck (Braunschweig: Friedrich-Gerstäcker-Gesellschaft, 2004).

DWB   Jacob and Wilhelm Grimm, et al., *Das deutsche Wörterbuch,* 33 vols., 1854–1971. Available online at: http://woerterbuchnetz.de/cgi-bin/WBNetz/wbgui_py?sigle=DWB.

WS   Friedrich Gerstäcker [Frederick Gerstäcker], *Wild Sports in the Far West, Translated from the German* (Boston: Crosby, Nichols and Company, 1861).

Figure 0.2. Friedrich Gerstäcker. Undated carte-de-visite, unknown photographer. Collection of Charles Adams.

Introduction

It is no exaggeration to say that drama, role-play, and costumes accompanied Friedrich Wilhelm Christian Gerstäcker from the moment of his birth. The man whose life would be an extended performance, with the world for a stage, was born in Hamburg on 10 May 1816, as the first son of two opera singers. Indeed, his father, who died when Friedrich was only nine, was one of the most famous tenors of the day. From an early age, Gerstäcker was a restless soul. Apprenticed at fifteen by his widowed mother to a merchant in Kassel, Friedrich ran away from the position after two years, walking over a hundred miles back to his mother's home in Leipzig. At eighteen, inspired by his avid reading of Cooper and Scott, and especially by his love of *Robinson Crusoe,* he announced his firm intention to travel to exotic places, with America as his first destination. His mother, fearing that her quixotic son would have no way to support himself in the New World, managed to delay his departure by arranging for him to spend nearly three years on a farm in Saxony to study agriculture. He endured the tedium of farm life for as long as he could, and in 1837, just a few days shy of his twenty-first birthday, he left Bremerhaven for New York.[1]

From the start, his time in America was marked by adventure and relentless movement. Upon landing in New York, he opened a tobacco shop on Broadway with a man that he had met on board the ship, hoping in this way to earn some money to support his travels. The venture failed after just a few months, and Gerstäcker set out for the wilderness, alone. Traveling by steamboat, train, and barge, but mainly on foot, he first went north to Niagara Falls, and then back south, pausing in Cincinnati before walking from there into Arkansas.

Over the next four years, he spent about thirty months in Arkansas, including two extended periods in 1839–40 and 1841–42. Toward the end of his life, he would look back with genuine fondness for the state and its people: "Arkansas! There I lived the best years of my youth, if I can even say that I had a youth. There I felt free and independent for the first time. There in the wilderness I found a home more beautiful and magnificent than any I could have then imagined. For me, the word itself was magic."[2] He traveled extensively throughout the state, hunting for his food and lodging with settlers when he needed companionship and something more than venison to eat. Most of his time was spent in the northeastern portion of the state, between the Mississippi and the White Rivers, and in the area west of Little Rock near the Fourche La Fave River. The latter region provides the setting for *Die Regulatoren in Arkansas.*

Gerstäcker returned to Germany in 1843, and (as he later claimed) was shocked to learn that he had become a writer. Unbeknownst to him, his mother had been giving Friedrich's descriptions of his American adventures to the editor of a literary magazine, *Die Rosen,* which published several sections during their author's absence.[3] Gerstäcker embraced his accidental career with enthusiasm, producing his first book in 1844. *Streif- und Jagdzüge durch die Vereinigten Staaten Nord-Amerikas* ("Ramblings and Hunting Expeditions through the United States of North America," translated as *Wild Sports in the Far West* in 1854) was based closely on his American diaries, and focused on his adventures in Arkansas, including a tavern brawl in which Gerstäcker saw a man knifed to death and his near-fatal struggle with a bear in which his hunting companion was killed. This thrilling tale of the American wilderness sold well, encouraging the fledgling writer to try his hand at fiction based on his experiences. *Die Regulatoren in Arkansas* was published in 1846 in a three-volume edition that also became a success. His career was launched.

For the rest of his life, Gerstäcker followed a pattern of alternating periods of obsessive writing in Germany with extended journeys to faraway places. In 1849, he left his wife and young son for a three-year expedition that included stops in the California gold fields, South America, several Pacific islands, Java, and Australia. In 1860, he escaped yet again, now for two years, visiting various places in Latin America, and subsequent trips during the 1860s took him to Africa and back to North, Central, and South America. Gerstäcker married twice (his first wife died while he was on his way home from South America in 1862), and he had five children, but his heart and mind were permanently engaged elsewhere, roaming through prairies, tropical rainforests, and South American pampas.

In the spring of 1872, his baggage was already packed for yet another adventure—this time to China, Japan, and India—when, at 2 AM on 31 May, he died of a stroke in the arms of his second wife, Marie Louise. He had collapsed, appropriately, next to his desk, where he had been working on a new novel, *Am Orinoco* ("At the Orinoco").

Gerstäcker's Work

Gerstäcker is a difficult writer to categorize, so vast and varied is his *oeuvre.* Although he was not the first European to write about the American frontier in the nineteenth century, he did so more extensively and passionately than others. Whether in fiction, as in *Die Regulatoren,* or in his numerous accounts of his experiences in the New World, Gerstäcker offers a unique and trenchant commentary on many facets of American life west of the Appalachians, including slavery and race relations generally, the nature of American communities, the peculiarities of religious life and expression on the frontier, lawlessness and violence, and the tensions inherent in matters of gender and class in the volatile society beyond the settlements.

Like many of his generation in Europe, Gerstäcker's notions of the frontier and its inhabitants were largely shaped by his reading of James Fenimore Cooper's Leatherstocking novels, the first three of which had achieved remarkable popularity in German translations by the time Gerstäcker left for America.[4] Cooper's powerful images of the upright hunter and his noble Indian brothers living in simple freedom amidst the natural splendors of the American wilderness were eagerly embraced by Gerstäcker, whose imagination was fired by the writings of Goethe, Schiller, and Defoe, among others.[5] Moreover, an idealized image of America had been popularized by several German-speaking novelists of the 1820s and 30s. A particularly important contemporary and model was the Austrian novelist and journalist Karl Postl (1793–1864), better known under his *nom de plume* Charles Sealsfield. A former priest, Postl spent many years living in the United States, interrupted by longer stays in Paris or London or Switzerland, and eventually became an American citizen. Postl's extensive travels in the American South became the basis for his best-known novel, *Das Kajütenbuch oder Nationale Charakteristiken* (1841; "The Cabin Book, or National Characteristics"), a series of tales told to a group of wealthy Southerners in Natchez, Mississippi. More explicitly political than Gerstäcker,[6] Sealsfield combines his admiration for American democracy and freedom with atmospherically dense descriptions of the American "prairies" that must have resonated with Gerstäcker, as would have the story of the remorseful murderer and his botched hanging that is at the center of the best-known tale in *Kajütenbuch,* "Die Prairie am Jacinto" ("The Prairie near the San Jacinto River"). But whereas Sealsfield, despite his long exposure to America, writes about the southern landscapes from the perspective of the outsider—someone who wants to impart a lesson in American history and politics to his readers back home—Gerstäcker immerses himself fully in the world of his characters. Perhaps the principal source of interest in Gerstäcker's work is his effort, carried on in various ways throughout his literary career, to reconcile these early fantasies about the frontier, and about America generally, with his actual experience of the place and its people, ordinary people, that is. As indicated by the title of one of his relatively early works, *Wie ist es nun eigentlich in Amerika?* (1849; "What Is It Really Like in America?"), he understood that the purpose underlying much of his writing about the United States was to mediate for his German readers between the imaginative power of "Coopers reizende Erzählungen" ("Cooper's charming stories") and the real thing.[7]

This is certainly an important motive of his first published book, S*treif- und Jagdzüge durch die Vereinigten Staaten Nord-Amerikas.* Here, amidst the stirring accounts of bear hunts and other adventures, Gerstäcker bluntly relates the less attractive features of American life: the poverty and cultural deprivation of the isolated individuals or families living in the deep woods, the severe difficulties of carving a life from the sodden swamps and craggy highlands of Arkansas, and the crime and violence always haunting frontier society. A remarkable feature of this book is the author's willingness to portray himself as driven by an almost surreal urge to kill everything that does not manage to get up a tree or into a thicket in time: from foxes and deer to bears, whose meat he particularly relishes. "We were all bear-killers," exults Gerstäcker, looking back on the crazy, near-suicidal hunts in which he participated, including one which required them to enter a dark, seemingly endless cave in search of a bear with three cubs. He at first only wounded the bear who pursued them, and, when she finally died, had to be pulled out by means of a rope around her neck. No unpleasant detail is left out of Gerstäcker's narrative, proof that he had indeed experienced all he wrote about: how the young bear cubs' brains had to be bashed in so they would not make a sound and betray the men's presence; how their mother's spine had to be broken "so that the carcass might lay better across a horse"; or how the skin of a cougar the men, constantly hungry for more meat, killed a little later was so riddled with bullets "that it almost looked like a sieve."[8]

In Gerstäcker's world, companionship between man and beast is possible only after death. In one of the caves, they find the skeletons of a man and a bear "lying peaceably within three feet of each other."[9] The dead man's foot-steps were still visible in the moist earth, even though Gerstäcker concludes that his body must have lain there for several years. Masculine bravado goes only so far in the West. Gerstäcker is struck by the number of widows he finds in the swamps of Arkansas: women must, he decides, be better suited to the climate. For all his fascination with frontier life, he has a clear sense of its limitations as well, and even as his English improves, he cannot shake the feeling that he comes from a superior culture: "The Americans in general," he writes, "have little feeling for German music; they are a people who live in a hurry, and everything must go fast, even music; when they hear any which has not the time of a reel or a hornpipe, they say they do not understand it."[10] His first two novels, *Die Regulatoren in Arkansas* (1846) and *Die Flußpiraten des Mississippi* (1848; "River Pirates of the Mississippi") give fictional form to the same commitment to render the wild side of the antebellum West.

These books also suggest that Gerstäcker had read Cooper more carefully than those Europeans who regarded the American writer mainly as a purveyor of "charming stories." A gothic world of lawlessness and terror haunts all of Cooper's tales of liminal societies, particularly *The Prairie* (1827), the climactic tragedy of the Leatherstocking series, and the one that most evidently influenced Gerstäcker. In Gerstäcker's hands, this mood is deepened and darkened into a portrait of a world where virtue is a relative thing and survival becomes the principal goal of both the good and the bad. Those who last in the wilderness do so not because of divine providence but because they have managed to avoid making stupid mistakes. In a crucial scene in *Wild Sports*, a bear finally exacts his revenge on Gerstäcker and his companion Erskwine, who rashly attacks the furious animal armed only with a knife, an error for which he pays with his life. Gerstäcker's later tales and sketches of American life—whether of the Mississippi and the Ozarks, or, subsequently, of the gold rush days in California—all illustrate with stern realism the point that Gerstäcker makes in "What Is It Really Like in America?": "If [the reader] finds many of my descriptions painted in less brilliant colors than those with which his imagination may have possibly misled him ... he should consider that America is not at all an ideal place, but rather a very materialistic and a very pragmatic land."[11]

As an unflinching observer of American customs, Gerstäcker continues to occupy an important place in the history of German popular culture, which has long been fascinated with a country Goethe famously thought "had it better" than the Old World.[12] There is no doubt that he influenced his prolific competitor, Balduin Möllhausen (1825–1905). Almost ten years younger than Gerstäcker, Möllhausen arrived in New York in 1850. He lived with the Ojibwe in the Great Lakes area, hunted in Illinois, and traveled west with Duke Paul of Württemberg, a naturalist and adventurer with a knack for getting them entangled in life-threatening situations. After becoming engaged to the mixed-race Pawnee Amalie Papin, Möllhausen returned to Berlin, where he became the protégé of the elderly Alexander von Humboldt. During a second stay in the US, he joined an expedition led by Lieutenant A. W. Whipple, which was intended to explore a route for the future transcontinental railroad. All of which is to say that in terms of adventurousness and personal derring-do, young Balduin was more than a match for Friedrich.

In terms of productivity, he would soon surpass him.[13] Möllhausen published his first novel, *Der Halbindianer* ("The Half-breed"), in 1861, fifteen years after Gerstäcker's *Regulatoren*. Over the next four decades, he went on to release one novel almost every year, returning again and again to his favorite theme, German–American relations. While he arguably never reached Möllhausen's level of insight into native cultures, as manifested not only in the latter's writings but also in his watercolor sketches of tribal life,[14] Gerstäcker's novels stand out for their rapt attention to ethnographic detail—the clothes, shoes, dishes, food, and other objects of everyday use. As Wolfgang Hochbruck has shown, Gerstäcker, a realist by inclination and necessity, inserted a new level of factuality into the familiar genre of the adventure novel, which he introduced to a German readership. He also reinvented it, moving the events he described from a mythic past invoked by his predecessor Cooper into the present, or at least a present pretty close to the reader's own experiences.[15] And thus he stirred adventure, anecdote, crime reportage, ethnography, and frontier humor into one powerfully addictive mix that lets the reader ignore the frequently careless writing, the repetitions (one does lose count of how many times his characters "laugh" at each other when they converse), as well as the long-winded nature descriptions. Incidentally, the latter are a hallmark of Möllhausen's writing too, and it is there that Gerstäcker's influence is most palpable. Like his model, the more romantically-inclined Möllhausen loves to invoke the play of light on the leaves of stately trees, the sounds their branches make when rocked by the wind, the many-fingered vines that lovingly loop themselves around them: "Solid as rocks they stood, the grey, partially wrapped tree trunks," he writes, in a passage that could have come straight out of Gerstäcker's *Regulatoren,* "as if equipped with unshakeable self-confidence their proud tops reached towards the glowing rays of the sun, while motionless hung from the patient branches of trees the wondrous vines."[16]

As the first German Western, *Die Regulatoren in Arkansas* stands at the head of one notable strand of German fiction, made famous worldwide later in the nineteenth century by the work of Karl May, who had never been to the United States when he fabricated his frontier tales. Indeed, it is impossible to imagine May's literary project without Gerstäcker's example; May borrowed liberally, and sometimes literally, from his predecessor, and the enduring German fascination with the American West can be traced directly back through May to Gerstäcker's writings.[17] Along with the work of May and Charles Sealsfield, Gerstäcker's rendering of America and Americans shaped German, and more broadly European, images of the US well into the twentieth century. Indeed, his eye for what mattered in American culture is illustrated by his remarkably prescient decision to translate Herman Melville's *Omoo* within months of its publication in 1847.

The Setting

Arkansas has had a complex and varied history, as unsettled as its name, the definitive pronunciation of which ("received by the French from the native Indians") was not settled before 1881, when both houses of the Arkansas legislature voted that it "should be pronounced in three syllables, with the final *s* silent, the *a* in each syllable with the Italian sound, and the accent on the first and last syllables." With more than a trace of annoyance, the legislators added: "the pronunciation with the accent on the second syllable, with sound of *a* as in man, and the sounding of the terminal *s*, is an innovation to be discouraged." And innovations were indeed not often welcomed during the early history of a territory that had to brawl its way into statehood, in the words of one of its most astute historians, the poet John Gould Fletcher (1886–1950), born in Little Rock.[18] The debate over the correct pronunciation reflects the uncertainties surrounding the state's genesis. One of the first Europeans to visit it, in the mid-sixteenth century, was the Spanish explorer Hernando de Soto. But it was French explorers who created the first permanent white settlement, the Poste aux Arkansas or Arkansas Post, in the late 1600s, adding a French twist (the silent *s*) to what is believed to be an Algonquian word for some of the area's original inhabitants, the Quapaw.

Arkansas became part of the United States through the Louisiana Purchase in 1803, emerging as a separate entity—the Arkansas Territory—in 1819. Much political maneuvering had to take place before the state's boundaries could be definitively established, with some of the wrangling still going on after Andrew Jackson, on 15 June 1836, signed the bill that made Arkansas the 25th state of the nation. Then, as now, the territory of Arkansas is bordered by the state of Missouri to the north, the prairies of Oklahoma and Texas to the west, the pine forests of Louisiana to the south, and the states of Tennessee and Mississippi to the east, with the shifting Mississippi River serving as an unreliable dividing line. As if to resist the flux and volatility suggested by its beginnings and uncertain borders, Arkansas culture, for the longest time, remained resistant to outside influences. Even as the cotton industry and chattel slavery of its southern neighbors spilled into its lowland regions, the mountain culture of the northwest, marked by the Ozarks and the Ouachita Mountains, continued to dominate the image of the average Arkansan for much of the nineteenth century and beyond. As Fletcher pointed out, well into the twentieth century the prototypical Arkansas resident was "far more likely to be a frontier settler in a coonskin cap, blanket cape, and buckskin trousers—or its modern equivalent of blue denim jumper, checkered shirt, blue overalls, and greasy black hat—than a planter in a broadcloth coat, satin vest, and ruffled shirt."[19] Self-sufficient to a fault, Arkansans were known for grinding their own corn, making their own clothes, building their own log cabins, whittling their own furniture, and, last but not least, distilling their own whiskey.

As Gerstäcker's narrator notes, the "city folks in New York" seemed far away to a settler on the banks of the Fourche La Fave: "let each region establish its own laws, and they will fit" (p. 135). In the absence of a strong and effective government, residents preferred to settle their own disputes, wrestling, gouging, pummeling, and kicking their way to the justice they felt they deserved. Many controversies were settled not by the courts but by the famous "Arkansas toothpick," the Bowie knife residents carried strapped to their belts (p. 24). In the backwoods, "Judge Lynch" rather than the courts prevailed—a nod to the famed Virginia planter and his improvised, rough method of dealing with suspected British loyalists, which included a swift trial by a hastily assembled court and a variety of quickly administered punishments, ranging from enforced oaths of allegiance to whipping or, certainly in the case of Arkansas vigilantism, hangings.

Friedrich Gerstäcker lived in Arkansas precisely during what Fletcher called the "dueling, knifing, brawling period" of the state's history, entering a world that was markedly different from that known to his artistic parents in Germany.[20] One of the most remarkable aspects of *Regulatoren* is the evident regard Gerstäcker has for the local vigilante movement. It is important to remember that during the months he spent in Arkansas, he fully participated in the lives of his new friends and neighbors. He did not share, as Robert Cochran has pointed out, the reservations of prior visitors such as Henry Rowe Schoolcraft, who were shocked by the rough manners of the Arkansans and would complain about everything from the absence of proper gardens to the inhabitants' "contempt of labor and hospitality."[21] Gerstäcker was twenty-one when he arrived in Arkansas. A survivalist equipped with better than average hunting skills, he, like his neighbors, had little patience for the emerging bourgeoisie in the state's new capital of Little Rock. His anti-authoritarian streak—fueled no doubt by the dismal political situation in his home country, divided into small chunks of land ruled over by greedy aristocrats—found ample affirmation in his daily encounters with Arkansas frontiersmen. Like the settlers he met, he lived off the land, eating meat when the hunt had been good or sucking on sassafras leaves and ingesting acorns when nothing else was available.[22] His descriptions of the trees in the Arkansas forests—the oaks, mulberries, papaws, cypresses, and pines—come from the pen of someone who has eaten their fruits, felled their trunks, or rested in their shade, someone who was not merely a visitor but, in the true sense of the word, an inhabitant. In 1835, the population of Arkansas had barely reached 52,000; by 1840, it had nearly doubled. *Regulatoren* recreates the intensity of these first crucial years after statehood when new settlers streamed into the new territory. What Gerstäcker's book captures, like few other documents from this period, are the twists and turns of fate that helped clarify who was suited for life in the woodlands and who was not. At the end of the novel, the punishments meted out to horse thieves, murderers, and liars seem less relevant than the community feeling proper residents gain from hunting down those, who, by their own behavior, have shown that they do not belong.

Die Regulatoren: Adventure Novel, Ethnography, Morality Tale

Gerstäcker's novel is set in the 1830s, in the area drained by the Fourche La Fave River, a tributary of the Arkansas flowing through modern Yell and Perry Counties, about 50 miles west-northwest of Little Rock. The plot turns on the conflict between a band of horse thieves and a group of vigilantes, "The Regulators," determined to impose their improvised justice on a frontier from which formal law is absent. As Gerstäcker explains in the preface, his descriptions are loosely based on historical events, and he claims to have witnessed instances of vigilante justice during his time in Arkansas. The Regulators are portrayed sympathetically, more or less; their justice is crude and their punishments brutal, but their actions are represented as a necessary evil if the lives and property of this primitive society are to be protected.

The hero of the story is a Regulator named Brown, the embodiment of the nineteenth-century romantic hero, both in his stalwart commitment to bringing order and a rough justice to the settlement and in his eventual marriage to the heroine of the piece. But there are also two more unexpected characters in the novel—the villain of the drama, a particularly devious and brutal man named Rowson, and the Indian who plays a pivotal role in bringing him to justice, Assowaum, or the "Feathered Arrow."

Until he is exposed toward the end of the novel, Rowson has a public face as that of a pious Methodist minister, well respected by the members of his flock, and disliked for his tedious zealotry by the less devout denizens of the Fourche La Fave. Alternating between casting out devils at boisterous prayer meetings and rustling horses under cover of darkness from his fellow worshippers, he even manages to become engaged to the novel's heroine before his double life is exposed. Lest we forget the source of his villainy, Gerstäcker's favorite designation for him is simply "the Methodist." Rowson's undoing is his brutal murder of Assowaum's wife, Alapaha, after she accidentally discovers that he is the horse thieves' ringleader. The Indian—openly lamenting the loss of his lands, his people, and now his wife, all a result of the white man's coming—patiently determines the identity of his wife's killer and exposes him to the white community, asking only that he be allowed to exact justice on Rowson apart from the beatings and lynchings suffered by the rest of Rowson's band. In a powerfully rendered scene of horrific (and avowedly non-Christian) revenge, Assowaum burns a bound Rowson alive in the very hut where he murdered Alapaha.

As even this summary suggests, the novel draws from several traditions in early nineteenth-century literature, especially the gothic novel, the sentimental romance, as well as the adventure novel. Moreover, several scenes throughout the book incorporate elements of the tall tale "Southwestern humor" tradition, and it contains as well many vivid "local color" descriptions of the manners and conditions of the people of early Arkansas. The themes are richly textured and varied: for instance, Assowaum's sympathetically rendered blood vengeance gives a startling twist to Cooper's (and others') sentimental concern for the vanquished Indian, and Rowson's life of lies demonstrates a degree of authorial hostility toward frontier piety unusual (though not unique) for the literature of this period.[23] Assowaum is a composite of different stereotypes associated with Native Americans—the strong, moody brave holding onto the shreds of his disappearing world—and his tribal origins remain murky. The Indian phrases Gerstäcker inserted into his text were likely invented and are not recognized by linguists as belonging to any known indigenous language.[24] At the same time, equipped with superior wilderness skills and unwaveringly committed to uncovering the truth, Assowaum does occupy the moral center of the novel. In his quest for the murderer of his wife he needs no gang of semi-lawless Regulators around him to accomplish his goal.

But this is not where the complexities end. Consider, for example, the obvious disconnect between Gerstäcker's heartfelt compassion for the Indians in his story and the virulent disdain for African Americans that pervades the text. When Gerstäcker describes blacks, he delves deep into the toxic lexicon of frontier racism, emphasizing their facial features, "scorched" hair, rolling eyes, and nodding heads. In Gerstäcker's narrative, they are mostly caricatures rather than characters, holding the reins of their master's horses or filling their food bowls and lighting their home fires, unless they, however unsuccessfully, attempt to aid and abet the horse thieves (chapter 26). To be sure, Gerstäcker was no friend of slavery and elsewhere wrote eloquently about the "horrors of the system." But that did not prevent him from also believing that the treatment of the slaves "was generally better than it is represented by the Abolitionists and missionaries," since it was, he pointed out, replicating an all-too-familiar argument, to the advantage of the owners to keep their slaves healthy.[25] Ultimately, human society interested Gerstäcker far less than the wilderness. While his characters throughout the book raise issues of law and/or justice on the frontier and debate the extra-legal measures of the Regulators, Gerstäcker makes clear that for him moral significance resides mostly in the natural world—by turns benign, menacing, and indifferent—which enables his story and which he explores with surprising subtlety.

As much as *Regulatoren* is about a certain group of people, it is also heavily invested in the world of things. Much time is spent on describing objects—what they are made of and how they are used. Of course, things—in the case of this novel, a button made of horn, a penknife, a neckerchief—carry special significance in detective stories, since they are potential clues. But it seems that Gerstäcker delights in describing them for their own sake, with an ethnographer's covetous zeal as well as a lover's eye. Sometimes things interest Gerstäcker more than individual people, who often, once they have been capriciously named (Cook, Hopper, Moos), again fade out of the narrative. And then there's the food, of course, the fresh meat, the wild turkey and honey, sweet potatoes, pumpkin mash, warm cornbread and sour pickles, the bowls of steaming coffee, and small bottles of whiskey greedily partaken of by settlers who don't take their survival for granted.

A startlingly progressive feature of *Regulatoren*, apart from the fervent critique of religious hypocrisy, is the emphasis Gerstäcker places on the role of female agency. Alapaha wounds Rowson, an act completed, more decisively, by Ellen, whose intervention saves Assowaum's life, as the "Feathered Arrow" himself admits. Since *Regulatoren* is at heart a detective novel, driven by the hunt for a murderer and thief, it is symbolically important that it is Mrs. Roberts who, after being prompted by Assowaum, unmasks Rowson in a key scene in chapter 33. The book's central clue, a horn button ripped from Rowson's coat by the dying Alapaha, is a piece of evidence procured by a woman for use by another woman. Thus, while the female characters are still frequently represented in ways that mark them as conventionally feminine (they are shy, timid, and tend to grow pale), their actions ultimately complicate that picture. By the same token, conventional masculinity often appears besieged in the novel: Assowaum's authority is challenged by Alapaha's conversion to Christianity, which sheds an interesting light on the brutality of the revenge enacted on a Christian minister, while other men—such as Roberts and Bahrens—lose themselves in tangents when they talk. Consider their random garrulousness during the ineffective siege of Rowson's cabin at the end of the novel, when the unarmed Roberts, making a ruckus outside the door, demands that he be let in. It does not seem altogether surprising, then, that the guardians of the Lynch Law are not the fierce avengers one would have expected: the one hanging they order is completed in their absence, and the most gruesome manifestation of frontier justice is carried out by Assowaum, who is not a member of their group. As Gerstäcker explains in *Die Flußpiraten des Mississippi*, the sequel to *Regulatoren* in which the action moves from the Fourche La Fave to the Mississippi, the Regulators' justice fails to deter wrongdoing. One of the perpetrators, Jones, insufficiently chastened by his flogging, unrepentantly continues his nefarious ways, while another one, Henry Cotton, escapes and subsequently murders two people.

In *Flußpiraten* Gerstäcker completes the cycle of justice, but only barely so: Jones is buried alive, though this is a case of mistaken identity rather than an act of deliberate punishment, and Cotton is presumed to be on the steamboat filled with fleeing river pirates that explodes at the end of the novel, though we are not in fact told that he is dead. And, quite unexpectedly, the mulatto Dan, after also escaping from the Regulators and continuing to assist Cotton in his misdeeds, shows up at the end of *Flußpiraten* all chastened and reformed, an obedient servant to one of the good guys in the novel, James Lively. Thus, alone among the gallery of criminals in both novels, a black man is ultimately found to be "ein recht wackerer Bursche" (quite a valiant fellow).[26] All of which further proves the point that there is more to Gerstäcker than meets the casual reader's eye.

The Translation

As the first German Western, and one of the very earliest European efforts to give fictional shape to the American frontier, *The Arkansas Regulators* deserves to be more readily available to English-speaking scholars and general readers. And as a seminal European response to Cooper and other writers of the American West, it offers an important perspective on early America that is effectively invisible to Anglophone audiences at this point. Readers with an interest in the history and literature of the lower Mississippi Valley, and the "Old Southwest" especially, ought to have access to this essential text.

However, the 1854 translation by Francis Johnson is extremely difficult to obtain. The text was published as *The Feathered Arrow, or, The Forest Rangers*, and WorldCat lists only eight copies of this volume, all of them housed in non-circulating library rare book collections. Portions of the Johnson translation were published under different titles. For instance, in 1857, the translation was broken into thirds and published serially by Dick & Fitzgerald of New York. Chapters one through twelve appeared as "The Regulators of Arkansas," while chapters thirteen through twenty-five were titled "Bill Johnson, or, The Outlaws of Arkansas." The final third, chapters twenty-six through thirty-nine, was dubbed "Rawson the Renegade, or, The Squatter's Revenge."[27]

The book was again published serially in thirds in New York in 1870, this time by Beadle & Co. The first portion was titled "Alapaha the Squaw, or, The Renegades of the Border"; the second part appeared as "The Border Bandits, or, The Horse Thief's Trail"; and the final installment, chapters twenty-six through thirty-nine, was named "Assowaum the Avenger, or, The Destroyer's

Doom." The baffling proliferation of titles is bad enough; the fact that these various portions of the book are accessible only by visiting one or more of a small handful of rare book rooms, or by obtaining microfilm or photocopies from these collections, means that none but the most determined will read it.[28]

More importantly, though, the Johnson translation is problematic in several respects. Some of these problems are relatively trivial, if annoying. For instance, the names of characters are changed frequently, and for no apparent reason except perhaps to Anglicize them: Gerstäcker's Rowson becomes Rawson, Heathcott becomes Heathcote, Bahrens becomes Barker, Pelter becomes Patton, Smeiers becomes Steele, and so on. Chapter titles are altered, sometimes dramatically. Worse, the language of the German original is regularly cleaned up and watered down, presumably to make it more palatable to a mid-nineteenth-century American readership. The changes may be at the level of individual words, as when the German "Schufte" is translated as "men," though a more accurate rendering would be "scoundrels" or "villains"—even "bastards" would not be too strong. Similarly, Rowson is at one point called a "soul-merchant" by one of his gang, but this was apparently too harsh for Johnson, who allowed the Methodist minister to be called merely a "horse thief" instead. But some such changes involve more extensive rewriting of the original, as when a bawdy and humorous anecdote about a stallion and some mares is reduced and recast almost beyond recognition.

Worst of all, the Johnson text commits the cardinal sin of translation—it silently excises several passages from the original, while occasionally actually adding text. Many of the eliminated passages are fascinating portraits of frontier life that Johnson, or an editor, apparently thought were too long-winded. Others feature "songs" sung by Assowaum, presented as poems that were perhaps considered too provocative; one is a song of vengeance fulfilled, which the Indian chants over the charred body of the Methodist. The few interpolated passages appear intended to explain aspects of the story to the reader, but no distinction is marked between Gerstäcker's original and the interpolated commentary. Whatever the motive, these silent deletions and additions, coupled with the "polite" translations deemed necessary by Johnson or his editor, underscore the need for a new and more faithful translation.

In the middle of the twentieth century, Earl Leroy Higgins (1896–1981), a history professor at the Arkansas State Teacher's College in Conway, became so enamored with Gerstäcker that he translated both *Regulatoren* and *Die Flußpiraten des Mississippi*. Higgins's translations were never published, though the typescripts may be found in the archives of the University of Central Arkansas. Higgins's version of *Regulatoren* has the great virtue of following the original text very closely. Arguably, it is too close. Seeking to mirror Gerstäcker's meandering and often unpredictable syntax, Higgins's prose becomes stilted and confusing. A number of simple translation errors and the inexplicably missing chapter titles do not improve matters. While Higgins's word choices are lexically correct, he had a knack for settling on the one option, among several plausible alternatives, that obliterates the humor and energy that fuels much of Gerstäcker's writing.[29]

Gerstäcker as Translator

Now, every translator of Gerstäcker must confront an important fact: that Gerstäcker was a translator too. Between 1844 and 1849, he frantically published translations of works by J. Tyrwhitt Brooks, Charles Fenno Hoffman, Seba (Elizabeth Oakes) Smith, and Charles Rowcroft. Most of these are perhaps mercifully forgotten today, with the exception of two works, one of outstanding literary merit, Herman Melville's South Seas tale *Omoo* (Gerstäcker's translation appeared in 1847, only months after the original), and the other of at least enduring literary notoriety, George Lippard's gothic novel *Quaker City, or the Monks of Monk Hall* (1845; translation, 1846).

Gerstäcker was an important and prolific mediator of American literature in Germany, offering his renditions of American writers "hot off the press," so to speak. As a translator, Gerstäcker was, well, Gerstäcker, and that is putting it mildly. In modern translation theory speak, he always came down in favor of "domesticating" the original, that is, he did what he could to transform it into an idiom and a form he thought German readers would recognize and that would also satisfy his own stylistic preferences as a writer. Good examples are the frequent passive constructions in *Omoo*, which are part and parcel of Melville's consistent attempts at concealing or obfuscating agency in the book, a strategy that reflects his narrator's often comical befuddlement. These passive constructions Gerstäcker typically transforms into active, assertive statements. Likewise, he combines or bundles Melville's short chapters to form longer sequences, a tribute presumably to the greater stamina of German readers brought up on a diet of Goethe and Jean Paul. In addition, he unabashedly poeticizes where he thinks Melville is too bland. See this example from the first chapter of *Omoo*: "The day was drawing to a close, and, as the land faded from my sight, I was all alive to the change in my condition."[30] This is not a complicated passage: it is getting dark, and as the island where Melville's hero, Tommo, was held captive vanishes into the distance, the narrator's mood also changes. If there's anything remarkable about Melville's writing in this passage, it is his use of the odd phrase "I was all alive to" where a simpler phrase such as "I became aware of" would have sufficed. But Melville's choice does make sense, given that Tommo thinks he has escaped certain slaughter by the skin of his teeth: "all alive" indicates his heightened state of consciousness as the fact of his own survival sinks in. In Gerstäcker's busy hands, this comparatively pedestrian passage turns into the following: "Der Tag näherte sich nun seinem Ende und das Land schwand mehr und mehr in blaue Ferne—träumend aber starrte ich auf die wogende See hinaus, die uns umgab." Rendered back into English, this "improved" sentence would read: "The day was drawing to a close and the land was fading more and more into the blue distance—in a reverie I stared out on the billowing sea that surrounded us."[31]

Melville's next sentence—"But how far short of our expectations is oftentimes the fulfillment of the most ardent hopes"—Gerstäcker changes completely, offering his readers the much-truncated: "Alle meine Wünsche waren erfüllt" ("All my wishes were fulfilled") perhaps because he disapproves of the rather intrusive, philosophizing comment in the original, which also (clumsily, he might have thought) anticipates more than it should, at least at such an early point in the narrative. Gerstäcker was no fool. Since he imagines Melville's novel from the inside out, as if it were a story *he* might be telling, Gerstäcker on occasion manages to be even more authentic and, in a dark sense, funnier than Melville. For example, when one of the sailors on board the *Julia* dies, the ship's doctor observes, "He's gone!" Gerstäcker has him say, "der ist fertig!" ("He is done for").[32]

Gerstäcker's version of the radical Philadelphia writer George Lippard's tremendously successful novel *Quaker City*, a combination of hard-hitting social exposé, satire, and sensationalist shlock, was not even identified as a translation. Publisher Wigand without further ado put the book out under Gerstäcker's name, an unforgivable offense even then. Gerstäcker claimed he was shocked by Wigand's act,[33] but the truth is that he had modified Lippard's original text so much that he could have legitimately claimed to have written the book himself. He does keep the novel's plot and satire and atmospheric details intact but cleverly manipulates its sensational and sexual references, for example by carefully re-orchestrating the (nearly) incestuous relationship between the depraved Father Pyne and his alleged daughter, the voluptuous yet innocent Mabel. Thus, when in Lippard's original Father Pyne sees before his watery eyes not Mabel but "a marble statue of an intellectual and voluptuous maiden, with all the outline and shape, which gives fascination to the face and form of beauty, without the warm hues, which tint the lips with love, and fire the cheek with passion," the same girl to Gerstäcker's Father Pyne merely appears as if in "einem süssen heiligen Traum" ("a holy sweet dream").[34] And while Lippard's lecherous minister, his flabby hand resting on his presumed daughter's bosom, asks her to kiss him, father and daughter in Gerstäcker tamely shake hands.

Why these radical changes? Not out of squeamishness, it seems. At the end of the same chapter, Father Pyne, to the reader's relief, goes on to disclose to "Devil-Bug" that Mabel is his daughter only in a "spiritual" sense, and it seems that Gerstäcker, experienced hand at novel-writing that he was, did not want to lose any of the more squeamish members of his audience en route to this important revelation. In a later chapter Mabel, under the influence of a drug expertly administered by the Reverend Pyne, responds to her alleged father's caresses, and here Gerstäcker proceeds to *add* details that Lippard did not include. This is Lippard's description (sufficiently nasty, one would think) of the kisses that the drugged-up "daughter" offers to her unholy "father": "She extended her arms and kissed his lips,—Faugh! Those lips were gross and sensual, though they *were* a Parson's lips! She kissed his lips again, and yet again."[35] But Gerstäcker turns up the heat even more: "sie streckte die Arme aus, und küsste seine Lippen—huh—in ekelhaftem Zittern begegneten ihrem Rosenmund die seinigen—geschwollen und zuckend—wenn es auch eines Pastors Lippen waren; —aber wiederum presste sie die ihrigen darauf, und wieder und wieder." Lippard never mentions any trembling ("Zittern") or twitching ("zuckend"), neither on the Parson's nor on Mabel's side, and the "ekelhaft" (nauseating) serves to horrify the reader even further, as does the "wieder und wieder." In the next few lines, Gerstäcker adds "schwammig" ("bloated") to Lippard's description of Pyne's face, and when the puffed-up parson, in Lippard's original text, gathers his arms "more closely" around Mabel's waist, the German equivalent in Gerstäcker's translation-novel goes a step further and "legte sein Antlitz liebkosend an ihren Busen" (i.e., he "rested his countenance caressingly against her bosom").[36] These are clear examples of the translator feeding "on the original for his own increase," in the words of George Steiner, of committing a "betrayal upward."[37]

When Gerstäcker translates, the writer he seems most beholden to is Gerstäcker. This sometimes improves the original; more frequently, though, from our modern point of view, it does not. This is not to minimize the importance of the cultural work his translations did. But it also helps us define what is at stake for us as we are translating Gerstäcker's own work today. In our translation, we have tried hard not to domesticate Gerstäcker by making him sound more American than he was. If Gerstäcker occasionally makes Melville's sailors sound as if they had spent time in Hamburg, we in turn did not want his Regulators to speak as though they had never left the wilds of Arkansas. But we also did not want to foreignize him more than is necessary, by making him sound like a German trying to speak English.[38]

Of course, translating a novel written by an American about his own experiences in the South Seas for readers in Jena or Leipzig is a quite different task from translating a German novel that is already set in America for an audience of American readers, even if it is written by a German. Unlike Karl May, Gerstäcker *had* in fact seen what he wrote about. So, the challenge for us has been not only to preserve what Gerstäcker really wrote, but also to recognize that Gerstäcker, addressing German readers, was already pretending to be something like an American writer, an American writing in German, that is. Our hope is that this new translation of Friedrich Gerstäcker's first novel, in all its hybrid, scruffy splendor, its boisterous weirdness, will contribute to a richer understanding of a transatlantic literary culture in the nineteenth century—a culture that stands apart from both the nationalistic tradition championed by Emerson and the wider Anglophone tradition lionized by those on the other side of the ocean who preferred to see American literature as a derivative branch of the British canon. Significantly, a German edition of the novel was published in Philadelphia as late as 1880 or thereabouts, indicating the vitality throughout the nineteenth century of a multi-lingual literary culture in this country.[39] Long before the birth of Modernism and its well-known transoceanic literary culture, western literature was cosmopolitan in ways that remain yet to be discovered. Bringing Gerstäcker's work to the attention of contemporary readers will, we believe, help sharpen awareness of this lost tradition of American cosmopolitanism, a project that now seems more necessary than ever.

Notes

Some of the material discussed here was first used in Charles Adams and Christoph Irmscher, "Telltale Breezes and Swirling Bubbles: A New Translation of *Die Regulatoren in Arkansas* (1846)," *Arkansas Historical Quarterly* 53, no. 1 (Spring 2014): 56–68, and appears here with the permission of the journal's editor.

1. For these and other details of FG's life we are indebted to the standard biography by Thomas Ostwald, *Friedrich Gerstäcker. Leben und Werk: Biographie eines Ruhelosen* (Braunschweig: Gerstäcker-Gesellschaft, 2007), the revised edition of a work first published in 1976.

2. FG, *In the Arkansas Backwoods*, ed. James William Miller (Columbia, MO: University of Missouri Press, 1991), 6.

3. FG, "Geschichte eines Ruhelosen," *Die Gartenlaube* 16 (1870): 245–46. It is worth pointing out that no issue of this periodical has surfaced. In the absence of conclusive evidence, it is possible that FG, in a coy attempt at authorial pseudo-modesty, fabricated the story.

4. On FG's relationship with Cooper, see Wolfgang Hochbruck, "Leatherstockings and River Pirates: The Adventure Novels of Friedrich Gerstäcker," *The Arkansas Historical Quarterly* 53, no. 1 (Spring 2014): 42–55.

5. On FG and Schiller, Kathleen Condray, "The *Kerl* in the Wild West: Friedrich Gerstäcker's *Die Regulatoren in Arkansas* and Friedrich Schiller's *Die Räuber*," *The Arkansas Historical Quarterly* 53, no. 1 (Spring 2014): 69–77. In his study in Dresden, filled to the ceiling with memorabilia from his travels and other outlandish items, including tomahawks, a stuffed bird, exotic plants, and arrow points, he also kept a small replica of the Goethe-Schiller monument in Weimar on his writing desk (see Bernd Steinbrink, *Abenteuerliteratur des 19. Jahrhunderts: Studien zu einer vernachlässigten Gattung* [Tübingen: Niemeyer, 1983], 139). In an autobiographical sketch

from 1870, he credits Defoe's Robinson Crusoe with having inspired his *wanderlust*; see FG, "Geschichte eines Ruhelosen," 244.

6. For a slightly different view of FG's political interests, see, however, Jeffrey L. Sammons, "A Plea for Taking Gerstäcker More Seriously as a Writer about America," *The Arkansas Historical Quarterly* 53, no. 1 (Spring 2014): 2–16.

7. FG, "Amerikanische Skizzen: Die Indianer," *Das Ausland* 54 (February 1846): 213.

8. *WS*, 315, 320–24, 333. The English version, the work of an unnamed translator, takes some liberties with the German original (see FG, *In the Arkansas Backwoods*, 27) but nevertheless preserves the enthusiasm that drove the young author. Since it is more easily accessible to the American reader, it will serve as our reference text throughout.

9. *WS*, 337.

10. *WS*, 199.

11. FG, *Wie ist es denn nun eigentlich in Amerika? Eine kurze Schilderung dessen, was der Auswanderer in Nordamerika zu thun und dafür zu hoffen und zu erwarten hat* (Leipzig: Wigand, 1849), iv.

12. The first line of Goethe's late poem "Den Vereinigten Staaten" (1827), *Goethes Werke: Hamburger Ausgabe*, 14 vols., ed. Erich Trunz (Hamburg: Christian Wegener, 1948), 1, 333.

13. See Andreas Graf, *Abenteuer und Geheimnis: Die Romane Balduin Möllhausens* (Freiburg: Rombach, 1993), 246.

14. Andreas Graf, "Nachwort," in Balduin Möllhausen, *Geschichten aus dem Wilden Westen*, ed. Andreas Graf (Munich: dtv, 1995), 296–97.

15. Hochbruck, "Adventure Novels," 49.

16. Möllhausen, "Präriebilder," 1867; Möllhausen, *Geschichten*, 51.

17. On May's borrowings from FG, see Josef Höck and Thomas Ostwald, "Karl May und Friedrich Gerstäcker," *Jahrbuch der Karl-May-Gesellschaft* 1979, 143–88; Andreas Graf, "Von Öl- und anderen Quellen: Texte Friedrich Gerstäckers als Vorbilder für Karl Mays 'Old Firehand,' *Der Schatz im Silbersee*, und 'Inn-nu-woh,'" *Jahrbuch der Karl-May-Gesellschaft* 1997, 331–60.

18. John Gould Fletcher, *Arkansas* (1947; Fayetteville, AR: The University of Arkansas Press, 1989), 1.

19. Fletcher, *Arkansas*, 5.

20. Fletcher, *Arkansas*, 55.

21. Robert Cochran, "The Gentlemen and the Deerslayer: Contrasting Portraits of Pioneer Arkansas," *The Arkansas Historical Quarterly* 53, no. 1 (Spring 2014): 32.

22. Kimberly G. Smith and Michael Lehmann, "Friedrich Gerstäcker's Natural History Observations in Arkansas, 1838–1842," *The Arkansas Historical Quarterly* 53, no. 1 (Spring 2014): 17–30.

23. For FG's reservations about Methodism, see also Evan Burr Bukey, "Frederick Gerstäcker in Arkansas," *The Arkansas Historical Quarterly* 31, no. 1 (Spring 1972): 3–14.

24. Personal communication, Marianne Mithun (UC Santa Barbara) to Charles Adams, 15 May 2017.

25. *WS*, 379–80. The juxtaposition of noble Indian and cartoonish African American continued to interest FG, as demonstrated, for example, by his story "Die Leichenräuber" (The Corpse-Snatchers), published in 1846 and set in Illinois. Here an African American boy named Sip, who is good at imitating Indian war whoops, offers to help a group of residents prevent the desecration of an Indian grave by the town's dubious Irish doctor. During the nightly raid, however, Sip flees in a panic when he encounters the son of the dead man who has also shown up. He was, as the narrator reminds us, "not the boy to stand up to a real Indian" (FG, *Heimliche und unheimliche Geschichten* [München: Borowsky, 1980], 256). For FG's later views on Recon-

struction, see Irene S. Di Maio, "Introduction," *Gerstäcker's Louisiana: Fiction and Travel Sketches from Antebellum Times through Reconstruction,* ed. and trans. Irene S. Di Maio (Baton Rouge: Louisiana State University Press, 2006), 12–15.

26. FG, *Die Flußpiraten des Mississippi,* 4th ed., 3 vols. (Leipzig: Costenoble, 1862), 3,18.

27. *The Feathered Arrow; or the Forest Rangers* (London: Routledge, 1857); *The Regulators of Arkansas, A Thrilling Tale of Border Adventure; Bill Johnson, or The Outlaws of Arkansas;* and *Rowson the Renegade, or The Squatter's Revenge* (New York: Dick and Fitzgerald, 1857).

28. Francis Johnson, trans., *Alapaha the Squaw, or The Renegades of the Border;* and *The Border Bandits, or the Horse Thief's Trail;* and *Assowaum the Avenger, or The Doom of the Destroyers* (New York: Beadle and Co., 1870; reprinted in 1881 by Beadle and Adams [3 vols. in "Beadle's New York Dime Library"]).

29. "The Regulators in Arkansas by Friedrich Gerstäcker, Translated by E. L. Higgins," M89–22, box 1, folders 7 and 8; "The River Pirates of the Mississippi by Friedrich Gerstäcker, Translated by E. L. Higgins," M89–22, box 3, folders 2–4; Earl Leroy Higgins Collection, University of Central Arkansas.

30. Herman Melville, *Omoo: A Narrative of Adventures in the South Seas* (London: Murray, 1847), 4.

31. Hermann Melwille [sic], *Omoo oder Abenteuer im stillen Ocean mit einer Einleitung, die sich den "Marquesas-Inseln" anschliesst und Toby's glückliche Flucht enthält. Aus dem Englischen von Friedrich Gerstäcker. Erster Theil* (Leipzig: Gustav Mayer, 1847), 5.

32. Melwille [sic], *Omoo oder Abenteuer,* 72.

33. See Ostwald, *Friedrich Gerstäcker,* 73.

34. George Lippard, *Quaker City, or The Monks of Monk Hall: A Romance of Philadelphia Life,* 2 vols. (Philadelphia: The Author, 1847), vol.1, 248; George Lippard and Friedrich Gerstäcker, *Die Quäkerstadt und ihre Geheimnisse. Amerikanische Nachtseiten* (1845, 4th ed. 1851; München: Hanser, 1971), 350.

35. Lippard, *Quaker City,* 272–73.

36. Lippard, *Quaker City,* 272–73; Lippard and Gerstäcker, *Die Quäkerstadt,* 350.

37. George Steiner, *After Babel: Aspects of Language and Translation* (Oxford: Oxford University Press, 1992), 423.

38. For more on the theoretical problems inherent in domestication and foreignization, see Douglas Robinson, "The Limits of Translation," *The Oxford Guide to Literature in English Translation,* ed. Peter France (Oxford: Oxford University Press, 2000), 15–20.

39. FG, *Die Regulatoren in Arkansas: Aus dem Waldleben Amerikas* (Philadelphia: Morwitz & Co., 188–?). Edward Morwitz (1815–1893), originally from Danzig, Prussia, was a physician and newspaper publisher who had settled in Philadelphia. Among the several hundred German and English-language newspapers he eventually controlled was also the Philadelphia *Jewish Record* (from 1875 to 1886). See Leland M. Williamson et al., eds, *Prominent and Progressive Pennsylvanians of the Nineteenth Century: A Review of Their Careers* (Philadelphia: The Record, 1898), 318–20.

Map 0.1. "Gerstäcker's Arkansas." Original map by Thomas R. Paradise, University of Arkansas, 2018. Courtesy of Thomas R. Paradise.

Foreword.

A few words will suffice to introduce this tale from the western woods of America to the reader, and to prepare him for what, after all, he may expect from it.

Arkansas, which the United States received into their union only in 1836, acquired, in its early years, the same reputation California has now: namely, that in its trackless woods and swamps all manner of ne'er-do-wells from the East and the South had found a safe haven from the punishing arm of justice, and that there each could live on his own, free terms.

This reputation was not entirely undeserved, since law and justice were powerless in these woods. Before the Sheriff could catch a criminal, that person would have fled, on the back of his own or someone else's horse, to another county, never to be seen again. And if he were actually caught, it proved to be an even greater task to keep him imprisoned. Either the criminal would blaze his own trail out of the log cabin in which he had been locked up, or he would, during his first night in jail, see himself liberated by a band of his friends, who perhaps would not even think it necessary to paint and disguise their faces, and he would then resume his natural course.

Horse theft was a particular specialty of these clans. Since animals and the herds of the pioneers were, according to western custom, allowed to forage freely for food in the woods, no one exerted even a modicum of control over them. Moreover, when the death penalty for horse theft was abolished in 1839, residents in different parts of the state turned it into a thriving business. The backwoodsmen finally saw themselves compelled to act and enforce strict rules.

The law alone was not sufficient to protect the residents on their respective farms, which were often several miles apart from one another. The "men of Arkansas" consequently founded *The Regulators Association,* seized whatever seemed suspicious to them, whipped their prisoners till they had confessed their trespasses and the names of their accomplices, and hanged or shot the culprits as soon as some form of evidence sufficiently confirmed their guilt.

It may be easily imagined that, given this rather reckless process, much wrong was done too. Several times innocent people were dragged from their peaceful cabins and flogged. Their proud Arkansan blood rebelled against the undeserved abuse, for which they then sought revenge, not through the legal channels, but using their own approach, shooting and killing their judges either secretly or publicly. Generally, though, the pioneers' implementation of frontier justice did the trick. After the *Lynch Law,* as the Regulators called their version of justice, had claimed its first several victims in different parts of the state, the horse thieves realized that there were safer and cozier places for them in America than Arkansas.[1] Many found refuge in the "Indian Nation," mingling with Choctaw and Cherokee, but the majority of the thieves moved to Texas, and currently the state has been pretty much cleared of the dregs of a free people.[2]

My tale takes place at a time in which this havoc had reached its highest level and self-protection had become a necessity for farmers and hunters. Most of the events are not invented but have really taken place, if in different places and over a more extended period of time; the Methodist especially is a historical character. I myself witnessed several of these scenes and, on one specific occasion, wrote down the names of twenty-six honorable people that the Regulators had extracted, with the help of the black hickory, from a suspect they had apprehended.[3]

The kind reader may now, if he has enough patience, follow me back, for a brief period of time, into the beautiful forests of this magnificent region. If he, after perusing this book, might not immediately saddle up and "make tracks" (as the backwoodsmen say) to these far regions of the West, it is still my hope that he, next to some less agreeable characters, will encounter several very good, gentle and lovable people, who might compensate him for the darker and shadowy aspects of the rest.

Notes

1. There may be a connection between the extra-legal summary justice of Lynch Law and a historical group of vigilantes who called themselves "The Regulators." According to one theory, the term stems from meetings held along Lynch Creek in South Carolina by a group of "Regulators" in the 1760s. See James E. Cutler, *Lynch-Law: An Investigation into the History of Lynching in the United States* (New York: Longman's Green and Co., 1905), chapters 2 and 3.

2. FG uses the German term "Hefe," which is more conventionally translated as "yeast," commonly employed in the production of bread and alcohol. Biologically speaking, yeasts are single-celled microorganisms classified as fungi. What FG has in mind here is the sediment that remains when, for example, wine has been drained from the glass; see the entry "Hefe 3) b)" in *DWB,* vol. 10. As "faex civitatum" or the dregs of society, the phrase first occurs in Cicero's oration *Pro Flacco* (section 18).

3. "Hickory" appears in English throughout FG's text. Such a beating of a horse thief is first described in *Wild Sports* (*WS,* 361–62).

Chapter 1

The Reader Makes the Acquaintance of Four Worthy Fellows and Learns More about Their Circumstances.

May's genial warmth had driven off the wild storms of spring. Flowers and blossoms pushed through the bed of yellow leaves thickly covering the ground, broken only here and there by tufts of lush green grass. Blossom upon blossom sprang also from the branches of the low dogwoods and spicebushes; blooms and buds hung from the luxurious liana vines that ran from tree to tree, turning the wilderness into a garden, and filling with their sweet aroma the forest roof, shaped by vaulting fir and oak and sassafras trees.[1] Even when sunlight pushed its way through the thick-leaved tops of the giant trunks, that tangle of vines and shrubs allowed only here and there a furtive ray to reach the earth, so that twilight reigned in this lower world even as the sun glowed high in the sky.

The half-light seemed to suit the three figures seated at the foot of a massive pine, for one of them, stretching his limbs, looked up at the green roof towering above them and said:

"A magnificent place for our secret gatherings – a really splendid place, as if it had been made for such things. The canebrake toward the river will stop any sensible Christian coming that way, and the thorns and greenbriers hereabouts are not exactly inviting. No one would venture in here without good reason – and there can be no good reason indeed, since we've taken care that there's no more game to be found around here."

The speaker was, as far as one could tell, since he was stretched out lazily among the leaves, a man of over six feet,[2] of muscular build and with frank and open features. But his eyes had something strangely wild about them, and darted rapidly this way and that, while his overall appearance was slovenly in the extreme. An old battered felt hat had fallen from his head, and his hair stuck up, coarse and unkempt. His rough beard had been neglected for at least a week, and his well-worn blue woolen hunting shirt, from which hung the remnants of a faded gold fringe, was spattered with both new and dried blood. A freshly skinned deer pelt by his side explained the stains. The fellow seemed, in short, very much at home in the woods. His rifle lay near him on the ground; his legs were stuck in a pair of heavily patched leather leggings or gaiters, and a pair of cowhide moccasins completed his thoroughly unbecoming outfit.

His companion sat next to him with his back against the pine's trunk, using a long knife (called an "Arkansas Toothpick"[3] in the language of the region) to whittle a bit of wood. He was a little different from his rude neighbor, and the difference was much to his advantage. His clothing was cleaner, and his leather hunting shirt, if just as old and worn, seemed to have been made with more care. Indeed, his whole appearance suggested a better upbringing than that of the wild woodsman, or at least indicated that he had more recently left his parents' roof. The latter was very likely the case, given his evident youth; he could not have been more than seventeen.

The third man was nothing like the others; if they displayed an abundance of wildness and zest for life, he seemed to offset it by gentleness and affability. His clothes marked him as one of the class of well-to-do farmers. The blue frock-coat, made of the best wool – the customary outfit of American rural folk – the salt-and-pepper trousers, the neat yellow vest, the carefully blackened shoes, the new broad-brimmed hat: all showed that he prized his appearance, and that – while he obviously belonged with his current companions, and might agree with them in certain matters – he did not share their disdain for decent, clean dress. He leaned, one leg thrown over the other, against a small oak tree, and looked pensively at the speaker, who after his last remark had let his head sink lazily back against the moss that covered the roots of the tree.

"Or, more likely, take much better care about it now, Cotton," he ventured, answering the hunter in a slightly nasal voice, "though it's hardly right to violate the holy Sabbath by roaming around without pressing need, shooting the peaceful animals of the forest."

"Oh, go to the devil with your preaching, Rowson," replied the hunter with an irritated laugh, as the youngster cast a sneering glance at the grave figure of the moralist – "save your moral for the settlement, and spare us your nonsense out here. – But what can be keeping Rusch? – I'll be damned if I understand it. He promised to be here at dawn and the sun's three hours high – the plague on his neck!"

"Your blasphemous cursing won't bring him here any faster," replied the farmer, shaking his head – "but," he continued more brightly, "I too feel that we have dawdled here too long. I must be at the prayer meeting at ten, and still have six miles to ride."

"Both errands agree very well with you!" cried the hunter with a scornful laugh – "Preaching and horse-thieving – hmm, they complement each other, and it's good that one can do them both, since the 'Sabbath,' as you call it, is otherwise a bad day for our trade. By the infernal Trinity, drop that nonsense here in the woods! 'Tis – to say the least – boring."

"Well, don't fear, you won't be pestered much longer," laughed the farmer, slowly digging a pinch of snuff from a box made of shell. "But look," he said sharply, "your dog's cocked his ears – he must scent something."

A grey and black brindled bloodhound was curled up a few steps away from the men in the only patch of sunlight created where a fallen tree had ripped a hole in the leaf canopy. He raised his nose to the wind for a moment, growled softly, made a faint effort to wag his tail, and fell back into his former posture. His master, who had been watching him closely, sprang to his feet with a contented look and cried, "At last! – it's about time he got here. Deik knows him well enough too, but he doesn't want to leave his warm spot over there. Hallo – there he is already! – come, Rusch, you must think that we like sitting here among the mosquitoes and ticks. What the hell kept you from getting here on time?"

The newcomer revealed himself to be a man of middle age, dressed like the farmer in clean and decent clothes. Though not wearing hunting clothes, a shot-pouch hung from his right side and a long rifle was thrown over his shoulder.

"Good morning, gentlemen,"[4] he said, turning to the men who greeted him, "good morning, and please don't be angry that you had to wait on me – I couldn't get here any sooner. That young dandy, Brown, and old Harper, along with that damned redskin, were all creeping along my path, and I didn't want them to see me come this way. Those old boys are getting too clever for their own good, and that skulking Scalping Knife is always sniffing around these woods. Hell and damnation! Why do we put up with that Indian here in our neighborhood? – But I have a hunch that the bullet's been cast that will help him on his way to the happy hunting grounds."

"And I believe, Rusch," said Cotton, "that *that* chunk of lead would be put to an excellent use."

"Listen here, Cotton," said the newcomer, turning angrily toward the hunter. – "I wish you wouldn't call me by that accursed name again. – You're going to use it in front of strangers some day, and then I'll be in the devil's kitchen. – Say 'Johnson,' even when we're alone – you'll get used to it that way."

"Whatever you say," Cotton laughed. "Rusch or Johnson, you won't dodge the rope, any more than the rest of us. But we'll be jolly, as long as we're together. Now, let's get to business. We haven't made a penny in the past two weeks, so it's time to get something going."

As he spoke, he pulled a small bottle of whiskey from a woolen blanket, twisted out the cork, and nodded at Rowson with a smile. "Cheers," he said, as he smugly put the bottle to his lips. After enjoying a very long draw, he handed it to Rowson standing next to him and cried: "There – fortify yourself for your sermon this morning – you'll be needing it. Damn me if I wouldn't have to have three such bottles in me to listen quietly to you, and even then only on the condition that I could fall asleep before you began!"

"Thanks," said Rowson, declining the offered drink – "thanks very much – but I'd rather not reek of whiskey this morning. – Give the bottle to Johnson; he's casting some longing looks at it."

"There's nothing better than a hot drink in the morning," said the newcomer, briskly paying his respects to the hunter. – "But, Weston," he continued, turning to the youngest of the group – "what's eating you? You're scratching at yourself like a snake trying to slough its skin. Did a mosquito bite you?"

"Just *one?*" asked the young man angrily, stepping forward and taking the bottle from Johnson's hand. "Just *one?* The air around here is thick with them. I now almost believe that Harper was right to say, not so long ago, that there are so many of the cursed sharp-faced fellows here, that when you sit down to dinner you'd only have to slice the air once with your knife, and you'd have a plateful of wings and legs."

"Ho Ho!" laughed Cotton – "you'll get used to it. Of course, you've come here straight from the Missouri hills, where I've heard that a man can sleep outdoors without smoke, which would be hard to do here."

"Gentlemen, let's remember why we're here," remarked Rowson somewhat impatiently. "We're losing time, and I really must be going. Anyway, this place may not be particularly safe if Johnson really saw the Indian and his companions creeping around here. So I suggest that we get to work without further delay and decide what we actually came here to decide."

"Bravely spoken, O great prophet!" cried Cotton, pounding his heavy fist on the speaker's shoulder so that he winced and cast a malicious sidelong glance at his all-too-affable companion. Stifling his anger with considerable self-control, Rowson looked deliberately around at each man, and continued: "Thanks to the meddling bastards roving around not just the village but the whole county – yes, the whole state! – calling themselves 'The Regulators,' we've been lying around idle for weeks and haven't cleared a penny. Yesterday, as you all know, a messenger came from the island[5] wanting a shipment of good horses that will be used for an overland trek or something like that, and we're stuck here with our hands in our laps. This can't go on – I need money – like all of you, and it's absurd to work for years growing corn and raising pigs to earn just table scraps. So let's get to it. Now, through the good name that I've managed to earn for myself, though I am, truly, but a weak and sinful man –"

"Oh hell and damnation, stop that twaddle!" cried Cotton, stomping his foot with irritation – "jabber your pious rubbish when you're at Roberts', but give it to us straight here."

"Now, through the good name that I've earned," repeated Rowson, making a conciliatory gesture toward Cotton – "I can come and go at many, very many farms. Naturally, this has given me the opportunity to figure out exactly how many cows and, especially, how many horses each owner has. *My* view of the matter is that there's no more lucrative area than *Spring Creek*, on the other side of the Petit Jean.[6] Husfield over there has some fine animals, and I'm dead certain that we can make off with eight horses from his farm alone. If we do that, I guarantee we'll have a two-day head start."

"Not bad," Johnson allowed, "but also consider that this takes us nearly fifty miles farther from the Mississippi."

"Thirty-five at the most," replied Rowson, "and two days and two nights head start. – Around here they're on our trail within the hour, and that's troublesome, to say the least."

"How would it be if we put the venture off until next week?" suggested Johnson, "I'd like to take a little ramble up the Ouachita."[7]

"Not an hour!" cried Rowson – "why waste time, when we need all the time we can get?"

"What's the hell's got you in such a damned rush all of a sudden?" asked Cotton, with amazement. "Usually you let things happen in their own good time."

"I need money," Rowson said tersely – "my land has been surveyed, and if I haven't paid the full sum by the first Monday in June, it'll be sold out from under my nose, as you all know very well. What is more, there are some amiable souls in the neighborhood who would take a special delight in doing me this kindness. – There's this Mr. Harper, among others – the plague on his head!"

"Ha ha ha ha," roared Cotton, "if Mrs. Roberts hears that you wished the plague on the skull of a fellow Christian, her pious opinion of you would spring a serious leak."

"Go ahead and laugh, Cotton, you've earned the right – 'tis your daily bread, but I tell you truly that there are some living around here that I'd love to take a knife to – but that's beside the point," he continued, quickly controlling himself – "say, now, are you going to take my advice or not? We can make three hundred dollars a man in eight days, and that's more than honest ways and means will bring."[8]

"Good, that makes sense to me!" cried Cotton. "But this time, *you* two go; we two, Weston and I, risked our necks last time."

"Yes, yes," agreed Weston – "'tis true, we came awfully close to getting caught – it's our turn to get to rest."

"Oh wait, not so fast," Johnson interjected, "first, we have to work out the plan, and then I'd ask you two gentlemen to consider the burden we had with the sale, and that I'm still not entirely free of suspicion. So, first the plan – how do you see it, Rowson?"

"Well, look," he replied, drawing a broad Bowie knife from under his vest and beginning to whittle – "two of us – (no more, no matter what, so that we don't arouse suspicion in case we're seen accidentally) – two of us, then, go carrying rifles – and three or four bridles each, which must be concealed somehow, from here over the Petit Jean toward the mill on Spring Creek. The bridles I mention so that we don't have the trouble we had last time selling the horses, when the green bark made their mouths bleed so smartly that the cutthroats on the island wouldn't pay us what they were worth. From the mill it's not much farther, maybe a couple of miles, to the Husfields'. At the first fence corner,[9] you take a quick left onto the first footpath; it looks like it runs back into the woods, but it just winds around a couple of fallen oaks and turns back toward the farm and goes straight to the paddock, which on its other side is directly connected to the house."

"Husfield has about twenty-seven horses, all told, including foals and stallions, eight of which he fodders. – These we must leave alone, since he would miss them the next morning, and he's too good a woodsman to miss our trail. The others are turned out to forage freely with a young stallion, a three-year-old, leading the herd."

"He shouldn't let a stallion run free so early in the year," Johnson broke in.

"I know that," retorted Rowson, – "but he does. Now, at least, I'm sure that the stallion is out, and that *every* evening he comes like clockwork to the paddock fence – to see a couple of mares. He trots all around it the same way every time, neighs his love song, and then heads back into the woods to find his customary place to sleep. The whole gang follows him, and that's the time to grab them, since the household doesn't pay much attention to the animals. I've stopped there twice, and I'm sure of it."

"If we could get the mares out of the fold," suggested Weston, grinning, "then we'd have the whole herd and could ride as fast as the beasts could run."

"Sure, and the next morning have about ten or twelve of the bastards after us with rifles and Bowie knives as long as your forearm, on a trail that a blind man with a cane could follow," countered Rowson loudly. – "No, we must be wary; getting away with it isn't enough, we have to be above suspicion, and that means doing the job as carefully as possible from the start. The ones who steal the horses can't be seen at the mill either. There's almost always someone from Husfield's around there, and faces from Fourche La Fave,[10] except mine maybe, don't have a very good reputation in the northern settlements. The best thing is to go straight to where the road meets Spring Creek and wade over to the other side. That's best for two reasons: it'll make anyone who happens to run into you on the road think that you're riding across to Dardanelle,[11] and it'll make it less likely that you'll meet up with someone you know. At the corner of the fence, right where the path branches off to the left, the ground is very rocky, so you can hardly see a track on the path back. I don't have to tell you what to do when you get to this point, you know well enough."

"But who's going?" grumbled Cotton morosely. "You're giving us good instructions, as if you weren't a member of the gang yourself. – We took the risk the last time, it's only right and fair that two others stick their necks out this time."

"Moreover, you know the area so well," exclaimed Weston. "Others of us will waste a lot of time looking for paths that we've only heard described."

"True – true in many respects," said Rowson, grinning. "But, young man, Johnson and I, as was said, faced more fear and danger last time than you two, who only *collected* the horses. But, all right – I volunteer to be one of the 'collectors' if you'll name the other. But only on the condition that I take the goods to the Maumelle,[12] and no farther; that is, to the ridge that divides the waters of the Maumelle from those of the Fourche La Fave. We'll rendezvous at the springs of the creek that flows out below into the big salt lick. From there, the other two must take the horses to the island."

"Then it's best if you and Johnson take the first part. Weston and I will then take the horses to safety."

"Hold on, there," – cried Johnson – "I won't willingly set foot on that scoundrel Husfield's land – maybe you don't know it, but he and I had a fight a couple of weeks ago, and I – the damned pistol snapped, and the bastard knocked me down. – I owe the scoundrel one for that," – he continued, gritting his teeth, – "but I don't want to settle it on his home turf, that would be against me if it came before the law. – No, let chance say who goes; we can draw blades of grass."

"Nonsense, blades of grass," sneered Cotton – "the hunt should decide it. – Let's say that tomorrow morning all four – or, rather, we three, since Rowson is a volunteer this time, we three start from different grounds, and meet back here on Thursday morning. Whoever shoots the most deer tomorrow, or has the best hunt overall, is free."

"Good!" cried Rowson, "that's a great idea, and I'll go too, if only for the sport."

"Fine with me," said Johnson, "we're all good hunters, and luck will decide which of us will haul horseflesh on this or that side of the Maumelle. So, early tomorrow morning it is. But we've each got to pick a ground to hunt, so we don't get in each other's line of fire. For my part, I'll go up the river a bit and hunt the bottoms."

"Then you'll be on my ground," said Weston – "I *have* to go up that way, since I've pitched my camp there, with blanket, cooking gear, and two deerskins."

"All right – then I'll go on over to the Petit Jean; Jones, from over there, told me yesterday that he'd seen lots of tracks."

"I'm going there too," said Rowson, "but I won't be able to hunt all day, since I've promised Mrs. Laughlin that I'd come over in the evening to hold a prayer meeting."

"And where will you leave your gun meanwhile?" laughed Johnson.

"Why, at Fulweal's, I think. Cotton's sister is there too, so when I ride home in the evening I can pick it up again."

"Rowson, Rowson," cried Cotton, laughing and wagging his finger – "I think something's fishy about this affair with Widow Fulweal. You're always creeping and wheedling around her, and when I showed up unexpectedly at your prayer meeting the other day, the two of you were kneeling awfully close together."

"Nonsense," said Rowson.

"And when the Holy Spirit came over the young widow," Cotton continued, ignoring the distraction, "when she started jumping and screaming and rejoicing, she didn't fall down until she knew she was right next to you, and Mr. Rowson naturally caught her, so that she whom the Holy Spirit had thrown to the ground might not come to further harm – oh, Rowson!"

"Nonsense!" Rowson said again, though he started to blush and turned quickly toward Weston, saying loudly: "By the way, young man, you can't count the two skins you've already got in your camp!"

"Heaven forbid" – he retorted – "no tricks – tomorrow morning early, when it's light enough to see the rifle bead, let the hunt begin."

"It's time to break it up," said Rowson, shoving his hands into his pockets – "so gentlemen, here's to a happy reunion!"

"Wait! One more thing," cried Cotton, as Rowson turned toward where he had tethered his horse outside the thicket – "we can't split up until we're clear about what we'll do if – the – the damned Regulators get on our trail. Hell and brimstone! If it were up to me, not one of the bastards would be alive this time tomorrow evening!"

Rowson turned back and, biting his nails, stopped next to Cotton. – "I almost forgot to tell you something," he said after a brief pause, during which he threw a sidelong glance toward his husky companion, "but now that Cotton's mentioned the Regulators, it's come back to me."

"And what is that?" asked Johnson keenly.

"No more and no less than that the sheriff of Pulaski County[13] has a warrant in his pocket for good old Cotton here."

"The devil!" shouted Cotton, "and what for?"

"Oh – I don't know if anything special was mentioned, rather it was a number of things. I heard some whispers about a fifty-dollar bill, and a wedding engagement in Randolph County,[14] and a man who went missing for a long time, and whose corpse was later found – and some other little things."

"A plague!" cried the hunter, stomping his foot. "And *that's* what you almost forgot? And let me go blindly into the settlement? I think it's about time that I get out of here – Arkansas's getting a little too warm for me, or I'm becoming a little too well known here."

"So you're pretty widely known, are you?" grinned Rowson.

"Very," said the hunter – lost in thought and barely hearing the question. "But so what," he said abruptly, drawing himself up, "so what – in a few days our business will be over, and with the money I can get to the Mississippi and from there get to Texas easily."

"Why don't you go from here overland? It wouldn't cost you a cent and it's not even a tenth the distance."

"True enough, but I have my reasons for not coming too close to the Indians living up north."

"Oh, my – yes, Cotton – tell us the story," begged Weston, "I've heard much said about it, but I want to know the whole story. What happened with you and the Cherokee?"

"You think this is the time to tell a story?" Cotton growled.

"They say," Rowson said snidely, "that your arms still carry the marks of the irons –"

"To hell with your childish babble – we've got things to do. It's not just me they're after, it's all of you. The Regulators have got wind of us from some bastard or other and they've got us in their sights!"

"Not me," laughed Rowson – "no one looks for a wolf in a godly and god-fearing Methodist preacher."

"No one?" Cotton asked with a derisive smile. "No one? What did Heathcott say the other day, when he called you a liar and a scoundrel?"

Rowson's face blanched and a deathly pale replaced his earlier ruddiness; his hand jerked toward his concealed knife.

"What charge did he bring to light?" persisted the hunter in a harsh whisper, taking a step toward the other, who trembled with rage and wrath. "Eh? Wasn't the word soul-merchant used? And you took it without a peep. – Bah! I was ashamed for your own soul –"

"Cotton," said Rowson, struggling to control himself, "you've plucked the right string – *that* fellow's dangerous to us. Not only does he have a hunch who *I* am, just the other day he dropped some hints about Atkins."

"What, Atkins? – he's never had a hand in a theft, he just quietly helps us out from his farm."

"Precisely that Atkins. Only the – devil knows how the bastard knew to look in our direction, but it's true. So when I put up with *liar* and *scoundrel*, I had my reasons. As a preacher, if I had lost control, and let the bastard have it –"

"He would have knocked you to the floor," laughed Cotton.

"It would have dealt a serious blow to my customary God-fearing ways," continued Rowson, without losing his temper.

"It would have been a blow, all right," said Cotton, "to your head, or right between your eyes."

"To hell with your jokes," shouted Johnson – "we're not here to listen to your antics. Rowson is right; if he's a preacher, he must act like a preacher –"

"And steal horses," laughed the obstinate Cotton.

"Do you want to talk seriously about a serious matter or not? – Tell me, because I'm sick of your nonsense," shouted Rowson angrily – "we're here together to work together to make a plan together, not to squabble. – And I know something more besides – the Regulators will be meeting here today or tomorrow."

"Here? Where?" they all shouted at once.

"At Roberts' or Wilkins' or someone else's, I don't know – but that they're coming is certain – and then – they have in mind to establish that always popular Lynch Law again."

"They can't do that!" cried Cotton – "the laws against it were just tightened up!"

"What can't they do in Arkansas," Rowson smirked, "when twenty or twenty-five of them get together in earnest? Do you think the governor will send a militia against them?[15] Absolutely not – and even if he did, it wouldn't do any good. They can do *all they want,* and they want our kind – I don't mean our quiet, friendly family circle – our sort, I say, wiped out. That done, all their horses will come home at evening, and they won't have to watch out for men who carry a Bowie knife, a couple of pistols, and a snaffle bit under their waistcoats."

"Put that way, I can't really blame them," grinned Johnson – "but as it no way suits our view of life – what's that animal doing there? He's been lifting his nose very strangely for the last couple of minutes – is something coming this way?"

"No, it's nothing," said Cotton, glancing at the dog, which had curled up quietly again – "maybe he smells a turkey cock, and wants to point it out without doing anything about it."

"But as it no way suits our views, we have to fight it with force or cunning. – As for force, we're too weak, for when push comes to shove, few will stand with us. So we must save ourselves by cunning. And, I think, with the help of Atkins, who couldn't live in a better place for our purposes, we can lead them all round by the nose, especially with this arrogant fool Heathcott in charge –"

"Heathcott's their leader?" Rowson asked sharply.

"Yes! That's what Harper told me just the other day, when I met him at the mill."

"Then these must be the last horses we lift from these parts," muttered Rowson thoughtfully, as if speaking to himself. "'Tis too dangerous. – Next time, I think, we get them from Missouri; Weston will be our leader there, and I'm well-connected on the Big Black and around Farmington."[16]

"Really *known?*" asked Cotton.

"You bet," returned Rowson, ignoring the other's malicious meaning. "*Really* known, and I've won the affection of the people there by my God-fearing way of life."

"And, of the horses," said Weston, laughing. "When he left there, three fine beasts followed him out of pure devotion."

This time Rowson joined in the laughter that followed this remark, but quickly recovered his earnest look, and cried loudly: "Gentlemen, this can't go on – think about it, our necks are on the line! There's a time for everything, in jest and in earnest – so now listen to my plan. I've changed my notion of the matter: we *won't* take the horses directly to the island, since it's possible that they'll stay on our trail, despite all our cleverness. That will spell trouble not just for us, but for the river folks too. Instead, wait for me above where Hoswells keeps his canoe – about a half mile higher, there where the Hurricane[17] starts. From there I have a plan that will let us lead our hunters by the nose and keep us safe. I'll set them off on a false trail, and that has to be done at the river. But more of that later – first we have to see who wins the hunt tomorrow, and I'll arrange it with him then."

"What if they follow us to Atkins' and find our last hideout?" Cotton asked doubtfully.

"Maybe we don't need to go to Atkins' at all!" exclaimed Rowson, laughing. "I've lived in the woods long enough to know how to lead a couple of yapping hounds[18] off the trail. Settle among yourselves who's to go with me, and you others get to the appointed place on time. Never call me Rowson again if I don't keep my word!"

"That's a mighty vow!" jeered Cotton – "maybe in a few weeks you'll be willing to pay God knows *what* – to have any name but Rowson. Well, I at least have the comfort of knowing that I run no greater risk than any of you. But now, let us swear we won't betray each other, in danger or death. – He's a bastard who's false with either look or breath, and our vengeance will find him wherever he runs, even into his mother's arms."

"A bloody death to the rat who betrays us!" shouted Weston, jerking his broad knife from its sheath, "and may his arm and his tongue wither, and may he go blind."

"That's a mighty oath," said Johnson – "But I'm with you!"

"I too," Rowson intoned, "but I hope such a vow isn't needed to bind us close and fast; mutual advantage has been enough until now, and that's stronger than any oath or bond. If that ever changes, then I'll wish I were in – Texas!"

"Do you think that one of us would be so vile as to betray his friends?" demanded Weston vehemently. "Just to think it is a betrayal and a violation of our friendship."

"All right, all right, I believe that you are being honest, Weston," said Rowson, extending his hand, "but you're still young, very young, and you don't know the troubles that a man can face."

"Torture itself couldn't force a word from me, that –"

"I'm happy to know that you think so, but now – good bye gentlemen[19] – adieu, Johnson – where shall we meet early tomorrow morning for the hunt?"

"Where Setters Creek[20] flows out of the hills; a grove of walnut trees stands on a little rise –"

"I know the place."

"Good, so that's the spot – until then, good luck. – Just don't get the poor people too excited –"

"Or the widow!" Cotton called after him – but Rowson no longer heard him as he quickly vanished into the thicket that tightly circled the clearing, the branches of which closed behind him.

Cotton stared after him for a long time, silent. At last, without saying another word, he shouldered his rifle and turned to go.

"You think Rowson's not straight?" asked Johnson, giving him a sharp look.

Cotton stood still, staring for a long moment into the other's eyes before declaring roughly and firmly: "No! – to answer truthfully, no! The slinking creature – you *cannot* trust a man who can keep smiling in spite of the crudest insults. Fire and brimstone! The fellow hates Heathcott like sin – wait – that comparison wasn't well chosen – like he hates virtue, more like it in this case, and you should have seen how they reconciled – I mean, Rowson walked up to Heathcott, shook his hand, and assured him that he bore him no grudge. I'd be hacked to pieces alive before I could do such a thing. The dog would feel my knife, not my hand. But as far as I'm concerned, it's in his interest to be with us, so I believe he'll be true. Anyway, it wouldn't do him any good to betray us – there's no price on my head. Ha ha ha, the ink-lickers think they can find Cotton in the woods! That'll be hard to manage, and could *only* be done by treachery, truth to tell."

"You think too poorly of Rowson," Johnson assured him. "He has his faults, naturally, as we all do, but he's loyal, and I'm convinced that the Regulators would skin him before he'd let the name of one of his friends pass his lips."

"Yes – but first they'd have to show that I'm one of them," Cotton said laughing. – "But farewell, Johnson – *you* mean well, I know, and a man can count on you in case of need – fare you well! The day after tomorrow, early, we'll gather here again, and we'll have a couple of hundred dollars in our pockets – then life will be better and safer. There are many here among the settlers who are shooting their mouths off in a terrible manner, bawling about theft and sin, but close their lips with a five-dollar bill and they'll show you nothing but the happiest of smiles. – Anyway, take care – time grows short – here's to a happy reunion soon!"

The men now parted ways. Cotton and Weston went together toward the bank of the river, but Johnson turned north, through the bushes. He crossed the county road carved from the woods, and disappeared in the steep, pine-covered hills.

The meeting place of the "Horse Traders," as they called themselves, lay silent and abandoned in the tranquility of the Sabbath. – For a full quarter of an hour, nothing broke the silence except the faint chatter of the squirrel and the sprightly cry of the jay. Then, without the slightest sound, the bushes parted, and the dark shape of an Indian stepped into the deserted space.

He listened warily on all sides before crossing the open space – just as a deer, stepping from the darkness of the woods to cross a path, stops and looks right and left to be sure that no danger threatens. Then he glided forward a few noiseless steps, his eyes fixed on the ground. Suddenly, he stopped, very likely alerted by the many footprints, and surveyed carefully the narrow opening. He examined in particular the place where the dog had lain, and then traced a wider circle around the small clearing, as if counting the tracks that led from it.

He had a powerful and handsome frame, this red son of the soil, and the flimsy checkered cotton hunting shirt that covered his torso – torn in numerous places by the thorns – could not entirely conceal the broad shoulders and brawny arms apparent beneath it. This shirt was cinched around his waist with a leather belt, which held a small sharp tomahawk, and, after the fashion of the whites, a broad knife. His legs were sheathed in leather leggings died dark, supplemented with a fringe a full two-inches wide, and around his neck he wore a large round silver medallion, cut to resemble a shield. On it was engraved, simply but not unskillfully, a stag. He wore no other ornaments, and even the bullet-pouch, which hung on his right side, lacked the glass beads and colored strips of leather with which the natives normally like to decorate their hunting gear. His head was similarly unadorned, and his long black lustrous hair hung in bangs over his temples and down to his shoulders. His gun was a common American long rifle.*

For a few minutes more he pursued his investigation, then stood up straight and brushed aside the hair from his forehead. Throwing another careful look around, he disappeared into the thicket, in the opposite direction from which he had first stepped into the clearing.

Notes

1. Lianas, Tarzan's preferred mode of transportation, are long-stemmed, woody vines rooted in the ground that use trees to climb through the forest canopy to reach sunlight. Other travelers were impressed by them, too. "Gustave Aimard" (the pseudonym for the French writer Olivier Gloux, 1818–1883) mentions them in *The White Scalper*: "All these trees, fastened together by lianas which envelop them in their inextricable network, serve as a retreat for a population of red and grey squirrels, that may be seen perpetually leaping from branch to branch. . . ." (*The White Scalper: A Story of the Texan War*, ed. Percy B. St. John [London: J. & R. Maxwell, 1861]), 23. The phrase "wilderness into a garden" echoes Isaiah 51:3: "For the Lord shall comfort Zion: he will comfort all her waste places; and make her wilderness like Eden, and her desert like the garden of the Lord."

2. There were slight differences between the German and the American metric system. An Austrian textbook from 1848 lists the length of the foot in Saxony, where FG had lived before he left for the United States, as 0.283 m, whereas the American equivalent is 0.305 m. FG was writing for German readers, so likely he was envisioning Cotton as being about 170 cm tall, taller than most male Germans around the middle of the century, whose average height, during a time of economic downturn, would have been around 160 cm. See the table in Franz Mozhnik, *Lehrbuch des gesammten Rechnens für die vierte Classe der Hauptschulen in den k.k. Staaten* (Wien: Verlag der k.k. Schulbücher, 1848), 131, and Sophia Twarog, "Heights and Living Standards in Germany, 1850–1939: The Case of Wurttemberg," in *Health and Welfare during Industrialization*, ed. Richard H. Steckel and Roderick Floud (Chicago: University of Chicago Press, 1997), 285–330.

3. "The Arkansas Toothpick" ("Arkansas-Zahnstocher"), a dagger about twelve to twenty inches long, was invented by James Black, who also created the Bowie knife.

4. FG frequently uses the English word "gentlemen"; future uses will not be specifically documented.

5. The "island" is the abode of the river pirates, the subject of FG's next novel, *Die Flußpiraten des Mississippi*, in which some of the plot elements of this novel will be continued. FG's sequel replaces the loose network of rogue criminals in *Regulatoren* with the nightmare vision of an organized underground society, conducting murderous raids on passing steamboats and rafts from the safety of their island. In 1963, FG's novel was turned into a Eurowestern with the same title, starring Hansjörg Felmy and Horst Frank.

---

* FG's note: "Rifle, called thus from rifled, *gezogen*." The word first appears in the early 17th century, derived from the French *rifler* (to groove), which is itself probably derived from a Germanic source.

6. The Petit Jean River, a tributary of the Arkansas River that flows east through the Ouachita Mountains of western Arkansas. FG's spelling throughout the original text is Petite-Jeanne. Spring Creek flows south and joins the Petit Jean River near present-day Danville, Arkansas.

7. The Ouachita River ("Washita," in FG's spelling) originates in the Ouachita Mountains about thirty miles south of the Petit Jean and flows east and south to the Black River in Louisiana.

8. $1 in 1840 equals roughly $28 in current value, based on, for example, the inflation conversion factors provided by Robert Sahr; see http://liberalarts.oregonstate.edu/spp/polisci/research/inflation-conversion-factors.

9. "Fenzecke" in the German original. FG's "Fenz" is borrowed from the English word "fence"; it is possible that FG had encountered it in one of the German dialects he heard spoken in the United States; consider the example from Pennsylvania German provided by H. L. Mencken: "'Mein *stallion* hat über die *fenz geschumpt* ...' (My stallion jumped over the fence ...)"; *The American Language: An Inquiry into the Development of English in the United States*, 2nd ed. (New York: Knopf, 1921), 398.

10. The Fourche La Fave, named after the La Feve family that settled near its mouth, rises in the western Ouachitas near the Oklahoma border and flows east until it joins the Arkansas River just above Little Rock. "Fourche" is French for "fork." The region of the river around present-day Perryville was FG's favorite hunting territory.

11. Dardanelle, a town on the south bank of the Arkansas River, near present-day Russellville, Arkansas.

12. The Maumelle River ("Mamelle" in FG's spelling) flows east through the Ouachita Mountains to empty into the Arkansas River just above Little Rock.

13. "Pulasky County" in FG's spelling. Its county seat is Little Rock, incorporated just a few years before FG first arrived and the state capital since 1836, when Arkansas gained statehood.

14. Randolph County, in the northeast corner of Arkansas; its northern boundary lies along the Missouri state line.

15. Militias were self-organized, paramilitary groups of private citizens who could be mustered by the governor. They provided their own weapons and returned to their homes when the crisis was resolved.

16. Farmington, Missouri was incorporated in 1836. The Black River flows through southeastern Missouri and northeastern Arkansas.

17. Hurricane Creek, rising south of Little Rock, flows south into the Saline River in south-central Arkansas. "Hurrikane" in FG's original spelling.

18. Here and subsequently in his text, FG uses the English word "hounds."

19. "Good bye gentlemen" and "adieu" are in English and French in FG's original text.

20. We have been unable to identify Setters Creek.

Chapter 2

Several New Persons Make Their Appearance on the Stage. Wonderful Hunting Adventure of "The Little Man."

On the county road that same morning, and barely five hundred paces from the thicket described in the previous chapter, rode along two horsemen who appeared to belong to the better class of farmers of that country. As different as they happened to be in their character and overall appearance, they otherwise seemed to be in perfect harmony, as they carried on together like the best of friends. The young slender man on a spirited chestnut pony – which submitted only with obvious displeasure, and frequent efforts to rebel, to the slow pace to which it was reined back by its master – laughed loudly and often at the jokes and observations delivered for his benefit by his short, portly companion.

The latter was a man somewhere in his forties, with a very full and very ruddy face, whose features offered the friendliest and jolliest expression that could possibly be ascribed to a man's face. His rotund, compact figure was in perfect keeping with his face, and his small lively grey eyes sparkled at the world with such happiness and good humor, as if they constantly wanted to say: "I am so very cheerful, that if I were any more cheerful it would simply be unbearable." He was clad, from head to foot, save only his highly polished black shoes, in snow white cotton. But his small cotton jacket could no longer be buttoned in front for all the treasure in the world, it had so shrunk in the washing – or, more likely, his round body had so expanded and "mayorized," as he liked to call it. A bright yellow straw hat shaded his face, and a thin bright yellow kerchief held together his open shirt collar, through which a stretch of his broad, sunburned chest was visible. Showing that he was not without some pride, or even a little vanity, the corner of a fiery red handkerchief peeped out of the right pocket of his trousers, which would have been capacious enough to hold and hide a half dozen of them.

His companion was a young and imposing man with a free and open expression, and dark, fiery eyes. His costume was that of a western American farmer, including a blue woolen frock-coat and trousers, and a black-striped vest made of the same material. His head was covered by a black and quite well-worn felt hat, and in his hand he held a heavy leather riding whip. He wore no shoes, just clean, simply made moccasins after the Indian custom. These, as well as his glance – continuously though calmly roaming over his surroundings – marked him as a hunter. As it happened, neither he nor his companion carried a rifle.

"A damnable fellow, my brother," laughed the small man, continuing some story already begun, "and he had a mania for buying old stuff – to drive you mad! When I was in Cincinnati last autumn, his wife complained to me about her predicament: the whole house was filled with old furniture and crockery and kitchen utensils, ten times more than she could use, and every evening the devil ran around to the auctions and bought every cheap thing he found. Once he had a thing, he never looked at it again. So I gave my sister-in-law some advice, that she should secretly take some of the junk right back to the auctions, just to get rid of it. She could put the money away and someday get something useful with it. It was a good plan – I discreetly hired a man with a cart, and one afternoon when my brother was at his business, I took the whole mess down to Front Street, and before it was dark the house was empty. My sister-in-law felt a weight lifted from her shoulders, and when her husband came home very cheerful at his usual hour of nine-thirty, she whipped up some capital punch. – By the way, Bill, we must brew some punch for ourselves here some time – the confounded folks in these parts are most of them loyal members of the temperance union. So – but where was I, ah yes, the punch. We sat together over the punch until eleven, and my brother told one funny story after another – he could tell some wild tales, my brother! I asked him several times why he was so jolly, but he wouldn't say a word. The next morning, he went off at six o'clock and what do you think he brought to the house in three wagons? All the junk that I had moved out the night before! Not a piece was missing, and he boasted besides about the monstrously good bargain he had made."

"Not bad, uncle," laughed the young man, throwing a quick sidelong glance at him, "nay, splendid – if it were true."

"Is that so, accursed boy – have I ever lied to you? Never. In the future, when I tell you a fact, you don't need to grin so, and stretch your trap from one ear to the other – do you hear me, Meesyer?"[1]

"Now, my good uncle, you mustn't think so ill of me. When you start a tale, I am always looking forward to the end of it, since it's usually something funny – which is why maybe I laugh sometimes a little too soon –"

"Funny? Just listen to that fop. I tell no funny stories – have you ever heard me tell a funny story? This last was serious – bitterly and sadly earnest. My brother will bring himself down with this accursed passion – he cannot help but ruin himself!"

"But your brother is said to be a very clever businessman, and if indeed he has a rather peculiar hobby in this regard, he makes up for it in other ways ten times over."

"A clever businessman? God bless you, young man – there's not a more cunning merchant than my brother – only too cunning sometimes, only too cunning! – I remember only too well the time when we were hunting together in Kentucky, how he used to con the peddlers with old possum skins – he sewed raccoon tails on them and sold them as coonskins. We drank several quarts of whiskey this way. – But I must tell you of a trick that he once played on me on Cane Lake.[2] We were paddling around the lake together in an old canoe, partly to harpoon fish, and partly to shoot deer as they came for a cool drink at the water's edge. It was singularly hot, and the sun grilled us in the most unpardonable way, so to make myself more comfortable, I decided to take off my hunting shirt. But as I took off my powder horn to start (a capital powder horn made from bone, with an airtight stopper), my finger got caught on the cord, and like a flash it slips overboard and sinks into the water."

"There I sat. The lake was clear as crystal, and though it was maybe fifteen feet deep, I could see the horn as plainly as if I could grab it with my hand. George was always an excellent jumper and runner, as well as a swimmer and diver; when he saw the embarrassment I was in, he offered to dive after it, and without further ado jumped overboard. Powder was monstrous expensive in those parts, and awfully hard to come by as well. The bottom was soft and muddy, and when he hit it, the water clouded up, and he had to wait a second until it cleared up. Meantime, I had gotten my hunting shirt off and was sitting on it; but when finally it occurred to me that he'd stayed under there just a bit too long, and I peered a little anxiously over the edge – what do you think he was doing down there – huh?"

"Well, I haven't got a clue what anybody would do in such a circumstance, other than try to get back to the surface as fast as possible."

"Off the mark!" cried the old man, and in his excitement checked his pony for a moment, as if overwhelmed by the memory. "Misfired! – He was just standing there – as calm as if he were standing on dry ground. He was bending over, so that I might not see what he was doing, but I saw it well enough! – The rogue was secretly pouring my powder into his own horn, and when he came up again, my horn was half empty. – Now, you don't need to laugh as if you're about to fall off your horse. – This one isn't true either, after all? Has your old uncle ever told you a lie – Eh?"

"No, Uncle Ben, now don't be angry, I believe every syllable! But – hey! – do you see that red thing yonder? – Over there – beyond the fallen spruce – just there, between the mulberry and the oak?"

"Where now? Ah, there – yes, that's a deer – sure enough; if Assowaum were here with his rifle, he could shoot him easily. If he remains behind the trees, he'd probably let one come within fifty or sixty paces of him."

"Where is Assowaum, anyway?" asked the young man, raising himself somewhat impatiently in the saddle and looking back toward the road, as though he expected to see the figure of the Indian there. "He slipped into the woods all of a sudden – I thought he had seen game, though the dear God knows what might have distracted him again. – What a great shot he could have taken from here," he continued, in a hushed voice, "I wish I had brought my rifle."

"The Roberts would give you a fine welcome if you showed up on the Sabbath with a gun – Mrs. Roberts won't even allow the Indian to do that, and he – but the devil take me – the creature is mighty tame – he must not hear us at all."

The two men had, meanwhile, been riding quietly along the road, and had come very close to the deer. He was standing at one of the countless salt licks found on both banks of the Fourche La Fave, but especially on the northern side, and he seemed to have no inkling of the danger nearby. Once, he lifted his head, but more likely in order to scent than from any fear that something extraordinary was about to happen. For the men saw that he had been licking in a deep hole in the clay bank of a small brook, hollowed out through frequent usage by horses and cattle and especially by deer. He paused in this position for a few seconds, frequently lashing his tail at the swarming flies, his back turned toward our two friends. Then, he again bent down to enjoy anew the salty taste of the rich soil. His newly sprouted horns were not quite four inches long and did not much hinder him in pursuing his object, so that he soon pushed his head into the hollow again, twisting it sideways, and using his long tongue to draw out the saltiest bits from deep inside.

"Where on earth can the Indian be, Bill?" said Harper in a whisper, barely concealing his desire for the hunt. "I do believe that a man could sneak to within five paces of the stupid thing, it would never know. – Ah, Bill, you should have seen me stalk them when I was young, I was once –"

"If you stay behind the root of the hickory, Uncle, I think it could be done," whispered the young man, smiling.

"Nonsense, boy! Do you think that I'm going to crawl around the woods on a Sunday with my old bones, frightening innocent creatures? I don't think so." – Despite this dismissive remark, Harper had jumped off his horse, which stood patient and motionless while the short fat man tiptoed ahead, clad all in white, face flushed with anticipation, keeping the roots of a fallen tree between himself and the creature. Apparently his sole intention was to enjoy the mighty leaps of the animal when it finally scented him so close by. But the creature did not seem to scent him, since it once more raised its head, stretched for a moment, and then returned to its tasty repast.

William Brown, or Bill, as his uncle called him for short, now also began to take an interest in the situation, for, sitting motionless on his horse to avoid making the slightest sound, he watched with rapt attention the progress of his uncle, who at this moment reached the tree roots and found himself within ten feet of the deer. Here he stopped and stood for a moment, and looking back at his nephew, screwed his face into a wonderfully comical grin, as if to say: "Well, Bill, ain't I a hell of a fellow?" Then, however, he hesitated for a few seconds, either because he was astounded by the inexplicable carelessness of the young deer, or because he was just as afraid to go any further in his clean shoes, since he was where the so-called "lick" or salt lick actually began and where the little brook that trickled through the soft clay soil had been trampled into a soft sludge by the tracks of countless deer and other animals. His old passion for the hunt at last, however, outweighed every other consideration, for now the possibility seemed to enter his mind for the first time that he could actually grab hold of the deer, and without a second thought he stepped lightly and carefully into the soggy muck, destroying the shine of his well-blacked Sunday shoes in a truly irresponsible manner. Nearer and nearer he came to the beast; Brown raised himself up in his saddle, breathless with anxious anticipation, and the heart of the old man beat (as he would later relate a hundred times or more) so loudly that he thought at any moment the deer must hear it. Now the latter raised his head; but before he could move a muscle in panic at the proximity of this gleaming white object, Harper threw himself forward, Sabbath and Sabbath clothes forgotten, and grabbed hold of the animal's hind legs with both hands at the same instant that, frightened to death, it reared up on those legs to escape, with a single leap, such a dangerous neighborhood. – It was too late. The old man hung on as with iron clamps to the fated beast, even as the desperate exertions of his prisoner jerked him forward. At full length he was drawn into the muddy earth, pulled into it despite the animal's desperate convulsions. In vain he raised his head as far as his short, fat neck would allow in order to keep at least that part of his body out of the mud bath. High into the air shot the liquid mass as he, like a ship launched from its slip, plunged in and submerged, then surfaced again.

"Hold tight," cried Brown, shouting with joy and giving his customary hunting cry – "hold tight, Uncle – hurrah for the old fellow, that's what I call a hunt!"

The encouragement was not at all necessary, for nothing could be further from the old man's thoughts than to let go at that moment, as he had already put not only his entire Sunday best but his whole person at risk. A cry for help he could not chance, indeed, for to open his mouth in these circumstances could have the most unpleasant consequences, and thus he held on as though his soul's salvation depended on it. Doubtless, at this moment his face expressed an iron resolve and strength of will, as with pinched eyes he was dragged jerkily through the salt lick, but his ancestral soil had so encrusted his entire physiognomy that to recognize any expression at all was really unthinkable.

Brown sprang quickly enough to his aid, but the sight was so comical that he threw himself down into the leaves at the edge of the lick and laughed convulsively, so that great tears ran down his cheeks, and for a full minute he could not pull himself together. But just as he was finally getting up again, he heard the sharp crack of a rifle, and for the last time the badly wounded animal leapt up, tore its fettered limbs from the old man's grip and, convulsing in its death agony, tumbled back into the mud.

Harper had heard the rifle's report, and struggled to his feet, shouting in a fierce voice, "Who shot?" Since he could not open his eyes, he turned the wrong way, to where no one was standing, provoking yet more irresistible laughter from Brown.

The hidden marksman did not wait long to reveal himself, for the Indian then stepped from a small sassafras thicket, and, when he glimpsed the sad condition of the otherwise so earnest and respectable man standing before him with fingers spread wide and eyes closed, loudly exclaimed with comical amazement, "Wah!"

"Bill – Bill – accursed boy – Bill – come here and lead me to the spring. By Jove, shall I stand here the whole day, until the muck gets so hard that the devil himself can't crack it? Bill, I say – you scoundrel, will you abandon your old uncle here?"

Bill really needed a few seconds before he could collect himself, then he stepped to the very edge of the white slime and handed the poor little man a dry branch lying just there, which the latter quickly grabbed. His obedient nephew straightaway steered him to the brook, where he first of all washed out his eyes so that he could see what was going on around him.

The first thing that met his glance was the figure of the Indian, who, poker-faced once more, was reloading his rifle.

"So, Mr. Red-hide – so do you believe that I crawl around in the mud here on Sunday mornings, and hold deer by the hind legs for you, until it pleases you to come around and shoot them down at your convenience, eh? If I've risked my life to capture a deer *alive*, do you then have the right to shoot it *dead*? Why don't you also go to my house and gun down the cows and pigs?"

"But, uncle, we're going to be late for church!"

"The church may go to the devil – do you believe that I'm going to church in such an outfit? – no, first I'm going to give this redskin a proper piece of my mind. Is it right and proper to sneak up on a Gentleman in this damned Indian fashion and shoot the game right out of his hands?"

"But, uncle, you couldn't have held the deer two seconds longer!"

"Not two seconds longer? And what does this young whippersnapper know about how long I could have held him? Didn't my brother once hold a bear the whole night long –"

"But you surely didn't want to capture the deer alive?" interrupted the nephew, who not without reason feared a long story.

"And why not? – don't I have a fence high enough to keep in a *herd* of deer, and is it any of the Redjacket's concern what I intend to do with my own property? Now, what is there to grin about, eh?"

The Indian, at whom all these angry expressions had been hurled, was meanwhile busily and without a word of reply loading his rifle, which he had already partially wiped out and cleaned. But while doing so, his face curled into a broad and friendly smile, revealing two rows of dazzling white teeth, and he replied in broken English:

"My father is very strong, but a deer is fast, and once out of the white man's hands, he never again would have pressed his tracks into the soft earth of the Fourche La Fave. My father wanted meat – here it is."

"The devil is your father!" grumbled Harper to himself. "If I have anyone to thank for the meat, it's these two bones," and with this he presented his burly arms. "But isn't it a fact, boy," he continued, becoming friendlier as the recollection of his heroic deed grew stronger, "that no one will do it quite so splendidly again, right? It was a stroke of luck, by the way, that you were both here to see it, for the devil take me if Roberts had believed me on my word alone. Despicable folks, here, as if I'd ever told a lie! But there, they smirk and smirk and look at one another and nudge each other in the ribs, as if they constantly wanted to say: 'Now you've told us another extraordinary story!' But I must wash myself now, this stuff will soon dry –"

"But we will be too late for the sermon!" said Brown, somewhat impatiently looking at the sun.

"Oh, go to the devil with your sermon – what does it matter if we hear that hypocrite Rowson preach? I can do it as well, and as for the fellow's piety –"

"Do you want to first ride home again, then?"

"That's understood – but you go on ahead, I'll be there in good time."

"But what about the venison?"

"What about the venison, Meesyer Nosy? That's easily said – that marches on my pony into my kitchen – I think I've earned it fairly enough. Just so, Assowaum, that's right" – turning now to the Indian, who was dragging the dead beast by its short antlers to the brook, to rinse off the thick mud – "wash him up, so that an upright Christian man can take it on his horse with decency; but, hallo – what's that, Mr. Scalping Knife – what the hell are you doing?"

This exclamation was in reference to the present actions of the Indian, who now, with the greatest cold-bloodedness, was disemboweling the deer and had begun skinning one of its haunches. "I don't want the skin off, do you hear? The fellow's deaf."

Assowaum, though, did not let himself be interrupted, but rather in perfect silence and with the utmost calm cut away one of the venison haunches and hung it with a strip of hickory bark over his shoulder. Only then did he very quietly reply: "The white man is alone in his wigwam, and Assowaum is hungry."

"Oh, take half of the meat, for all I care. But I'll get all bloody."

"But not any dirtier," replied the Indian laconically, threw his rifle once more on his shoulder, and walked quickly up the road, leaving further care of the game to the two men. Brown helped lift the mangled deer onto his uncle's horse; the latter then swung himself into the saddle and, his good mood straightaway restored, made his nephew swear that, above all, he would not tell the story to Roberts before he himself got there. He would just ride home quickly, change his clothes, and not stay long. Brown promised him, and then trotted quickly after the Indian, who through the young man's tarrying had gained a considerable advantage.

Notes

1. "Meesyer" is our rendition of FG's "Musjö," a popular corruption of the French "Monsieur."
2. Cane Lake: perhaps Cane Creek Lake, near Pine Bluff, Arkansas.

Figure 3.1. "Le Peau-Rouge – Assowaum" (The Red-Skin – Assowaum). From *Les Brigands des prairies*, a partial French translation of *The Regulators*, by Bénédict-Henry Révoil. *Journal illustré des voyages et des voyageurs* (October 1858). Image courtesy of the translators.

Chapter 3

The Indian and the Methodist. –
An Invitation to a Wedding.

Assowaum, the Feathered Arrow, belonged to one of the northern tribes of Missouri.[1] Several years earlier, as game grew scarcer in the more and more densely populated hunting grounds of his people, he became acquainted with the two white men, Harper and Brown, and migrated to the south. But not for game alone had he left his tribe; rather, he was also forced to escape the vengeance of his enemies, for he had slain a chief who, drunk with the fire-water of the Europeans, had assaulted his squaw, and as she cried for help, he became her savior and avenger. With her, he had raised a little wigwam[2] not far from Harper's home and lived by the hunt. His wife, though, braided the slender reeds that grow in the lowlands of the South into graceful baskets, and wove the supple bark of the pawpaw tree[3] into soft mats that Assowaum then carried along with his pelts down the river to Little Rock and traded with the merchants of that still young city for powder and lead or other necessities of life, and, though very seldom to be sure, for hard cash as well.

Here, then, his wife had been converted by the Methodist minister, the so-called "circuit rider"[4] (since he preached in almost all the settlements of this and the neighboring county), to the Christian religion. With Assowaum, however, all such efforts had failed, though Rowson strove constantly to entice "The Unrepentant," as he called him, to abandon the faith of his fathers and to bring him within the arms of the "one and only soul-saving church" of the Methodists. The Indian insisted that he wished to die in his faith, and would not let any of the fanatical preacher's exhortations and threats deceive him.

Alapaha,[5] Assowaum's squaw* started early that morning for the white man's settlement to hear the holy man preach, and Assowaum had followed her there, in part to take her home, and in part to take with him to his wigwam a load of otter pelts that he had bagged several weeks earlier in that region, and that he had stored at Roberts' house. Incidentally, the greater part of the

---

* FG's note: "Squaw – Indian name for wife."

settlers happened to be amicably disposed toward the two Indians, since they behaved themselves and were pleased to oblige when they could offer anyone a service. Still, the brave was always much graver and more reserved than his wife, who loved to busy herself with the children and never seemed to grow tired of their wild games.

"Well, did you ever come across a man who looked as funny as my uncle just did?" asked the young man, laughing, as he finally overtook the Indian.

"Looked like a mud turtle," said the latter with a broad grin, "only much dirtier. – The old man will have big story to tell when he gets to the huts of his friends."

"And *what* a story he will tell! It was strange, though, that he could hold the animal so long; I wouldn't have believed it if I hadn't seen it with my own eyes."

"Kahween Shaugweewee-See,[†] his bones are iron," replied Assowaum. "But the deer is also strong, and if Assowaum had come a minute later, he would have found no other flesh in the salt lick than the little man's."

"Could be; but he denies it vehemently, and now swears surely that he could have held the deer all night."

"The old man has big words," said the savage.

"Do you know old Bahrens, who just built a little house on the Petit Jean?"

The savage laughed and cast a sidelong glance at his companion.

"Have you ever spoken with him?" asked the latter.

"He has told of his hunts on the Bayou de View and on Cache River[6] – he shot nineteen deer in one day, and the smallest skin was eleven pounds, dried, without the pelt."[‡]

"Yes, he is mighty in such matters," laughed Brown, "I would like to see Uncle and Bahrens together one time."

"Me too," said Assowaum, who seemed very pleased by the thought. The two men now moved along the wide road in silence without encountering a single person, until from a distance echoed the shrill and drawling tones of a hymn. To these the Indian first listened for a few seconds with keen interest, but then quietly moved on, saying only: "The pale man" (as he called Rowson, due to his striking facial pallor) "has a very loud voice; he is like a young wolf. – The old howl as they may – you always hear the young."

"So you can't bear the preacher, Assowaum?"

"No – Alapaha loved the Great Spirit – she prayed to the Manitou, who had protected her fathers, and was an obedient wife. She never crossed

---

[†] FG's note: "He is not weak." On FG's use of "Indian" phrases, see the introduction, p. 10.

[‡] FG's note: "Pelt is the thin hide which the American hunter commonly will strip with the deer's fur and let dry, so that, sold by the pound, it will weigh more."

Assowaum's path when he went on the hunt; and when, in the first dark night, she drew her Matchecota§ around the freshly-planted mondámie (corn) field,⁷ the worms and preying animals avoided it, and the crop was blessed. Alapaha now laughs at the Great Spirit of Assowaum, and the game disappears from his path when he goes into the woods."

The Indian did not seem disposed to further conversation. He stepped quietly and quickly onward, until they reached the outer fence of Roberts' farm. From here lay a wide path leading between two cornfields to the main building, from which the singing that they had heard so long now sounded clear and distinct. When he came to the house, William Brown hung his horse's bridle over a fence rail and entered the room where the worshippers had gathered.

The hymn was just ended, and the whole congregation was on their knees, backs turned to the preacher and supporting themselves on the seats of their chairs. But Rowson, whom we earlier encountered under very different circumstances in the woods, stood erect in their midst, and, with eyes devoutly closed and in a harsh and repulsive voice, said a loud prayer, in which he laid before the Almighty the appalling sinfulness of those present, and prayed for mercy and compassion, rather than the punishment that they so richly deserved.

Brown, who belonged to another sect and could not be persuaded to sink to his knees, stood with folded hands and listened solemnly in the threshold of the door, but did not step closer. Vainly, Rowson made several friendly gestures to him to take a place at his side; he seemed not to notice and stared silently ahead. Finally the preacher finished his prayer, all stood up, and the service was ended.

Brown now greeted several of those present with whom he was acquainted, and who had congregated here from throughout the community.

"You've come quite late, Mr. Brown," said Marion Roberts, old Roberts' lovely daughter, who had been engaged these past six months to the pious preacher Rowson.

"Have you missed me, Miss Roberts? – then I indeed regret having missed most of the service."

"Now Mr. Brown, that is not well spoken. I have too good an opinion of you to believe that you'd attend such a sacred event for any reason other than the service itself."

"I'm not a Methodist."

"And what does that matter? Are we not all Christians?"

---

§ FG's note: "An outer garment customarily used by the northern tribes to ensure the fruitfulness of the fields and intended to keep predators away from the crops."

"Your *bridegroom* thinks otherwise about it." Brown emphasized the word "*bridegroom*," and gazed into the beautiful girl's eyes searchingly. But she avoided his look and replied: "He may sometimes have views that are a little too strict; I, in any event, think about it much more leniently and – Father, the same. Mother is, of course, very strict, especially in this regard. Mother and Mr. Rowson have, overall, very similar views."

"This time the blame isn't mine, Miss, I was on the way in plenty of time – but my uncle – an accident kept him, and he had to go back home."

"Surely he's not sick?" asked the girl quickly and anxiously.

"Hearty thanks for your sympathy and interest in him," replied the young man frankly – "it will give my old uncle great pleasure to hear of it. He thinks *very* highly of you."

Marion blushed at her somewhat too ardent question, and said evasively, "But why didn't he come with you?"

"He had an adventure," laughed Brown, "which he has forbidden me to relate, since he wants to tell it himself. You know his passion for storytelling."

"Oh, I'm looking forward to it!" cried Marion, clapping her hands, "it will be delightful!"

"And may one know what will be delightful?" asked Mr. Rowson, stepping forward and greeting the young man cordially.

"Something amusing that happened to my uncle, or rather a heroic feat that he performed, and –"

"Did you see it yourself?" asked Marion, laughing. "You know your good uncle –"

"Now, Marion," admonished Rowson gravely, "is it right, that so soon after service to your God, you concern yourself with worldly, profane matters? It would greatly grieve your mother, should she hear of it."

"Mr. Rowson," said Brown, uneasy at being a witness to a rebuke that brought a yet deeper blush to the girl's cheeks, "as Miss Roberts' betrothed and the preacher in this county, you have a double claim on the young lady. But I should think that an innocent jest, a cheerful word, cannot be displeasing to a loving God. Everything in its time – pious at prayer and joyous at table."

Rowson surely would have had replied to this, but at just that moment old Roberts stepped toward them, and heartily shaking young Brown's hand, he cried, "It is good, my lad, that you've come here once more – the dev –" His remark might have ended in a manner unbecoming the Sabbath, had he not met the preacher's grave and austere look just in time. Changing course, he continued: "for four weeks – how long have you actually been in Arkansas now?"

"Seven weeks," replied Brown.

"Well, for the past four weeks or so I've hardly seen you twice; in the early days, you were here every day – but, my – it's not so very amusing here on this lonely patch of land that a man can easily do without good company. Harper comes here more often – but where is *he* today?"

"He'll be here soon."

"By the way, Brown, so I don't forget – I invite you to my daughter's wedding, four weeks from today – you and your uncle – you must be there or it won't do, and then –"

"Forgive me," replied Brown quickly, half-turning away from him, "in – four weeks I'll – scarcely still be in Arkansas."

"No more in Arkansas – what? I thought your uncle had bought himself some land, and wanted to stay here forever?"

"Yes, my uncle will do that, but I – I'm going to join the Volunteers who are going to Texas. I heard a few days ago in Little Rock that they want to free themselves from Mexico and – need American muscle."

"Foolishness!" cried Roberts, grasping the younger man's hand in friendly fashion, "let them fight their own wars in Texas and stay here with us. We need able, brave fellows on the Fourche La Fave too, to even out the many scoundrels in these parts, and – all the girls in the world will come to the wedding, it'll be the dev – it'll be very strange if you don't find something for yourself among them. – Oh – don't worry," he went on, laughing, when he saw Brown shaking his head slightly – "there are some grand girls here, only they live so scattered about. A man like you, indeed, who goes nowhere and makes no visits, never gets to see them, though. But truly, here comes Harper; lightning and – hmm – how red he looks!"

It was truly this worthy gentleman, arriving at a lively trot. Apparently, he feared that Bill would tattle, and cried to them while still at a distance: "Well, young man, have you kept your mouth clean?"

"Mentioned not a syllable of it, Uncle."

"That's good! – Children, this morning I had a frolic – had a hunt –"

"A hunt, Mr. Harper?" reproachfully cried Madame Roberts, who had joined them and greeted the two men warmly, "a hunt on the holy Sabbath?"[8]

"Without a rifle, Mrs. Roberts, without a rifle, quite innocently. But I must tell it from the start, since a man doesn't do something like this every day. – Bill – stop – stay here, lad, you're my witness – where is Assowaum?"

"He's gone into the field, to the burning tree trunk, probably to roast a bit of meat for himself."

"Good, he'll be here later – I must have witnesses, or folks won't believe it – they all want to see it themselves, have a hand in it themselves – you should have heard my brother tell stories."

"Or old Bahrens!" laughed Roberts.

"Bah – who is old Bahrens? I always hear about old Bahrens; I must pay him a visit. He must be a marvel, then?"

"We'll be in his neighborhood Tuesday, to check on feral hogs," said Roberts; "come with us, Harper, if you like. We'll stay overnight at Bahrens'."

"First rate!" cried Harper – "but now for my story."

While the little man related, with great pleasure, his wonderful adventure to an attentive audience, Rowson, who did not consider it becoming his dignity to join in the general gaiety so soon after concluding his sermon, went out the back door of the house into the field – or rather the cleared land, since no corn had yet been planted nor the felled timber entirely moved out of the way. To best clear the large trunks, Roberts had laid a fire under several of them, and Assowaum was making use of one such spot to roast several pieces of the deer that Harper had captured. Alapaha, though, had noticed him here, and was now preparing a meal after the Indian custom.

Sprawled carelessly on his outspread blanket, drawing tobacco smoke from his short self-fashioned cane pipe and slowly blowing it out again, the powerful form of the red son of the forest lay outstretched next to the enormous trunk of an oak, the symbol of his distinctive race. Only a short time ago the tree had proudly and bravely overlooked the wide land as its own property, and now, after it had fallen to the ground, the white intruder did not know at once by what means he could most quickly and securely move it from the path. As the embers worked upon the trunk of the tree, so worked the firewater on the root of the warrior; at first slowly but steadily spreading and rending throughout, it destroyed the beautiful, noble fiber of life, the healthy marrow of the tree, and left only ashes and coals behind. The graves of the warriors fertilized the earth that the white man tore open with his plow, and the hearthstones of their council fires became so many headstones for their fallen and faded glory.

Such thoughts very likely crossed the mind of the brave Assowaum who, unlike thousands of his race, had not allowed the vices of the whites to enter his heart, as he stared daydreaming into the smoldering coals. His wife rose suddenly from her work and went toward the house. She had seen the figure of the preacher approaching and hastened to meet him. He, however, extended his hand to her and said a long and unctuous prayer over her. Meanwhile the meat sizzled on the coals and scorched on one side.

Alapaha was one of those few Indian beauties, in which the distinguishing characteristics of the race, not otherwise pleasing to the eye of the white, are a source of charm. The protruding cheek-bones lost themselves beneath the full cheeks, brimming with health; the ripe lips swelled lusciously; the black eyes flashed forth with a barely subdued fire from the dark complexion of the forest beauty; the ivory brilliance of her teeth would shame a negress; and the slender, voluptuous body was by no means so veiled by the close folds of her finely tanned leather robe or wrap as to conceal a hint of her beautiful, flawless figure. Her graceful feet were wrapped in carefully worked moccasins, her hair was tied up in a bright red cloth on the top of her head, and glass beads adorned her ears and neck.

"Alapaha!" now cried Assowaum to his wife, in a stern though not unfriendly tone, "Alapaha – does the Great Spirit of the Christians tell you that you must neglect the duties that you owe to your husband and chief?" Alapaha flew back to her work with quick steps, and Rowson drew near the red warrior, who, greeting him with only a slight nod of the head, remained lying quietly.

"Don't be angry with your wife, Brother Assowaum," he addressed the Indian in a friendly manner, "don't be angry with her, if she listens to the words of the Lord. It is her own soul's salvation that she rushes to embrace, and you should be the last to place an obstacle in her path."

"Assowaum is not angry and does not hinder her in the practice of her faith," answered the savage; "but he is hungry, and the meat burns. Alapaha is the wife of the red man."

"I have long wished for yet one more opportunity," said Rowson with a friendly glance, "to make very clear to you the blessings of Christianity. You have always avoided me – may I make use of the present occasion?"

The Indian did not reply; he took the meat that Alapaha served him on a crudely made wooden platter and began his meal. The venerable preacher now recalled to him all those potent places in the Holy Scriptures where attention is drawn to the sins of man and the mercy of the triune God, in the course of which he did not forget to relate to him the many wonders that Christ had performed on earth, until he died on the cross for the reconciliation of all flesh. He probably believed that through these colorful stories he could best appeal to the sensual nature of this son of the forest. The Indian calmly continued to eat; but even when he had finished his meal, he still did not interrupt the speaker with a single syllable, or a single glance, and listened attentively to his words. Rowson, encouraged by this, continued to harp on the Christian religion with increasing zeal, using themes that he believed, not unreasonably, must have the greatest worth in the eyes of his savage auditor.

"And has the pale man finished?" asked Assowaum at last, when the other exhausted himself and fell silent.

"I have," answered the preacher; "and what says my brother to it?"

Assowaum threw off the blanket that he had partly wrapped around himself and spoke, stepping close to the Christian:

"In ancient time, the Great Spirit – the one *you* call God – created the world, and out of the world he made men – Indians. – They did not come from across the sea. He spread a cover over the earth and put the men under it; all the tribes were gathered there. But one tribe among them sent one of its young people up to see what was going on above, and this one found it all very bright and rejoiced at the beauty of everything. A deer ran by, and an arrow was stuck in its side; he followed it and came to the place where it had fallen and died; he saw other tracks also, and soon came the man who had shot the animal. – It was the creator himself, and now he showed him how he should strip off the skin of the deer and cut up the meat. God then ordered him to make a fire, but the Indian did not know how. – God must do it himself. God then called him to stick a piece of meat on a stick and roast it; but the Indian did not know how and burned it on one side, while the other remained raw."

Rowson made a gesture as if he would speak, but the stern glance of the savage checked him.

"After he had thus taught the red man how to kill the wild animals and use the meat and skin, he called the others out of the earth, and they came tribe after tribe and each chose a chief."

"God also made Good and Evil – they were brothers. The one went out to do good; the other to destroy his brother's work. This one made the stony, gravelly places, let poisonous fruits grow and caused disaster. The Good wanted very much to destroy the Evil, but not with violence, so he proposed to him that they would run a footrace, after which the loser should leave the land. Evil agreed and –"

"Stop!" now cried the Methodist, rising ardently from the tree trunk on which he had been sitting to this point, "it would be unbecoming for me to listen to such stories on the holy Sabbath. Poor blinded heathen – your disastrous superstition leaves you hanging in this web of lies – chase it away from you! Jesus Christ –"

The Indian spoke not a word during these expostulations of the Methodist. He did not interrupt him with a single syllable, but fixed on the preacher a look so fierce, so brimming with rage and wrath, that he ended his speech out of fright, and looked back toward the house, which was not far off. But Assowaum quelled the raging storm in his breast, and merely looking darkly at the alien apostle, he spoke in a firm but quiet voice, while the other fell suddenly silent:

"I have listened to your words. You have told me of the chief who turned sticks into snakes and squeezed water out of the rocks; of the fish that kept a man in its belly for days and then spit him back on the land; of the prophet who drove to heaven on a fiery wagon; and of him who was sacrificed and died and then later came back to earth alive. Assowaum has believed it all. Now I tell you how the Great Spirit on *this* side of the world made his children, and you call me a *liar*. Go!" he said, stretching his arm toward the somewhat ashamed preacher, "the eye of the pale man sees only the side where his own wigwam stands – everything else is black."

Without waiting for any further response, Assowaum stepped toward the house, leaving his squaw to bring their belongings.

Meanwhile, Harper had finished his story to the laughter and displays of sympathy of those remaining in the house, who for the most part, as noon approached, dispersed to their various dwelling places, in order not to miss their meals. Only Harper and Brown had been invited by old Mrs. Roberts, as her "right rare guests," to partake of the simple meal.

Before the table was spread, however, Roberts once more beckoned to young Brown to come with him to the fenced field where he kept his best horses; they were the objects on which all of his pride and ambition converged. No man in the state could have better horses than he, and whoever bargained with old Roberts could be sure to come out on the short end, since no one had a surer eye for the flaws or virtues of this noble animal than he.

Yet before we become better acquainted with this old man, it is perhaps necessary to mention a small habitual weakness of his conversation. Namely, he always got carried away and rambled on at sixes and sevens, as they say: no matter how a sentence started off, he could never bring it to an end. Those who knew him best knew of this, and always interrupted him at the right moment so that he could quickly find his way back to his original theme. But if one let him go on undisturbed, he would lose his way and come at last to a sudden stop, without being able to remember a single word of what he wanted to say.

Arriving at the so-called "lot,"[9] he made the young man particularly observe several of the animals, extolling them to him – how cheaply he bought this one, how dearly that one; how much that one had won on a bet; how many minutes it took another to cover the track. He was so completely in his element here. Even better, Brown very clearly gave him to understand that he had thought to buy a horse from him in the next few days – a strong and sturdy one, to be sure, and suitable for the war for freedom in Texas.

"You can get that from me, Brown, you can get that!" cried the old man joyfully, completely forgetting for the moment that by doing so he would lose the young man from the neighborhood. "That chestnut horse there is a force of nature – you can't kill him – just as frisky in the morning as in the evening, and just four years old – but – what's come over me? You want to go to Texas? Hang it all, we can't bear it – I'd love to sell a horse, but I'll be – " He instinctively looked around to see if by chance his wife were nearby and could hear his cursing.

"No, Brown, this is nonsense. Texas is a land where no Christian man can thrive; – only the Indians – and what a gang that is! I remember right well how those from the Creek Nation came through here; then corn cost two dollars a bushel, and we couldn't get enough for them.[10] Of course now it's cheaper, and anyone who goes to Little Rock –"

"This quiet life here doesn't do it for me; I must see a little of the world," interrupted Brown – "I'll come back later."

"From Texas, eh? No one comes back from there – no *decent* chap at least – every rogue and scoundrel is heading there now, and the saying, 'go to hell' is entirely out of fashion; people are meaner now, and wish folks a trip to Texas. The soil there is no better than ours; I have some below the canebrake that I wouldn't sell for ten dollars an acre, and the fattening – you should take a look at my hogs next winter; I've also bought a new kind for myself from Atkins – with uncloven hooves. Atkins let me have two, and I would have taken more, but his brother – he's a lawyer in Poinsett County, and only recently settled there – but do you know how many people have moved to that swamp now?"

"It'll be right quiet for you at your house soon," said Brown, who had been staring out in deep thought for a moment – "Your son is in Tennessee, and when – Marion is married –"

"Yes – that's true; it'll be strange for me. Well, I'm not to blame for it, I've grumbled enough against it. I don't know, I can't stand preachers."

"Other than that, he seems to be a decent, quiet fellow!"

"Quiet? Yes – very quiet; but – between us – he doesn't seem to me to be much of a man. Heathcott said some things to him recently that *I* would have run a knife though his guts for, but he didn't say anything back. That Heathcott is a savage fellow, to be sure; his father was one of the old Virginians, who back then –"

"What did you tell me, the wedding is in four weeks, right?"

"In four weeks – yes – I told him that he can't have my daughter until he's bought the land where he lives, and anyhow until he's arranged things so that he can at least feed a wife properly. We don't need much here in the woods, but, still, a little capital is necessary; cash is generally a mighty rare thing, and the banks –"[11]

"Really, how does Rowson feed himself? He gets no ready money from his preaching."

"No, heaven forbid; but he does have some assets in Tennessee, eight or nine hundred dollars, as he told me. He expects one part of it in three weeks – after that I've promised my consent – her mother is completely crazy about the union. I would have nothing against it, but – I don't like how the man looks at you. It's strange, how that first look can create an impression. In Tennessee, where I lived before, and where my father had eighty acres on the Wolf River – you know the Wolf River, don't you? – splendid land, and in Memphis, not quite a half mile away, is an excellent market for every sort of produce. – Now how long has it been that I've been away from Memphis? Dear God, how the time flies, that was in the days when the first steamboat came along – the 'New Orleans.' Yes, yes, that must have been 1811 – 1811! Then came the war, and we marched down to Louisiana, but we got there too late; Old Hickory had already thrashed the British. – A clever idea, that with the cotton bales[12]; I spoke later with one of the Kentucky riflemen who had fired fifty-one times and gave me his word that he didn't miss his aim a single time. They're crack shots, those Kentuckians. Then later, in 1815, was the hard frost that ruined all our fruit – such a frost has never happened again in my lifetime. But Brown – what are you thinking about, truly? You're staring at nothing; is something wrong with you? – what was I talking about just now?"

"Me? No – nothing – a slight headache – I believe I laughed too much this morning about Uncle Ben's adventure. Right, we were talking about our horse deal."

"Oh, some other time for that! – But hello – who comes there? One, two, three, four, five, six men on horseback, and every one with a rifle and a knife? Now, that will be a fine letter of introduction to my wife; Heathcott and Mullins and Smith and Heinze, Lord bless us, it's the 'Regulators' – something's burning somewhere. Well, we'll hear about it soon."

The old man quickly opened the gate and Brown followed him out to greet the riders, who now approached at a slow trot along the wide path that ran westward among the fields.

Notes

1. FG is vague regarding Assowaum's tribal origins. Here he is described as a member of one of the "northern tribes of Missouri," which might refer to the Missouria, Illini, Ioway, or possibly Osage peoples. But in chapter 38, he sings a song of the Ojibwe, an Anishinaabeg tribal group traditionally occupying territory in the upper Mississippi region (mainly present-day Michigan, Wisconsin, and southern Ontario). By the time FG resided in Arkansas, indigenous peoples like the Caddo, the Quapaw, and the Osage had been "removed" to reservations in Kansas, Louisiana, and Indian Territory (Oklahoma). New groups from the Southeast (Cherokee, Creek, Choctaw, Seminole, and others) had passed through the region as part of the "Trail of Tears" (1830–1850), and a number of them had stopped in Arkansas rather than continue to Indian Territory. Given such complexity, we cannot be more precise about Assowaum's identity than FG.

2. For one of the earliest uses of this word—derived from the Eastern Algonquian phrase *wĕkou-om-ut* or "in his house"—see the "Third Remove" of *A Narrative of the Captivity and Restoration of Mrs. Mary Rowlandson* (1982).

3. The pawpaw tree (*Asimina triloba*) is a fruit-bearing deciduous tree common throughout the eastern United States. Pawpaws are the largest edible fruit indigenous to the United States.

4. "Circuit rider" is in English in FG's text.

5. Alapaha may have been named after the ancient village in southern Georgia, situated along the river with the same name. In the view of some linguists, the word is derived from the Timucuan word for "bear." See John H. Goff, *Placenames of Georgia: Essays of John H. Goff*, ed. Francis Lee Utley and Marion R. Hemperley (Athens: University of Georgia Press, 2007), 240.

6. "Bayou de View" (FG writes "Bai de View") and the Cache River (FG's "Cashriver") are both in northeastern Arkansas.

7. "The freshly-planted mondámie (corn) field": in the original text, FG adds "Mais," the German translation of the Ojibwe word for corn.

8. FG frequently applies the honorific "Madame" to his frontier ladies, thus comically French-ifying his tough Arkansas women.

9. The term "lot," meaning property, appears in English in FG's original.

10. The Arkansas River Valley was a major route on the "Trail of Tears."

11. Roberts uses the inaccurate German plural "Bänke," normally reserved for "bench" as a piece of furniture; see Heinrich August Schötenbeck, *Grammatik der neuhochdeutschen Sprache mit besonderer Berücksichtigung ihrer historischen Entwicklung* (Erlangen: Ferdinand Enke, 1856), 111.

12. During the Battle of New Orleans in 1815, the 7th US Infantry, commanded by General Andrew Jackson ("Old Hickory," 1767–1845), successfully held their position against the British forces from behind a breastwork of cotton bales; hence the nickname "Cottonbalers."

Chapter 4
The Regulators. – Squabble and Struggle.

Lynch Law – that is, the exercise of justice by persons with no legal authority, and the punishment of criminals by individual citizens of the state – had recently become alarmingly prevalent once again in Arkansas, and to curb such excesses, the laws had been made more stringent, and even stiffer penalties had been imposed on the creation of these arbitrary juries. But little did any of this help in a state where still hardly a path had been cut through the wilderness, and the arm of justice could not reach into even the nearest settlements. Moreover, Arkansas had become, at the time, the gathering place for all those bands of thieves that had formerly wrought their mischief on Missouri, Illinois, Kentucky, Tennessee, and Mississippi. The settlers there had justifiably come together and entered the field as one against their arch-enemies, who threatened to destroy the peace of their dwellings. But as everything has its light and dark side, so here as well. On the one hand, some villains were hauled quickly and unexpectedly before a tribunal and handed over to their just punishment, without anyone troubling the Justice of the Peace or the Sheriff; on the other, it sometimes happened that personal hatred and a thirst for revenge turned the crowd against a lone innocent, and let him feel the power that was, for a moment, in the hands of his enemies. Thus in White County[1] the Regulators ripped a respectable and hardworking farmer from the heart of his family and bound him to a tree before the eyes of his wife, who fainted and was thus luckily spared the worst, and amid the moans and wails of his children. They whipped the unfortunate man in a horrifying manner, in order to force from him a confession to a crime that he had not committed. To be sure, he later proved his innocence and shot the ringleader of the gang, but the shock and fright had so affected his wife that she succumbed to a fierce fever and died a few months afterward. It was said, moreover, that Heathcott was one of the Regulators at that time and had had to leave White County as a result. In any event, he was a savage and crude fellow, with whom no one wanted to have dealings – a Kentuckian to the bone, boastful and belligerent, though otherwise honest and upright.

The other men were for the most part farmers from the neighborhood, all dressed in their hunting shirts, and armed with rifles, Bowie knives, pistols, and tomahawks. Heathcott, especially, was studded with guns and daggers, and warranted Roberts' comment to Brown that he looked like a privateer who had gotten all his weapons on deck and was ready to board.

"Hello, gentlemen," now cried the old man, welcoming them. "Whither bound? Whither the journey? Are the Indians coming, that you're so frightfully equipped with knives and shooting irons?"

"Indians? No!" cried Heathcott. "But something much worse; the horse thieves are on the loose again; they've stolen four of them from Judge Rowlove up on the Arkansas, and the tracks led southeasterly. But the damned rain night before last has washed them out, and we can't tell whether they go toward the hot springs[2] or farther easterly. We searched the woods yesterday in all directions, but to no avail, and we could do no more than send Hostler down the river and Bowitt over toward Hot Springs County.[3] Now the rest of us are going down to Wilkins', to talk over our next steps. Do either of you want to go?"

"Thanks much!" said Roberts. "You young fellows sort this out among yourselves. My old bones are no longer suited to running through the woods!"

"But you also have a lot of horses. Who knows when the bastards may pay you a visit; you'd come with us after that," laughed Heathcott.

"I'll wait for it; I must be in a right inconvenient place for them here, or else I'd be missing things already. It's quite remarkable how they've spared *me*."

"Might almost look suspicious," grinned the Kentuckian.

"No, no," laughed the old man good-naturedly, "that's not it. But wouldn't you like to go to the house, gentlemen, and have a bite to eat? Good morning, Heinze; good morning, Mullins; hello, Peter, that must be a new horse you're riding there? – I've never seen it – handsome animal."

"We'll gladly accept your invitation," said Heathcott, climbing down from his horse, while the rest of them followed his example, "anyway, Wilkins never has anything to eat, and it's surely better that we stock up now. But don't make a fuss – the horses can rest a bit in the meantime."

While Heathcott spoke, Brown had greeted each of the men with whom he had become acquainted during his short sojourn, and he now walked with them to the house, where the little Negro girl was busily working to bake some cornbread and roast some pork for the unexpected guests.

"And you, Mr. Brown," asked Heathcott, turning now to the young man, "don't you want to lend your arm and your eye to a good cause? We can hardly be too many, since with the law against us, we must prove to the state how earnest we are about the matter."

"I must ask you to forgive me," replied Brown; "first, I'm only a very brief visitor to this region, and not yet very well acquainted with the forest or the circumstances of the country in general, and then I must tell you honestly that I don't like the Regulators' style of justice, it too often tends to mischief."

"Sir!" said the Kentuckian, somewhat irritably – "But surely you'd also concede that we around here know best where the shoe pinches?"

"Naturally – naturally," replied Brown amiably. "I wouldn't presume to offer an opinion about that, but I also reserve the right to conduct myself as I see fit."

"A man never knows where he stands with you gentlemen who are always flitting from one state to another," said Heathcott, casting a side look at the young man that was anything but friendly. "One day you're in Missouri, another day you're in Texas, and everywhere you go you have friends and acquaintances. – Maybe you don't join the Regulators out of consideration for your friends?"

"Mr. Heathcott," responded Brown very earnestly, but also very politely, "I'll choose not to understand this innuendo of yours, since I don't feel that it applies to me. As for my conduct, my travels from one state to another, I'm bound to account for that to no man but myself."

The other farmers now joined in the conversation and prevented Heathcott from saying anything more that could wound the young man's feelings. They had all become very fond of him, whereas they feared their leader more than respected him.

"In here, gentlemen, right in here!" Roberts cried out to them from the open house door. "You must make do with something I've prepared quickly for you, so you don't need to wait until lunch to eat. So, sit yourselves down and – help yourselves."

The men didn't need to be told twice, and after they had greeted the ladies of the house, they sat themselves down at the richly laid table without further ado – indeed, without laying aside all the many deadly weapons that were attached to them. They were just about to tuck in, when Rowson, who had been standing next to Mrs. Roberts by the fire, stepped to the table, hands folded, and began to say grace.

The farmers – some of whom were Methodists themselves, while the others respected the customs of the house – lowered the knives they had already grasped and looked down reverently at their empty plates. Heathcott, however, glanced up angrily at the preacher, who appeared not to notice him at all, and calmly continued to exercise his duty, as he called it.

Had the women not been present, the crude man's wrath probably would have exploded at this, but he controlled himself – or, at least, saved it for a more suitable occasion – and began his meal even as the preacher was still saying "amen." Needless to say, such behavior deeply wounded Mrs. Roberts. She sat down on her rocking chair with great bitterness and muttered something about "crude, sinful men," which, however, reached only the ear of the preacher, who had stepped back to her side and now nodded his head and sighed in agreement.

"Mrs. Roberts – you wouldn't have a sip of whiskey in the house?" asked Heathcott after a brief pause, wiping his mouth with the sleeve of his leather hunting shirt. – "Over there at Bowitt's we drank such damned harsh stuff that it almost burned my guts."

"I keep no whiskey," replied Mrs. Roberts, irritated anew as much by the question as by the profane swearing[4] – "Mrs. Bowitt would likewise do better not to allow such drink in her house."

"Yes – I told her so myself," laughed Heathcott, who either misunderstood, or chose not to understand, the old woman's meaning. "It's a shame. For a dollar a gallon, she could get the best brew in the world from the peddler on the Petit Jean – real Monongahela."[5]

"Mr. Heathcott really should see," said Rowson mildly, "that a conversation about whiskey is not at all pleasant to Mrs. Roberts' ears."

"Mr. Rowson would do well to mind his own business," answered Heathcott sharply.

"I've given the horses some corn, gentlemen!" cried old Roberts through the open door as he was now returning from the stable with Harper and Brown.

"Thank you! Thank you!" shouted Smith and Heinze, happy to have an excuse to rise from the table and interrupt a conversation that could only end unpleasantly.

Smith stayed back for a moment as the other men stepped out, and said to Mrs. Roberts in a friendly tone:

"You mustn't take Heathcott's crude talk so hard, Madame. We had a brisk ride this morning, and when we got to Bowitt's, he drank a little more than he really should have."

The old lady did not reply, and only rocked herself more fiercely. Rowson, on the other hand, thanked his neighbor for his good intention, and assured him that he bore Heathcott not the slightest grudge. "He's a rash young man," he continued, smiling pleasantly, "and doesn't always mean to be as wicked as he sounds."

"I will be much obliged to him if he never again graces my house with his presence," Mrs. Roberts finally blurted out. "I raise my child to be God-fearing, and don't want her to see an example of evil within my own four walls, nor –"

"But, mother!" pleaded Marion.

"Nor that pious people," continued the old woman, ignoring the interruption, "who preach the pure word of God, are insulted under my roof – say that to Mr. Heathcott." And once more the old lady began to rock in her chair, as though she had resolved to see how far she could go without flipping over.

Smith, a quiet, peace-loving man, and himself a Methodist, was too much in agreement with everything that Mrs. Roberts had said to object to any of it, and followed the others silently out the door. There they had seated themselves, partly on chairs and partly on tree trunks and troughs, and spoke of what most concerned them, the horse-stealing that was becoming more and more common.

"The rascals must have a middleman here in the county, otherwise I can't figure out how it's possible for them to fool us every time," said Mullins.

"Yea, and where they hide the stolen beasts is still a mystery to me," cried Roberts. "A horse isn't a bird that can fly over the ground without leaving any tracks."

"Be patient!" assured Heathcott. "Just be patient; everything comes to an end, and we'll catch those guys some day when they least expect it, but I'll be damned if I let a single one of the dogs live. It's a crying shame that they abolished the death penalty for horse-stealing here in Arkansas last year – that's saying to folks as plain as can be: 'Now, help yourselves – we won't do it anymore.'"

"I don't know, it will always be hard to take a man's life for a horse," interjected Brown.

"Hard? Then you go to hell!" shouted Heathcott, thrusting his giant knife into the bark of the trunk on which he sat. "Whoever steals my horse – steals a piece of me. – I've just sold three and I'm carrying the money on me – you could say it's my whole fortune, with which I was planning to buy more property. – If someone had stolen the horses, this would be the same as destroying my whole plan for life, my future, and that's worse than if he had shot me to pieces. No, death to the bastards! – Just let them see that we're in earnest, and we'll soon run them out of Arkansas – that is, the ones we haven't hanged."

"You seem to hold a man's life of little account," interjected Brown.

"Very little," answered Heathcott, playing with his knife again.

"Then you value your own very little," laughed Harper, "eh? Otherwise you wouldn't weigh it against that of every scoundrel."

"Highly enough to – let him taste nine inches of cold steel, whoever I thought – could be dangerous to me," cried Heathcott, looking wildly around the circle. – "This is a free country, and every man has his views, but I'll be goddamned if don't defend my own above all – that much is sure. – Aha, there's Mr. Rowson again," he continued scornfully, as he noticed the venerable figure of the man standing in the doorway with his hat on his head and his prayer book under his arm. – "Another one of the cheats, strutting around in his sheepskin and letting the fox show through only now and again."

Rowson turned toward the Negro boy who came to the house just then, and asked him to hold his horse; but Heathcott, incensed by the disregard of the preacher, who pretended not to have heard a word, sprang up and shouted angrily: "Now, Mr. Hell-Stomper, I thought I was worth an answer, even if I am a sinner!"

But before Rowson could say a word in reply, Brown jumped up, put his hand to Heathcott's chest, and flung him so fiercely down onto his seat that he went over the log backward, hitting the ground so hard that he was bleeding. The others leaped up in fright, and with them the Kentuckian. Gripping the knife that had fallen next to him, he sprang over the fallen tree with a single bound, and was about to throw himself on his assailant, when the other – without budging an inch from where he stood – held out a cocked Terzerol revolver.[6] Heathcott, who had supposed him unarmed, ran back to grab his rifle, but the other men grabbed him by the arm and shouted as one that they would allow no murder here.

"Stand back," shrieked Heathcott, – "Back! Let me at the bastard – that calls for blood! – I must have his heart's blood – damn you all – the eyes out of his head."

"Let him go," said Brown, now pocketing the Terzerol and drawing from under his vest just such a knife as Heathcott wielded – "let him go, and we'll see right away who the best man is."

"For God's sake, Mr. Harper, stop this terrible thing!" begged Marion, rushing from the house with a deathly pale face and taking the old man's hand in a trembling grip. "That wicked Heathcott will kill him."

"Be calm, dear child," Harper soothed the pleading girl – "and above all go back into the house. – This is no place for a young woman at present – once the bullet leaves the barrel, no man knows where it may go."

"He will kill him," wailed the maiden.

"Who? Your bridegroom? No. – His fight is with my nephew."

Marion buried her face in her handkerchief, and meekly allowed herself to be guided into the house by Rowson, who had stepped to her side.

"Back, I say!" shouted Heathcott in a frenzy – "give me my rifle – I must blow the dog to pieces!"

"Let him go!" again cried Brown, his fighting spirit blazing up. – "Set him free – he has knives enough about him to hazard an honest fight – out of the way, men of Arkansas! Would you stop an even fight?"

"Good!" said Mullins – "you may fight it out, but he can't have a gun. – We won't allow murder; – a fight is something else."

Heathcott found himself free in the next instant, and the men made a circle around the two. But the Kentuckian, so wild a moment earlier, seemed to be mightily subdued by the cold, fearless gaze of his opponent, and though he still frantically clutched the knife in his hand, and threw his foe looks of angry determination, he did not attack, but stood his ground as though in a trance. An awkward silence ensued; the men stood around the foes and hardly dared to breathe, while Marion gazed out from the doorway of the house at the circle with deathly pale cheeks and a fixed stare, convulsed with excitement. Her hands folded over her breast and trembling with fear, she awaited the triumph of the loathsome man.

Heathcott found himself in an awkward position; he obviously feared the steel of the enemy, but even more the ridicule or the derisive laughter of his comrades that he believed must follow if he did not accept the offer to fight. His friends here interposed, and stepping between the two men, separated the combatants.

"Come, Heathcott," said Heinze. "You're both in the wrong, and it's a sin and a disgrace for two decent fellows to carve up each other's carcasses when there're enough vermin in the woods that you could loose your fury on. Come – it's about time for us to get started; it's not right either to spoil the Sabbath of the folks here who have received us so kindly."

"That's the only thing that has so far stopped me from whipping the greenhorn," said Heathcott, grinding his teeth. "But wait, laddie – I'll find you, and God help you if ever you end up in front of my barrel."

"Heathcott – Heathcott," Mullins cautioned, "that's wicked and dangerous talk – very dangerous words."

"Let him," Brown laughed contemptuously, returning his knife to its sheath – "let him boast; it's the only pleasure he still has in life."

"Come, Bill," said Harper, as he pulled his reluctant companion toward the house, "come, Bill – let the fellows run along – you've satisfied your honor, and I'm so pleased that my sister's son has behaved so bravely. But that's all for now – think of the women – Marion has just now fainted."

"Marion's fainted?" Brown asked quickly, as he hurried toward the house. "Ah, yes," he then said more slowly, stopping short. "Of course, her bridegroom is with her – I hadn't thought of that – she will surely recover."

Meanwhile, the Regulators had left the place, and Rowson too prepared to ride home. Harper, though, accepted Roberts' invitation and stayed at the house so as to join in the promised hunt the next morning, and to visit old Bahrens, of whom he had heard so much.

Rowson delivered another long prayer before mounting his horse, partly to beg the forgiveness of the Most High for the appalling desecration of the Sabbath, partly to thank Him that this cup had passed by without bloodshed. But before he swung himself onto his horse, he first went to young Brown and said:

"You've taken my part today, and I thank you. But though that knave is plotting revenge, fear not, Heaven will shield you; just rely on its protection."

"I thank you, Mr. Rowson, I thank you," heartily replied Brown; "but I rely more on the fellow's cowardice and my own strength than on anything else at all. He'll stay out of my way, that's for sure, and I'm not looking for a fight. So we'll scarcely come together again."

Notes

1. White County, located in south central Arkansas. The county seat is Searcy.

2. Hot Springs, southwest of Little Rock, in the western Oauchita Mountains, next to Lake Ouachita.

3. "Hot Spring County" in FG's spelling.

4. FG uses the verb "schwören" in German, an Americanism.

5. The Whiskey Rebellion was a popular uprising that began in 1791 and culminated in an insurrection in 1794 in the Monongahela Valley of Pennsylvania, triggered by the government's decision to tax whiskey. Old Monongahela Pennsylvania rye had a much higher alcohol content than today's Kentucky rye whiskeys.

6. Terzerol, a small muzzle-loading pistol with one or two barrels.

Chapter 5

Brown and Marion.

Rowson had ridden off, as he said, "to preach the Word of God in another settlement," and Marion was reclining, pale and exhausted, in an armchair. Only occasionally did great teardrops steal down across her cheeks and roll gently onto her delicate fingers, which she held folded in her lap; but a deep, deep heartache was revealed by the soft features and tightly pursed lips of the beautiful girl. Harper, Roberts, and Brown were seated around the fireplace, in which the Negro woman was lighting a fire, more from habit than any real chill in the air, and Mrs. Roberts stood near her daughter and stroked her nut-brown hair.

"Come, child – let go these cares and phantoms," she said soothingly to the dear girl, "see, it's all over now. Mr. Rowson can't possibly meet those men again today, he's taken an entirely opposite direction – get out into the fresh air, then you'll be better – perhaps Mr. Brown will accompany you and take you for a little walk. Look, you really do have a fever – how flushed you seem to be once more – come, come – you should be ashamed of yourself, such a big girl and crying so."

Marion had, at these last words, buried her face in her mother's breast and sobbed loudly. "Mr. Brown, won't you take that foolish child outdoors a little? I really wish that Mr. Rowson had been able to stay with us today, but of course – service to God comes before service to man."

Brown had already jumped up at the first hint that his company was desired, and he now approached the young lady, somewhat embarrassed at himself, to offer her his arm.

"So, that's right, child," encouraged the mother – "that's well done – chin up – you'll feel better outdoors, and walk vigorously, Mr. Brown, so that she gets some proper exercise. God forgive the wicked people who bring such strife and discord to the peaceful homes of His servants."

Harper had, meanwhile, become very pensive, and stared silently at the crackling wet wood, while Roberts, having begun a conversation about the recent quarrel, had come by his usual sequence of thoughts to the Revolutionary

War. He was just about to begin an anecdote from Washington's life, when the two young people left the house and wandered slowly and silently along the wide, cleared roadway that led up the river to the higher settlements.

The sun was sinking toward its setting, and the shadows of the tremendous trees fell across the road; flocks of cheerful perroquets* fluttered shrieking from tree to tree, grey squirrels sprang with bold leaps across the branches or squatted chewing on some hoarded nut, the shell of which then fell rustling down through the leaves. Warily lifting its beautiful head, a doe with a young fawn stepped softly across the road, paused for a moment to look up and down the wide thoroughfare, standing and then slowly disappearing in the thicket, as if she knew that those approaching threatened no danger. A quiet peace lay on the landscape, and the mighty tops of the pines and oaks rustled majestically in the southeast wind passing through them.

"We really owe you a very big thanks, Mr. Brown," Marion finally broke the silence that was becoming painful. "You so kindly and bravely took the side of my – of Mr. Rowson and – exposed yourself to great danger."

"Not so great as you perhaps believe, my lady," answered Brown hesitantly. "The fellow's a coward, and only picked a fight with Mr. Rowson because he could – because as a preacher he couldn't take it up."

"You meant to say something else? Speak it out – you think Mr. Rowson is a coward?"

"He's a preacher, Miss Roberts, and it would get him a very bad name in the community if he went around looking for quarrels."

"Not looking, but – it comes to the same thing – you stepped in on his behalf – it's very comforting to me to feel that you're such good friends with each other. Where did you actually get acquainted?"

"Acquainted? friends? Miss Roberts, I barely know Mr. Rowson – we exchanged the first words with one another today."

"And you risked your life for him?" asked Marion quickly, as she stopped in amazement and looked into the young man's big blue eyes.

"I heard that – he – was engaged to you – I saw you turn pale and – I'm of a somewhat impetuous nature. Anger got the best of me concerning the rude fellow; I was probably a little rasher than I really should have been; but my God, Miss Roberts – you are unwell again, wouldn't you like us to sit for a moment on this tree trunk?"

---

* FG's note on this French word: "A small species of parrot." (The French word is misspelled as "peroquet" in FG's original). The Carolina parakeet, the only parrot species native to North America. Now extinct and commemorated in one the most famous plates of John James Audubon's *Birds of America* (1827–1838), plate 26.

Marion let him lead her to one of the trees that had been felled when the road was cleared and then rolled to the side, there to decay in the course of time. Again there was a long pause, and Marion finally inquired softly:

"Do you wish to leave us, Mr. Brown? Father said a little while ago that you're going to join the struggle for freedom in Texas."

"Yes – Miss Roberts – it will be better for me if I find an occupation of that kind. – I would like to forget a number of things, and a campaign is probably the best place for that. – Perhaps then, too, it'll bring a sympathetic – I'll probably do a horse trade with your father."

"You don't seem to be happy," said the lovely girl softly, while she looked at him earnestly and thoughtfully. "You lived long in Kentucky?"

"I left Kentucky with a light heart!"

"And has Arkansas brought you such sorrow? That's too bad – I've loved this land so much until now."

"You'll keep loving it. – In a few weeks you'll celebrate a union with the man of your choice, and if with the love of one's heart the desert must become a paradise, how much more then the beautiful woods, the enchanting climate of Arkansas – ah, there are still some very happy people on the earth!"

"And whom do you count among them?"

"Rowson!" cried the young man and startled himself by the audacity of what he had said.

"The mosquitoes are very bad in this place," said Marion, as she stood up quickly, "let's go on, Mr. Brown. – We must soon turn around – the sun is no longer high."

Once more, silent for a while, they took their way.

"You live alone with your uncle, don't you Mr. Brown?" Marion asked at last, after a long pause. "Mother told me so, at least."

"Yes, miss – we keep a bachelors' household; a rough life."

"Your uncle is really a fine man – always cheerful – always ready with a joke; and has something honest, open in his look – I liked him from the first moment I saw him; – I've never seen him so serious, by the way, as he was today. – But you too seem to me awfully earnest today; the bad men are to blame for it all."

"Mr. Rowson's probably going to buy here in the area? I heard Mr. Roberts say that he's waiting for a portion of his assets."

"Yes," whispered Marion. "Father wanted it so – Father – was altogether against this union."

"That's not right of your father, Miss – he shouldn't stand in the way of his own child's happiness."

"But he maintained that I wouldn't be happy," said Marion, smiling sadly.

"Is not love the greatest happiness?"

"So they say."

"So they say? Don't you love your intended, then?"

"Mother's whole heart was set on this union. Taken by the godly man's pious way of life, she believed that she could not better care for me than to persuade me to take his hand. Indeed, I got to see many men here in the forest, but none had made an impression on me. – The wild, rough, roving hunters, the carefree river men – the otter trappers and even the simple farmers who settle here in our neighborhood, were all unsuited to win my heart. Mr. Rowson was the first to gain my respect by his decent, friendly behavior. He came often to this region, preached frequently here, and – Mother learned to value him. – She herself persuaded him to settle down among us and take a wife – he asked for my hand, and Mother – pledged it to him."

"Until then I had never thought about a union with him," Marion continued haltingly after a while, "I always saw him more as a fatherly friend than as a possible lover, and the proposal surprised me. And then – I can perhaps confess it to you – his eyes held something that filled me with horror, if I glanced at him quickly and unexpectedly; but if I looked at him quite seriously and steadily, there lay then something so mild and soft in his features that I was finally taken with him. Driven by my mother's never-ending exhortations, I at last gave my consent. But Father would not agree; he couldn't abide the still, quiet man, and had a couple of pretty serious run-ins with Mother about it. To tell the truth, it was all the same to me which of them was right, since I believed indeed that I would be happy with Mr. Rowson, although without him I didn't expect to be unhappy either. As, therefore, Father decided to yield the field to Mother, and only insisted as to the matter that Mr. Rowson must have enough property to give him a hope of supporting a wife without being dependent on preaching alone, I promised Mr. Rowson – to be his wife. – As he just told us today, he hopes to receive in a few weeks a sufficient sum of money not only to buy the land on which he lives, but also to get a start on cattle breeding, apart from purchasing all the other necessary farm equipment. Then nothing will stand in the way of the fulfillment of his wish, and I – will be his."

Marion spoke these last words with such a faint and trembling voice that Brown involuntarily stood still and looked down at her – she had turned her head away, and the bonnet that she wore hid from him her face.

"You will be happy," he whispered, and a deep sigh escaped from his breast.

"We must turn back, Mr. Brown," said Marion after a little while. "Don't you see, the tops of the trees are already reddening, the sun will soon be down, and in these dense woods it'll quickly be night – Mother might worry."

The two young people turned silently homeward; after a few minutes, Marion spoke smiling: "I've now told you my whole life story in a few words, and thus shown an astonishing degree of confidence; but confidence, as Mr.

Rowson says, awakes confidence, and now it would be only right and proper that I demand the same of you. That is – if you have no secrets to protect that a talkative child, such as I am, naturally shouldn't find out."

"My life has gone on quite simply," replied Brown, "almost too simply. Born in Virginia, my father moved us, while I was still a child, to Kentucky, where he founded the first settlements with Daniel Boone.[1] I was hardly strong enough to carry a rifle when I had to fight against the Indians, who at that time worried us day and night. For a long time we defied their tricks and superior force, but once, one ill-fated night, they cut my father off from our dwelling, attacked him, and killed him. At daybreak, we were awakened by their war-cries and the crackling of the flames that destroyed our log cabin. Our whole family fell to the tomahawk of the red devils, and only through a miracle I escaped their notice and the scalping knife. I fled and reached the next settlement. From then on, though, we fought to drive the savages from their hiding holes and forced them to leave us in peace. In those days much blood – much innocent blood was shed, and I still don't know whether the white man at that time had a right to be so hard and cruel to the natives from the moment he came upon them. Of course, the savages then took their revenge again in almost too horrible fashion, which couldn't be tolerated."

"Later I went with my uncle to Missouri, where we lived for several years, and hearing of the rich land and the healthy climate of the Fourche La Fave – we decided to wander this way. My uncle had always urged me to marry, for the bachelor's household that we kept had become a kind of burden to us both, but never did I find a being who matched the idea that I had formed for myself of my future wife. – I couldn't decide to take a wife without feeling that my heart was drawn to her – oh, I fully expected love to come, but I hadn't known it yet. Then I was riding late one evening – this was still in Missouri – through a neighborhood where I had never set foot before. Clouds covering the sky, I lost my way and came to a cabin where, though I found my way again, I lost my peace and quiet forever –"

"I saw a girl in this cabin – I saw – but why describe an angel that I was fated to find, only to know with certainty that I can never have her? This girl, Miss Roberts, was *engaged*. After that I stayed only a few days in Missouri, and then went on to Texas – went to Arkansas; from this, then, may come my often distraught condition, which you, Miss, must kindly forgive. It hurts when a man believes he's found his happiness for once, and then sees it dissolve into foam and fog; oh, but it was such a beautiful dream!"

Marion had bowed her little head, and hot teardrops welled from under her long silken lashes, but Brown saw them not, for close by the two, in the thick bushes of sumac and sassafras, there was a rustling and rattling, a light step was heard among the dry mosses, and in the very instant that the young man, fearing a possible danger, stood still and reached his hand toward his weapon, the thick branches directly before them parted, and a huge panther stepped into the path and looked up – by no means fearful, but rather wild and insolent – at the two humans who had the nerve to disturb his solitude.[2] With a soft cry the mortally frightened girl threw herself into the arms of Brown, who grasped her with his left while the right pulled from his pocket the Terzerol that he had already once that day pointed at the wild Kentuckian.

The panther, meanwhile, swung its long tail, half in anger and half playfully in the air, and struck his flanks with it, as if unsure what he should do – attack or leave the place. Brown quietly aimed at the animal's head and, just as it arched, as if to spring, squeezed the trigger. But because of the trembling of the beautiful girl that he held in his arm, and perhaps himself excited by the sweet burden, he missed the head, and the bullet passed over the right shoulder of the beast and into its flank. Up jumped the animal in terrible pain, but then, as if the unexpected bullet had erased any further desire to fight, it let out a sharp, piercing cry and fled with powerful bounds into the thicket.

"The danger is passed, Miss Marion – if any danger really threatened us – the animal has fled," said Brown softly, while he tried to gently lift the trembling figure resting on his breast. "My shot has scared it off – Marion – what's the matter with you? Marion, collect yourself – for God's sake – Marion!" The long-restrained feelings of the passionate Arkansas girl now broke forth in a violent rush from a heart closely guarded until this moment. Sobbing, she leaned into the shoulder of the beloved, and whispered softly, but in deep, bitter pain:

"Oh, I am so very – very unhappy!"

"Marion – you're killing yourself and me!" cried the young man, filled with the wildest anguish of soul. "Oh, that the happiest hour of my life must also be the one that shows me in an instant my whole misery! Yes, Marion, I love you, love you with all the warmth of a heart that on earth can know no other happiness than to have you, that sees only in you the star that can illuminate the course of its future life, and now looks back in despair to the last bright glow as it disappears at the horizon of its sky of happiness, from which it will never, for *him*, rise again."

"It's time that we part," he continued in a soft, subdued voice, "I shouldn't stay here; my presence would only cause unhappiness, only make you and me miserable. Tomorrow I shall leave Arkansas, and in the wild noise of battle I shall try to deaden the memory of you. – Forget you, Marion – I can never forget you!"

Sobbing, the beautiful girl leaned on his breast, and the lovers held each other in a long silent embrace. Brown finally led her again to the same trunk on which they had earlier sat, and in the deepest anguish Marion hid her angelic face in her hands.

"Do you love the man to whom you promised yourself?" asked Brown now quietly, while he grasped her left hand and gently pulled it toward him. "Have you ever loved him?"

"Never – never!" protested Marion, pressing her free hand to her heart. "I was helpless, didn't know anyone to whom I was inclined to be friendlier than him, because my mother clung to him with true devotion, and everyone else said he was a worthy, good man. I believed it was love that I felt for *him*. Then you came, then I saw you, saw your frank, open conduct, came to know your honest, faithful heart, and – became miserable. Sorrowful pictures of my future rose before me, a life of endless misery by the side of this man spread itself out before me, a man whom I now *couldn't* love any more, even if he hadn't behaved so cowardly and unmanly today; a dark fog enfolded all my dreams of happiness and satisfaction, and with you – the light of life takes leave of me. – But it *must* take leave," she continued, arising, "even our being here together is sin. – I am engaged to that strange man – I'm his be-trothed – so, let this be the last time that we see one another – it's better for us both. – Go easy on me, I'm really only a weak woman and the pain would destroy me."

"You're right, Marion – we must part, I owe this to your heart, to your honor. I'll only lead you back to your loved ones, then I'll never cross your path again. – But allow me to take one token of remembrance of this hour into my gloomy, joyless future; grant me a lock of your hair, so that my eyes have an object on which to rest when my heart sends prayers to the arbiter of our fates for you and your well-being!"

Marion bent her dear head toward him, and he gently severed with his sharp hunting knife a small lock from her forehead.

"Thanks, my dear girl," he then whispered, "thanks, warm, heartfelt thanks, and may the Lord strengthen you on your long thorny road; may Rowson make you as happy as you ought to be, and when you supplicate God, think sometimes about the poor wandering hunter whose heart's blood will have perhaps moistened that land of freedom, young Texas. Fare thee well, and God protect you!"

In fierce pain he embraced his beloved, and their lips met for the first time in a long, long kiss of farewell; then Marion tore herself from his arms and rushed with quick steps toward the not so distant dwelling. Harper and Rob-erts met them immediately after that; they had heard the shot and feared that something had happened to them. Roberts now took his daughter's arm, and Harper and Brown followed them at a short distance.

"Uncle," said Brown, after they had walked along silently side by side for a while, "Uncle, I set out early tomorrow!"

"Nonsense!" cried Harper and stopped, startled, looking his nephew in the eye. "Nonsense!" he then said once more, but in an uncertain, only half-doubting voice. "And where will you go?"

"To Texas."

"You want your old uncle to be left sitting alone here high and dry? Is that right?"

"I *must* go, Uncle!"

"You must? And who's making you?"

Brown was silent, and turned his face aside, though convulsively pressing the old man's hand.

"And so I really must stay behind here, gloomy and lonesome in my hut? Bill, that's hard – that's not half right of you. I'll disinherit you, Bill!" he continued, after smiling wistfully for a few seconds. "I'll disinherit you for sure!"

Brown seized his hand and looked into his eyes, his gaze obscured by tears. – The old man was poor, and all the land, cattle, and money the two now owned together really belonged to the nephew.

"Don't worry, Uncle – your old age is secure; as you know, I received a letter eight days ago from my lawyer in Cincinnati. – My lawsuit's been won, and the payment of the proceeds can't take much longer; this evening I'll write to Wolfey[3] and give him the order to forward everything to your address. – You'll take care of it until I come back, and – if I don't come back – well – anyway, we'll talk about this yet. Early tomorrow I'll go over to the Petit Jean, and from there to Morrison Bluff on the Arkansas, where I have business to take care of.[4] In a week I'll come by your house again on my way to Texas. In the meantime, make a deal for me with Mr. Roberts about the sorrel."

"Hello there!" now cried Roberts from the house, which he had reached with his daughter in the meanwhile. "Hello there! You're moving as though you had lead on your soles – come, Brown – supper's ready."

"You really will leave?"

"I'm setting out this second – I still have a letter to write and bullets to cast, and some bread to bake, so I can take some provisions with me."

"But you'll also be sure to come by here again in a week?"

"Here's my hand on it – and of course I have to collect the horse; until then – farewell, Uncle, I'll surely be here again in a week. – But don't say anything to Roberts about waiting for me to return – I – I couldn't spare the time to visit him, and he might take it badly."

"Hey there, Brown! – what's Brown doing in the barn, Harper?" asked Roberts, as he came to the house alone. "The meal is getting cold, my old woman's already been grumbling."

"He's set on going," Harper said sadly, "the good Lord only knows what's got into his skull."

"Going? This evening?" cried Mr. and Mrs. Roberts. "But what for?"

"He has business tomorrow on the Petit Jean and has to go home first. It would make him late if he stayed here tonight."

"Strange that this came to him all of a sudden," said Mrs. Roberts – "this afternoon he'd completely agreed to spend the evening here."

"He'd already spoken about it with me on the way," said Marion, as she turned away to take off her bonnet, "and he's very sorry that he can't stay with us. He must have very pressing business."

"Yes, and I'd like to accompany him," Harper threw in, "we've no cook anymore at home but me, and I must really look after the provisions. – It may be that he'll be on the road for several days."

"But Mr. Harper!" cried Mrs. Roberts, half-offended. "I don't understand you two at all – the evening meal is ready. – So eat just a little bite first."

"Thanks very much, Mrs. Roberts – thanks very much – early tomorrow, if you have nothing against it, I'll invite myself to breakfast, because I do want to go hunting with Roberts. – Jim, bring me my horse too – but quick," he then interrupted himself as he gave this order to a little Negro. "So, at seven o'clock I'll be here – shall I bring the Indian with me?"

"He can be of considerable use to us in hunting hogs," said Roberts.

"But, Mr. Harper – just *one* cup of coffee before you go. – You'll have nothing warm when you get home."

"That's an undisputed truth, Mrs. Roberts," replied the old man, as he stepped to the table and emptied the bowl of hot coffee proffered. "Unfortunately true – it's a sad life, is a bachelor's housekeeping – I think I'll marry!"

"Ha ha ha!" laughed Roberts. "That's a clever idea. Ride around here in the neighborhood and court the girls. But for that you must put on the new light-blue coat that the tailor in Little Rock made for you, eh? You've never even told me what it cost. Yes, the tailors in Little Rock are remarkably expensive. Recently, when I was down there –"

"Good night, Mr. Roberts – good night, Ladies!" Brown's voice cried from the front of the house, where he stood with his horse.

"But Mr. Brown – won't you come in here just for a little and drink a cup of coffee – your uncle –"

"Hearty thanks, Madame – I'm really not thirsty – good night once again to all!"

"Hold on, lad – I'm going with you," cried Harper.

"You, Uncle?"

"Yes, indeed – there's the horse already. – Now then, tomorrow morning, and, Roberts, don't take the small-bore rifle with you again, rather cast some bullets for the other one this evening – 'tis poor shooting with such miserably small lead – good night to all, then," he continued, as he mounted and seated himself firmly in the saddle – "good night!"

Mr. and Mrs. Roberts stood in the door – behind them, Marion.

"Good night!" cried Brown once more and waved his hat – once more he saw the figure of his beloved – he knew her eyes rested on him; for the last time, he called out his salute, and then drove his spurs into the sides of his faithful beast so wildly that it suddenly jumped up to one side, and with a few crazy leaps disappeared from the circle of light that streamed from the open door of the house.

"Hold there!" cried Harper to his nephew – "are you mad – do you want to break your neck and legs? – Nice and slow, if I'm going to keep step – nutty boy, that one – crazy boy, that –" And for a long while they heard the old man scolding and arguing as he drove his horse to catch up with his nephew's nervously prancing beast, frightened by the spur.

"Amazing!" said Mrs. Roberts, as she sat down to supper with her husband and daughter – "amazing! – that was really very strange conduct by the both of them – they could have ended the holy Sabbath in a more dignified manner than by riding home and –"

"Nonsense, old woman!" Roberts interrupted her – "that young man, that Brown, still has that escapade with that rascal Heathcott filling his head; you can't blame him. The knave threatened to shoot him down wherever he finds him, no doubt about it, and he's rotten enough to keep his word in this regard."

"Do you really believe that, Father?" – asked Marion, turning deathly pale.

"Well, the youngster will stand up to him like a man," continued the old fellow, without noticing. "An able, fine fellow he is – his heart is in the right place. Since the time when he came here with his uncle – it's now about six weeks, right? I think at that time I had just fenced the new piece of land, after we had lost yet another piece of ours to fire. Yes, the laborers be damned, and if it comes out of someone else's pocket –"

"Would you like another cup of coffee, Roberts?" asked his wife.

"No, thanks very much."

"Well, then we'll want to have our evening prayer," said the matron, and took down from the little shelf the carefully preserved Holy Scripture.

Oh, with what devotion the poor, unhappy girl prayed this evening; how ardently she implored from the Most Gracious One happiness and peace for her beloved! And when she finally sought her bed, she moistened her snow-white pillow with countless tears, and fell asleep like a child worn out with weeping, with folded hands and the name of the beloved man on her lips.

Notes

1. Misspelled by FG as "Boon." Invoking an association with Daniel Boone was a gesture of self-authentication in early American frontier writing; see the sketch in which Audubon claims to have spent a night "under the same roof" with Boone. They never actually met (Audubon, "Colonel Boone" [1831], *Audubon and His Journals,* ed. Maria R. Audubon, 2 vols. [New York: Dover, 1986] (2: 241–46).

2. The following scene was possibly inspired by chapter 28 of James Fenimore Cooper's *The Pioneers* (1823). Panthers are also commonly known as mountain lions, cougars, pumas, and catamounts. The scientifically accepted name is *Puma concolor.* The animal is the fourth-largest cat and native to the Americas.

3. "Wolfey" is likely Brown's lawyer.

4. Morrison Bluff, a small town on the south bank of the Arkansas in Logan County, once a significant stopping point for keelboats and steamboats.

THE PANTHER AT FAULT.

Figure 6.1. "The Panther at Fault." Lithograph after a crayon drawing by Harrison Weir (1824–1906). From Friedrich Gerstäcker, *Wild Sports in the Far West, Translated from the German* (Boston: Crosby, Nichols and Company, 1861). Image courtesy of the translators.

Chapter 6

Bear Baiting. – The Strange Discovery. – The Indian's Ingenuity.

The next morning broke bright and pure. In the east the first rays of light stole over the mountains; the whip-poor-will[1] still sounded its sad and monotonous song – the owls cried out from the thick overgrowth of the lowlands, and here and there the irritated gobbling of a courting turkey answered them. In the bushes the small songbirds came alive, and deep within the woods, in a lonely farmyard, a valiant rooster crowed his shrill morning song into the fresh, bracing morning air. The dew had fallen heavily; on every grass blade hung a row of clear crystal, and from the branches great bright drops fell sonorously on the moist leaves below. Meanwhile, the flowers and blossoms gave out such blissful invigorating scents that the breast breathed more freely, and with delight inhaled the balmy fragrance.

Two horsemen rode slowly along the county road. – It was Harper and Brown, both today in the garb of the western hunter: wearing leather hunting shirts, leggings, and moccasins, with rifles on their shoulders and their wide hunting knives by their side. Brown had confessed everything to his uncle; it would have weighed on his heart had he concealed it from his fatherly friend, and without exchanging a word the two were, each occupied with his own serious thoughts, approaching the area of the salt lick where Harper the day before had caught the deer. From there a small side path to the right led over the mountain ridge to the Cypress River and the Petit Jean, and here Brown stopped to take his leave of his uncle.[2]

"Well, farewell, my lad!" said the latter finally, after they had shaken hands heartily, "take care of your business and then come back with a cheerful spirit. You'll learn to forget that girl. – Well, yes, I grant you that it'll be hard to do, but, good God, one forgets a lot, for sure. I could tell you a pretty sad story about that, but no, we're both already upset enough without a second song of woe. Meantime, I shall take care of everything for you here that you want to have taken care of: I'll buy the chestnut, I'll get the blankets for you myself the day after tomorrow from Little Rock, or anyway leave it to a sure hand to get them; you should also get the bullet-pouch, and Alapaha must have by then finished tanning the skin for the new hunting shirt. Up till now only the deer brains have been lacking for her to finish, and we should easily be able to shoot four deer between us.[3] So – Godspeed, my boy – come back soon and watch out for yourself, and if you come upon any Regulators on the way – those chaps rode off that way – well, don't start a new fight with them. – It's no use, and it'll bring you no honor."

"Don't worry, Uncle – the fellow's already out of my way, and if he really pushes himself on me, well, I'll surely know how to get some space for myself. But now adieu – if the money from Cincinnati comes in my absence, well – you know what you're to do with it – adieu. – In eight days I'll be back again and – would you? – give *one* more greeting to Marion – the *last* farewell salute – then I shall accustom myself to forgetting her. Good bye, Uncle, when we see each other again, I hope that we'll both have recovered our old happy mood." The men parted, but Harper stayed on the road until the slim figure of his nephew, on the little rough-haired pony, had disappeared beyond the sharp-edged mountain ridge. Then he continued, shaking his head portentously, on his way, while whistling in a frightfully sharp and shrill manner an old song, without any thought of rhythm or attention to key. But his facial muscles worked mightily, and it was apparent that the poor old man was trying to assuage his pain over his nephew's unhappiness and loss. Soon thereafter he reached Roberts' house again.

But here there was more life indeed; another two hunters from the neighborhood had arrived and greeted Harper with a loud hello. The men rejoiced, the dogs howled, the geese and ducks cackled, and the spectacle so frightened the old rooster that he fluttered up to the roof and in great amazement turned his head this way and that, looking down at the raucous gathering.

The breakfast stood ready – hot coffee with fine cream and brown sugar, fried bacon and bear ribs – some venison, sour pickles, honey and butter. The men didn't have to be asked twice, and soon the empty bowls revealed how good it had tasted to them. Each then slung on his bullet-pouch, took his rifle, and mounted his horse, whether waiting outside the door or held by a Negro; but before he followed the others, Harper stepped toward Marion, sitting pensively on the hearth, and quietly pressed her hand. The maiden looked up at him in alarm, but as she met his gaze, she read there the farewell greeting of her beloved, and, sighing deeply, she hid her face in her left hand. In the next minute the hunters were mounted. The sound of the small horn hanging by Roberts' side brought all the hounds to the spot, where they were howling and jumping up at the horses, and away they went with a happy hunting cry into the green, blossoming, magnificent forest.

To be sure, Harper's sorrow vanished the moment his horse entered the dark shadow of the trees; he was now only a hunter, and an Arkansas hunter has no time for care, misery, or grief. When his green forest home embraces him; when even the horse that carries him, whinnying with wild and joyful desire, jumps willingly over brooks and fallen tree trunks; when the hounds in wild haste begin to search for the warm trail of a bear or a panther, sometimes gamboling behind a flustered and fluttering flock of turkeys nearby or standing howling with bristling hair next to wolf tracks; when the dew off fragrant bushes dampens the warm cheek; when finally the pack with wild barking follows the flustered beast and the hunting party hurtles after it in a wild clamor: who then still thinks about pain or grief, whom then could searing sorrow still oppress? "Forward!" is the hunter's only feeling. "Forward!" is the only thought of which he is aware. – Oh, it is a lovely life in the free, green woods!

The hunters made their way right over the mountain ridge that separates the waters of the Fourche La Fave from those of the Cypress, rode this little river upstream to its source, and then followed the mountain ridge up the Petit Jean, until they climbed down to it and entered the lowlands, the wide and fertile valley of this river.

"Now where on earth might the Indian be hiding, Harper?" asked Roberts finally – "didn't you say that he would meet us at the Petit Jean?"

"The dear Lord knows where the fellow's prowling around. Well, our tracks are wide enough for him to follow – but, Curtis[4] – what does Eddy have there? Just look how she's wagging her tail. – If only Poppy[5] were here – the cursed mutts have been loitering on the wrong trail."

Hearing these words, Roberts jumped off his horse and ran to the place where Eddy, a young bitch, apparently was preoccupied with the very interesting inspection of a still fresh track. A bear had taken his course by here this morning on his way to the river, about two miles away, and very likely must have sat on this spot for a little while, since the dog would not let itself be led away from the spot.

"Plague and thunder!" cried Curtis, who now had also dismounted his horse, "that must be a rough fellow, and he doesn't look too light either – just look at how his paws have pressed in. – Our poor hogs must have served him nicely – and yet – no – this here is definitely no bear track. – A man's passed there, maybe the Indian – and there's yet *another* one; that can't be Assowaum. Where the devil have these dogs gone? The bear can hardly have gone over the river already – blow on that horn, Roberts."

The latter blew a couple of loud, shrill notes on the simple instrument, and it was not long before he heard at once a panting and a rustling in the bushes, and then out sprang "Poppy," as the old hunter called him, into the small open space at the edge of which the men had stopped. The remaining hounds soon followed him, for Poppy was the leader of the pack; the whining dogs circled around the place where they smelled the traces of the enemy. Then a young tracking dog came upon a warm scent, let out a sharp howl, and shot like an arrow into the woods on the "back-track" to the hills. Poppy, lost for the first time in many years, now allowed himself to be led. He also sniffed the fresh trail and flew ambitiously after the younger dog, not wanting to be second in the hunt. The others naturally could not be stopped now, and in a wild tumult they quickly disappeared into a thicket more than a hundred-feet wide that ran along the foot of the hill.

In vain Roberts cried out, intermittently blowing his horn until his neck veins threatened to burst; in vain the other hunters joined their cries with his; the pack did not hear, or did not want to hear.

"Toadstools and rattlesnakes," old Roberts now cried furiously, as he flung his hunting cap to the ground in a fit of wild fury, "the devil take the scoundrels, they're running off on the back side – no, there's never been anything like it. Now we and our hunt have become a laughingstock!"

"So what's happened to the crazy dogs?" grumbled Curtis.

"That red beast is to blame," said the other hunter, a shopkeeper from the eastern states, who had just arrived at Curtis' and wanted to take part in a regular Arkansas hunt for once. "That red beast tore off for the hills first."

"That red beast be damned!" cried Roberts, who was most deeply annoyed, "it was Curtis' dog – the scoundrel has no more idea of a bear's track than a sheep has of the Cherokee language. – Curtis – if the dog were mine, I'd blow him to smithereens, God knows."

"Well, I only wish that Mrs. Roberts and Mr. Rowson were here to hear your prayer!" laughed Harper.

"Mr. Rowson should – mind his own business; in fact, I wouldn't be too embarrassed if he were here –"

"Nor Mrs. Roberts?"

"*She* won't be coming to the Petit Jean swamp. – But it's a fact, we're standing here like a bear in a plum garden, and don't know which way to turn first. The dogs won't be back for three or four hours, you can count on it, and after that they'll be as tired as – as dogs."

"Well, but your Poppy was also dumb enough to follow," cried Curtis, who was annoyed as well.

"Yes, well – when such a beast takes off first and makes such a spectacle, as if it had found God knows what; – now, Poppy, look forward to *that* thrashing!"

"Psst!" cried Harper suddenly, as he quickly stretched out his left arm while he laid his rifle in front of him on the saddle horn and with his right hand made a funnel to his ear. "Psst – I heard something that didn't sound like dogs barking – ha – there it is again – that's Assowaum, and I'll bet my neck on it that he's turned the scoundrels around. – Blow, Roberts – blow – he doesn't rightly know yet just where we are."

Roberts let his horn ring out again, and sure enough the note was answered by a long drawn out cry that seemed to come down from the not-too-distant mountain ridge.

"Hurrah – that was Assowaum's voice, and if he's met the hounds, he'll bring them back with him – Poppy knows him only too well."

Harper was right. After a short quarter-hour the Indian appeared driving the pack before him, still searching as always and apparently unwilling to quit the chase; Poppy, though, he brought on a thin lasso made from twisted leather straps.

"Hallo, redskin, where did you find the dogs?" Roberts called out to him joyfully.

"A great bear came over the mountain," said the Indian – "deep tracks and not hungry; not a stone has he picked up on the way to look for worms, no rotten wood turned over or scratched; his tracks led right to the river. In the cane thicket there is a quiet bed and not too many mosquitoes. Assowaum knows the place."

"But how did you come by the dogs?"

"When Assowaum finds the track of a bear, he also knows which side his nose is on; Poppy met me, and when he jumped up on me, I held him fast; when the bees swarm, they always follow one, the biggest, the smartest – so do hounds; when the leader leaves the track, the others also think it is no longer warm. Assowaum has many pieces of venison in his hut – they know him – Wah!" And he stretched out his arm and pointed at the scattered pack, which had now, with the exception of a few young animals, gathered themselves around the hunters.

"Capital fellow, that Assowaum," said Harper, rubbing his hands happily. "Capital fellow. Now we just need to put the curs on the right track, and like a bolt –"

"They will run back to the mountain again," – said Assowaum – "no – I will lead Poppy – the others will follow – once we have them going – Onisheshin![6] – after that they will not leave the right trail again."

The Indian's advice was instantly taken, and after just a few paces Poppy already seemed to understand fully that he had made a fool of himself a little earlier, so that he hung his tail and looked up dolefully at his leader. The latter, though, did not yet trust him, until he followed him a full two hundred steps along the trail, and saw that he could hardly hold him on the leash any longer. Then he let him loose, and, fired by his wild hunting cry that rang shrilly through the woods, the large, beautiful animal went whimpering and howling along the trail, and soon disappeared, followed by the loudly yelping pack, into the thicket.

"Now it's a matter of staying in the saddle," cried old Roberts, who at this instant seemed twenty years younger. "Huzzah! Aha Poppy – *hey ho!*" And he spat out the last syllable with such force that even the horses, catching the passion of the hunt, reared up in response to his cry.

Through thicket and swamp, over tree trunks and standing water, through places where the whole forest seemed to be bound together in a single web of thorny creepers, to the canebrake that surrounded the river for about three hundred feet, went the hunt. Up to now they had all stayed in the saddle pretty well, except for the shopkeeper, who just after entering the greenbriers* was pulled off by one of these or a grapevine. In any event, he called out to the hunters with such cries of heart-rending misery that at first Harper actually reined in his horse. But, to be sure, it was only for an instant, for in the next moment the faithful animal once more felt his spurs. It was no Arkansas hunter who, on a warm bear track, stayed by a fallen comrade.

But at the edge of the canebrake the others had to leave their horses, abandoning these to their fate; they leapt out of their saddles all together, and pushed into the great tangle of creepers and cane that in many places formed what were really walls, and through which a path had to be cut first with knives. Indeed, the hunters had good reason to push forward as fast as possible, for in the middle of the thicket, and not very far from them at all, now arose the most dreadful noise, of a sort that can only be *imagined* in a cane swamp. The dogs howled and barked, the dry cane snapped, the leaves rustled, and the men shouted to further incite the combatants, so that one could easily believe that a hurricane had come booming through the woods, or that the legendary Wild Hunter with his ghostly pack was playing a guest role in the primeval forests of America.[7]

The bear had been brought to bay; the dogs had surprised him in his lair, where he had apparently first settled a short time earlier, and he must have roused himself so late that the first ones, Poppy and Eddy, were close on his heels before he could recover from his first fright.

Eddy was only a hound,† and though an excellent tracker, was not worth much in a real fight. Poppy, on the other hand – rather more solidly built – knew no greater delight than to take a bear by the hind leg, since he very prudently avoided fooling with the front paws very often. So when Bruin, with a wild leap, nose close to the ground so that he could slide under the vines,

---

* FG's note: "Greenbriers, a thorny creeper; the worst hindrance to the hunter in the North American woodland."

† FG's note: "A tracking dog (*Brake*)." The "Bracke" or "Brackenhund" (*DWB*) is a type of scent hound used for hunting foxes and rabbits.

proposed leaving, Poppy grabbed him by the coat before he was aware of it, and held him so roughly that he turned, growling, to drive back the intruder with his powerful claws. But Poppy was by no means going to dally. As soon as he saw that the bear had stopped, his aim was achieved, and lightning-quick he flung himself to the side and thus away from the deadly blow, repeating the game anew as soon as the quarry turned the other way. Of course, he could not hold him long in this way, but now the other dogs came storming in as well, and Bruin had to think seriously about turning tail, if he didn't want to lose his skin in the hunt.

So, he fled toward the not very distant river, in which direction the thicket was also the most impassable; but over and over the pack threw themselves against him, swarming him furiously, though only a few dared to get nearer. At last, he saw that he was forced to choose an opening in the woods and make use of a shallow slew‡, the steep banks of which somewhat hindered the dogs from coming near him. In case of an attack, they would not be able to dodge him. Here he defended himself for a long time indeed from the teeth of his pursuers, but the hunters also got an opportunity to cut off his path, since they knew instantly from the howling of the pack which way the chase had turned. Just as the bear, not at all in the best mood, tried to jump to the left again in order to make a second effort to get to the river, Roberts broke out of the thicket next to him, leveled his gun, and fired. At the same moment, a second gun cracked, and Curtis' bullet whizzed toward the beast. Still, though both bullets landed, they nevertheless seemed to have little effect on the bear, who only gave a great leap and let out a weak moan that almost sounded like a sigh, but then, with a mighty bound, reached the edge of the slew. Here, with one blow from his terrible paw, he struck the hound that had hurled itself against him and flew toward the river.

Roberts had, meanwhile, made good use of his time; with a single leap that would have done honor to a panther, he threw himself over the slew, and, clutching his knife, was right behind the beast as he reached the edge of the river. Here a third rifle cracked, and at the same moment Roberts also reached the mortally wounded animal and thrust the broad steel into its flank. But in the heat of the chase, he had not paid attention to the place he found himself. The bear raised himself again in the final exertion of his death struggle, and rather than defend himself at all against the two dogs Poppy and Watch (Harper's dog) that hurled themselves at him, he sprang down the steep bank into the river, and bear, Roberts, Poppy and Watch disappeared simultaneously into the muddy, engulfing waters of the Petit Jean.

---

‡ FG uses the English word "slew" (as he will throughout the novel) and notes: "Flowing swamp water; in the lowlands a kind of small muddy brook."

"Wah!" said Assowaum, laughing, as he, holding fast with his left hand to a young tree trunk, looked down over the edge of the bank. "The white man holds on strangely hard." But before any of the remaining hunters could reach the battleground, those submerged surfaced again, and Roberts, in no way rattled by his admittedly rather unexpected plunge, pulled the bear, now dead, and the two dogs, who had not lost their hold even under the water, to the river bank. He only then took the time to look up at the spot from which he had come down so suddenly, and by no means of his free will. Here he met Harper's gaze, who looked down at him amazed, and cried:

"Hallo, Roberts, what the devil are you doing down there with that beast? Now how are we supposed to get him up again?"

"Yes, if I were only up there myself," answered the one questioned, laughing – "going down was remarkably easy, but now we may have a little difficulty."

"Wait!" cried Assowaum. "I have the solution."

"Wait?" said Roberts, with comical wistfulness. "I'd like to know what else I can do than wait; someone caught in such a trap as I am here might well wait."

"So is the bear fat?" asked Harper.

"Quite!" answered Roberts, feeling the flanks of the animal that still lay half in the water near him. "Wouldn't you like to be sure of it yourself?"

"Thanks a lot," laughed the other, "I'll take you at your word, I'm really not in a great hurry."

Assowaum had meanwhile felled a small hickory, which he then chopped off below its first branches, and proceeded to remove most of these from the stem, leaving those remaining not too far apart, so that it formed a sort of easily climbed ladder. Then he clambered up a small white oak that had grown up close by a cypress and cut from the latter a thin grape vine as high up as he could reach. First, he let down the slender trunk to Roberts, and then reached him the end of the vine, which he meant for him to use to tie the dogs one after the other securely to the tree. With the help of a belt and a pocket handkerchief this was easily done, and each, through the combined strength of the men pulling upward, was soon on top of the bank.

"But now how will we get the bear up here?" asked Harper – "the fellow weighs at least three hundred pounds, and without ropes we'll probably have to leave him below!"

"Uh-huh," nodded Assowaum – "that is all right too – do you see the two pieces of rotten wood here on the water's edge? Onisheshin – we'll roll them into the water – bind the bear fast to them, and Assowaum will go down the river with them. One and one-half miles from here lives Mister Bahrens. –[8] You others take the horses and ride down along the canebrake. By sundown we'll all be sitting at Mister Bahrens."

"A capital idea, Assowaum," cried Roberts, who now with great agility climbed up the slender trunk and soon was with the others again, "a capital idea. Besides, Bahrens has dug a trace down to the river, and there we can drop our booty on dry land with the greatest ease."

"But listen, Assowaum!" cried Curtis, as the Indian had already begun to execute his plan with great skill, "when you come to Bahrens' house, to the spot where we cut down the honey tree last summer, just tie up your raft somewhere along there for a while and go to the house first *without* the bear. Bahrens always boasts so dreadfully about the amount of game he shoots, and we'll just see what he has for provisions in the house. So be careful that he doesn't notice you with your fat cargo."

The Indian smiled and nodded his head, but said nothing more, and was soon busily occupied rolling the two logs into the river and then tying the bear firmly to them with pieces of stripped hickory bark. In less than a quarter of an hour he had everything in order; he laid his gun on the bear, which was held partially out of the water by the lightweight pieces of wood, and, partly swimming and partly wading, pushed the strange craft before him down the river.

"An Indian like that's not a bad thing to have in the woods," Harper said at last, after the redskin disappeared around a bend in the river – "very practical ideas those fellows have, and once they have got something into their heads, they make it happen. – But, hallo! – there comes Hartford, the shopkeeper; the devil fetch me if I hadn't completely forgotten about him."

"Now just tell me what strange things you're doing?" cried the man working his way through the bushes – "so where's the bear?"

"Assowaum's pushing him down the river to Bahrens' house," Roberts answered. "But we must go back to our horses and ride down the cane brake 'til we come to the narrow path that leads to the old hunter's home. That will be the best way for us to get there, since it's hidden so deep in the thicket that no one can find it except by accident, or in the morning, when the cocks crow."

"Ok, but what good is my bear hunt to me?" wailed Hartford, "if I never once get to see the bear!"

"You'll still get to see him, man," cried Harper, "and taste him too; but now onward! The sun will be up less than an hour, and I'd really like to get out of this thicket before it gets dark. Hallo there, dogs – up with you, this evening you'll have some proper food too – that's good, Watch, beautiful, Poppy – go on ahead of the others and set a good example!"

The dogs, who had bedded down, exhausted, were revived by Harper's voice, and jumped up and followed the hunters. At first, they made use of an opening that led down to the river and were starting to cross diagonally toward the hills when the shopkeeper suddenly stopped and gripped Roberts' arm.

"Psst – don't you see something there – that there?" he cried, speaking rapidly, but in a hushed voice.

"What then? where then?" asked Roberts.

"There in the bush – the red thing!"

"Ah – truly, a deer – he's just stood up. – Shoot, before the dogs scent him or it'll be too late!"

The shopkeeper quickly raised his rifle, took a moment to aim, and at the report the deer jumped into the air and flew with great leaps back into the expansive thicket behind him.

"He's hit – he's hit!" rejoiced the shopkeeper, who ran quickly toward the spot where he believed the deer had stood. "Do you see? There's blood, and Poppy, that fine animal, is already on his trail – he scents the blood."

The dogs were, indeed, behaving strangely. Eddy and one of the others, in any event, followed the fleeing deer. Watch, though, sniffed around in the bushes with great eagerness and care, without paying attention to the summoning howls of the other dogs, and Poppy just sat down on his backside, raised his nose in the air, and howled so that a stone would have pity.

"What the hell's the matter with the beasts?" cried Roberts, coming nearer in amazement. "Is he howling so because you missed the deer?"

"Missed?" said the shopkeeper with great indignation. "Look here – does that look like a miss? And there – and here! and over there – do you call that a miss?"

"Truly, there's blood enough," said Curtis, bewildered, "but – but didn't the deer run over there, where the dogs followed? Wouldn't I have seen his white tail shining through those greenbriers?"

"Yes, indeed," said Harper. "There between those two cypresses is where he went through."

"Then this is someone else's blood," exclaimed Curtis – "this one leads to the river."

"It's not possible – was the bear here, then?"

"No way – a good piece further up."

"Can't you see any tracks, then?"

"No – but yes – here's where the hunter went, that's a man's foot!" cried Curtis, bending down to the ground – "and there's yet another – there must've been two of them, and they were careful to keep on either side of the blood so as not to smudge the track."

"What does it mean, then?" grumbled Roberts to himself. "Anyway, the ground is soft enough here, and I can't find a single track in the blood!"

"I believe that, for sure," laughed Harper – "that's not game they're following, but an animal that they had *killed*. – Don't you see how deep their heels pressed in here? They dragged it to the river, and it wouldn't surprise me if it was Bahrens, and this evening we find a nice piece of venison at his house."

"Bahrens never wears anything but moccasins," Curtis said, shaking his head. "But this one here had on crude shoes, and the other one a pair of store boots like Brown brought with him not long ago from Little Rock. But it could be that they've taken their booty to Bahrens' house."

"Oh come, men, leave the tracks alone," cried Roberts now. "The sun is nearly down, and we really must get out of this accursed canebrake. If they took the game to Bahrens' house, and if old Bahrens really was there, then we'll find them there this evening and we'll have to listen to a big long story, that's for sure; so let's go!"

"But just look how strangely that dog is acting," said Harper – "Poppy – aren't you ashamed of yourself? That's a howl to drive a fellow crazy."

But for once Poppy didn't seem to pay any attention to his master, rather only sniffed from time to time at the drops of blood, and then began to howl so mournfully that the dogs returning from their useless pursuit of the deer gathered around him and, likewise lifting their noses into the air, joined their voices in a gruesome dirge.

"Gentlemen!" cried Roberts, suddenly stopping while looking sharply at his dog. "Something's not right here – Poppy's too clever an animal to betray such feeling about nothing; – there's something not right about that blood there – that's not animal blood, that's *human blood*!"

"The devil you say!" said Curtis and looked nervously at his companions.

"Let's follow the tracks to the river," Roberts continued, "where we will get an explanation, or at least we can mark the place and we can resume the search early in the morning. Here goes the trail – that's clear enough – all the small bushes are trodden down, the body must've been heavy. – Anyone carrying a bit of game would walk in front or behind it, single file, and here the tracks are on either side of the load."

"It terrifies me to look at the blood," said the shopkeeper, and turned away shuddering.

"That's because you haven't been in Arkansas very long," said Curtis; "once you've lived in the state for ten years, like me, then you won't care about such things. I've seen many a corpse since I've been here, helped to bury many a murdered man – you get used to it, really. Only once – one time was it too much for me –"

"Knock it off with your story now," cried Roberts impatiently. "We have horror enough to look at here without you trotting out your great 'autopsy' – let the dead rest in peace."

"You must tell me the story," cried the shopkeeper. "I love to hear about such things –"

"Another time," answered Curtis. "But there is the river, now we'll probably find what we're looking for."

"Here's where they laid their burden down," said Roberts, indicating a spot that was somewhat pressed down. "Deer or man, from there it must have been put in the river."

Curtis knelt near the place and bent his face close to the ground, carefully examining the slightest impression in the soft earth. He suddenly sprang up and cried:

"It was a man – there – there's the impression of a button in the soft earth of the riverbank. – You can see it plainly – there – right next to the black streak of blood – in front of the yellow leaf there –"

"Yes, truly," said Roberts, after he had also examined the spot. "It was a man – here's also the spot where his hand lay, there's the mark of a fingernail too, plain as day. Gentlemen, a murder's been committed here – there's no more doubt about that, and tomorrow we must come back here to look more closely into the matter – it's too late today. If we stay in this canebrake ten minutes longer, we'll be forced to camp here for the night, since it's impossible to get through the thicket in the dark. But tomorrow at daybreak we shall see if we can't find the victim or the culprit. Now let's get out of here; the place gives me the creeps."

The men did not need to be invited twice to leave the place. Silently they cut a path through the cane with their broad hunting knives, got back to their horses just at twilight, swung themselves into the saddle, and trotted briskly onward, taking advantage of the relatively open woods between the cane and the mountain range thick with bushes. They arrived before nightfall at the ford of the Petit Jean, on the opposite bank of which stood the little cabin of old Bahrens, who bore the less than honorable nickname of "Lying Bahrens" in the neighborhood.

Notes

1. "Whip-poor-will" appears in English in FG's text. In *Wild Sports*, FG describes how he spent his nights in the woods looking for game, "hearkening patiently to the hootings of the owls and the complaint of the whip-poor-will" (*WS*, 369). The whip-poor-will is indeed a true night bird, feeding, nesting, and mating at night. The males sing to defend their territory. The bird fascinated travelers; see, for example, Charles Sealsfield's description of a whip-poor-will sounding its plaintive song into the lightning-bug–filled silence of the Texan prairie (*Das Kajütenbuch*, ed. Gerhard Muchwitz [Leipzig: In der Dietrich'schen Verlagsbuchhandlung, 1956], 39).

2. FG's geography is unclear here. Cedar Creek flows through present-day Petit Jean State Park and empties into the Petit Jean River, but the nearest stream named Cypress is Cypress

Creek or Bayou; it rises in the highlands north of the Arkansas River and flows east into the White River.

3. See FG's notes on the "Indian method of dressing skins" in *WS*, 365–66.

4. Curtis, unidentified in the novel, but perhaps identical with the protagonist of FG's story "Curtis' Brautfahrt" (1846); see note in *RA*, 66n27.

5. See FG, "Jäger Stevans und sein Poppy" (1845); see note in *RA*, 66n27.

6. Likely meaningless exclamation, added for authenticity, which shows up again in this chapter and, changed to "Onishin," in chapter 33.

7. The "Wild Hunt" was a folk myth recorded throughout ancient, medieval, and early modern Europe. It featured a vision of ghostly hunters passing by. Seeing the wild hunt was thought to spell disaster and death to whom the vision appears.

8. "Lying Bahrens" appears in *WS*, 154. "Munchausen would have been obliged to hide his face before him," writes FG, alluding to the iconic literary liar popularized by the German writer Rudolf Erich Raspe.

Chapter 7

Two Genuine Backwoodsmen. –
Bahrens' and Harper's Stories.

The old man stood in front of the door and, evidently waiting for the hunters, looked over toward the spot where they would have to come out of the woods. Near him, Assowaum crouched and pulled on his moccasins, which he had taken off to walk through the water and fastened securely next to his rifle.

"Hallo down there," cried Roberts. "Is the ford low enough?"

"Ay, ay!" was the answer – "knee deep."

The men considered this assurance sufficient and drove their horses straight down the bank into the river. But Curtis, riding in front, nearly suffered grievously from the joke, since he sank instantly, and his horse had to swim with him to the other bank.

"Damn your black soul," he cried out with genuine anger once he had reached dry land, "what the hell are you doing, chasing us into the water with your damned lies – eh – is this knee-deep?"

"Well, point taken," laughed Bahrens – "but don't you see the cypress knee* in the middle of the river? It's not even fully grown yet, but it's seven feet high –"

Roberts had stopped instantly when he saw Curtis immersed headlong in the current, and Curtis now called to him from the other bank: "Ride a little farther down in the river, Roberts – there, where you see the gravel, there you'll be able to pass and stay dry."

"If you know the way so remarkably well," laughed Bahrens, "why didn't you ride down farther yourself?"

"Because I was fool enough to take you at your word," he answered, and then galloped along the steep riverbank, jumped off his horse, and shook the old man's hand, who heartily welcomed him.

---

* FG's note: "Outgrowth of the root of the cypress tree, the top of which looks like a rounded knee, and often grows to a height of ten to twelve feet, but when they are low, they make riding in the swamps especially difficult. They are called cypress knees."

Bahrens was one of the true pioneers, or squatters, of the west. About five years earlier he had settled in Poinsett County, in the most frightful swamps and twenty miles from the nearest human habitation.[1] There he had lived for a long while, mightily pleased with the yields of his hunting. But then something happened about which he was reluctant to speak and which he referred to as a "family matter," but which forced him to leave the neighborhood. It was rumored among the inhabitants of the Fourche La Fave that it had something to do with a love of horseflesh, but this was groundless. First, they did not understand the region, for there whatever strayed near his cabin had become wild and was fair game for his gun; and second, Bahrens had always proved to be an honorable man, and none of his "neighbors" could say anything bad about him. That he sometimes "mangled the truth a bit," as Roberts put it, most of his acquaintances would freely confirm. But he himself persistently denied this and was always ready to swear by each of his stories, only – he would never put money on it, though he was otherwise never slow to take a bet. His main business was cattle breeding, and he cultivated only a very small piece of land, about five acres, to raise corn for himself and his family, and he had some horses, but not many. He believed that horses could not tolerate the air in Arkansas. His family consisted of his wife, two daughters, and one son, who no longer lived with his parents. Two years earlier he had wandered off, and since he could neither write nor read, naturally they had heard nothing more from him.

The house itself was one of those common log cabins of the American West, built of rough, unhewn tree trunks; its roof – roughly finished, short boards – was held down by heavy rods, so-called weight-poles.[2] Out of a chimney built of raw clay and timber came thin blue smoke, and Bahrens was just now busy chopping firewood for the evening, in order to keep a cheerful flame in the fireplace. Only a small low fence kept a litter of young piglets from disturbing the peaceful solitude of the household; squealing and grunting, they ran around the hampering enclosure as if expecting their usual evening meal, a few ears of corn. In a small pen close by, the eldest daughter, a handsome dark-eyed girl, milked a great white cow, while the younger held back a little calf by a rope, so that it would not disturb her sister in her work and instead would wait until its own turn came. Near the house, however, on huge tree trunks felled by the farmer's axe and still lying in the merely half-cultivated field, sat a large number of vultures, as if they either had been scared away from their loot, or had only left it in order to resume their disgusting meal the next morning.

The three hunters now also rode up to the house, and Roberts called to the old man while still some distance off: "I've done you a real injustice, Bahrens. We believed that we'd find you out of meat, but the vultures over there tell us that something must be on hand, unless a cow has fallen."

"Good evening, boys,[†] good evening, you've done well to pay Old Bahrens another visit. – Cow fallen? Roberts, no meat in my house? Then you don't know Old Bahrens very well. When I lived on the Cash River, I could kill, let's say on average, between eight and nine hundred pounds of meat a day – Curtis knows that, right, Curtis?"

"Yes, indeed," he laughed. "Tame creatures!"

"Tame? – Wild animals, buffalo, and cows running wild included, of course, but get down, get down, make yourselves comfortable. – Betsy, throw an armful of corn in the trough for each of those animals – do you hear – but stand by them until they're finished, and keep off the swine so they don't turn the trough over, like yesterday."

"Bahrens, truly, there must be carrion nearby!" cried Roberts, once the initial greetings were over – "by my soul, it smells to me like rotten flesh."

"Rotten flesh? God bless you!" laughed Bahrens. "You have good noses – there's nothing here nearby – those scoundrels, the vultures, always come when you slaughter –"

"Slaughter?" asked Curtis, horrified. "Something you've slaughtered reeks like that? What's the matter with you, Assowaum? The fellow's making a face as if he wanted to laugh."

"Mr. Bahrens has slaughtered a small hog," said the Indian, and it was obvious that the situation delighted him immensely. "But buzzards are dumb animals; the pig was killed a week ago, and they're still coming today."

"And we're supposed to eat it?" Roberts cried, laughing. "So, where's the deer?"

"What deer?"

"The ones you shoot every day, like you just said."

"Oh, I've sprained my foot and haven't been able to hunt for three days."

"Bahrens – here's a friend of mine, Mr. Harper – one of my neighbors, who'd really like to make your acquaintance – Harper – Mr. Bahrens, the man I've told you about many times – I think you'll become good friends." – The men shook one another's hand, and Bahrens swore that he'd be damned if Harper didn't have a remarkably amiable face.

"But, Bahrens," Curtis now interrupted them. "Early tomorrow, at daybreak, we have to go to the little slew. There, where the three dried-out cypresses stand, a murder's been committed; at least it certainly looks that way."

"A murder? That'd be awful!"

"It can hardly be otherwise; – we found the marks too plainly, but we didn't have the time to look into the thing more closely. It's not far from here, by the

---

[†] FG's note: "'Boys,' *Knaben*, the customary greeting, something like 'my lads.'"

way, and early tomorrow we can easily get to the bottom of it. Today, of course, it'd be impossible to chase the culprits."

"My goodness, that's strange!" cried Bahrens. "I passed by there only this morning and didn't notice anything!"

"I thought you'd sprained your leg?" laughed Curtis.

"Well, yes – three days ago – blockhead! – Do you think I'll have to limp my whole life, then? – But come in here, boys, the fog's remarkably damp this evening, and we'll be more comfortable sitting in front of the fire."

"No, old chap!" said Roberts, clapping him on the shoulder, "since you're so poorly stocked with provisions, we'll get our own supply; Assowaum, let's have the bear. We can't keep it under wraps any longer, or we'll go hungry for it. Besides, it's getting dark."

To Bahrens' surprise and delight, the Indian soon came swimming up with the fat barbeque. Through the men's united efforts they dragged it up out of the water in front of the house, and soon a few of the best pieces were handed over to the women for preparation.

"Good evening, Mrs. Bahrens," said Roberts, stepping into the house and greeting her. "How are you? Long time no see; still alive and kicking?"

"Well, have to be – Mr. Roberts," the woman answered in a friendly way, pushing back the large cotton bonnet that she wore while cooking, to protect her eyes from the heat. "It's good of you to visit us; and next time I'll come over to see you. But my old man really doesn't like to be taken away from home."

"My old lady's been expecting you and your daughters for some time, Mrs. Bahrens," answered Roberts, shaking the hand she offered him. "How are the girls getting along here in the woods – eh? But they're used to a lonely life already, for it was not any livelier in the Cash River swamps. Wretched place, the Cash swamps, when I was there the last time and rode by Strong's. – You know Strong, don't you, the one who owns the large farm? Truly, he settled on the best place there, and will –"

"Stop him – for God's sake stop him!" cried Bahrens jovially. "There he goes again without a bridle; if we let him go, he'll be talking about the Revolutionary War in five minutes. God help us, Roberts, you don't speak a word of sense. – But, children, since you've taken such good care of the provisions, you deserve a reward; here, Lucy – hand me that medicine jar from under the bed – take good care, lassie, God help you if you break it! Now, boys, we'll enjoy a merry evening, bear meat and whiskey – hey *ho*!" And the old man let out his hunting cry; the dogs outside got excited and began to howl.

"Bahrens, the beasts outside are biting each other," said Curtis finally – "ours are hungry too; where do you keep the hog meat? We should give it to the animals; it's not fit for humans."

"My good meat?"

"Ah, to hell with your meat – I thought you were able to shoot so many deer? –"

"Yes, but my leg!"

"Now he brings up his leg again, the capital fellow! But, Harper, you sit there so silent and don't say a syllable; maybe you're thinking about the murder?"

"Yes! To tell the truth, I can't get the blood stains out of my memory. It looked too horrible!"

"Horrible, Mr. Harper? Then you should have lived on the Cash River a few years back," answered Bahrens. "I'll be damned if every day two or three corpses didn't come floating by – and what corpses! Some without heads."

"But where did all the people come from?" asked Harper, half appalled and half disbelieving. "I thought it was such an unpopulated area?"

"The people? Well, was I supposed to worry myself about it? and what was it to me?"

"Stop – save your conversation until after dinner!" said Roberts, laughing. "Let's first of all see to the horses; after that the food will taste better too."

This advice was instantly followed; and, sure enough, as they were returning from the fodder trough, the lady of the house was already calling them to the evening meal, and soon the men sat on upended barrels, boxes that had been dragged over, logs, and roughly fashioned armchairs around the narrow table, on which a huge bowl full of roasted bear ribs and thinly sliced meat provided the centerpiece, while cornbread, boiled pumpkin, some honey, and milk made up the remaining ingredients of the meal. The whiskey flask meanwhile went round in a circle, and even if not a further word was spoken, the clatter of knives and the cleanly gnawed ribs that were increasingly conspicuous everywhere proved how delicious the meal was to the hungry men.

When they were done, they stood up from the table one by one as each finished, and the women, who had very wisely put aside a few pieces, sat in the emptied chairs without taking the trouble to exchange the greasy plates for clean ones.

Old Madame Bahrens, somewhere in her forties, still showed signs of an earlier and not unremarkable beauty, but her slim figure was wrapped in a cotton dress that was far from clean and was no longer white. Her beautiful brown hair was pinned to her head with apparent carelessness, and her large, dark eyes lost much of their luster in the far from brilliant setting of a somewhat rough and dirty-looking face. The daughter carried herself better and more neatly, but her complexion too would have been improved by some warm soap water.

As the food was removed – or, better said, the plates, since the food had disappeared without a trace – Bahrens shoved the table back a little, allowing the chairs of various styles to be returned to a circle around the fireplace, and then called out cheerily: "Now, gentlemen, comes the best part – the stew."‡

"But you don't have any butter!" said his wife.

"My goodness, that's true – but hallo – why do we need butter, when we have bear fat – whiskey and bear fat go much better with each other – gentlemen, this is the land to live in – it doesn't get any better than Arkansas!"

"Ah, well, Mrs. Bahrens," said Harper, who, as he noted the preparations for his favorite drink, began to thaw out. "Ah, well, I really don't know – Missouri is also not to be scorned, I lived there for a long time, and –"

"Missouri?" cried Bahrens in amazement – "Missouri? May God help us; and you compare that with Arkansas?"

"Well, doesn't it border close enough on it?"

"Borders? It's exactly as if the dear Lord took his finger and had drawn a line between the two states, so that one would be fruitful and the other unfruitful – Missouri – nah, now listen, how long have you actually lived in Arkansas?"

"About six weeks."

"Oh, then that's a little different, that's why you don't know any better. Sir, here the soil is so rich, that when we want to make candles, we just dip the wicks in the puddles – it burns just as well. – If a man in Arkansas tills his field with diligence and attention, he can count on getting a hundred bushels an acre off it."

"That'd be a bunch!"

"A bunch? That's nothing, really – if he makes *no* effort with the land and lets the corn grow up untended, he'll still get seventy-five bushels, for sure; and if he doesn't plant *at all*, then – then he'll still get fifty – the land can't be made fallow!"[3]

Harper moved around a little on the box on which he sat, and Roberts and Curtis cast stolen glances at each other.

"And another advantage is," said Bahrens, "the first time we need to plant is June, the corn grows so remarkably fast. Just think, last year it pulled the beans that I had stuck in between out of the ground by the roots. And the pumpkins – ten men can circle a *single one*."

"Amazing country!" said Harper – "but, then, everything about it is magnificent, since *these* mosquitoes and *these* wood ticks are really unparalleled."

"Everything magnificent?" asked Bahrens, now fully astride his hobby horse, bragging about the land in which he lived – "everything magnificent?

---

‡ FG's note: "A much loved drink in the western woods, consisting of whiskey, hot water, spice, sugar, and butter."

Let me tell you something; in the hot days of summer, the mosquitoes are so thick that they often get stuck together with blood and fall out of the air in clumps. With my own eyes I've seen the wood ticks rise on their forelegs from a piece of wood when they hear the cowbells, and in the evening the fleas go regularly to the river to drink, just like the other animals. And *what* rivers we have! Lord have mercy on us – with all their might they push the sea back a long way when they flow into it."

"But they don't go into it," said Harper.

"Don't go into it? Where do they go then?" asked Bahrens indignantly – "do they just evaporate, eh? So where does the Petit Jean run to?"

"Into the Arkansas."

"Well, and the Arkansas?"

"Into the Mississippi."

"And the Mississippi?"

"Into the Gulf of Mexico."

"As if this weren't all the same thing. – You take for instance the southern part of Missouri – has anybody been to the southern part of Missouri?"

"All of us, probably," answered Roberts.

"And up to the Eleven Point River[4]? – Gentlemen, I don't want to exaggerate, but it's so rocky there that we had to lift the sheep up by the hind legs so that they could pluck up a little grass between the sharp stones; the wolves got so lean and weak that they had to lean against a tree if they wanted to howl. Now you see the difference between Missouri and Arkansas. For example, how did we get on in the winter, when we had nothing for the poor cattle to eat? well? take a guess."

"Let them run around wild in the woods maybe?" asked Curtis.

"What use would that have been to them, I'd like to know? The ground was so dry that bark wouldn't even grow on the trees and the bushes – no, I hit upon a very different way. You know Tom, Roberts – the one who later had to take a business trip to Texas in a big hurry – heh – Big Tom, surely you remember, he was so tall he had to kneel every time he wanted to scratch his head. – All right – in his former life, in Philadelphia, I think, he was a mechanic, and had brought with him a bunch of tools; – I got him to make me a batch of big, green spectacles; I put these on the cows, gave them wood shavings to eat, and I'll be damned if they didn't take them for grass and get fat."

"Lord have mercy on us!" cried Harper.

"So we have it better here," continued Bahrens happily, "here we sit on moss, as it were, and the hunting –"

"Hello!" cried Harper now, breaking in. "As for that, I won't hear anything about Missouri. There's nowhere better."

"Better?" laughed Bahrens scornfully – "better? when a bear here has only three inches of fat on his back, he's called lean – the deer –"

"One catches by the legs!" laughed Roberts. Bahrens looked at him in astonishment, and Harper wore an unusually amiable look.

"Well, Roberts, you must tell that yourself," continued Bahrens – "but Betsy, the water's boiling; now brew the drink, my girl, you know how we like it – you must admit it, Roberts, in hunting I have no equal here. Small game I don't *shoot* anymore, since I have my own ways of catching them!"

"Like our young ones," said Harper, "who catch rabbits in traps."

"Traps?" laughed Bahrens disdainfully, "are traps still needed for that? – Come to Arkansas if you want to learn something. If there's a little snow lying about, then I go out into the woods, just far enough that I can't see the house anymore –"

"That's not far," said Curtis.

"All right – there I stick little pieces of beet in the snow and sprinkle snuff over them – in the morning the rabbits are lying dead all around them."

"Do they eat the snuff, then?" asked the shopkeeper, amazed.

"Eat? No, they sniff it and sneeze so hard they break their necks."

"Speaking of breaking necks," said Harper, "I remember what I did with an owl recently. The scoundrel had carried off one of my chickens three nights in a row, and I'd been slipping around to catch him, but to no avail. Finally, on the fourth day, early in the morning, it rained a little, and it came flying to the house. I noticed it as soon as the chickens started fluttering weirdly here and there. I grabbed my gun quickly, and ran out, but soon found that the owl was sitting in a little, thick-leaved hickory, and I could only see the head of it, and as I didn't want to shoot it dead right away, rather give the dogs some fun, I went around in a circle, looking for a good place to shoot. – But the leaves were equally dense all around, and meanwhile the owl peered steadily at me with its great rolling pop eyes. I'd gone around the tree three times in that way, with my gun aimed, when all at once something rustled in the branches, and the owl came down. The devil take me if it hadn't, by keeping its eyes on me, twisted its head off unawares."

"That's nothing," cried Bahrens, who didn't think to doubt the truth of the story. "When I was still a young fellow, I could take any turkey on the run, and if it started to fly and didn't climb too high, I had him for sure."

"As for running," said Harper, "I wish you could have seen my brother when he was after partridges."

"You don't mean to tell us that he caught partridges on the wing!" cried Bahrens, rising in alarm.

"No," said Harper, "not that, but I'll be damned if he didn't pull a handful of feathers out of their tails every time they sprang."

"Gentlemen, here comes the stew! God bless it, Betsy – you've made it strong!" cried Roberts – "no, I thank you, no more water in it, it takes away the spicy aroma, it must be cooked with it. But Bahrens, you really were right – the bear fat tastes wonderful, so smooth yet so fiery!"

The conversation was now suspended for a moment, and the men gave themselves over entirely to enjoying the drink. Finally Curtis broke the happy silence and said, grinning: "Mrs. Roberts and Mr. Rowson should just see straight-laced Mr. Roberts sitting here drinking whiskey stew, they would pull quite a face."

Mr. Roberts, who was already on his third glass and was beginning to grow warm, put down his drink and cried out: "Mr. Rowson may go to – pasture. This *I* know, that he'll not lecture *me* about my business! – With my wife and daughter, he may do as he wishes, or – as *they* wish, rather."

"I believe *they'll* do pretty much what *he* wants," said Curtis.

"I'm afraid so – the smooth, slick sneak has always been a thorn in my side – forever ranting about the Roman Catholics – damned if I think he's a pinch of snuff better!"

"Rowson's damned crazy about the girl, your daughter?" asked Curtis.

"Well, naturally – in four weeks they'll go to the Justice of the Peace and get hitched – it's all right with me!"

"Listen, Roberts, I was once wildly in love too," said Bahrens, grinning. "It was a girl from the city – from St. Louis. At that time I was trading with the Osage[5] up there, up towards the Missouri and Yellowstone rivers, and was camped about three miles from the city. Would you believe it? Every three days I got a long letter, in which there was much written about pure love and faith. What a pity that I couldn't read them myself, and the Indian with whom I was living couldn't tell the difference between the inside and the outside of a letter. But there must have been a fiery love buried in the things, it was dreadful – I bound them together and shoved them, as I went out, into a leather pouch, and when I came back home and opened it again, there was nothing more than ashes inside."

"But, folks, I thought that we were going to bed!" cried the shopkeeper, yawning. "We have to get going at the crack of dawn tomorrow, and I'm beginning to feel as if I were getting tired."

"Yes – it's getting late," said Roberts, who was standing in the door and looking at the stars – "it must already be past ten o'clock."

"Just another moment!" protested Harper with a slightly thicker tongue; "since we were speaking of love just now, I thought of a story about my brother, when he was still a young fellow. – You should've known him then – a cussed beggar; eighteen years old, and already engaged to three girls. So he meets a Quaker in Philadelphia, and, strangely enough, it's the brother of one of the girls. He recognizes him, but he's still very friendly and invites him to stay for dinner with him; but after the meal he gets up, pleads some business as an excuse, and leaves the house to go get the constables and have my brother taken in. But what do you think he found when he came home again?"

"Well, he'd probably flown the coop –"

"Yes – but not alone, he'd gone off with the Quaker's wife."

"Ah, how the man can lie!" Bahrens quietly whispered to Curtis, standing next to him.

"So, to bed now – where will we sleep then, Bahrens?"

"Well, we must organize that. There are only three beds; the girls must have one, one for me and my old lady, and the third should be for the elders, so Roberts and Mr. Harper – Mr. Harper will sleep well after all his stories – and the other three gentlemen, Curtis, Mr. Hartford, and Assowaum, well, they'll find skins enough. So, that's good, Betsy – make them a proper bed, and tomorrow we'll take off first thing."

Assowaum, who had not spoken a single syllable the whole evening, though he nevertheless seemed very amused by the two men's stories, and afterwards partook of no small quantity of whiskey, now also wrapped himself in his blanket. But as he stepped to the place where he meant to lie down, passing close by the corner of the hearth near the fire, he stumbled and nearly fell.

"Hallo, Indian!" laughed Harper. "Got too much whiskey in your head? That's not good."

"It's not good, too much of anything," said the "Feathered Arrow," as he stretched himself out and shoved a block of wood lying nearby under his head. "But too much whiskey is just enough"; and with this truly philosophical remark he lay himself on his side and in a few minutes quietly dozed off.

"Is there a side of the bed that you especially prefer, Roberts?" asked Harper when they had undressed.

"No," said the other, in all innocence.

"Well, then you can sleep on the *underside*," said Harper laughing, as he crawled under the tanned deerskin spread across it.

But Roberts did not seem to be in complete agreement about his spot, for he quickly lay down by Harper's side, and in a short time nothing more than the soft crackling of the fire and the deep steady breathing of the sleepers could be heard.

The night passed quietly and without disturbance; except one time, when Curtis jumped up and, cursing wildly, drove out the whole pack of dogs. For these had crept in, one after the other, and, seeing the hunters outstretched on the floor, had settled themselves on top of and alongside them.

Notes

1. Poinsett County is in northeastern Arkansas, near Jonesboro, just west of the Mississippi.

2. "Weight-poles": FG uses the original English word.

3. The exaggerated promise of agricultural yield echoes the tall tale/southwestern humor tradition, as in one of the best-known examples, Thomas Bangs Thorpe's "The Big Bear of Arkansas" (1841): "the sile is too rich, and planting in Arkansaw is dangerous."

4. Eleven Point River, now in the Mark Twain National Forest, Missouri.

5. The Osage dominated areas south of the Missouri River, including parts of northern Arkansas and northeast Oklahoma. In the early 1800s, the Osage were forced to convey their lands in Missouri to the United States and moved west to northern Oklahoma.

CALICO ROCK ON WHITE RIVER, ARᵏ

Figure 8.1. "Calico Rock on White River, Ark." Lithograph after a drawing by David Dale Owen. From David Dale Owen, *First Report of a Geological Reconnoissance of the Northern Counties of Arkansas, Made During the Years 1857 and 1858* (Little Rock: Johnson & Yerkes, State Printers, 1858). Image courtesy of University of Arkansas Special Collections.

Chapter 8

Morning in the Log Cabin. – Searching for the Traces of Blood Found the Previous Evening. – Assowaum Dives for the Corpse.

On the thickly leaved peach trees that surrounded the log cabin, the cocks crowed and announced the approaching dawn; out in the woods the wild turkeys answered, and in the east the friendly stars began to grow somewhat pale. Now arose from their beds, in the cabin that we wrote of in the previous chapter, the three women, Mrs. Bahrens and her two daughters. Forced to share a room with so many strangers, they wanted to dress before it became lighter. Carefully, they stepped over those lying by the fire, and once more blew the dying embers to a livelier glow. Soon a warming flame, fed by brightly glowing pine chips, flashed; the large tin coffee pot was placed on coals raked to the front of the fireplace, and hastily mixed bread dough was beaten flat and placed on iron lids leaned in front of the blaze.

"I've told Father a good fifty times now," grumbled the wife, as she put the roasted coffee beans in a tin can in front of her on the hearthstone and pounded them with the handle of a tomahawk – "he should bring me a coffee grinder from Morrison Bluff or Little Rock, but no – God forbid. He thinks about his hunting gear, but when one time it's something for me, then I can tell him who knows how many times. – Yesterday he was over there at the store again; the whiskey jug – he didn't forget that, oh no – but the coffee grinder –"

"Stop grumbling, old woman!" – cried Bahrens from the bed. – "Stop arguing!" –

"Well, it's true –"

"No, it's not true – reach over there in the corner, by the salt gum – to the right – there – what do you call that thing?"

"Oh, my soul, a coffee grinder, and you let me stand here pounding away forever!"

"When my eyes are closed, how should I see what you're doing?"

"Listen up, Roberts," said Harper now, sitting up in bed, "sharing a bed with you is quite a trick – you're not impudent *at all*, are you?"

"Well, you'll allow me half the bed, won't you?" mumbled Roberts, still half asleep.

"Indeed," answered Harper, "but not the middle half, so that I have to lie on both sides of you to have my half – that's against all international law."

"Allons, boys – get up, get up!"* now cried old Bahrens, who had stepped to the chimney and was holding the whiskey bottle aloft. "Here's a stomach medicine – who wants his bitters?"

That did the job; all sprang to their feet, and only the Yankee shopkeeper still lay snoring, as if the whole house was as quiet as the grave. Curtis poked him in the ribs for a long time, but in vain, and at last swore that the fellow was so tall that he could only be awakened piece by piece. When the sun sent its first beams through the brightly glowing tree tops, the men sat around the breakfast table, while outside the girls fed the horses and shooed the pigs and chickens away from the troughs.

"But tell me, Bahrens," asked Roberts as they ate, "what's going to become of our hog hunt? If we want to look into the murder, we have to let the pigs go, and my old lady's going to grumble mightily."

"Well, you can surely come over here again another time; besides, I think we'll come across pretty much all of them – except those that get eaten by the bears, naturally[1] – about two miles further down the river. Day before yesterday, I saw a lot of them with your mark, and by the way – the sow that belonged to your father, Curtis, the one whose neck the bear took a chunk of fat out of."

"What, she's still alive?"

"Yes, and has eleven of the most adorable piglets with her."

"The devil you say!" – cried Curtis – "Listen, Bahrens – keep your mouth shut about it. I spoke day before yesterday with the old man about the sow, and he takes her for dead – I'll buy her from him, 'as she runs in the woods,' as they say, whether found or unfound. I'll get her for a silver dollar and then I'll drive her home."

"Not bad!" laughed Harper, "now he wants to cheat his own father."

"That's not really a cheat, is it?" the shopkeeper defended him – "whoever earns an honest dollar cheats no one. For sure, his father isn't a bit obligated to buy the sow from him."

---

* "Get up, get up!" appears in English in FG's original, with a footnote offering the German translation: "Steht auf, steht auf!" "Allons" (French for "Let's go") and "boys" likewise appear in the original language.

"And that would be the last thing a Yankee would condemn," said Bahrens, who had listened quietly. "But now let's go, boys – the sun's up, and we mustn't lose any more time. If a murder really was committed here, it might still be possible to catch the culprits; but I still think you've made a mistake. First off, I rode by there yesterday morning, and then Mr. Brown must've come in the same direction."

"Brown?" Harper asked quickly – "Brown? What's he doing then in these parts? He was going to head over to Morrison Bluff."[2]

"That's what he said, and if he came straight from the Fourche La Fave, then this was rather a round-about way. – But away – away. We can probably be home again by mid-day."

The hunters now took leave of the women and rode across the lower ford, with Assowaum mounted behind Harper so as to be the first across, and thus get moving more quickly. They went off at a sharp trot to the place where, the day before, they had found the suspicious marks.

"Stop! There's the spot!" cried the Indian as he sprang from the horse, "we must not ride any farther, so that we don't trample the ground any more than is necessary."

The riders quickly dismounted and tethered the horses to the low-hanging swaying grape vines so that they could not tear the reins. Assowaum, though, strode forward and stopped at the track that was pressed into the soft earth. He bent down carefully over it, and closely examined every overturned leaf and each blade of grass, then stood up again and followed the tracks with light steps to the place where the blood was first visible. But he had hardly cast his eyes about the spot when he let out a loud, deep "Wah!" that quickly gathered the hunters around him. He pointed around the area, and there could be no more mistaking the atrocity that had taken place.

The place lay just at the foot of a fallen spruce, from whose root hole a thick tangle of blackberry bushes and thorny climbers had grown. A horse had tried to go around this little thicket; the hoof marks led half way around it, as if something must have stopped the rider – probably the murderous bullet. There lay the first blood; but the unfortunate man had not yet been thrown from the horse, which had made a leap.

"The bullet must have hit the horse," said Roberts, "otherwise the rider would have fallen off, right?"

Assowaum pointed silently to a hickory nearby, on whose light grey bark, a full eight or nine feet from the ground, telltale blood marks were visible.

"I see!" cried Harper in horror – "he hit his head against the hickory – and here's the place where he fell too."

The ground there was marked with numerous footprints – the murdered man apparently must have defended himself, for several branches revealed where he had clung with a last, desperate effort, stripping the leaves. There had he sunk down on one knee – thick, dark blood covered the ground here – never again to arise. But yes, once more – there where the red sap of life hung on every bush, flung as if from a ruptured vein against the trunk of the spruce. That may have been the last flicker of the last spark of life. Under this cypress he died, and here too the body had remained for a while, back bent over a sharp root, a position no living man could have endured for long.

The men stared silent and shuddering at these terrible tokens of murder; for *murder* it was – no battle had taken place, at best a desperate defense. The dead man was either shot or pulled from his horse, and then beaten to death.

"Come!" said Assowaum, and now followed the tracks to the bank of the river, carefully examining each footprint on the way. "Two carried him."

"We already found that out yesterday – the tracks go to the river bank."

"He lay here, and two stood here – what is that? There's a knife – bloody."

"A penknife, by the eternal God – surely they could not have killed the man with that?"

"Show me the knife," said Roberts, his hand stretched toward it – "maybe I'll recognize it!"

Harper leaned forward, and both inspected it carefully; at last the former said, nodding his head: "I've never seen the thing – it's still new."

Harper did not recognize it either, and it was unknown to the rest of them too.

"I'll take it with me," said Roberts finally – "maybe it'll give us a clue; but I'll wash the blood off. It looks much too terrible –"

"A-tia," now cried Assowaum, and pointed to a freshly dug place in the bushes, not far from the place where the body had lain – "what is that there?"

"That's where they buried the body," cried the shopkeeper.

"No, God forbid," said Curtis, who had walked over there, "the hole's not nearly big enough to bury a possum in, much less a man. – But something's been dug here, and with a broad knife at that – but the earth that was taken out of here isn't there anymore; what need would they have just for dirt?"

Assowaum looked closely at the area between the spot where the body had lain and the little grave, then said, straightening up: "When air is found in the clothing, sometimes a body floats and gets hung on some protruding bush or tree – if the body is filled with earth, it will sink down."

"Horrible! Horrible!" cried Roberts – "so that explains the little knife – to slice open the corpse. Gentlemen, this is a terrible deed. – Who can the unfortunate man be?"

"The stream hides that," answered Harper dully – "who knows if it'll ever come to light, but – what's the Indian doing? What are you trying to do, Assowaum?"

"To make a rope and dive," he said, as he peeled the bark from a small paw-paw tree standing not very far off and tied the strips together.

"Dive? After the corpse?" asked Roberts, horrified.

"Jau e-mau," whispered the Indian, pointing to the water – "he is there!" And with that he threw off his hunting shirt, leggings, and moccasins and was just about to jump into the water.

"Stop!" said the shopkeeper, who had observed these preparations with great interest, and now understood what he had in mind – "if you mean to tie the rope to the corpse, it'll take too long – here's a fishhook." With this, he took from his pocket a small package containing every possible type of fish-hook and handed the Indian one of the larger ones.

"That is good," cried the latter happily, quickly fastened the hook on the end of the tough pawpaw bark, glanced back once more at the spot where the body was thrown into the flood, and in the next instant disappeared into the dreadful place. – A deathly quiet reigned for several seconds – no one dared to breathe. The river was once more completely smooth above the submerged fig-ure of the red hunter, since it was quite deep here, and only air bubbles rising quickly one after the other revealed his location. Then the black glistening hair emerged again, and instantly the head of the warrior rose above the surface. – Taking just one deep breath, he struck out for the shore where the men stood. He clambered up the steep bank while still holding the hook in his hand.

"And the corpse?" asked Roberts.

"I felt it," was Assowaum's answer – "my hand touched it as I groped around after it. But the water lifted me again too quickly – it's down there!"

"Will one of the white men give me a stone?" he asked after a little while, as he threw himself exhausted under a tree – "I'm weary and would like to rest!"

"Are you going down there again?" cried Harper, astonished. The Indian only nodded his head, but Hartford walked quickly to the gravelly bank nearby and dragged back a fairly heavy stone, around which Curtis straightaway tied a short rope, to which in turn he tied a noose.

"So, Indian," he said then, "if you hang this, the way I am showing you now, on your left wrist, it'll take you under, and if you want to come up again, then you just need to slip it off – like this, see?"

The Indian required little instruction; he quickly followed the white man's advice, this time leaving the end of the cord made of bark in Curtis' hand and taking only the fish hook in his right, thereby taking care not to get entangled with it. Then he slid down the steep clay bank and dove into the river for the second time.

This time his stay underwater was longer than the first, since he was forced by the heavy stone to move slowly along the bottom and to feel with his foot for the object of his search. Finally he jerked on the line that held the hook;

numerous foam bubbles welled up, and once more the dark head of the Indian appeared. He quickly paddled to the bank, climbed out of the water, and looked back with a shudder. His face had taken on an ashen color, and as he swept his long raven-black hair from his forehead his eyes stared with a vacant and spectral look, as though he no longer belonged to this earth, as if he were the spirit of his original tribe rising from the dark depths because he would not share a watery grave with the enemy of his people.

"The line's fastened," cried Curtis, holding the end in his hand, "Assowaum's found the body!"

Now, as the Indian silently looked out upon the surface of the water, the men on the riverbank above pulled on the line slowly and carefully, so as not to break it. Thus the body to whose clothes the hook was fastened rose up, and soon a dark object was visible in the water. – The water parted and shrank back, as if shuddering at its eerie burden, and in the next instant Assowaum grabbed the corpse by the shoulder and pulled it to dry land. The men had jumped down, and as the Indian turned the corpse over so that the pallid face was visible, every lip sounded a cry of horror. With one voice, the hunters cried: "Heathcott!"

"Heathcott," Harper then breathed.

For several minutes the men stood there silently and looked with terrified eyes upon the dreadful spectacle. The body of the unfortunate man was cut open and filled with dirt and rocks[3]; on his forehead gaped a wide wound, though the bullet appeared to have gone through his chest. Roberts bent down to the corpse and examined the bullet hole.

"How many bullets does Brown's rifle fire?" he asked softly, as if hesitant to speak the name of the young man in front of the body.

"Thirty," whispered Harper back. Roberts pointed silently to the hole torn by the bullet in the dead man's chest.

"Do you think he's guilty?" Harper now asked, looking nervously around the circle.

"Guilty? No, by God, no," cried Curtis; "no jury in the whole of Arkansas would say he's *guilty* after that one there spewed such threats at him as Smith told me he did. – I'd have shot him too. I'm sorry to see such a vigorous fellow lying there like this, that he wasted his life in such a way when he could've become a useful citizen of the state; but a plague and death on it! When such fellows, who are known to keep their word about fighting and killing, say in no uncertain terms that they're going to shoot someone or other dead the next time they see him, then they deserve nothing better than a rifle bullet – that's what I think. – Only – the – he could have done without the belly ripping – the vultures would have finished him off just as well and even faster; just look how they're coming here in droves. – But this time you're mistaken; *that* meal will be taken away from you. I suppose we must make a report about this, or should we leave him lying here?"

"No, by no means," said Roberts – "we can't do that; the best thing to do would be to cover him here with branches and report it to the Justice of the Peace; then he can send his constable. I'll have nothing more to do with it – what are you looking for, Hartford?"

The shopkeeper had knelt down next to the corpse and was very carefully searching the leather hunting shirt that clung in wet folds to the dead man's chest.

"This man here," he said at last very earnestly, standing up – "carried with him in his leather pouch, – the one you see here – four hundred and seventy dollars in bank notes, all as good as silver[4] – I saw them myself yesterday morning at Bowitt's house, and he couldn't have lost them since the button on the pouch is hard to undo – someone's opened the pouch and – taken the money out of it."

"Who here dares to say that my nephew has robbed a dead man?" cried old Harper, as his face turned deathly pale and he jumped up, ripping his knife from its sheath. – "Who calls my Bill a thief?"

"Hold on, Harper," said Roberts kindly, laying his hand on the other's arm, "we have every reason to believe that Brown shot Heathcott. The money could've been taken by someone else – there were two of them in the business."

"But who else could've been with him?"

"Only God knows that – not us; but here are the footprints of two men, one with boots and the other with shoes, that's obvious, and if Brown did this for revenge, the other could've easily found the opportunity to secure the money for himself."

"Brown would've never allowed it."

"If he even saw it; but that's all the same; the money was there, since he had already mentioned outside my house that he was carrying the price of three horses with him. – Brown heard him, for sure, but I consider the young man to be honest, and as I've said, who knows who helped him?"

"This is terrible!" cried Harper, as he covered his face with his hands and leaned against a tree, shaken by the most violent emotions. At the foot of the same tree, Assowaum sat thoughtfully, feet tucked under him, chin in his left hand, his elbow propped on his knee.

"So let's get to work then," said Curtis, as he began to drag branches to the spot – "this place makes me shudder, and I can't spend another minute with that scary face."

"Right you are, Curtis," said Roberts, helping him drag to the corpse a rather heavy branch that had broken off and fallen – "another few more pieces like this one here and then some ordinary branches on top, and the ravens and vultures should leave the place alone for a while; besides, the wolves won't come here in the daylight."

Curtis, Roberts, and Hartford soon finished the temporary grave of the murdered man, cutting down enough branches with their heavy hunting knives to fashion a roof; Harper and Assowaum stood by and did nothing. At last this sad duty was fulfilled, and the men got ready to depart. Of course, Harper followed them as they left the place, but he appeared dazed; the old man's spirit seemed broken. He did not complain, but his pale cheeks and stony gaze told only too clearly what was in his heart. He himself did not doubt for a moment that Brown had committed the murder; that, though, would bring him no shame in the eyes of the world, and least of all in Arkansas; but the money – the money – that was terrible! He knew men who were only too inclined to think the worst of everyone, even when the worst did not have such blatant evidence in its favor; but here, where even an impartial person must waver – it was dreadful! He climbed into the saddle and dropped the reins on his horse, which slowly followed the others; he never once noticed that the Indian remained in his thoughtful pose at the foot of the tree.

Assowaum stayed there for many minutes after the others had disappeared into the thicket, sitting and staring dreamily at the ground before him; but then, as the last sound of the hoofs and the last yapping of the dogs had died away, he rose softly and began again his examination of the tracks and marks. With the small knife that he carried in his belt, he marked on the handle of his tomahawk the exact length and width of the footprints; then, after he had convinced himself that nothing had escaped his notice, he shouldered his rifle and plunged into the thick woods, in the opposite direction to that which the hunters had taken.

Notes

1. In fact, the vast majority of a bear's diet consists of plant foods.

2. "Morrisons Bluff" in FG's spelling.

3. Perhaps an allusion to the fairy tale of *Little Red Riding Hood,* popularized by the Brothers Grimm.

4. "As good as silver": the silver standard was not replaced by the gold standard until 1900. This amount is equivalent to about $13,000 today.

Chapter 9

The Gang of Four Negotiates a Business Matter. – Rowson's Righteous Indignation at the Murder, and Marion's Weakness.

We must take the reader back to the thicket in which we opened this story, and where on the same morning in which the hunters fished the corpse out of the Petit Jean, the four conspirators met and discussed the next step in their plans. Cotton and Weston were the first on the scene, though Johnson and Rowson did not keep them waiting long and were welcomed by the other two with a cheery "hurrah."

"Psst – psst!" said Rowson, hushing them. "Don't make so much noise as if you were on a country lane and didn't care who heard you."

"Well, I really don't care," laughed Weston – "what would it matter if someone finds us here together?"

"Nothing, of course, for you all – but it would for me. – My mother-in-law's a very pious woman, and she would consider it of little honor to herself if I were to count you two among my acquaintances."

"Your mother-in-law?" asked Cotton, astonished – "no, tell me, Rowson, is it true then, what people are prattling? are you really thinking of marrying old Roberts' daughter? It's true, I've heard about it, but I couldn't yet believe it."

"And why not, Mr. Cotton? This is the last business of this sort that we'll do together; – I'll make a respectable man of myself."

"It's about time, that's for sure!" laughed Cotton – "almost a little too late already; but God help the poor girl!"

"Mr. Cotton, I won't tolerate any offensive talk; there's no joking with me on this subject."

"Quiet!" said Johnson. "We didn't come here for you to start your old banter again – our purpose is a more serious one. – How'd your hunt go, Cotton?"

"Four deer and a fox."

"You might have spared the fox its life; and yours, Weston?"

"Two deer and three turkeys."

"Then I've got the least," said Johnson; "actually, I have a valid excuse. I fell yesterday morning off one of the mountain ridges, that is, a stone gave way and I slid and cut my whole arm; that's really slowed my hunting down a lot."

"Hold on there – that doesn't matter," cried Weston – "it doesn't matter in a horse race either if one of the horses comes up lame. No, a level field and everyone takes their own chances –"

"Where do you keep your skins, eh?" asked Johnson, half angrily.

"They're hanging near Cotton's cabin. – If you don't believe us, come on; but I rather thought –"

"Yes, yes – it's all right; it was really just a joke; so Rowson and I will begin the dance. God help us, what a stir it'll make in the settlement. But with twenty-four hours head start, the whole of Arkansas shan't find the animals again. Rowson has an admirable plan; so don't forget the place above Hoswells' canoe, and you, Weston, keep your horses and wait for us that evening at the ruined cabin on Horse Creek,[1] and make as few tracks as you can. – But you'll be clever enough as to that."

"Where would I best stay in the meantime?" asked Cotton, "I don't want to just lie idle during all this. – Ah well, I'll go over to Atkins'; I can rest a little there."

"There's sure plenty of game in that area; you won't want for meat," said Johnson.

"And the Regulators?"

"Can go to hell – by the time they catch the scent, it'll be too late, and for all their wit they'll have missed their best chance. There'll really be quite a stir here in the county for quite some time after this."

"If my plan succeeds," said Rowson, "the Regulators won't have much on us. They'll be sure to come upon the false trail, and once one of the hounds has struck it, its howl will drag the whole yelping pack behind it. It would be a capital joke if we could fool that boasting Husfield especially."

"Well, we'll all do our best – but when will you start?"

"Straight away," said Johnson. "The sooner it's settled the better it'll be. The Regulators' meetings are starting now, and once the damned scoundrels have whipped the whole territory up into a frenzy, it'll be too late to get any sensible business going."

"In any case, I must go to Roberts' once beforehand," said Rowson, "and indeed this very morning – and, by the by, I won't even have to make a single detour. Meanwhile, Johnson can go through the woods, and we'll meet again at the springs of the little Cypress Creek, where the copper beech is."

"So we're going on foot?" asked Johnson.

"Of course," answered Rowson, "that is to say – *on the way over*, but hardly coming back!"

"No, hopefully not," laughed Cotton, "and now, boys, good bye – I must get going."

"When'll you get to the meeting place?" asked Weston, "you're not going to keep me waiting around there with the horses too long?"

"Well, *before* Friday evening in any event," answered Rowson. "That is to say, if nothing gets in the way. If we find on Thursday evening – we certainly wouldn't be able to get there on foot earlier – that there isn't a good opportunity, then it'll have to wait until Saturday; but I hope it'll all go well, and we'll be at the meeting place Friday evening at sundown; so, here's to a speedy – and merry reunion!"

"Until we meet again!" cried Cotton and Weston, and were lost in the bushes. – Rowson looked after them for a while and then, shaking his head, spoke to his companion: "Johnson, this has to be the last time that we have anything to do with that fellow, that Cotton. They don't want anything more to do with him on the island either; they've heard that he's always getting drunk and then blabs all sorts of stuff and picks quarrels."

"The youngster, Weston, is just as little to my liking," answered Johnson. "Truth be told, I believe that if his feet were in the fire, he'll tattle out of school. – I don't trust him."

"Let's hope that his silence is never put to the test," said Rowson with great seriousness – "who knows what any of us would do in such a case. It's pretty tempting to save one's own skin by sacrificing one or two others, *strangers,* for safety's sake. With us two it's very different, though; I don't think turning state's evidence* would help *us* much, and where –"[2]

"You know, the less we talk about that, the better," said Johnson very quietly, as he checked the powder in his pan. "Where do we leave the horses?"

"At Fulweal's again – Weston already knows that and will pick them up there."

"Good – then you go now, straight to the road and follow it, and I'll keep to the woods – it'd be better if we're not seen together."

"Good luck in the meantime!"

"Good luck!"

Rowson, who had now reached the spot where his horse stood tethered, swung himself up and trotted toward the road, where he gave his horse the reins and galloped quickly until he saw shining in the distance the bright roof of the peaceful home where his beloved lived. Here he reined in the animal again, approached the house at a measured pace, and dismounted at the door. But although he was welcomed by Mrs. Roberts with joy, and by Marion with friendliness, he did not tarry long with the women, but rather told them that he had only come to take leave of them for a few days. In part he was, he said, compelled by his calling to travel to the northern part of the county to preach

---

* FG's note: "If someone turns accuser of one's comrades and appears as a witness for the state."

the word of the Lord, but his business also required him to go to the Arkansas River, where he would receive a sum of money that he was expecting.

"Soon, my dear Marion," he continued, taking the maiden's hand tenderly in his own as she paled slightly, "soon the most ardent wish of my soul will be fulfilled, and with the help of our Lord Jesus Christ we will set up our house together in peace. It is not good that man be alone; this unsettled life is bad for my health, the eternal riding around often forces me to seek a night's lodging in places that I'd rather happily avoid."

"The men of Arkansas," whispered Marion softly, "like to sleep in the open – Mr. Rowson perhaps has not yet tried it?"

"Oh, yes, dear Marion, of course, but it doesn't suit my constitution – I'm past my youthful years; why should a man seek out hardships that he can avoid? But farewell, dear child – may heaven protect you in the meantime. But first we should pray fervently to the Lord just once more, that He will bless our poor endeavors and be gracious to us."

With that, he pulled out his little prayer book, bound in black, that he always kept in his pocket, and began his devotion in a loud voice. The women knelt at their chairs, in the manner of Methodists, and Marion looked up with moist eyes over her folded hands at the clear, pure heaven above. Her thoughts drifted far, far away – she did not hear the harsh voice of the hypocrite at her side, who intoned his monotonous memorized phrases with the same feeling, perhaps, as the hurdy-gurdy man listens to the song he's played a thousand times – her gaze was fixed on the cheerful dome of the Lord, and though her lips pressed silently on her tender fingers, her heart was speaking to God.

"Rub the horses down a little – in an hour I must be off again!" said Roberts' voice outside, to the Negro – "come in a minute, Harper, and rest yourself – what could you do at home now? Come, I'm tired and I'd like to rest a minute myself – but hello – it's prayer time again, forsooth," he continued softly, turning to his friend. – "The devil take that preacher! – as if a man had nothing else to do but slide around on his knees all the time – I wonder if that could give the Lord above any pleasure? – Tom, get us a couple of chairs from the house," he then cried in a louder tone again to the Negro, who was just then taking the saddles from the horses. But Rowson had heard the arrival of the two men, and broke off his prayer just as the Negro came into the room. The two men then stepped in without further ado.

"Good morning, ladies!" said Harper – but he seemed pale and miserable, his eyes sunk in their sockets, his knees barely able to support the weight of his body – he sank wearily into a chair.

"Mr. Harper – for God's sake, what's the matter?"

"Nothing – I thank you – it'll pass – a glass of water, if you please."

Marion took the long-stemmed gourd bottle which lay in the water pail and handed it to the old man.

"A murder has been committed," Roberts now said, as he moved his chair over to the chimney and stared at the floor before him. "A murder – a terrible murder – Heathcott has been killed."

"Heathcott?" cried Rowson, staring at him. – "Heathcott? who says so?"

"I've seen the corpse – Brown's killed him! What's wrong with the girl? Marion – what foolishness – why does she have to pass out when someone mentions murder; certainly, this not the first that she's heard of." Harper approached him softly.

"Don't mention the money here," he whispered to him – "let's see first if we can't find the trail of the other one."

"Don't worry," answered Roberts – "as for that, I myself believe in Brown's innocence."

Rowson had stood for a moment as if sunk deep in prayer, but now he sighed and raised his eyes, and said shuddering: "It's terrible – horrible – still so young and already a murderer and a thief."

"Thief?" Harper started wildly.

"Didn't Heathcott say here that he carried a substantial amount of money on him? Do you think his murderer would bury the money with him?" Marion looked over at her father in anxious expectation, as if she waited on his answer. Roberts did not speak but stared silently into the blazing flames in the fireplace.

"Heathcott was a sinful man," Rowson continued in a stern voice. "But to die like *that*, to depart *thus* in his sinfulness, that's terrible. Where was the frightful deed committed, Mr. Roberts?"

"On the Petit Jean – we found the tracks, and Assowaum pulled the body out of the river."

The preacher was silent several minutes and stared down before him, deep in thought, then raised up suddenly and asked, his eyes fixed steadily on Roberts: "But how do you know that Brown is the murderer?"

"He was seen in that neighborhood on the same morning," said Roberts, sighing, "and there were two who did the killing. – And then Brown had a quarrel the day before with the murdered man, who spit out these mighty wild threats against him at the time."

"Shameful – shameful," cried Rowson in pious indignation – "I'll go myself to the Petit Jean – maybe we can still catch the murderer."

"Mr. Rowson, it was on *your* account that the unfortunate man's fight with the deceased began," said Marion earnestly, gazing at her betrothed – "it becomes you very little to sit in judgment over him."

"Marion!" cried her mother, indignant at the audacity of the otherwise so gentle maiden. "Marion – how dare you?"

"Leave the child alone – Sister Roberts," replied Rowson mildly. "She judges from superficial impressions, and who can blame her for it? – God alone sees the heart and knows how to weigh it."

"It would help you little to apprehend my nephew," said Harper now, standing up angrily – "we're all ready to testify to the threats that Heathcott made against him here. – A jury *must* and *would* acquit him – in any event, he'll come back here in eight days or so and defend himself."

"He's coming back?" asked Rowson quickly.

"Thank God – then he can't be guilty!" cried Marion with heartfelt joy.

"Miss Marion seems to take a lot of interest in the young man," remarked Rowson.

"In *anyone's* innocence!" said the lovely girl, at the same time blushing at the zeal with which she supported the cause of a man she hardly knew.

"That is fine and praiseworthy," answered the preacher in a friendly tone – "may the Lord bless you for it, my good child, and keep you in your pious faith. You have not yet had the bitter experiences that we have – may they never come to pass!" With this, he stepped toward Mrs. Roberts and quietly said something to her; then he kissed his bride respectfully on the forehead and went outside with the two men, who, after a few brief words of farewell had swung themselves back into the saddle. Here he mounted his small lively pony and rode slowly up the wide road that led between two cornfields to a smaller path that ran, further on, northwest to the Arkansas River.

"Mother," said Marion after a silent and painful pause, when they were alone together, "Mother – I *cannot* love that man. – My heart doesn't hold any of the emotions that I would have to feign at the altar."

"Child," cried the matron fearfully, as she grasped her daughter's hand – "pray! There's nothing in the world as reviving as a fervent prayer, when the tempter draws near. – You know that Mr. Rowson has your word and mine – you know that his entire happiness depends on it, and that by the side of such a pious man you'll be able to purify your soul to an extent that's so completely missing in you now. Mr. Rowson hopes, as he just now confided to me, to see his business finished before the time agreed on earlier, and as soon as that happens, it's wedding time. – Be my good child, as you've always been, and you'll be as happy as you deserve to be." Her arms slung around her mother's neck, Marion sobbed aloud.

Notes

1. "Horsecreek," in FG's original. Possibly a reference to present-day Horsehead Creek, across the Arkansas River from Morrison Bluff.

2. "State's evidence" appears in English throughout FG's original text.

Chapter 10

The Sheriff's Election in Pettyville. – A Lack of Rosin. The Pursuers Are on the Trail.

It was election day in Pettyville[1] – That is to say, a Sheriff and a Clerk* for the county were to be named, and three candidates had announced for the first post, two for the second. One, a well-to-do farmer from the neighborhood by the name of Kowles, had tried to bring voters over to his side by giving a banquet on the previous Fourth of July, the anniversary of the American Declaration of Independence. Even now he regularly carried a small bottle of whiskey in one pocket, and a piece of chewing tobacco in the other, and it was said that he dispensed both very freely where there was even the slightest hope of getting a vote. The second was a German,[2] though he had been in America quite a long time, and ran a small store farther up the river; the third, by contrast, was a farmer from the Arkansas River, who had held the post once before, though he was not re-elected because he frankly drank a bit too much for the good folk, who were generally quite indulgent in this regard. "Being a little 'slant' three times a week," many had said, "they could easily put up with, but every day, that's too much." In any event, he must have reformed, and there were many voices supporting him. Indeed, Vattel was a really good-hearted fellow who loved to join in the fun, and who never took offense at a joke, but who also stood his ground when it was necessary to assert his authority.

The election was supposed to begin at two o'clock, and the farmers and hunters who had already gathered in the little house, where the table and the writing materials stood, were killing time as best they could. The house was an ordinary log cabin with one bed in one corner and a table in the other. Rifles leaned against the walls everywhere, and on every nail, or rather peg (since there was no great abundance of iron in the whole building), hung bullet-pouches and powder horns. Several backwoodsmen lay outstretched, some on blankets and some on the raw floorboards, and they talked in great

---

* FG's note translates the original "clerk" as "Gerichtsschreiber."

detail about pastures, game, and a soon-to-be-discovered gold mine in the mountains of the Fourche La Fave.

But the strangest group by far lay on or near the bed. On the bottom edge of the bed, left foot pressed against the floor, sat the tall, thin figure of a man in a badly worn, light blue woolen frock-coat, the back of which was made of a material very unlike that of the collar and sleeves. On his head he wore an old felt hat, in which he had cut holes on three different sides to let in fresh air. A similar experiment had been carried out on his shoes, but here, it seemed, less for the sake of air than for his corns. His trousers, which were really only held together at the knee by various straps of deerskin, were as multicolored as a map of the United States itself, of which it was Robin's pride to count himself among its free citizens. An old worn-out leather bullet-pouch hung from his right side, and a very small knife with a wooden handle was stuck in the front of his belt, which kept the aforementioned trousers from completely leaving his body, to which they seemed indeed only partially to belong.

But in spite of his very independent appearance (if one may use the word independent to describe a man about whom everything, truly, was *dependent*), he sat very happily on his very uncomfortable, sharp-edged seat and scratched away on an old violin in such a dreadful manner that the dogs, who were sunning themselves outside the hut, paced back and forth in their places, apparently divided as to whether they should abandon their nice warm spot or go on listening to the screeching. The men inside the cabin, however, seemed not to notice the ear-splitting noise; they chatted and laughed and paid no further attention to the player. Only one seemed to take a special interest in the completely self-absorbed artist: a young blond-haired farmer – who gave every indication of the greatest comfort as he lay outstretched at full length on the bed, feet pointed toward the player – whistled along with the melody, following it perfectly, though in an entirely different key. But the player stuck to one and the same song, and fiddled the verse a full fifty times, always from the beginning, until at last even his patient listener had had enough.[3] Giving him a gentle poke with the end of his foot, he called out to this second Paganini:[4]

"Damn it – Robin, I've been lying here now a half an hour, whistling the same song forever – can't you do another one? – well – that's right, Yankee Doodle." – And falling back again onto the pillow from which he had just risen for the first time, he commenced to whistle the new piece with all his might.

"So what happened then with the body?" asked a farmer from the mouth of the Fourche La Fave – "I haven't heard a thing more about it."

"Well, nothing more's happened with it," answered another – "the men that found it covered it with branches, and we all went out to find the trail of the other fellow who had a hand in the business. But you know how it started to rain so bad that afternoon, and so nothing more could be done."

"So Brown really shot him up?"

"Well, naturally," said the justice of the peace, walking over to them, "that was to be expected. Who the devil would put up with such threats to his life? But I'd like to find the second one – that fellow definitely had no grounds, and no one really has a notion at all whom to rightly suspect."

"It was a hell of a thing for that Indian to dive down just to put a hook into a body. – I don't know what somebody would have to give me to make me do it!"

"Ah, the redskins are used to such things – without him we couldn't have found out who the dead man really was, since no one would have thought of Heathcott –"

"If the Indian hadn't behaved himself so well in the matter, I'd have suspected him himself," said the judge – "Brown and the redskin are always hand and glove together anyway, and it would've been no wonder if they were pulling on the same yoke here. But it doesn't appear to be so, since Assowaum would want to guard against lending a hand to something that must be dangerous to him and that could not have been done without him."

"Have the Regulators already chosen another leader?"

"They're to meet on Sunday at Bowitts' and talk it all over. – They're on the trail of several who live here in the area."

"So is it true that they robbed the dead man?"

"He had money on him that very morning, that I know for sure," said Cook, who lay on the bed and had stopped whistling for a moment – "he had money, namely in a little red leather pocketbook buttoned inside his hunting shirt – but it was gone when they found him; naturally they whisked that away –"[5]

"Not Brown, I'd swear to that!" said the judge. "Brown I take for an honest fellow, and it strikes me as quite strange that he'd need anyone else to help him dispatch the braggart."

"Robin," said Cook from the bed, on which he now turned halfway around and administered a second friendly poke with the end of his foot to the forenamed individual – "Robin, if you don't stop soon with your Yankee Doodle, I swear I'll fetch the dogs in here, for sure; can't you do more than those two pieces, then?"

Robin began to play Washington's March,[6] and Cook quieted down again.

"Gentlemen," the judge now cried – "it's time that we get started; it must be two o'clock. By the way, we need a clerk. – Who among those present can fill that office, eh? Cook – you can write!"

"Yes – my name; but since I'm not on the candidate list, it won't likely be needed."

"Smith – you then – or Hopper – or Moos – what the devil, can't any of you make a list?"

"Here comes Hecker out there – the German, he can write," said Robin, pointing with his violin bow toward the open door.

"Hey, Hecker!" cried the judge. "Do you have an hour to spare to make up a list of names?"

"Yes – two or three," answered the person addressed, as he appeared in the door. "I just want to be at the salt lick over on the other side of the mountain by the time it gets dark; if I leave here by five, I'll get there in plenty of time."

"Good – then put your rifle there in the corner – is it loaded?"

"Do you think I carry an empty barrel around in the woods?"

"Well, just lean it carefully – I always worry about the damage those damned short things can do."[7]

Hecker, a young German who supported himself by hunting in the area, and who was clothed exactly like the local backwoodsmen, moved a chair to the table, drew from its sheath the large wide hunting knife that made it uncomfortable for him to sit down, laid it in front of him, and asked Smith, who sat next to him:

"Is it not possible to get either Robin or Cook to stop their frightful music? It'll make the dogs sick."

"It'd be hard," laughed the other, "they both think it's a wonder how beautifully they do it. – But there comes Wells[8], sure enough! What brings *that* man here? He doesn't usually pay any mind to elections."

"He's caught some wolves, by God!" cried the judge. "Bravo, Wells, that's clever of you; the beasts have done enough damage!"

"Good evening to all," said the hunter, as he stepped into the cabin and threw three bloody wolf scalps on the table – "good evening, Judge – there – just give me the certificate[†] or buy them from me; I'd prefer the last, since I don't much bother with taxes."

Wells was a slim well-built man with lively grey eyes, but otherwise his whole appearance was more like that of an Indian than a white man, and many claimed that his veins carried as much red blood as white. In his clothing, too, he was indistinguishable from the half-civilized red sons of the wilderness. Like these, he left his head bare, so that his long, black, glossy hair floated about his shoulders, or at most it was held fast, in very windy weather, by a strip of tree bark bound around the temples. Some told tales of adventurous deeds in his life, especially those of recent years, which he had spent in Texas

---

[†] FG's note: "For the scalp of a wolf you would receive a reward or premium of three dollars in Arkansas, though the amount is not paid in cash but in the form of a voucher, which is accepted for state taxes."

for the most part. Now he lived very quietly and peacefully on a well-established farm that he looked after with his two sons, young lads of nine and eleven. But he worked only in the summer, and even then only in the few weeks of planting time – the other months he hunted and set traps for predatory beasts, especially wolves. Otherwise he was harmless and was regarded fondly throughout the region for his friendly though rough demeanor, as well as for his boundless hospitality.

"Listen, Wells," laughed Hecker, as he wiped the wolf's blood from his ruled sheet with the sleeve of his hunting shirt – "if it's all the same to you, lay those sopping things under the table – it'll be easier to write –"

"Oh, I've gotten the paper dirty – I'm really sorry. – Well, you can still write on it anyway; it's just on one corner up there. – Here, Judge – three times three makes nine –"

"Yes – nine dollars for three wolf scalps, that's well enough, but you must first swear that you killed them yourself and in this county."

"I can't do that – I only trapped them, my dogs chewed them to death after that."

"It's the same thing – whether they were killed by your hand, your dogs, or your traps – swear that to me –"

"Well, I'll be goddamned if it isn't true –"

"Good – by God!" cried Cook from the bed, as he dealt Robin another light kick. "That deserves a Yankee Doodle –"

"Dear Wells," laughed the judge, "that's not the correct oath. But the clerk will take it from you; but now, about our election – so, Hecker, you'll write, and who're my two fellow judges‡? Aha – Smith and Hawkes – just sit down, we can get started."

"What's the date today?" asked Hecker.

"The twenty-seventh."

"And what day?"

"Well, grace be to God, don't you even know the day? Friday."

"When a man's out in the woods for a couple of weeks, he gets mighty confused," laughed Hecker – "I thought it was Sunday."

One of the farmers stepped forward – Hecker wrote down his name – "good evening, Heslaw – he doesn't need any further identification, right?"

"No – not him –"

"Whom for sheriff?"

"Vattel."

"And clerk?"

"Hopper."

---

‡ FG's note: "To determine voter eligibility, three citizens of the state are named as judges."

"Robin, for God's sake stop that scratching, won't you," said the judge, now half angry – "it sounds awful!"

"I don't have any rosin," said Robin quietly, but otherwise continuing without interruption – "Smith – reach under the table there. There's a little leather bag hanging from one of the legs, there must be some in that."

"Oh, better yet, stop your fiddling, it gives a man a headache."

"Oh? – better yet, close your ears if you don't want to hear it, and go to hell!" cried Robin, highly offended, and angrily departed the room.

"Your name?" Smith asked the second man who had come to vote.

"Kattlin."

"How long in the state?"§

"Seven months."

"How long in the county?"

"Eight weeks."

"Can you swear to that?"

"Yes indeed!"

"Administer the oath to him – clerk."

The latter prompted the man with the set phrases of the oath in a rather rapid voice, held the Bible out for him to kiss, and ended the vow with the customary, solemn vow: "So help you God."¶

"He could use that, for sure," said Cook yawning, as he turned himself about in bed.

The voting now continued off and on for two hours, until all those present had cast their votes and the two clerks were about to sign their names in closing – for the record must be kept in duplicate, to avoid any mistake – when those standing outside announced the arrival of old Bahrens, who came trotting up on his little pony.

"Not yet closed, gentlemen?" he cried out as he stepped into the room, "not yet closed – well, but, surely it's early enough. – Hurrah for Vattel – that's the man, boys – he loves a piddle sometimes, that's true, but that's not worth mentioning, afterwards he's always on the job. – Write down Vattel, I say –"

"'Tis time you came, Bahrens," said Hecker, "I was just about to leave. It's already past five o'clock, and I still have half an hour to travel."

"Where to then?"

"To the next salt lick. Want to come with me?"

---

§ FG's note: "To be qualified to vote, men must have resided in the state for six months, and in the county for six weeks."

¶ Original in English; FG's note offers this German translation: "So möge Euch Gott helfen."

"Oh, the devil take your salt lick; we'll stay here together, right, boys? – This evening we should have a spree.** – I won't go home until I – can't go any more, and then I'll stay here for sure."

"That's good, Bahrens!" cried Cook, who had stepped to the table. "I'll go for that. I've brought two deerskins with me that we'll put toward drinks. Damn it,⁹ not every day's election day. Have you shot anything?"

"I? No, I watched a hunt this afternoon that made me forget all about shooting. Wait, Hecker – you must hear the story first. – You'll get to your damned salt lick soon enough – you won't shoot anything anyway –"

"Now, what was that?"

"Yes, well – what did I see? You see, about an hour ago I was coming along, right above here by the steep cliffs of the Fourche La Fave, and what did I see? An eagle that keeps flying along in a circle above the water. I stood still and got ready to shoot, since I thought it would maybe come within shooting range, and if it hovered in the air just right, beating its wings, you could put a bullet in it beautifully; but all at once it dove down like lightning, made a wide turn and lashed the water with his broad wings in the blink of an eye, then straightaway climbed back up and – God strike me, if it's not true – carried an eel in its claws."

"Well, is that really so remarkable? I've seen it several times before."

"Hold on there – not so fast, Meesyer, from over the water – seen it several times before? Let me finish speaking first, if you please. For an eagle to catch an eel, that's not a miracle, I'll grant you, and anyone who's always out in the woods and lying about rivers and lakes may see it, but just keep listening. The eagle kept climbing, took the eel in its beak, and gulped it down. Now, I thought it was all over; I uncocked and shouldered my rifle, when all at once – God strike me, if it isn't true – *the eel slipped out again.* The eagle must not have noticed it at first, then suddenly was aware of it – it followed, and – yes, just watch – before it was in the water, had it again by the collar."

"Bahrens!" cried the judge.

"And do you really think that was all?" cried his interlocutor, without letting himself be distracted – "no – the eagle and the eel couldn't settle things between them. As soon as one thought he had the other down, the other was on its way again."

"And what became of them finally?" asked Hecker.

"What became of them? – do you think I had nothing else to do than watch all afternoon to see if an eagle can digest an eel? I left them to their business and I went away."

** Original in English, with FG's note added: "An American expression for a 'merry night.'"

"May I go now?" asked Hecker.

"You with your grinning face may go to the devil, for all I care! Boys, who'll fetch the whiskey? I can't sit in the store over yonder, it's too gloomy for me there. – Well, come on, Hecker – have a drink first, since sitting there dry all night's no joke. – God bless us, if I can't shoot my deer in the daytime anymore, I'll give it up; to lie out there in the open at night by the side of a fire that I'm not allowed to get myself warm at – to be worried always that I'll doze off and that my fire will go out, that a deer will come to the salt lick and hear me snoring – no – that doesn't suit me at all. – Good – I won't keep you – do as you please – I won't have to care for you when you get sick, but wait – you must hear what happened to me once at a salt lick in Texas."

"Only make it quick," said Hecker, shouldering his gun, "I really don't want to waste any time here."

"And it'd be a shame if your hide doesn't feel the thunderstorm that's blowing up over there, it'd be a real shame – ah well. – I too lay one night (at that time I was just such a fool as Hecker is now and stayed outside day and night) with my rifle at a salt lick. There was a great quantity of game in the area, and I had gotten myself on the spot a bit early so as to shoot down a goodly number of skins that night. – Well, it was barely dusk as I was hunkered down near a great heap of pinewood and under a stand that I had thrown together. Then, all at once, I heard, not far away, a frightful din and clamor, as though a few thousand panthers were howling. The whole woods shook – I no longer *heard* the noise, I fairly *felt* it – and (but here I must first point out that I was about a quarter hour from a big cotton field, and lying in a very low swampy area) before I was fully aware of it, it boomed all around me, and came down on me like a thunderstorm. But what do you think it was?"

"The devil only knows."

"Wild geese – a few thousand at least. My stand they destroyed, my little fire that I had just kindled, they put out with their wings, and as for me, they acted as if I didn't exist at all. But I wasn't lazy; I pulled out my hunting knife and began to strike back. The ones next to me now saw clearly that they had barked up the wrong tree, but too late, for before they could recover from their fright and give the alarm call, I had thinned them out pretty well. As they were leaving, I counted fifty-one geese and fifty-eight heads that stayed behind."

"What? Seven more heads? So where were the geese?"

"The ones that belonged to the heads? I found them the next day. They were flying so thick that the dead ones were carried with the living birds into the air for a full five hundred paces – good night, Hecker, good night – the fellow's running! And how he flings his legs!"

"Bahrens, you're still the same old fellow!" – laughed the judge. – "Nothing but nonsense, and you can lie so well the windows fog."

"That would be a trick now!" Bahrens cried scornfully. "Fog the windows? – I don't believe there are two panes of glass in the entire county, excepting those that Smith wears on his nose there. – But what good's my story if you don't believe a word of it? – Why don't *you* open your mouths? Well, there's the whiskey at least."

"If it didn't come right on the heels of Bahrens' story," said Curtis then, "I'd like to tell you all what happened to me yesterday – but upon my word 'tis true, and you don't need to grin so about it, Bahrens."

"Did you ever hear me make such excuses in advance about one of my experiences? Never – that always makes people suspicious," answered Bahrens, shaking his head.

"*You* really don't need to do that," said the judge, laughing, "with you it's always near at hand. But go on, Curtis, go on, and be so good as to allow me another drop of that stuff in the cup there."

"I was at the Petit Jean again yesterday evening," Curtis began – "to see about the hogs that Bahrens had told me about the other day when we were held up by the search for the corpse. Well – I crawled around the whole day in the bush and saw that they'd run everywhere, but never found as much as a pig's tail. Finally towards evening, as it was already getting dark, I saw something light standing in a little paw-paw thicket, and sure enough it was the old sow with her piglets (though I only saw ten – Bahrens talked about eleven – well, maybe the bear caught one). Once I'd convinced myself that it was really father's brand that she had on her ears – a hole in the left and a slit in the right, I was satisfied, and left them alone so as not to make them more nervous than necessary. But as there was nothing more to do with them that evening, I just threw them a few corn cobs that I had brought with me in my bullet-pouch and looked around for a good place to sleep.

"I am sick of the Petit Jean swamp. Everything was wet and damp, and the mosquitoes were so thick that you couldn't see through them. After a long hunt, I found a dry place, lit a fire, rolled myself up in my blanket, and lay down. I hadn't taken any dogs with me since I didn't want to scare the hogs, and anyway I wasn't intending to hunt, and tired from all the to-ing and fro-ing, I fell asleep fast enough. How long I might have lain there, I don't know, since the trees stood so thick that I could hardly make out a few stars above me, but one time I woke up, and it seemed to me that I heard something creeping softly around me. I listened long and hard, and had my rifle cocked beside me. But then I couldn't hear it anymore, and I persuaded myself that I'd just dreamed it, and lay down again; but I couldn't get the thing out of my mind. Without a dog, I'd have found myself in a mighty uncomfortable spot if an old panther were to jump on my neck just to be friendly, such a one as Dipolt over there had met on the Ouachita not long before. Half asleep, half awake, I lay thus and kept listening for the slightest sound, when I thought I heard the very same noise again. Softly I pulled the blanket from my face – it seemed to me that I heard something breathing – clearly and nearby, and almost at the same instant I felt the hot breath of some living creature on my face. Despite the darkness, I could make out a black object bending down right over me, and completely overwhelmed by fear and surprise I lay there dead still and awaited whatever the mysterious creature above me would do next. It couldn't have been a panther, that I knew, since it would have had me by the throat long before that. But that was the only thing I could think of. I never thought once about the knife in my belt that would have at least given me something to defend myself, but instead I lay there as if dead and stared up at the dark object close above me, whose shining eyes I could barely see gleaming in the darkness."

"I don't know – usually I'm not a bit fearful, but here I was really as if bewitched, and so helpless that I would have been the sure victim of any predator that would take the trouble to gobble me up."

"And the beast?" everyone asked.

"All at once I could see the stars above me again and no longer felt the hot breath – and right afterwards I heard the soft footsteps moving away. My visitor had left me, and I breathed freely again, as though I had been raised from the dead."

"Yes – but – wasn't the fire still burning?"

"It still barely smoldered, since the evening before I had dragged together nothing but dry hickory wood."

"Well, what did you do then?"

"I can't exactly remember any more. – First of all, I needed to get up and stir the fire, then I thought to pull my knife out of its sheath and lay it next to me or hold it ready in my hand, then I decided that I should lean my back against a tree to keep myself sitting upright, but I don't know how it happened – I must have fallen asleep again, because when I fully came to, it was broad daylight."

"That's strange, for sure," said the judge, "what could it have been? Didn't you see any tracks?"

"Strange," grumbled Bahrens. "If I'd been telling the story, there'd have been talk of nothing but 'nonsense and lies' – and now it's all 'strange.'"

"Naturally I looked for tracks," answered Curtis, "but I couldn't see any right there, since the ground was dry and the leaves were piled high, but some distance away I came on the trail of a remarkably big bear, and in all likelihood that must have been my night watchman."

"These beasts will do that," laughed Smith. "I know from experience, since two years ago I had a pet bear that got up several times in the night, came to my bed, and looked me right in the face – they're funny animals!"

"By the way, Curtis," asked the judge now – "you've promised to catch a small bear for me this spring; my wife would really like to have one. Is it no longer possible then?"

"Well, it's really too late now; by May the little rascals can already run like horses. – Besides, that's why I crept around out in the woods in every direction for six weeks in February and March, even went twice over to the Magazine Mountains[10] to look in a few caves that I know there, but nothing doing. – I'd like to have a little pet bruin myself – they're so awfully sweet."

"Foolishness," said Bahrens. – "They get to be clumsy things. Even before they're one year old they throw the glassware and dishes off the shelves, pull the tablecloth off the table with everything standing on it, drag the bee hives around, scuffle around with the piglets, and shake the peach trees. – No, there're lots of other animals that are harmless and just as much fun. In North Carolina I had a pet herring that chased me all over the house."

"Wait, Bahrens – don't trip yourself up," laughed the judge, "how long would a herring live on dry land?"

"Live!" cried the old hunter with great gusto – "live! An animal can adjust to anything. It'd been thrown onto a sandbank in its youth and had never seen water again – I only had to give him fresh sand every day. – Now I've got a little piglet," Bahrens continued, without allowing a second interjection, "a wonderful thing – and not at all *strange*. – Though it looks speckled like a fawn, and its little tail is twisted so remarkably tight that its hind legs haven't touched the ground for three weeks now."

"Hurrah for Bahrens!" cried Curtis.

"I almost caught a cub[††] for you the day before yesterday, Judge," said Cook, as he moved his chair to the table – "hello, Castley, why the devil don't you bring a little pine wood or dry shavings in here, it's getting pitch-black in the room, and I can't see if I still have anything in my cup anymore."

"Where then?" asked the judge.

"I was going over to Lewisburg,[11] to the open plains about eight or nine miles from here; – 'tis kind of a small prairie. – I was riding through it when I saw to the left of it, in the dry bed of a little stream, an old she-bear who was happily looking for worms with her young; she had only one with her. Well, of course I was carrying my rifle on my shoulder, but it wasn't loaded. That's why I was going to Lewisburg, to have some new screws put in for me, since the lock had flown off once already when it was fired. I pulled my horse up for a moment now and didn't really know what I should do. I didn't feel like riding back to get a rifle, since the next house was four miles away, and who knew

---

[††] FG's note: "Junger Bär," offering the German translation of a phrase given in the original English.

where the bear would be by the time I could get there again, even in the best case. So I gently leaned my weapon on a tree, which considerably lightened my load, and decided to have some fun. – That is to say, I wanted to see how the old girl would look if she suddenly got wind of me. So I rode carefully through the scattered bushes, right up to her, and since the leaves there were damp and didn't rustle, and the two animals were so busy with their worm investigations, they didn't notice me until, when I was not quite ten steps away, my pony scented them and snorted. The old lady jumped up like a bolt of lightning, and forgetting everything but herself, she reached a great oak with a few powerful strides, grabbed it with her forepaws, pulled herself up on it and looked back to see whether she needed to climb the tree. But I was so close on her heels that when she stopped, my little pony, who's used to such chases, jumped right over a tree trunk lying nearby and almost touched the old lady with his nose. Now, you should've seen the old she-bear tear out – God help me, the way she threw her big hind legs when she heard my loud hunting cry close by."

"So what became of the young one in the meantime?"

"Well, just listen – after a few strides the idea suddenly went through my mind that, if the old lady abandoned her young one in such a cowardly way, I might really be able to catch it at last, since it was still a little thing, born about the middle of March. No sooner thought than done; I quickly turned my horse around – which, by the way, I must say, really showed no particular desire to leave off the chase – and set out after the cub. Up until now, it had been sitting bewildered near the tree trunk it had been scratching on, but as it saw me coming it started scurrying away with all its might. Naturally, it couldn't run fast enough to keep pace with my horse. Soon I'd caught up with it and cut off its escape, so then it wedged itself under an old tree trunk, crying out with fear. I was just about to jump out of the saddle and claim my prize, when I heard something snorting, and here came the old lady, with ears pinned back and jaws open – her red tongue sticking out God knows how far. – Hello – how I turned my little pony around again, so this time too he didn't wait very long at all to be asked, and fast as a flash of lightning I went through a hawthorn hedge into the bushes with the old lady on my heels. I'd have gotten the short end considerably in a fight, since I had no other weapon with me than my little scalping knife. So I was pretty happy that the old beast, after she'd got me going at such a really delightful speed, let me go or, better said, stopped running, and went grumbling on her way again with her cub."

"Something like that happens every time a man is without a gun, or at least a loaded one," said Smith – "the same thing has – wasn't that a shot just now?"

"Yes – I think I heard it too. – It must have been Hecker; the salt lick that he's at this evening hasn't been guarded for a long time, and I wouldn't be at all surprised if he got off a few shots."

"The same thing," continued Smith – "happened to me too once before – although in the Cherokee plum orchard – you know the place, Cook – up on the Arkansas, at least that's what they call it there –"

"Hello in the house!" a voice suddenly cried outside the door, and the dogs let out sharp and piercing barks.

"Someone's calling there," said the judge.

"Hello in the house!" repeated the voice outside, though this time so loudly that it drowned out the barking and howling of the dogs.

"Hello out there – what is it?"

"Bring a light here – will you?"

"Who's there?"

"Husfield from Spring Creek and friends. Can you get pine wood here, or a few pounds of wax, to make some big lights out of them?"

"Yes," called Eastley – "Wax I don't have, but I have enough pine. But it has to be split, and meanwhile you'd better get down and come in. Quiet, dogs!"

"Husfield? what the hell brings you around here in the night?" cried the judge, who, followed by Cook, stepped to the door. "Whom do you have there with you?"

"Friends from Spring Creek!" answered the one spoken to, who exchanged a word with his companions, then dismounted and came in the house.

"Good evening, Gentlemen! – Is there any one among you who knows the fords of the Fourche La Fave and would like to be our guide for a few hours?"

"What's going on then, are you on someone's trail?"

"Some vile bastards," called Husfield, "stole six horses from me in the night, between Wednesday and Thursday. Luckily I noticed it first thing in the morning, while it was still night, really. What happened was, several of my foraging horses came to the house, which they almost never do if they aren't frightened by strangers or wolves. Naturally, I couldn't pick up the trail in the dark, but still I called my neighbors together before daybreak, and with the first light we started the chase. The tracks were naturally broad enough, but shortly they separated, and three went to the right while the others went left. We supposed, and not without reason, that this was just a trick to mislead any who wanted to follow the trail. Now there were five of us there, so to be completely sure we split up, and were led over the northern mountain ridges of the Petit Jean and through the Magazine Mountains in such an atrocious way and back and forth through such frightful stony stretches that even now I don't understand how the horses stood it. That naturally took us a lot of time, since the bastards were zigzagging, and in fact, to throw us off the trail, were riding in circles in places where a man could barely make out a hoof print. – But they must have thought themselves safe finally, since at the head of Panther Creek,[12] where it runs down south to the Petit Jean, they had joined up again, and from here rode through open woods toward the river until they reached the road, which they probably did yesterday evening. From there they followed, as brazenly as could be, a long stretch of the high road. It looked as if they waited for first light to strike into the woods again and, in order to give themselves and their horses a little breather, made a camp and foddered the animals – God knows where they'd come by the corn, stolen in any case. We had to rest for a little while too, and didn't want to push our animals too hard, since we seemed to be on to the fellows now. Anyway, it was only by good luck that since nightfall we had followed the road which they'd entered again a few miles from here, and we now thought it better to take it slow and sure and stay on the trail through the night with torches. But since they've crossed the river in any event, we'd like to have someone with us who knows the ford, so we won't have to stop without cause."

"You do well to stay on the trail," said Cook, "since it'll rain before tomorrow morning anyhow. – The sun went down in a most ominous way."

"I think so too," answered Husfield. "Just one more reason for us to speed up the chase – oh, that's enough pine – Eastley – that'll do it. – If the scoundrels only stopped overnight on the road, which I don't doubt for a second, we'll surely catch up with them by daybreak, or at least not be any farther behind them."

"But why should they follow the road?" asked Cook. "I think it's impossible really for them to lead the horses over to the hot springs. Their only hope of coming through all right, if they aren't followed at once, is to reach the Arkansas. But they must have reckoned on a quick pursuit and gotten ready for it."

"That's true," said Husfield thoughtfully – "but we shall see for sure when we're on the other bank of the Fourche La Fave. If they want to get to the Arkansas they have to strike out from there through the woods to reach the lower road. So there's really nothing we can do but wait until first thing in the morning. But if they've followed the road on the other bank, it's a good sign that they're headed for the hot springs, and then we can ride very easily along the open road."

"If only we knew how to find the Indian," said the judge – "he's excellent on a trail and would be of great use. But God knows where he's hiding."

"Maybe that was him that we met up here by the salt lick who spoke broken English. – It was already pretty dark, and I couldn't rightly see his face."

"No, that's a German – but did the tracks go by there?"

"Yes – within four hundred paces. They must have still been in the area. He told us that he'd seen the men when he'd just arrived and still had no fire, but he hadn't been able to recognize them, though the figure of one of them seemed very familiar. – Just think, just two of the scoundrels made off with all of six animals. They must know the business from the ground up."

"How did you find the German?"

"We came on down the road, saw the pine fire burning at the stand, and took the chance to ride in and question him. The hunter himself was sitting outside the light, of course. Our presence didn't seem particularly pleasing to him, though, since naturally to him we were keeping the game away from the salt lick; so we didn't stay there long."

"But who could it be?" said the judge – "I shouldn't be surprised at all if that rascal Cotton had a hand in the game. He was seen some time ago here in the area, and the constables had even received an order to put him in jail. He must have gotten wind of it, since he was off all at once, or at least he hasn't let himself be seen in public."

"He won't escape prison," said Smith.

"Prison?" asked Husfield angrily – "do you think we'll bother with him for long if we catch him with the horses? Do you see this here?" With these words he pulled out a thin cord of twisted leather, which he held out toward the judge – "as my name is Husfield, the bastard'll hang on the same tree we catch him under. He'll have as much time to say his prayers as I need to make a noose – not a second more. We must show the scoundrels once and for all that we're serious, or they'll keep skinning us alive."

"But the laws," said the judge, shaking his head.

"The laws are right good to be used where they're made, and in the towns; here in the woods, though, it's a little different. Just imagine if we backwoods-men sat ourselves down here and made laws for the city folks in New York – they couldn't use half of all those we scraped together, and we'd forget seven-eighths of what they absolutely need there. No, let each region establish its own laws, and they will fit. If I set out to buy a ready-made sheath in a shop, well, yes, I'll find a thing that it'll go into in a pinch for sure, but usually it never fits tight, and before I know it I've lost it in the woods. So it is with the laws. – It looks as if they fit, until you get into the woods; then there something's wrong in every nook and cranny. So long as we have to take care of ourselves, we'll have jurisdiction over ourselves too, and – should I ever have to rely on someone else's protection – then I'll take myself farther west. – So who's going with me?"

Cook, Curtis, and several others were ready at once, and led by Curtis, who as an old settler knew every footpath there, they soon reached the road that crossed the Fourche La Fave from north to south; they followed it, and here soon found hoof prints in the soft earth that Husfield swore he could pick out of thousands as those of his own horses.

The sky had meanwhile completely clouded over, and a fine penetrating mist began to fall. But even if it gradually soaked the men's clothing through and through, it still had not yet destroyed the tracks.

Notes

1. "Pettyville": the actual place was Perryville, Arkansas, on the Fourche La Fave.

2. The German who "can write" is likely FG's self-portrait; see *RA*, 103n44.

3. Perhaps an allusion to the folk tale of the "Arkansas Traveler," which is believed to have originated around this time. The story revolves around one Colonel Sandford C. Faulkner (d. 1875), who was travelling in Pope County, Arkansas, in 1840 when he met a sullen mountain fiddler who became friendlier only after the Colonel was able to complete the tune he was playing.

4. Niccolò Paganini (1782–1840), famous Italian violinist and composer, whose playing left audiences spellbound.

5. "Mr. Cook" is the name of the blond, whistling farmer mentioned a few paragraphs earlier. Among FG's Arkansas acquaintances was a man named John Cook (*RA*, 100n47).

6. A likely candidate for "Washington's March" is a catchy tune composed by Philip Phile (Pfeil) in 1789, in honor of Washington's inauguration as the first president of the United States. It has been known under various names, among them "The President's March" and "Hail Columbia."

7. FG himself exchanged his double-barreled short rifle for a longer rifle, of the kind he believed was carried by Hawkeye in James Fenimore Cooper's *The Deerslayer* (1841); see *RA*, 106n46.

8. John Wells, also a friend from FG's Arkansas days; see *RA*, 107n48.

9. "Damn it": English in FG's original.

10. Magazine Mountain, or Mount Magazine, the highest mountain in Arkansas, in the Ozark National Forest in the Arkansas River Valley. See Figure 30.1.

11. Lewisburg, Arkansas, once a thriving town on the Arkansas River and the seat of Conway County, about fifty miles west of Little Rock. It was abandoned in 1883; the present-day city of Morrilton is on the site.

12. Panther Creek, White County, near Searcy, Arkansas.

Chapter 11

Assowaum, the "Feathered Arrow," and His Squaw. – Weston and Cotton Impatiently Await Their Comrades.

On the same afternoon on which the election described in the previous chapter took place, Assowaum, "the Feathered Arrow" – his blanket on his back, his rifle over his shoulder, and followed by his squaw – stepped silently through the woods along the bank of the river. Alapaha carried, according to the Indian custom, the few cooking utensils that these children of the wilderness needed, as well as a woolen blanket and two dried deerskins, and lightly walked in the footsteps of her husband and chief, who slowly and carefully scanned both banks of the little stream, as if he were looking for something and couldn't find it.

When he thought that he had gone up high enough, he turned around again and began his search anew, though with no better result than the first time.

"Is this not the tree to whose root the canoe was usually tied?" he asked his wife after he had finally stopped, pointing to an old, storm-ravaged sycamore, whose snow-white branches seemed to reach like the ghostly arms of a giant up toward the dark and towering masses of clouds behind them.

"Assowaum can see a piece of the bark to which it once was attached," said Alapaha, as she leaned over the steep riverbank and pointed down at a projecting root of the tree on which a few strips of bark were still hanging.

"The canoe is gone," replied Assowaum, "and we must swim across if we want to camp on the other side."

Without saying another word, Alapaha rid herself of her pack, rolled two fallen branches into the river, with the chief's help, with which to ensure the dry passage to the other side of the few belongings that they had with them, and soon both were climbing up the steep bank that lay opposite.

"And which path does Alapaha take?" asked the Indian now, standing still, as he calmly regarded his beautiful wife.

"A half mile up the river we cross a path – it leads straight to the house of Mr. Bowitt, and Mr. Rowson has promised to hold prayer hour there tomorrow. – Will Assowaum not once listen to the words of the white man? – He speaks well – his words are honey, and his heart is pure like the sky in autumn."

"Alapaha, it would be better if you also – ah – what is that?"

A soft rustling in the dry leaves was heard, and straightaway a stately deer stepped out of the thicket, lifted his beautiful head high and looked around calmly and confidently, not suspecting any danger. At the first sound of the crunching leaves, Assowaum had gotten his rifle ready to fire; he now raised it slowly to his cheek, and in an instant the deer, struck by the fatal lead, leaped high in the air and expired with a shudder.

"Good!" said the Indian, as he stood quietly and loaded his rifle again – "very good – Mr. Harper has no more meat and is too sick to follow the tracks himself – Alapaha will take meat to his house –"

"And does not Assowaum know that I am on my way to hear the word of God?" whispered his wife, as she bowed her slender body and softly murmured a prayer.

"There was a time," said Assowaum, staring bleakly before him – "there was a time when Alapaha heard the music of the 'Feathered Arrow' and in it forgot the soughing of the tree tops or the song of the ghost-bird.[1] There was a time when she turned her back on the God of the white man and lifted her hands to the Manitou of the red man. There was a time when she braided the sacred wampum[2] for her husband, and with mysterious symbols ensured him good fortune in the hunt. That time is past – Alapaha is dead, and a Christian has arisen in her place – Maria. – She still wears the same moccasins in which she left her kin and followed her husband into exile. She wears the same cloth around her temples that Assowaum once ripped from the shoulders of that savage chief of the Sioux to adorn the forehead of his squaw at home. She wears the same string of sacred snake rattles, and their sound should remind her of her home, of the land of her fathers. But no – her ear is closed – it does not hear – but even more closed is her heart – it does not feel."

"Assowaum!" said the beautiful woman in a soft, pleading tone. "Assowaum – don't be angry with me. – Look, our life is short, and I see spread out wide before me the most beautiful, brightest future. – Oh, you don't know how wonderful, how delightful the heaven of the whites is – would you rob me of what is still most holy and precious to me in this life, besides my duty to you?"

"No!" said Assowaum – "Alapaha may go and serve the God of the whites – it is good."

"And will you then never listen to the voice of the holy man, from whose lips the Manitou himself speaks?"

Assowaum stretched out his right arm and was about to say something in reply. But another thought seemed to take hold of him at the same moment, and he lifted his rifle to his shoulder and said: "Alapaha cannot just *pray*; she has to *eat* too. – Not far from here, on the bank of the river, stands a small, uninhabited hut – we will carry the meat in there, and Alapaha may dry it this evening. – The house will protect her against the gale and thunderstorm tonight, and tomorrow morning it won't be far to the settlement of the whites, where the pale man tells stories of his God." ·

"And Assowaum?"

"Has given the little man his word to seek out his son – he will keep it. The white men speak evil of their brother because they do not hear his footsteps among them. – He is far away – he will come back, and the wrongdoers will be silenced and look up to him."

"But he is evil –"

"What serpent has breathed its poison into Alapaha's ear? She has listened to the voice of Machinito[3] and casts dirt on the hand of the one who has done good to her."

"Mr. Rowson said that the son of the little man killed a brother and then robbed him."

"The pale man lies!" cried the Indian, straightening himself up, as the blood rose to his temples and his eyes burned – "The pale man lies!" he repeated – "and – he knows it!"

"Assowaum is angry with the Christian because he made Alapaha turn from the faith of her people. Assowaum is good and noble; he will revile no man because he thinks otherwise than he."

"We will carry the meat to the hut," the Indian said, breaking off the conversation – "it grows late. Assowaum must still walk miles more before it is dark."

With a practiced hand, he now cut open the dead deer; he removed the shoulder blades, neck, and head, which he left for the wolves or the vultures, and then hung the rest on a quickly hewn rail, one end of which he grasped while Alapaha laid the other on her shoulder, and thus they walked on silently again until they reached, after not a very long march, the place already mentioned.

It was a crudely constructed log cabin built by an earlier settler and abandoned again after a short occupancy, as the land around it was too low and thus very much exposed to flooding from the river. The roof and the walls were still in fairly good condition, but otherwise it offered not even the slightest comforts, since even the chimney had fallen in and a plank floor had never been laid. But the missing chimney was in no way an obstacle to building a fire indoors, since the open cracks everywhere in the walls offered a passage to the smoke in every direction; the wind rushed and roared very strangely through the wide gaps between the logs, rattled the pieces of bark hanging loosely from them, and whistled over the mossy roof on down to the river that wound its way very close by the inhospitable site, though still separated from it by wild overgrown bushes.

Assowaum now reached this place with his wife and carried the meat into the dwelling. The door had been broken off the wooden hinges and lay flattened in front of the door, thus in no way hindering entry. Assowaum looked around for a moment in the empty building and then said:

"The house is good and will afford Alapaha protection. When she comes back from her pious travels, she will carry the meat to the cabin of the little man. – Assowaum will be with her before the whip-poor-will has sung for the third time." – With that he turned around and stepped silently with head bowed into the woods.

Alapaha meanwhile did as her husband commanded, cutting thin poles with the small delicate tomahawk that hung by her side so as to construct a rack on which to dry the meat; carried wood in order to maintain a gentle fire for drying the venison and, at the same time, to maintain a warming fire for the night; then cut the meat in strips, put them on cane poles cut for this purpose, and hung it over a fire kindled with the help of dry leaves.

Meanwhile the sky had become more and more overcast, a damp dusting of mist fell, and the wind rushed wildly and eerily through the tops of the trees hanging over the roof of the hut. Alapaha crouched down beside the flickering fire, softly hummed a hymn that she had learned from the whites, and awaited the approaching darkness to prepare a bed for herself. But she kept a watchful eye on the curing venison so that it would be dry enough the next morning to be bound together and stored.

But the region was not as completely lonely and deserted by humanity as Alapaha might have believed to begin with. At the same time that she was so intently occupied with her work, a young man stepped out of a thicket on the path that lay a short half mile farther up the river on the opposite bank, and looked impatiently over to the other side, as if he awaited someone from there. The air was by no means warm, and he now rubbed his hands together, now shoved them under his arms, now leaned himself on an overhanging sycamore, and several times seemed about to walk back and forth on the leaf-covered ground, but straightaway paused each time and looked doubtfully at the area where he had stepped, as if the tracks he left were too conspicuous and easy to recognize.

Another man now joined him; wrapped in a woolen blanket, an old, badly worn felt hat pulled down low on his forehead and gun tucked under his arm to protect the lock as well as possible from the mist, he approached the young man quietly and laughingly inquired:

"Well, Weston, it's getting to be a long time here for you, eh? You're freezing – why didn't you bring your blanket with you? – I told you so. – Heard anything yet?"

"Not a hint," morosely answered the one addressed – "and I really don't think they're coming this evening; now that'll be great fun. If I have to stay here all night without blanket or fire, by morning I'll be a corpse."

"That'll be at least a twenty-dollar loss for the sheriff," laughed Cotton, for he was the worthy companion of the young man. "Anyway, I hardly think that we'll have to wait much longer. – Rowson's familiar with every nook and cranny there, and Johnson too for that matter, so they couldn't run into too many difficulties. Besides, you said yourself that Rowson's called a prayer meeting tomorrow at mid-day in the settlement over there. That right there'll guarantee that he'll do everything in his power to be on time and not attract any possible suspicion. I can't stand the hypocritical bastard, but in terms of business he's first-rate, that's for sure; you can see that he comes from the Yankee states."

"The story of Heathcott's death is causing quite a sensation among folks now," said Weston – "Brown's supposed to have done him in – your name was also mentioned in the matter."

"Mine? Goddamn it, why do they have *me* in the matter? I've never seen the popinjay in my whole life; must I be guilty of every trick that's played on them here?"

"It must be all the same to you now," laughed Weston – "by the way, they don't put the murder on your shoulders, just the money."

"What money?"

"The dead man's supposed to have had the cash he got for three good horses in his pocket, four or five hundred dollars – and it's gone."

"Thunderation – that would've been worth the trouble! – Two birds with one stone, a Regulator and a pile of cash. – Brown's not stupid – but – listen, Weston, Brown's never had anything to do with us in his life – what would he have had against the Regulator, then?"

"Some other things I know about. The women up in the settlement claim that Heathcott and Brown were courting the *same* girl; hence their fight. – But that's all beside the point, the main thing is that we're rid of Heathcott; how and in what manner is all the same to us."

"Now listen, Husfield isn't to be fooled with, and if he wants to sniff us out, it'll be serious. – Anyway, I don't rightly see how we can mix up the tracks, so the scoundrels can't find us again. One thing's for sure, if *I* were on your trail it'd be hard on you."

"You can forget about that," Weston flashed a sly smile, "the thing's underway and damned clever, Rowson's worked it out. See – before they get to the river they'll ride along the open road again."

"Along the open road?" asked Cotton, astonished.

"Yes indeed – along the free and open road, so their tracks are clear and unmistakable – then into the river and then – not out of it again."

"But where to? They can't stop in the river, surely? Where then?"

"Down the river, until they're too far to track, and then into the wide world."

"The animals can't manage that long swim, can they?"

"That's why I've hidden the canoe there – look there – under the clump of cane that's leaning over – and there, right next to it, another one. That's from down at the mouth of the river, from the Stewarts, who probably think it's broken loose and floated into the Arkansas. Using both canoes, we can get the horses down lower splendidly, until we reach the place that Rowson described to me, and from there *you* must take the lead, since I don't know the way to the 'island,' as you call it. Meanwhile, Johnson is supposed to get the trackers onto the false trail, and if that works, we're both completely out of danger, especially if tomorrow's a rainy day. Then we'll shoot through the woods with the animals, and once we reach the Mississippi bottoms – say good night to the pursuit. – Johnson has assured me that there we'll find shelter and help everywhere, and the bastards up here know that very well – they won't follow us nearly that far."

"Yes, all that's very pretty and sounds very fine. But those from Spring River won't be such asses and believe that we've flown away with the horses through the air, as I saw the other day in a picture over there at the Germans'."[4]

"We're not expecting them to think that either, for here comes the very best part. – Below here in the canebrake – that is, not *in* the canebrake, rather *below* the canebrake, on a slab of rock in the river bed, stands my horse, yours –"

"Mine?"

"Your horse and Johnson's two white ones. – Once we've started on our journey with the fresh shipment, these horses will be brought up the short stretch of the river where it's shallowest to the landing; there Johnson mounts up and gallops with the beasts straight out onto the road, as if he's going to the hot springs. If the trackers first show up tomorrow or the next day, and it's rained hard in the meantime, this'll really be unnecessary; but if they're close on the hoofs of the – let's say, – collected horses, which I rather fear, they'll naturally believe that the hoof prints that go into the ford of the river on this side, and that lead out on the other side, are one and the same and follow them without thinking or – and this is the main thing – without dismounting and looking more closely into the matter. Then if they catch up with Johnson, quite naturally he doesn't have *their* horses, and doesn't know anything about them, and they'll see too late that they've been chasing after the wrong animals."

"But if they don't catch up with him?" inquired Cotton.

"So much the better – then he takes the horses by a roundabout route to the island, reports the shipment soon to follow, and sells ours."

"What – my horse?"

"Don't be a fool, Cotton," laughed Weston, "first of all, you get the money for it –"

"Yes, but how much? Not half the price!"

"And then," continued Weston, ignoring the interruption, "you mustn't let yourself be seen by a single person, and you must leave these parts in a *very* short time."

"But what does all that have to do with *my* horse?"

"It means that I know you too well to believe that you'd take leave of the Fourche La Fave on your *own* horse," laughed Weston.

"You're right there, Weston – that was smartly said," crowed Cotton, "and you well know –"

"Don't yell so, the devil knows if someone's not slinking around here. Besides, I heard shooting around here this afternoon."

"Do you know, I've already picked out a horse that just tickles me to death?"

"And that would be?"

"Roberts' stallion – a splendid animal."

"You know, Cotton, you're not so stupid. On him you could thumb your nose at every pursuer. – Huh – that'll raise another rumpus!"

"The plan is good, by the way," said Cotton thoughtfully – "yes, yes, when it comes to business, Rowson's first-rate – and how wonderfully he leads the women-folk of the settlement around by the nose. – Their eyes would pop out of their heads if they saw him this evening galloping through the woods with a couple of horses on a line."

"Mrs. Roberts takes him for a real saint – well, I don't care. Only it's a shame about the pretty young girl that has to marry him; I wouldn't want him for a husband!"

"I don't dare blab about it," replied Cotton mysteriously. "Too many are involved in the affair, and I wouldn't like my tongue to be the one that gets burned on it. – This much I can trust you with, that it lies in the Mississippi, and that the people *there* are friendly minded toward us. – I haven't set foot on it myself yet."

"Bah, there're lots of islands in the Mississippi – and friendly minded – half of Arkansas is friendly minded toward us, and five-sixths of Texas; no, tell me something more particular – what number is it in the Mississippi? You know, don't you, that the islands in the stream are all known by their numbers from upper to lower?"

"Don't I know that!" his old fellow traveler laughed scornfully. "But I can't reveal any more to you – anyway, you'll learn the whole story soon enough now, since we'll be there in a few days. Until then, don't be too curious. But wait! – listen – what was that?"

"Quiet!" cried Weston – "that was a whip-poor-will – Rowson was going to give the signal this way – could it be them? – I'll answer in any case, since everything's secure here."

He held his fingers to his mouth and imitated just as deceptively the shrill call of that small bird.

"Whoopee!" Johnson's voice screamed, as all at once the rapid clatter of horses became audible; the next moment the ones they had anxiously awaited stopped on the bank and waved their hats over toward their comrades as a sign of their happy success.

Notes

1. The "ghost-bird" is likely the whip-poor-will.

2. Wampum: beads or shells, strung or braided together and used for trade. Excavations confirm their presence in early Arkansas. FG's reference to Alapaha's "weaving" of a sacred artifact is an anachronism; the use of wampum had ended in the early 18th century.

3. "Machinito" was a generalized name for an evil spirit, which FG could have found in one of several works dealing with Native American mythology, including an essay by John Greenleaf Whittier published in *The Democratic Review* in 1843, "The Inner Life – The Agency of Evil."

4. Perhaps an image of the fall of Phaeton, the subject of several popular lithographs of the time.

Chapter 12

The Horse Thieves' Trick. – The Surprise. – Alapaha and Rowson.

"Hurrah!" replied Weston, forgetting all his earlier caution at the sight of the magnificent horses that came down the opposite bank at that moment and stopped at the water's edge. – "Hurrah – that's what I call horses!"

"Are you two crazy?" Rowson called over angrily – "do you absolutely want to attract the attention of anyone who might be sneaking around here? Shut your traps and save your outbursts of joy for the time when you're good and done with carrying out your duties. Where are the horses?"

"At the appointed place below here," said Weston.

"Good! Bring them quickly – but look lively and don't leave any tracks on the bank; stay in the deep water."

"Aye, aye – I know that – and Weston wasn't dropped on his head either."

The young chap jumped quickly down to the spot below where he had left his horse and returned in a very short time, carefully keeping the beasts in the middle of the current, which could hardly be three feet deep.

"Now where are the boats?" asked Rowson – "it doesn't matter if *these* horses trampled the ground here for a while, since if they actually follow us they'll think that we couldn't decide whether to try the crossing. But if we let the other animals stand on the opposite bank and make lots of tracks, they'll be forced to examine the tracks more closely, and then they might discover that they're different tracks. Also, Cotton's horse has such unreasonably large hoofs."

With that, Weston disappeared with Cotton into the canebrake, and, after a short delay, they came gliding across the margin of the brake in their canoes.

"Stop!" cried Johnson. "No farther – they mustn't see the print of the boats on the banks – so – come out into the middle – now gather in the horses here – better get in, Rowson. – So, two in the big canoe and one in the small. – Stop there – let me change horses first; ah – that's a load off my mind, now that I'm sitting on the back of my own horse again."

"Now just show that you can ride, Johnson," said Rowson, as the other got ready to climb up onto the bank – "let the horses run as best they can, they've been rested. – Give them the spur and the whip and remember that every quarter hour that we take the trackers off the *right* trail is worth its weight in gold."

"Never fear!" laughed Johnson – "they'll have to ride hard if they want to catch me, and *if* they do catch me, I'll laugh at them. I've done the spade work and told several of my acquaintances how I'm going to take my horse and a few others into the southern part of the state where I hope to get a huge amount of money for them."

"So go," replied Rowson, "the devil may trust you. Who knows how soon they'll come clattering in here, and they would find us just now in a very interesting situation. – God bless me, we would be a pretty sight, all of us together."

"So what about the provisions?" asked Cotton.

"I don't need them!" Johnson called back, just as he reached the top crest of the bank. "The horses have to rest now and then, after all, and that can be done just as well at a house."

"But just not tonight, so those following don't discover the horses' colors so soon. The two white ones might make them wonder –"

"Don't worry – they'll have to hold out until mid-day tomorrow – to a happy reunion!" With that he let out his hunting cry, buried his heels in the sides of his horse, and in the next instant disappeared into the woods.

"That's been taken care of then," said Rowson, "now, Cotton, we must see how we're going to arrange things with these animals. Above all, we'd best get away from here and go down the river about a half mile. Here on the road we're not only liable to be seen by every traveler, but we may also expect the damned Regulators to come for our necks at any moment. So leave off tying them up for the moment; we can take them down the short stretch of road so, and anyway they'll probably have bottom land the whole way. At the first sandbank we'll get everything arranged and have the whole scheme over and done before it gets dark."

There was too much truth in these words to require any further response. All the necessary precautions were quickly made, and a few minutes afterward the boats, each with three horses attached, glided around the bend of the river that made it impossible for them to be seen from the road.

"Well – for the first time now I'm feeling a little easier," whispered Rowson. – "It's getting darker and darker, and if our trackers really keep coming after us in the night, well, they'll fall into the trap we've set for them, without a doubt. – Hurrah! When I think of those fellows galloping along the trail with bloodthirsty looks, more eager by the minute to chase the supposed thief – itching to see him, digging their heels into the sides of their horses with one last effort, and then – their dumbfounded faces – the cursing and ranting, and Johnson's innocent sheepish look as he regrets being the unwitting cause of the criminals possibly having been deprived of their just punishment – ha ha ha – the very thought is delicious!"

"Here's the gravel bank," said Weston, as he pointed over toward the left bank; "the animals have ground under their feet, and it'd be better to tidy the bridles and halters now. Also we have to better distribute the horses among the boats, since right below here, just as soon as we get around this river bend, the current gets deeper and the horses will have to swim that whole stretch. I checked it out carefully this morning, as I was on the way up here."

"If I'm not mistaken," said Cotton, looking up at the bank, "there's a little deserted hut somewhere near this gravel bank. – About three years ago we camped in it, at the time I went with Johnson to the Nation.* But now the bushes have grown up so much around here, that you can't see it any more at all. Yes, this is the place," he continued as they landed the canoes, "I know it by the fallen sycamore tree; it fell in the same night that we camped here, and if it had taken a different direction we would've been done for."

"Arkansas wouldn't have mourned," laughed Rowson.

"No, not a lot – and some – but we'd best not talk about that – what are you going to do there?"

"We have to tie the small boat to the larger one," said Rowson – "after that we can take two horses on each side and two behind; and we won't have much need to row since the current's quite strong. At any rate, one of us can help a bit, mainly by steering, and the other two can then watch the horses so they don't get tangled up. We ought to be at the 'Devil's Crook' by about twelve; there I'll get out and leave you two to your fate. Don't spare the horses and avoid the wide-open road only when the woods are scattered enough to get through just as fast. But if they find the right track by tomorrow – though that's not likely, and in fact almost impossible, except by accident – well, you have about twelve hours head start and sound horses – Cotton, do you know the way?"

"Well, I should think so," he grumbled – "I've been chased often enough – one time with five guys on my heels. Once we get to the Mississippi swamp, where I know paths through all the bayous and lagoons, then we're safe. There's one special place where if I get through it and drop a tree on the spot from the other side, it'll take the trackers a whole day on horseback to get through to me. – I've always kept the place in mind for an emergency."

"But how do you come by an axe there?"

"Just last month I hid my axe there in a hollow tree; if the need arises, a tool won't be lacking."

---

* FG's note: "In Arkansas, the 'Nation' almost always means the Cherokees."

"So that will do it for now," said Rowson, who had just finished rigging the canoes, "now, Cotton, another word with you about your part, and then off to work. Weston knows the place where you should first touch land; it's there where the broad stone slabs run high up between the trees. That'll give us an advantage, since our tracks up from the water can't be seen at all. About a hundred paces down the river, where a spruce and a pawcorn[1] tree have fallen crosswise toward the stream bed, Atkins has hidden a sack with corn and other provisions –"

"So why don't you go with us as far as that place?" wondered Weston.

"My tracks could be found there," replied Rowson, "that's not possible at Devil's Crook; if I take a little roundabout route from there over the mountains, I'll come back into the settlement again from a completely different direction. I don't trust that damned Indian, especially if they should set him on our trail; therefore I'll be as careful as possible. But Cotton – don't you have anything to eat with you? I'm terribly hungry. – As we came here it seemed to me that I smelt roasted venison – I wish I had a piece now. – Why on earth didn't you bring a single provision with you – one can't think of everything."

"My kerchief with corn bread and venison's up in the canebrake, where the horses stood," said Weston, "but I'm ashamed to say that I forgot it – now it's probably too late to get it again."

"The devil – you should have thought of that earlier – no one could find it, I suppose?"

"No, it's hanging out of sight – but shouldn't we get going?"

"Just wait until Cotton's repaired the bridle," said Rowson – "if it should break on the way we'll be more delayed, and we might not finally be able to fix it in the dark."

"So how'd you actually catch the horses, Rowson?" asked Cotton, who was busily working to restore the broken halter, "tell us now, since once we're underway we won't have much time to chat, and we won't learn about it afterwards at all."

"I can do that in a few words," replied Rowson with a grin, as he very calmly cut off a large piece of chewing tobacco and shoved it in his mouth. "Luckily, we didn't meet anyone we know on the way, and got to the spot at the corner of the fence, where Spring Creek flows close by, just as it got dark – well, somewhere around that time. We'd gone neatly around the mill, and when the first owl called we were standing at the enclosure where the mares were kept. I wasn't easy about the business, since according to my reckoning the free-ranging horses should already be there; but that couldn't be helped, and Johnson and I climbed up a couple of trees, for one thing to guard against surprises, but also to be able to see everything coming that way sooner. It was lucky that we did it, since we had hardly settled ourselves when, God damn me – Husfield himself – did you say something, Cotton?"

"No – why?"

"I thought I heard a noise – Husfield himself came by there from the hunt with a whole pack of dogs. If we'd been on the ground below, the beasts would've tracked us down, and then good night, Johnson, since Husfield has a particular beef with him; the bridles we'd carried with us would have given us away in any event. But the damn dogs only sniffed around under the trees, lifted their noses in the air, and scented for a while in a way to make us nervous and fearful, but then they followed yelping after their master, who meanwhile had already ridden down the way a stretch."

"Both of us were sweating blood, but anyway our misery ended at that point, since a moment later the horses came up. We picked, since it wasn't completely dark yet, the ones that we liked best, bridled them up, swung ourselves up on them, and away we went like a hurricane through the woods, so fast that a couple of times I thought surely we'd break our necks and legs. To lead them astray, we also zigzagged around on stony ground for a while, struck out in several directions, and then, thinking ourselves safe, set out at last with less caution but therefore all the faster."

"Weren't the other horses frightened when you fished out a portion of them?"

"Yes – they snorted mightily, and as soon as we had nabbed the last of them by their manes, the rest of them took off blowing and neighing and galloped around the fence, then probably into the woods again. – The chestnut here spun me around in a circle about six times before I could bring him to a stand."

"Well, Husfield will rage nicely," laughed Cotton, "never in human memory have *six* horses been stolen from a farmer all at once –"

"And the pious Rowson in the lead!" exulted Weston.

"But listen, Rowson," said Cotton now, as he squinted over the bridle at him, standing there smiling, "what theme will you preach about tomorrow? It's such a shame that I can't hear it with the others; something like that would be worth the trouble."

"Goddamn it!" cried Rowson angrily – "tomorrow I'd rather not deal with that nonsense, I'll be so distracted, so anxious about what's – become of you."

"Of the horses, you mean?"

"Well, yes, of the horses too, and then I must stand there and babble prayers and bawl boring silly songs."

"And after that the 'Glory' calls and the fainting of that fat widow!" laughed Weston.

"And the pious conversations with the beautiful Indian woman," interjected Cotton – "listen, Rowson, you don't have such bad taste –"

"Damn it!" cried Rowson, "let's get going and get out of here, I'm beginning to get cold and the horses are freezing as well. – Doesn't anyone have a drop of whiskey? – Johnson, that scoundrel, has my bottle in his pouch and doesn't say a word. – Oh, to hell with you, leave a drop in it already, you suck on it as if you want to suck out the air too!"

Cotton handed the bottle over to him, and Rowson took a long pull; then he corked it again and gave it back.

"That's refreshing, isn't it?" asked Cotton smiling – "yes, and warming as well – I put a whole handful of Spanish pepper in it – that gives it some heat."

"It does you good tonight, for sure," said Rowson, shivering – "this light rain chills you to the bone."

"So – now we can get going again!" cried Cotton, as he placed the mended bridle on his horse. – "Quick now, let's get out of here; it's getting darker all the time, and up there – up the – ere – plague and damnation!" he added quickly, whispering – "what is that? There's a light shining in the bushes!"

"Where?" Rowson barked furiously.

"Up there – it must be in the hut."

"There's something light crouching in the brush!" called Weston now, whose sharp eyes had noticed the outline of a figure nestled within the dark shrubs that bordered the river bank.

"Death and the Devil," shrieked Cotton – "this is treachery!" And like an arrow from a bow he flew with a few strides up the bank, followed by Rowson, and in the next instant stood opposite the solitary being who had observed from above everything the men had been up to – had heard every word.

"Alapaha!" cried Rowson, horrified.

"The red-skinned woman!" Cotton said, gritting his teeth, almost as much astonished as alarmed.

"You're alone?" Rowson asked the Indian woman quickly. "You're alone? Where's Assowaum?"

But the poor woman was unable to reply; for a while she stood rigid and upright, and looked into the cold face of the unmasked preacher with an expression so spiritually earnest, yet fearful, that he dropped his eyes bashfully – he could not bear her gaze. But the proud daughter of the forests only for a moment glared condemnation at the man who had stolen her belief in her God and her love for her husband. Then the thought of her boundless, terrible misery overcame her – how she had renounced the Great Spirit that her fathers had venerated in the rustling of the mighty forests, in the rippling of the quiet brook – how she had listened to the words of a man whom she had taken for a saint, and who now – her heart shuddered as she gazed before her at him – was a thief and a robber.

She buried her face in her hands, and large bright tears trickled through her tightly pressed fingers.

"The horses are getting restless!" cried Cotton angrily. "What are we going to do with this one here?"

"Go – leave her to me," whispered Rowson to him, and rose with a wild and devilish look.

"Leave her to you? I believe that!" laughed the hunter scornfully – "don't be so stupid – is this the time for such foolishness?"

"Go on with the horses," said Rowson in a subdued voice – "the river makes a bow here, maybe three miles around – but it's not a hundred paces straight over by land; you can cut off the whole bend that way. So go – Weston can't handle the beasts alone."

"And what'll happen with the woman?"

"Don't worry," Rowson whispered to him, "if anyone's in danger from her testimony, it's me –"

"So go to hell and – come quickly," cursed Cotton, "you'll bear the consequences if you make us wait." He sprang down the river bank again and walked over the loose gravel; a few seconds later the boats, with the snorting and blowing horses in them, glided into the darkness lying on the water.

Note

1. "Pawcorn": perhaps a corruption of "pawpaw."

Figure 13.1. "On avait volé six chevaux à la fois" (They stole six horses at once). Illustration by E. Coppin. From *Les Brigands des prairies*, a partial French translation of *The Regulators*, by Bénédict-Henry Révoil. *Journal illustré des voyages et des voyageurs* (December 1858). Image courtesy of the translators.

Chapter 13

The Preacher Unmasked by the Indian Woman. – The Successful Escape.

"Where's Assowaum?" the preacher asked in a soft but firm voice when he saw that he was alone with the young Indian woman. But the latter seemed not to hear his question, or did not want to hear it. – Nothing broke the still of the night except the sobbing of the poor woman and the minister's heavy breath.

"Where's Assowaum?" the latter finally asked for the second time after what was for him a painful pause, and at the same time seized with his right hand the arm of the weeping woman. But, as if touched by a snake, the unhappy woman jumped up, got herself free of the grip of the sinister man, and cried, shrinking back from him:

"Away – away – your breath is poison – your touch is death – your tongue is forked, and your eyes belie God while your breast harbors the devil. – Away – grass and flowers must wither wherever you set your foot; the birds must be silent when you step near them. – The smoke of the holy pipe must fly back from you and may not surround you. Your god is a god of lies, or else he would have long sent his lightning to smash your accursed body to pieces – away!"

"Where's Assowaum?" asked the preacher with a hoarse voice, without heeding the curses of the Indian woman.

"Oh, that he were here to punish you!" she said passionately, rising to her full height. "That he were here to redeem the shame that you have heaped on the head of his poor wife. – But woe to you – he will find you – he will strike you; his war whoop will sound in your ear – oh – you have not yet seen him in all his warlike glory," she went on proudly when she saw the American's scornful smile, "you have not yet seen him brandishing his flashing tomahawk, with his battle cry on his lips and the enemy's death in his eye, with waving scalp lock and glittering spear point. You have not yet seen his war dance with the death-heralding stripes on his face; have not yet seen him red with the blood of the slain and with the scalps of the defeated on his belt. – But he will come, he will return!"

"When – woman, when?" asked the preacher quickly, as his hand moved with a nervous jerk toward his side.

"When?" laughed the Indian woman triumphantly – "when? Too quickly for you at least – before the sun rises two times more in the east, he will be here, and woe to you if his path crosses yours!"

"But where is he now?"

"Ha – how you already tremble, you miserable coward, at the mere thought of his arm, of the sharpness of his weapon – ha, how you shake and look fearfully about, full of dread that he could step out of the bushes right now. – I am only a woman, but I am filled with pride when I look down on you."

"Where is he now?" asked the white man, gnashing his teeth but still not free of fear, since he could not believe that the Indian woman had left her wigwam alone and was camped here in the woods without the protection of her husband.

"Where would he be now?" Alapaha continued with a scornful laugh – "he will not come back alone – the strong hand will be with him, the one that slew him who had offended it – tremble, for your God will not protect you!"

"Ha!" exclaimed Rowson, as a devilish joy flashed across his face – "so he's over there to fetch his comrades; – yes, I thought so. – Good! Then you're *mine*, and neither god nor devil will snatch you from me."

"Back!" screamed the Indian woman, rising up in terror as Rowson tried to embrace her, and fled toward the hut – "back, devil! – Your eyes are glowing – back!"

"You're *mine*!" Rowson cried with a wild laugh. – "You're mine, and I defy the red-skinned bastard; let him come – but nothing will tear you from me – and as for making sure that your mouth won't betray us, I'll take care of that."

"So may then the Manitou of our people, to whom I belong once more from this moment on, give me strength!" called Alapaha, once again tearing herself from the arms of the furious man and grasping her tomahawk, which she carried by her side. – "Die, wicked man, at the hand of a woman, and may vulture and wolf tear your bones to pieces – die!"

With these last words she sprang with a wild jump on the terrified man as he tumbled backward and would for a fact have sealed his fate in the next moment had not the door that had fallen from its hinges caught her foot; she staggered, fell, and in the next instant found herself in the power of her enemy.

* * *

"If Rowson doesn't put an end to those screams soon," angrily grumbled Cotton to himself, "he'll bring someone down on his neck or ours. – I'm sure I heard shooting here somewhere this afternoon and wouldn't think it impossible that the redskin's still camped somewhere in the woods."

"I wish he'd come," said Weston, also annoyed – "just drifting with the stream is too slow going, and you really can't hold three horses and row too. Besides, the beasts will get restless; the water's cold, and the whole thing likely looks pretty unusual and strange to them."

The men listened for a moment, and again the Indian woman's cries for help pierced the quiet night, so that the owl in the dark pines on the river bank answered mockingly and flew inquisitively to the place from which these eerie calls came forth.

"A plague on the fool!" cried Cotton once more angrily. – "I wish by God she'd escape him, and – but only if we were now some fifty miles farther on. But if the redskin escaped now and gave the alarm, hell and damnation! I believe we'd have an army after us here tomorrow."

"He won't kill her, will he?" said Weston shuddering, as he listened breathlessly over in that direction. – "Everything's so deathly quiet all at once – it horrifies me, Cotton – he won't shed any blood, will he?"

"Fool!" grumbled Cotton – "would you put your own neck in the noose, eh? Are you hungry for the Regulators to hoist you up high from some convenient oak bough? Rowson will do what's necessary. If it can be done without bloodshed, so much the better, I'm no friend to it myself. But if that doesn't work –"

"Oh, no blood – no blood" – cried Weston fearfully. "I joined up with you to steal horses – that's no crime – but blood – I shiver when I think about it – I won't have blood on my conscience; and besides, that was only a woman."

"So much the more dangerous," laughed Cotton, "at least where it's a matter of keeping something secret. But don't be a fool – Rowson'll get it done – he doesn't do anything more than what he – watch out for that horse, he feels the bottom and wants to go to the bank – plague it, it's already pressed its hoof into the mud over there – take care, Weston – we don't know *who* will be on our trail."

"The devil may keep them in order," cried Weston angrily. – "Why's Rowson staying so long – the animals are getting impatient, and my hands are about to fall off from holding them so long already."

"There's the place where he wanted to meet us," said Cotton – "see there, where the root's in the water – right in front of you – I've often hunted here in the area and know the bend that the river makes well enough."

"Someone's standing next to the root!" whispered Weston softly. At that moment the call of the whip-poor-will sounded from the spot indicated, and immediately afterwards Rowson (for it was he) jumped from the stone on which he was standing into the water, which was only a few inches deep here, and waded to the boat, since its occupants could not stop to take him on board.

"Here are provisions," he said in a hoarse voice, as he threw an armful of venison cuts strung on stakes into the boat, "fine game."

"Where's the Indian woman?" asked Weston, looking timidly into the eyes of the vile man.

"Safe!" the latter answered laconically and turned away from the searching gaze of the questioner.

"Safe? You haven't done her any harm, have you?"

"Nonsense – mind your own business – what are *my* dealings to you? – All right, give me the horses and you take the oar a little – the water gets deep here, so we'll come away from the spot a bit faster."

"How far is it yet to the place where we land?" asked Cotton.

"Three miles – rather a little more than less."

"And how far are you going with us?"

"About two yet – we'll soon reach the ridge of hills which I'll get out at the foot of – but – Weston – come here yet once more and take the bridle, won't you – Cotton – don't you have an old cloth or something with you?"

"What do you want with it? – My neckerchief!"

"Give it here – or – just bind it around my arm – there – right there by my shoulder."

"Yes, but you must take off your jacket – even then I can't do it well – the cursed boat rocks so, and I'm afraid I'll turn it over."

"Good – then I'll wait another quarter hour until we get to a shallow place again and I'll walk alongside in the water – it'll work better that way."

"What happened to your shoulder then?" asked Cotton, as the other took off his jacket and slipped up his sleeve.

"Oh – the little witch snatched up her tomahawk, I don't know how, that I had already taken away from her and – but that's of no significance. – Down there, where it shimmers so brightly, the deep water ends, and then we can bind something around it."

Silently the men now once more pursued their course to the place indicated; then, after carefully feeling for the bottom with the short oar, Rowson climbed overboard, and as he walked along next to the slowly gliding craft, holding tightly to the side with his right hand, Cotton dressed his hardly insignificant wound.

"If only the moon would shine a bit," cried Weston after a while, "so that we could at least recognize the point where we have to land!"

"There you go again, yearning for the moon," grumbled Cotton, "not a thing more is missing. – I wish it would rain all that wants to come down from heaven."

The boats now glided past a steep line of hills whose rugged rocky edges extended right into the stream, while a few dark cedar bushes grew out of the vertical cliff wall and long sinister crevasses stretched up to the top of the mountains. The crest was crowned with tall swaying spruces and pines, and cedars and hickories formed the thick, dense, and nearly impassable underwood.

"We're not very far from the end!" said Rowson. "Right there below is the place where I left you, and Cotton – you certainly know the spot where you get out!"

"Don't worry – I can't miss it. – But it doesn't matter – about a quarter mile farther down there's another place like it. But wait – what's that? A fire on the bank? Someone's camping there."

"Calm down," whispered Rowson – "whoever it is, the cane won't let him get close to the bank here, and the tree cover will likely hide us from any curious eyes."

A yapping dog now struck up on the bank, and they could even hear a voice quieting it. But the cane thicket was, as Rowson had rightly observed, so thick and tangled it would have been impossible to get all the way to the river at this spot, or to see through it from the place where the fire was burning, and soundlessly the men floated in the current, which was here quite deep.

"Damn the horses, the way they sway about," whispered Cotton after a while.

"It's time they got to firm ground" – answered Rowson, "besides, here's the place where I have to land – so – keep a little bit closer in so that I can jump off – well, do your part wisely – now sit tight!"

With these words he swung himself out of the rocking boat onto a projecting rock, waved his hand at them one more time, and disappeared in the darkness.

But it took a practiced canoeist like Cotton to prevent the swaying vessel from being overturned by a person jumping out. For him, though, the maneuver presented only slight difficulties. The small craft rocked for scarcely a few seconds and then glided, without one drop of water having been taken on, farther along its course.

Weston spoke not a syllable more; since the last frantic scream of the Indian woman, which still rang in his ears, a strange and insurmountable fear had taken possession of him. – He started at the slightest sound, and his heart pounded with feverish blows.

Without exchanging another word with one another they soon reached the place indicated by Rowson, where wide, smooth rock shelves ran halfway out into the river and extended up to the bank above, which was overgrown with thick low bushes. Here they stopped and led the snorting and impatiently stamping horses onto dry land.

"Yes, just trample," laughed Cotton – "you'll soon be warm enough. Hold them a moment, Weston, I must first sink the one canoe so that no one finds it and becomes suspicious; the other can float on, no one knows it, and if they do know it they'll think it broke loose."

With that, he quickly threw off his clothes so as not to be hindered if he had to swim, filled the canoe with rocks, paddled it to a deep place, and let it sink.

"So," he said, as he sprang back onto dry land beside Weston and threw his clothes on again, "so – no one will soon get a look at that, at least not soon enough to cause us any harm. But now let's go, the ground here is burning under my feet."

"And do you know the way exactly?" asked Weston apprehensively – "at night it takes a capable woodsman to keep to a straight course in the forest."

"Don't worry one bit," cried Cotton, "besides, we have to keep somewhat to the mountain ridge, since there's the least undergrowth and so it's impossible to lose the way. Especially once we're out of the cane thicket, and it's hardly five hundred paces wide here, then there's no more worry. So back in the saddle, Weston – by the way – what kind of saddles did you bring with you from home?"

"For you, an old Spanish one, for me, none at all – I'll take the buffalo skin here. How far is it then?"

"Well, thank God," laughed Cotton – "we don't get there tomorrow or the next day; still, who cares? A man who takes up such a business mustn't particularly look for comfort. Besides, Rowson's plan is capital, and I think we'll get to the Mississippi swamp untouched. But I wonder if they'll leave Johnson unscathed."

"If I only knew that Rowson had done the Indian woman no harm!" said Weston, sighing.

"Oh, a plague on your Indian woman, what do we care about *her*! Hell and damnation, it's starting to rain again. But wait, I won't swear, it's all right and can only be good for us, Johnson especially, since it means they won't be able to find out where he came from with the horses. But let's go now – through here, Weston; this is the mouth of one of the little brooks, and free of cane at least."

Weston had meanwhile put the aforementioned skin on the back of one of the horses, swung himself up, and, leading two others, followed his companions, who during this time had already entered the thicket and disappeared into the darkness. For a few moments one could still hear the breaking and crashing of dried and withered cane as the horses pushed their way through it, then this too died away; a deathly quiet lay on the wilderness, and the darkness of night shrouded sin and crime.

* * *

But the reader must now return with me once more to the ford where we found ourselves at the beginning of the previous chapter.

It was not so very long after the four accomplices had disappeared under the dark shadows of the trees that the horsemen from Spring River came blasting along the road, with pine torches in their hands and their number increased by the farmers from Pettyville.

"Here they are, down below," now shouted Husfield, bending low in his stirrups and holding his pine stake as close to the earth as possible, "that's my horse – I'll be damned if their impudence isn't boundless; galloping down the middle of an open county road as if they were riding their own nags. But wait, you scoundrels, wait – you won't escape punishment this time."

"It's very doubtful that they'll wait," laughed Cook, "the tracks certainly don't look much like they would; thunderation, how they've torn it up here – Husfield, we'll have to ride hard if we want to catch up with them tomorrow."

"If we ride hard – and if I have to kill *these* horses too; I'm willing to lose them all, but I must see the vermin hanged – hanged – or I'll never sleep soundly again."

"Seems like I heard a cry as we rode around that fallen oak up there," said Curtis – "didn't you too?"

"Yes," answered Husfield – "I heard something, but it'd probably turn out to be a panther; there're definitely still some here in the cane brake."

"Oh, enough," cried Cook – "especially here in this area. I shot one eight days ago, and here there're tracks galore."

"How's the ford then," Husfield asked now, turning back in his saddle. "Is there any deep spot there that could be dangerous?"

"Yes – on the other side," replied Curtis, "just let me ride on ahead, I know the spot."

With that, he let his horse slowly descend the steep bank and rode, followed by the others in single file, to the other bank.

"Do you see the tracks there?" asked Husfield, who was last in the train.

"Yes indeed – of course," Curtis called back – "there's no other way they could go up – straight ahead on the road, as my name is Curtis. They rely on the quick hoofs of their beasts."

"Wouldn't it be better if we threw the torches away now?" asked Cook; – "if we actually get near them, they'll see the bright fires from a distance."

"That's true!" affirmed Curtis, "let's extinguish the torches; if they've stayed on the road, which now I don't doubt for a second, then we'll catch them, and in that case the burning pine stakes can only do us harm, so away with them!" And without waiting any longer for the others to agree, he hurled his torch over into the damp foliage, where it went out instantly. Cook followed his example, and only Husfield still searched the ground with his light to find the familiar hoof prints again.

"They're up here," he called to Curtis – "the tracks are right here in the road itself."

"You've trampled on everything," said Husfield; "well, on in the dark then, for all I care. We can't very well lose the way."

"It's not possible," replied Cook, "at least not tonight, since it'll be pretty bright before we get to the place where the path starts to be unclear."

"Good – forward then," cried Husfield, as he too threw away his pine stake, "forward, and he among you who lays the first hand on the bastards will get barrel of whiskey from me."

The men loudly cheered this reward, and they flew along the road at a full gallop toward the "hot springs" – following Johnson's tracks.[1]

Note

1. "Hot springs": if this is a reference to the town of Hot Springs, Arkansas, it would be a way of indicating that the thieves' trick has worked, since Hot Springs is nearly in the opposite direction from the Mississippi.

Figure 14.1. Cover illustration for *Alapaha, the Squaw; or, The Renegades of the Border*. From American Tales no. 67 (New York: Beadle and Co., 23 July 1870), Francis Johnson's translation of the first part of *Die Regulatoren in Arkansas*. Image courtesy of University of Virginia Library Special Collections.

Chapter 14

Brown on His Way Home. –
The Mysterious Meeting. – The Indian. –
The Old Farmer. – A Canoe Trip.

It was in the twilight of the same evening described in the last chapter when the Pittsburg ferryboat,[1] rowed by two strong Negroes across the Arkansas, landed on the opposite, southern bank of the river. It dropped there its only passenger, a pale young man who held his small rough-haired pony in the boat by its bridle. The traveler paid the required fare and, throwing the bridle over his horse's neck, let it jump from the boat by itself. It managed this very cleverly with a short leap, then ran about twenty paces farther up the river bank and stopped there to bite off and eat the sparse grass sprouting from the sandy soil around the roots of a few solitary birch trees.

"But Massa,"[2] said one of the ferrymen, a true Congo Negro, whose appallingly wide nostrils seemed to vie with a narrow wooly moustache as to which of the two could extend farthest down over the corners of his mouth, and whose hair appeared to be more scorched by the sun than curled, "I already told you there's not a house for seven miles and Massa'll have to spend the night in the open air and the rain."

As he spoke these words, he shoved the half dollar fare that he had received into a small, filthy, leather pocketbook, and then buried this with great care in the single wide pocket of his cotton trousers.

"I know that," the stranger replied indifferently, "but how long has the cabin been abandoned, the one that stands not far from here at the edge of the little prairie? There were people in there before – settlers from Illinois."

"Oh, since a long time, Massa," answered the Negro, "the wife died and – the two children too. Then the man went off again, but sold the little piece of land with the cabin to my master in Pittsburg, and I heard over yonder that he must've gone home, up the Mississippi."

"The house is still standing?"

"Yes, Massa – but –"

"Well – but? – Is there no roof on it?"

"Oh yes, Massa – a good roof – everything still in good shape – but – the folks over yonder say – things aren't quite right in that house."

"Not right, how so?"

"Well – the wife, who's buried there under the five peach trees, she is –"

"Maybe still haunting the place?" smiled the stranger.

"Uh-huh!" the two blacks now nodded together very significantly, and looked nervously up and down the desolate river bank.

"Why do they believe that?" asked the white, as he turned to go. "Has anyone seen the ghost?"

Both Negroes nodded their heads again in a life-threatening manner, since it seemed almost impossible to execute that movement with such force without breaking one's neck in the process. Indeed, it required a second question to discover some details about the ghostly house, and the one who had spoken first then stated that people told all sorts of terrible stories about the place, among which the most common of them was: "The man first murdered his wife, whom he wanted to be rid of, and after that the two children, and then took his way down the river in a steamboat; where to, no one knew. After his flight, however, the grave was opened by two doctors in the presence of law officers and found their suspicions confirmed; somehow, one of the doctors is said to have stolen the corpses of the two children, and the mother now searches for her children at night and only returns to the grave at first light."

The Negro now seemed to believe that he had said as much about such a gruesome subject as the proximity of the place and the steadily descending darkness allowed; without waiting any longer for a reply, he wished the stranger a good night and pushed off from the bank, and at once the wide and clumsy vessel glided under his slow but powerful oar strokes back across the river.

Brown, for the stranger was no other than our young friend, who was on his way back to the Fourche La Fave, looked after it long and thoughtfully. Farther and farther it floated into the damp fog that lay on the surface of the water, and finally seemed only a vague dark speck, across from which yet came the sharp and clear sounds of the measured strokes of the oar. Finally this too disappeared; the boat had reached its destination, and as if waking from a dream, the young man sighed heavily and sorrowfully, then mounted his grazing beast, grasped its reins, and walked slowly up the narrow footpath that led from the ferryboat landing to the area directly above it.

Having arrived there, he paused for a moment, standing and silently looking out over the landscape overhung with gloomy rain clouds. For a few hundred paces away from the river the rising water had churned up the earth, covering it with many feet of the white sand peculiar to it. In many places even the trunks of the birches and the cottonwoods were half swallowed by it, and the earth itself, with its long wave-shaped ridges, resembled a swelling sea. But farther on, where the force of the swollen stream had been slowed by the thicket of pawpaws and sycamores, the dazzling white coating of sand lay like an even blanket of snow on the primordial fertile soil, and stretched far away to where the land, rising higher, had set a dam against the greedy stream. There lush green grass formed the soft carpet of a kind of prairie that ended at a broad and enormously vast wild plum orchard. Such "plum orchards" are found not infrequently in the western states; their low bushy fruit stock had all been planted in earlier times by the Indians, especially the Cherokees. The early owners of these tracts had been driven from their native land and transported farther west, and their garden had become a desert.[3]

At the edge of this "Cherokee plum orchard," as the place was still called among the inhabitants of the district, lay the aforementioned little house that, according to the Negro's testimony, supposedly sheltered such eerie guests. Nonetheless, Brown turned toward the place and reached the infamous spot as darkness fell.

It was one of those small settlements as are found by the thousands in the American far west: a low log cabin with a clay chimney now fallen in, a small overgrown field about two acres in size, the fence of which was felled partly by rot and partly by fire, a half-collapsed side building that had probably served as a kitchen or pantry, and a toppled well, whose opening was covered by a sawn-off piece of a hollow tree. The place seemed to have been abandoned for many years, but something so wild and eerie reposed on the deserted site that Brown involuntarily paused as he was about to step over the fallen fence and looked over at the nearby grove of trees as if conferring with himself as to whether a night camping in the open, under the green trees of the forest, were not preferable to the dry but by no means inviting habitation. But a stronger gust of wind from the west that pushed a mist of fine, cold drizzle in his direction put a sudden end to his indecisiveness, because he now, without further delay, drew the faithful animal into the inner enclosure and along to the little side building that he first of all examined and found still usable. To be sure, he found it necessary to lift a couple of far-from-light beams out of the way to allow his pony entrance; but then he had the satisfaction of knowing that the brave beast that had already carried him a long, long way that day was dry and fairly protected from the cold northwest winds. Now quite satisfied at having found this site, he pulled over a trough lying in the corner, fetched the small sack that he had brought with him strapped to his saddle, and poured out a meal of hulled corn for his happily whinnying pony.

With that taken care of, he then thought of his own bed and stepped into the house in order to rest his weary body under the sheltering roof and strengthen it for new endeavors. However desolate and empty it may have seemed from the outside, the young hunter nevertheless soon found that it must have provided another wanderer protection and shelter only a short time before, since ashes lay in the chimney, and under these even a few coals still glimmered. He could not easily have come across anything more pleasing, and he quickly carried in an armful of broken fence posts, cut thin shavings with his hunting knife, and to his satisfaction soon afterward saw a bright, warming fire blaze up.

Saddle and blankets he had brought in with him; the latter he now spread out before the friendly glow, took for his very frugal supper a small piece of dried venison, and then threw himself down onto a bed that was hard but welcome enough to him.

To this point, the preparations for his own comfort, and for his animal's, had laid claim to all of the young man's mental powers. He had been busy, and little time was left to him to reflect upon himself or his situation. But now, as he was stretched out before the crackling coals, in the tight, unsteady circle of light from the flickering fire, his heart opened up, and alongside the few blessed moments of his recent past, his destiny passed before him, seriously and gloomily, into a dark future. He saw himself in heated combat with Mexican mercenaries, defending the freedom of a young nation; he saw himself storming the enemy's batteries amid the roar of guns hurling death and destruction his way – he saw himself bleeding among those fallen in mortal struggle, but lying on a triumphantly won battlefield, and an almost exultant smile passed over his pallid features as he convulsively seized the rifle resting next to him and with a proud and death-defying look half lifted himself from his bed and stared out through the fallen chimney into the dark starless night. Now suddenly the image of his beloved pressed itself before his mind's eye as she, like a beautiful martyr, laid her hand in that of her appointed husband – he saw her grow pale, saw how she anxiously looked around for help – for *him* – heard her half-suppressed cry of pain, and – the proud strong man broke down under the impact of the deadly feelings that assailed him. He buried his face in his hands, threw himself back onto the rough bed and wept – wept as if his heart would break.

But this wild raging pain at last gave way to a gentle, calming melancholy; his hand on his pounding heart, his burning forehead pressed against the rough bearskin saddle blanket that served him as a pillow, he prayed – for the happiness of his beloved, for calm in his own overburdened breast, and with the precious girl's name on his lips the god of sleep at last took him in his gentle arms and carried him away to the heart of the one he so fervently desired.

It must have been past midnight when he awoke from his sweet dream and found himself in sad reality: no more in front of the warming fire, but rather before the open chimney, through which the wild storm drove its cold, cutting wind in on him. The coals were, of course, completely burnt out – not another spark was to be found, and shivering he moved his bed into a far corner of the building that was better protected from the wind and rain, and here awaited the longed-for daybreak.

But hardly had he done so when it seemed to him that he heard voices outside the house. This quickly recalled to his mind the Negro's story, which he had already almost forgotten about, and, supporting himself on his right elbow, he first felt carefully for his rifle and knife to see if his trusty weapons lay by his side, and then, holding his breath, listened with rapt attention in the direction from which he believed he had first heard the sounds. But no more was to be heard, and he was about to sink back onto his bed, smiling at his own fear of ghosts, when he once more distinguished human voices, and very close by indeed. Almost in the same instant someone tore open the door and entered the narrow room, while a rough voice cried out:

"Damned dump! I was about to think I'd never find it again on a dark night. – But what a weather – good for business though."

"But not wet enough," replied another, "it's washed things out a little, but not enough."

"The devil take me if it's not enough for me at least. – It makes me shiver so that my teeth bang together; if we could only light a fire."

"With what then?" asked the other. "Everything's sopping wet, and I don't even have a tomahawk with me to get some dry shavings. When I was here this afternoon I had a little fire, in fact, and I covered it with ashes too as I was leaving so as to keep the embers, but now," he said, feeling around in the fireplace with the point of his foot and pushing aside the ashes, "everything's dark as night. We can't stop here too long anyway, at least I can't, since I must be home again tomorrow evening; our neighborhood will find itself in a bit of an uproar next week. As soon as the storm lets up a little, I'll go."

"But our horses won't break loose, though? It would've been better to have brought them here."

"Don't even think about it – in such weather they stand still and don't move. – No, I haven't brought them into this region on purpose, since I wouldn't like to have any horse tracks here at all. But now to our business; time is precious, and we must use the short half hour we've been granted. When do you think you'll be back again?"

Brown, who had actually experienced a certain paralysis following the initial surprise, was further perplexed by the mysterious words praising this weather as "good for business," and he really did not immediately know what to do: whether he should allow himself to be known or remain lying quietly. But the thought of playing the eavesdropper was awkward to him, and he was about to reveal his presence by calling out when a statement by one of them again made him waver in his intention. The aversion of one of the strangers to horse tracks near the cabin made him wonder.

"Could these men belong to the band that the Regulators were formed to eliminate?" was his first thought, and their continued conversation was apt to strengthen this suspicion in him still further. He therefore gently drew his knife from its sheath, since if he were discovered he must be prepared for an attack and be equipped to defend himself; holding his breath, he nestled back into his corner in order to hear what schemes had led these worthy fellows here, and whether it might be his prerogative to defeat their efforts.

"When can I be back?" answered the other one thoughtfully. "Well, given the nature of the work, it could take fourteen days to three weeks. – The place is far from here, and I must go to work very carefully."

"Just don't forget to be cautious at the little stream before you get to my house," replied the other one to him. "If the tracks lead back to my house and the goddamned Regulators get wind of it, then an investigation would seem inevitable, and that could bring trouble for you too."

"To me? How so then?"

"Well, if they catch your horses, do you think I'd later pay you a share of the profits, or more likely, the losses?"

"Yes, right – I thought you meant something else; no, don't worry, I know the routine precautions well enough. But wait – I just thought of something else: it's likely that I won't be able to get the horses all the way to you myself. I have business at exactly that time that hopefully will bring me more; if that's finished, then I'll stop off at your place and we can settle up with one another. One more thing: trust the man who brings you the horses in every respect, only – only don't give him any money for me."

"Don't worry. – But will he know the place where he has to turn off the road before my house?"

"Of course – he described the place to me first."

"Do I know him?"

"I don't think so."

"But then how will I know if he's the one I can trust my secret to?"

"Hahaha – he knows it well enough, but wait – just so you'll feel surer of him, he might ask about the Fourche La Fave. – To that, you'll answer him that it flows near the house. His next question then should be: 'How's the pasturage in these parts here?' And if he asks you for a drink of water the third time, then open your gate and door to him – it's the right one."

"Good – such caution is necessary indeed, since not only do I frequently entertain visitors from the neighborhood, but my foster daughter lives in the house with me and likewise mustn't find out anything about it. – The devil trusts a woman's tongue; 'tis already dangerous enough that my old woman knows. But now good night – the rain's let up and I must get home. It'd be better for you too if you leave this place again as fast as possible. I am amazed that you have the heart to come here, if only half of what they say about you is true."

"Children's tales," grumbled the other. "Anyway, it won't be dry long, we'll have a wet morning probably."

"Maybe not, my sense is that it's starting to get colder, and the wind is shifting –"

"Well, what's the matter?" asked the one as the other, disturbed by something, suddenly stopped speaking.

"It seemed to me as if I heard a horse stamping very close by," he said.

"Oh, nonsense," grumbled his comrade, "the animals are a quarter mile from here. – But come, it really seems that the weather's going to get better."

The door opened again – the men walked out, and a deathly quiet reigned over the desolate dark cabin anew. Long and motionless Brown lay, wrapped in his blanket, and listened to the storm that now whistled madly through the gaps and chinks of the house, played with the planks torn loose on the roof, roared in the tree tops, and took its course with awesome ferocity down along the wide surface of the Arkansas.

"But who could these men be, consorting with one another on such a night and in such a place?" That thought alone almost entirely occupied him. No good could come of their schemes, otherwise they would have chosen a better time and opportunity – but who were they? *One* voice especially Brown thought he recognized; he was sure that he had heard it before sometime. But where or when, here in Arkansas or in Missouri, even over across the Mississippi, it was impossible for him to decide. In thinking it over, his ideas became confused again – he closed his eyes and pulled his blanket over his head, so that, undisturbed by outward impressions, he could pursue that voice into the buried depths of his consciousness, and – in a few minutes he was dreaming again. The two voices thereby became steadily better known to him, more familiar, and at last he could even recognize the figures of the speakers – Marion and Rowson, as his beloved pulled back from the embrace of her unwanted intended – ever further and further away, as her pursuer steadily assumed wilder and more terrifying shapes and steadily came nearer and nearer – threatened to seize her, and the poor girl in utmost mortal anguish finally cried out for help into the dark, stormy night.

Terrified, he threw off his covering and sprang up – a cold sweat stood on his forehead, but – it was only a dream of course. Outside, though, a big owl[4] whooped its monotonous and eerie morning-song, a few wolves answered from farther away, and a faint light, coming from the eastern sky, announced the approaching dawn.

The air had become bitter cold, the wind had shifted to the northeast, and not the smallest cloud now marred the clear, blue firmament. Brown, to whom the events of the night now seemed almost like an actual dream as they merged with his own, stood thinking and brooding and tried anew, though again in vain, to connect these persons with scenes he had experienced in his past. To no avail – he finally had to give up the effort, and now, with a zeal all the greater on that account, set about the business of the moment in order to dispel and forget what he could not alter or fathom. With the last corn left to him he fed his pony, then led it to a small puddle formed by the wet weather to quench its thirst, saddled it, and was already on the way home at a lively trot before the sun had yet announced its arrival by a single beam of greeting.

Now the fresh morning air and the brisk ride gave his body as well as his soul a new energy, and the small plucky animal that he rode trotted, under the gentle pressure from his thighs, with joyous snorts through the flat swampy valley of the Arkansas until it entered the first low range of hills, and now, feeling firm ground under its hoofs, flew along over it as if yearning to greet its home pasture again quite soon.

Then the rider saw on the broadly hewn road that he was following a foot-traveler striding rapidly along it, and on coming closer he recognized, to his boundless astonishment, the Indian.

"Assowaum!" he cried, as he reined in his pony with a swift hand. It had stopped anyway on its own, since it knew the red warrior well enough and probably thought it self-evident that the two friends would chat with one another. "Assowaum – what in the world brings you this way? Where are you going?"

"To this place," quietly answered the Indian, as he grasped and pressed the hand extended to him.

"So have you been looking for me? What's happened?"

"Much – very much – and does my brother know nothing about it?"

"I? How would I – I wasn't – and yet – the two men last night – their mysterious meeting – who knows what connection there is between them and what you have to tell me? But out with your story – I'm burning with curiosity."

"And you know nothing at all?"

"Oh, hang it, Assowaum, don't pull such a deadly serious face," cried Brown, laughing. "When I'm on the other side of the Arkansas, how can I know what's happened on the Fourche La Fave?"

"But before you left –"

"My fight with Heathcott?"

"Heathcott has been murdered!" said the Indian gravely, as he looked searchingly into the other man's eyes.

"Good God!" cried Brown, reining back on his pony so that it reared up in sudden pain. "That's terrible, if true."

"Suspicion rests on *you*," continued the Indian, his eye fixed on him, "and they also justify you completely. The dead man spouted wild threats – perhaps would have made good on them – was possibly about to make good on them, and your deed was, as they say, justifiable as a result, only –"

"Assowaum!" cried the young man, interrupting him, as he sprang from the saddle and stepped up to the Indian, "Assowaum – by that blue sky spread out above us there – by the grave of my father – by this hand that I stretch on high, pure and free – I am innocent of this murder. – I haven't seen the unfortunate man again since the moment we separated in front of Roberts' house. Do you still believe that I'm guilty?"

The Indian stretched his hand toward him, smiling, and cried in a joyous tone: "Assowaum never believed it – at least not from the moment when he heard that the murdered man had been robbed."

"And they accuse me of this too?" the other asked, horrified.

"Bad men – yes – the good know you better. Mr. Harper and Mr. Roberts do not believe it."

Brown buried his face in his hands at Roberts' name and, sighing, leaned on the pommel of the saddle on the quiet animal standing next to him.

"Let me see your foot!" said the Indian now, as he pulled his tomahawk from his belt.

"For what? Have you measured the tracks?"

"Uh-huh," nodded the savage and held the handle of his weapon against his friend's sole.

"Three-quarters of an inch too long," he laughed to himself with pleasure, "but I thought so!"[5]

"I didn't even wear boots on the morning I left the Fourche La Fave," Brown said as he reached in his saddlebag. "These moccasins here. – Were they the *boot-tracks* that you discovered at the crime?"

"Uh-huh," nodded the Indian again, but more slowly than before, and it was almost as if a new idea had flashed through his mind. – He laid his tomahawk on the ground in front of him and appeared to compare the length of the handle with another measurement that he marked by spreading his fingers, but then suddenly looked up at the young American[6] with such a wild and vacant stare that the latter took a step back in shock and asked him what he had – what he had thought of.

"Nothing – nothing," smiled the savage mysteriously, "come – we must go back – time is passing. They regard you as guilty; bad men spread all sorts of rumors – and the little man has fallen ill – he lies alone; Alapaha listens to the preaching of the pale man and will not return to him until the evening. Does not my brother want to tell them himself that he is innocent?"

"But where'd the murder happen? How'd they find out about the dreadful thing?"

"Go – go; we can walk and talk – Assowaum must get to the Fourche La Fave."

With quick steps the Indian now hurried back along the way that he had just come, and Brown had to keep his pony to almost a slow trot just to stay by his side. In this way the latter made known to Brown all the proceedings that he had witnessed, and for his part now learned all that Brown knew about the nighttime rendezvous of the two men. In that connection, the Indian averred that that morning he had met a man on a large brown horse. But he could not recognize his face since he was completely wrapped in his woolen blanket, and upon seeing the savage had drawn it even more tightly around him.

"Maybe this was one of the two," Assowaum continued as he indicated the hoof prints that ran along before them, "maybe not; but here is the track, and we can follow it."

But from this they were deflected, for when they came into the Fourche La Fave valley the ground had been made so swampy by the rain of the previous night and the flooding of some small mountain streams that the Indian proposed that they take a straight course to the river, which was not very far off, and continue their way in a canoe that he hoped to get from a farmer living there. At high water the little stream shot with tremendous speed to the Arkansas, and even if the countless windings of the stream extended the trip by several miles, a light vessel could cover that distance faster than if the travelers had to continue slowly along their muddy road mile after mile.

Brown gladly followed the advice of his friend, since in this way he could go around Roberts' house. Avoiding therefore the swampy valley, they followed a so-called "spur"[7] or off-shoot of the hill that brought them directly to the bank of the river with dry feet, and the sun was still several hours high when they reached the dwelling of one of the older settlers on the Fourche La Fave named Smeiers.[8]

But as the Indian had expected, the river foamed in raging fury against the rock walls that constrained it; and the farmer warned the men not to trust themselves to the small unstable canoe, since they had to pass through places in which even a practiced swimmer would not be able to save himself. Nevertheless, he gladly turned the boat over to them and also promised to send Brown's pony with his oldest boy down to Harper's dwelling the next day, as it was Sunday. But Brown bought the canoe from him at once, since he wanted to keep it in the river at his uncle's house.

Their friendly host meanwhile laid on the table what he could to quicken and strengthen the tired travelers: wild turkey and honey, sweet potatoes, pumpkin mash, and cornbread, as well as a beaker full of real Monongahela whiskey, and the two did not need to be urged for long to partake of the kindly offered meal.

"Everyone's flown off again today," said the old man when a little Negro girl had carried in the last bowl and filled the guests' glasses with fresh delicious milk.

"Where to?" asked Brown, taking the glass from his lips.

"Prayer meeting is today!" interrupted the Indian, as he pushed aside the knife near him on the table and took a turkey wing in his fingers. "The pale man must not think much of the virtue of the whites if he makes them pray to their great spirit several times every week."

"'Tis true!" said the farmer, while he took a hearty gulp from the whiskey beaker and handed it over to the white men. "It's fast getting too bad for me. – My neighbor here – Smith – and his whole family all of a sudden got religious, as they call it, and then nothing at all would do but that my old woman must also go with them, and now she drags the poor girls over to the meeting, who nevertheless, it's true, would have nothing else to think about but prayer."

"Women more easily feel the need to turn to their God than we men," replied Brown – indeed, he thought of his beloved, how he had seen her so often in childlike pious devotions. "Our whole life and work, after all, leaves us far too little time to spare for opening our hearts to feelings that must be nourished and nurtured and couldn't, called upon suddenly, spring into life all at once. On the other hand, for women, confined to their narrow circle of domesticity, religion is almost a part of their being, and I wouldn't want to blame them if they're attached to churchly practices with a passion and reverence that the cruder male probably doesn't feel for them to that degree."

"Good sir," said the old man in a friendly tone, "may the dear Lord preserve me if I should bear the women any ill will or in any way hinder them if they want to pray: but I'll be damned if I don't also think that they have something else in the world to do than just pray. – The devil take the praying sisters – that's what I say, and that's the worst, I think, that a man with a good conscience can wish for the devil."

Assowaum smiled, nodded his head, and said: "I will send Alapaha up here – such preaching would be better for her than that of the pale man."

"Don't misunderstand me," replied Brown, "God knows how abhorrent false piety is to me, and it really seems as if it's getting the upper hand a little in this settlement, but – maybe the blame lies more with the people themselves than with the preacher. I believe, at least, that Mr. Rowson speaks with conviction and that he feels what he preaches from the very bottom of his heart."

"To speak frankly, I don't believe that," cried the farmer, shifting about impatiently in his chair, "I've just heard him once, to be sure, but he didn't please me then. – Rolling your eyes is a bad sign. When a fellow starts off looking like a sick chicken, then I can't think that he's capable of having great piety. Still – as far as I'm concerned – I won't be a bother to him again, but I really wish he'd give my women, just one of them at least, some time off, so it'd look like I had a home. But now they put on their great sunbonnets, take the books in hand, and off they ride. Then late in the evening, when every other Christian is thinking of sleep, they come home all at once like a tempest, and instead of laying themselves down respectably and properly, they go on sitting around in corners for hours and talk about their sins, and what lost and no good mortals they are, and how it's just by a very special grace that their dear God troubles himself about them at all. Lord! Truly, if I weren't so well acquainted with my folks, and didn't know that they're fine decent women and children – according to their talk, I'd have to take them for the most despicable pack of scoundrels that'd ever set foot on God's earth. But that's the fault of the preaching and praying, pure and simple. By thunder, I won't say I'm white as the driven snow, I've been up to a few monkeyshines, but that I should crawl around in the dirt for that and cringe and hold my mouth open in astonishment that the earth hasn't yet devoured me, terrible sinner – naw – that would be too much to ask. – Once not long ago the pulpit-thumper was here with us and wanted to hold a prayer meeting – but nothing came of it; I walked around the farm with him, of course, showed him all my livestock, my horses and cows, showed him my fields and my pastures, but that was all. As for preaching, he had to go on up to Halfers', and so I got rid of him for the afternoon at least. – But he didn't spare me the evening prayer; he slept here, and I'll be damned if he didn't stay on his knees there in the corner from nine o'clock 'til quarter to ten and recount to the dear Lord an incredibly long list of all the things he didn't deserve, but that he really wanted to have. – But you're ready, and seem to be in a hurry; well, my chatter won't keep you any longer. But take care with that nutshell anyway – the current's very bad and an accident could easily happen."

"Don't worry, sir," laughed Brown. "We both know how to get about in such vessels, and I even have an Indian there who'll manage the steering; it couldn't be in better hands. So the pony will definitely come down tomorrow?"

"To Mr. Harper's house. You can leave it there, safely" said the farmer. "Your name is Harper, isn't it?"

"Brown, sir."

"Brown?" asked the old man quickly and with alarm, keeping his eye firmly fixed on the young man, who meanwhile quietly met his gaze. "Brown? But not the one –"

"Of whom they say that he murdered the Regulator? The same, sir," replied the young man; "but," he continued, as he took a step forward and a deeper red colored his cheeks, "it's a disgraceful slander, and I am now on my way to refute that false rumor. I did *not* kill the man."

"He threatened your life," continued the farmer, still half doubtful.

"Yes!" Brown cried with noble passion. "And I would've killed him and then freely and openly made the deed known, had he opposed me in an honorable fight. But the man was, as the Indian here told me, ambushed by two men, assassinated, and robbed, and – do I look like an assassin, then?"

"No – God strike me, no," cried the honest yeoman, gripping the young man's hand, "no. – I know nothing more about you, but you have something honest, something fine about your face, and if you say yourself that you didn't do it, then I'll be damned if I don't believe it. My girls were down at Roberts' yesterday, and they tell me too that Mr. Rowson's bride had very much taken your part."

"Assowaum, we really must be going," cried Brown, turning suddenly to the Indian, who already stood in the door awaiting him.

"I'm ready – it is getting late," the latter replied, and once more the young man heartily pressed the farmer's hand, thanked him not only for his friendship and kindness, but even more for the trust that he had placed in him, and expressed his hope that his innocence would be soon and fully brought to light. The men then climbed into the boat; Assowaum seated himself in the back to guide the narrow cockleshell, while Brown took a place in the forward section, and both tied their rifles to themselves so that they would not lose them in case of an accident. Casting off from the bank, the sleek, light vessel, now propelled by two strong and skilled men, glided with almost miraculous speed over the boiling, foaming flood, and the next minute had disappeared around the projecting rocks that formed a steep promontory extending more than a hundred paces below the dwelling.

Fortunately, though, the two friends passed the most dangerous places while it was still daylight, especially those spots where birches and willows had washed into the river and could have easily become a danger to such an unsteady craft. Thus they arrived, just as it began to be dark, at the shallower but also wider part of the stream – a passage that, less darkly shadowed by overhanging branches, allowed each obstacle in their watery course to be easily discerned.

They were gliding silently now, no longer paddling but merely steering with the current, when Assowaum's hand suddenly pointed ahead and drew the attention of his companion, who sat with his back turned to the nose of the boat, to a bright light that was becoming visible before them.

"Strange – what can that be?" said Brown, turning toward it. "So far as the thick bushes allow it to be seen, it looks like a lot of lights or torches. What neighborhood might we be in? Is there a house here on the bank, then?"

"Yes!" said the Indian softly, steering the boat over in that direction. "Yes – an empty cabin. – Alapaha was here yesterday evening – let us land." And in the next moment the small light vessel had already shot to the river bank, where its occupants quickly tied it to the trunk of a young birch with the usual anchor cable, a slender grapevine.

Notes

1. Pittsburg, in present-day Johnson County, is on the north bank of the Arkansas River just downstream from Morrison Bluff.

2. FG uses "Massa" here and elsewhere in the original text. See the introduction to this volume for a discussion of FG's demeaning portrayals of African Americans (p. 10).

3. A reversal of the Biblical reference to the wilderness of the Garden of Eden at the beginning of the novel (see note 1, chapter 1). The Cherokee had been in the Arkansas River Valley at least since 1812, when the New Madrid earthquake prompted many living in northeast Arkansas to move to safer ground. The naturalist Thomas Nuttall described them as he traveled up the Arkansas in 1819: "Both banks of the river, as we proceeded, were lined with the houses and farms of the Cherokees, and though their dress was a mixture of indigenous and European taste, yet in their houses, which are decently furnished, and in the farms, which were well fenced and stocked with cattle . . . argue a propitius [*sic*] progress in their population. Their superior industry, either as hunters or farmers, proves the value of property among them." See the Cherokee entry in the *Encyclopedia of Arkansas*, www.encyclopediaofarkansas.net.

4. FG chooses the word "Uhu," a reference to the German eagle owl, not a North American species.

5. The old German "Fuß" was divided into twelve "Zoll." Each Zoll was equivalent to 1.029 British imperial inch. See William Alfred Brown, *The Money, Weights, and Measures of the Chief Commercial Nations in the World, and a Sketch of the Metric System* (London: Edward Stanford, 1899), 144.

6. "The young American": an awkward lapse in point of view by FG.

7. "Spur" is English in FG's original.

8. "Smeiers" was based on "Slowtrap" or "Meyers" from the Fourche La Fave, one of FG's acquaintances (*RA*, 152n63).

Chapter 15

The Prayer Meeting. –
The Terrible Message.

The sun had crossed the mid-day line by some two hours when various groups of people appeared from different directions but at the same time at a small log hut that lay secluded and alone in the vast and quiet forest. The owner of the same, Mr. Mullins, a new settler too, and an industrious, respectable man, in a very short time had already brought a quite handsome piece of land under cultivation. But nothing of this could be noted from the house itself, since this stood, contrary to the custom of American farmers, a half mile distant from the field, on the slope of a small rocky hill that formed the first rise of the mountain ridge separating the waters of the Fourche La Fave from those of the Petit Jean. Around the dwelling itself fallen trees and split fence rails lay scattered in wild disorder, which gave the place an appearance of newness that was, at the same time, uncomfortable and even doleful.

But however desolate and still it all had looked throughout the morning, it now came to life. Not a bush was without a tethered horse, not a fallen trunk was without a few men sitting on it, dressed in their Sunday clothes and comfortably chatting with one another, while the women stepped into the house to lay aside their bonnets and shawls. At the same time, of course, that gave them the opportunity, before the preacher arrived, to hold forth on the sins of their fellow mortals – at least just a little, and completely in confidence – and naturally with the very friendly purpose of fully excusing the same, but only in so far as this was compatible with a precise and thorough recounting of them.

"Strange that Mr. Rowson isn't yet here," said Madame Pelter to Madame Mullins, "he's usually very punctual, you know."

"Bet he's coming with Roberts," was the answer, "the wedding's in three weeks, so he mustn't leave his bride alone for too long."

"What? – a wedding?" asked three or four others, pressing close with curiosity. "Is it really true that Mr. Rowson is marrying Marion?"

"I have it from her mother herself, and she really ought to know – that they love each other has long been a well-known fact, besides. All the same, I must ask you not to do anything about it, since I don't know if it may be made public yet. – But I declare, here comes Roberts *without* Mr. Rowson; well, I don't know what in the world –"

"He did go to the Arkansas," said a relative of Bowitt's, "it might turn out he had so much business to attend to there that he just couldn't get back in time."

"That would be a real pity," sighed the young Miss Smeiers; "I was *so* looking forward to his sermon today."

"Oh, he'll come, certainly," cried old Madame Smeiers, a corpulent, friendly matron, "it's truly needful that we here in the settlements listen to the word of God right faithfully. Such sinfulness as *now* threatens to get the upper hand – only the Lord's mercy will protect us!"

"And as for that, there're still people who never think of praying," said Mrs. Bowitt. "People who never go to meeting, even if they're held in the next house – people who curse and swear –"

"Oh, if only I could stir my husband to go with me to hear God's word just one single time," said Mrs. Hostler, "every time he promises me he'll go, and he *never* sticks to it."

"You must do with him what I did with mine the other day," replied Mrs. Hennigs, "he had laid himself down in the afternoon to sleep quietly in the corner, and when he woke up, people were sitting all over the room and the preacher from over there at Petit Jean was just starting his prayer. You should've just seen what eyes *he* made; but he could no longer prevent it, and he had to bear it patiently. Another two or three times like that, and I'm sure he'll come on his own. – Oh, if they'd just once felt the sweetness and comfort of such a sermon, it'd always draw them in again."

"But Mr. Hennigs told my husband," averred Madame Smith, "that the next time he'll bring the dogs in to sleep with him so as to make a racket as soon as anyone comes."

"Just let him dare!" cried Mrs. Hennigs, indignantly. "Dogs on my bed, is it? No, I'd like to see that just once, who – good evening, Mrs. Roberts," she interrupted herself, since at this moment the person she named stepped into the house with her daughter, "how are you, Miss Marion?"

Customary greetings were now exchanged on every side, and the women had, in their excessive zeal to examine the finery of those who arrived one after the other, completely overlooked the fact that Mr. Rowson had meanwhile actually come in, and now suddenly stood in the midst them with a friendly salute.

But, great God, how he looked! His face was ashen, his cheeks hollow, his eyes sunken, and his voice noticeably trembled as, left arm thrust deep into his vest, he stepped across the threshold.

"Mr. Rowson!" cried the women, almost with one voice. "Are you sick? What's the matter with you then? – You look pale as death!"

"You must be sick!" said Mrs. Roberts, as she walked up to him. "Or has something happened?"

"No – nothing at all – I thank you," replied the preacher with a friendly smile, "I thank you all from the bottom of my heart for your concern, my honorable friends and sisters, but it's perhaps only a case of over-exertion. I've come down here from the northern settlements and have been riding the whole night to keep my word and be here at the appointed time. This may have worn me out a little too much, as my body isn't accustomed to such things."

With this, he walked over to Marion and stretched out his right hand to her in a friendly way, at which she noticed the strange position of his left arm and asked him solicitously whether he had injured himself in some way.

"A trifle," replied the preacher, "that will soon pass. My horse stumbled yesterday evening over a tree limb lying in the road and threw me against a tree, on which I grazed my arm a little. Since it was very trivial, I paid no attention to it at the start – but in the very damp and inclement night it indeed swelled toward morning, and my arm's now become a bit stiff. But, as I said, it will soon pass."

"Ah, Mr. Rowson – I have a splendid liniment," said Mrs. Mullins, going up to him, "if you'll let me –"

"Thank you, truly – deep thanks for all this kindness; but indeed it's not worth the trouble of worrying about in the least. – Nay, on my word, I must thank you, good Sister Mullins. Were it more important than it is, a slight passing chill, I could not let it be the reason to withhold the Lord for an hour longer from souls so full of piety and faith. Let us begin, honorable friends – you see in what numbers all these good folk have assembled. Do we want to stay in the house, or shall we go into the open? So that we have enough room, the open space is probably preferable."

"Only if it's not too cold for you in the fresh air!" said Mrs. Roberts nervously. "The wind is still blowing quite cold and damp."

"Don't concern yourself on my account," smiled the preacher as he pressed her hand, "I am in the service of the Lord, and in such service a man cannot be remiss. Anyway, movement will do me good, and I hope to be completely recovered again in a few days."

All further remonstrations were useless. The little table was dragged under the two mulberry trees that the farmer had left standing on account of their sweet fruit when he felled the rest of the trees that shaded his dwelling, and a short half hour later the sharp, widely-resounding voice of the preacher sent its prayers and *thanksgivings* up into the clear blue sky. – And the trees did not break and crash down on him at once, the earth did not devour the hypocrite

who lifted up his bloodstained hands to the Most Gracious, and *thanked* Him
that he had blessed his weak efforts with His fatherly benevolence and all – all
of his flock, pious and devout, who had come together here under the green
leafy roof of his cathedral! No avenging lightning bolt struck the lying traitor
to the ground, as he implored forgiveness for those who had neglected the
opportunity to hear the Word of the Lord, given the fact that they were otherwise zealously striving to put aside their sins and become worthy to be called
servants of their God. There he stood and did not blush as a cordial sunbeam
stole down through the dense leaf canopy of the underwood; there he stood
and did not blush as the women near him whispered, "a halo encircles the temples of the godly man." There he stood and did not turn his insolent eyes to the
ground as he met the pure pious gaze of his betrothed, who for the first time
felt drawn to him by a deep affection, for she too believed that the excessive
zeal for his pious calling had thus exhausted and transformed him. A woman's
heart is indeed often won by compassion, and the pale man had the expression
of suffering on his face to thank for what he was unable to attain through
months of trouble and effort. Marion believed this evening for the first time
that she could live by his side, if not happily, at least quietly and contentedly.

Rowson, meanwhile, concluded his holy performance with unshaken calm.
His lips did not quiver as he implored forgiveness from the Most High for
himself and his listeners; his voice did not tremble as he spoke the Amen and
the blessing. Only once, once only, when all around him were folded on their
knees rapt in prayer, there flashed through him a sudden terror and he faltered
for a few seconds; then high – high over the swaying tops of the oaks, four
vultures raced toward the northwest. He could not hear the heaving beating of
their wings, but he knew what place they aimed for with greedily outstretched
necks; knew what their meal would be before the sun sank down over there
in the west. Then, gathering himself with a mighty effort, he intoned a loud
"Hallelujah" as if in grim mockery of himself, and the congregation joined
in the familiar melody while he collected himself once more amid the loud
swelling voices, and gathered his strength for the conclusion of the sacred
service.

Meanwhile, not all the settlers that had arrived there appeared to take part
in the prayers, since a small group of them were collected about a hundred and
fifty paces away from the meeting. Among these, particularly, were Bahrens,
the peddler Hartford, Roberts, and Wilson, the last being a young settler on
the same river as the others, only on the opposite side. Their conversation,
which to this point the peddler had for the most part enlivened with com-
plaints about his poor trade, had nevertheless faltered in the last few minutes. For Rowson's loud and clamorous admonitions had reached them, and
Bahrens sheepishly shoved back into his pocket a small flask of whiskey that

he had just brought to light. But Wilson noticed the move and grabbed at the arm that was about to withdraw the refreshment from him.

"Hold on there!" he said, laughing. "That's against the laws of humanity; first show a fellow the 'real stuff,' and then you want to hide it again? – That'll never do."

"But Wilson – if Rowson should happen to look over here, or even one of the women!"

"Oh – what about it; they must have sharp eyes if they can tell what we've got through the bushes. – And even if – by thunder, what do we care for their jabber; if that were why we came here, we'd be sitting right in the middle of them."

"Well, don't let them see any more than's necessary," said Bahrens; "my old woman's singing with them, and I'll have to hear about it for a week otherwise."

"Don't worry – granddaddy," laughed Wilson, as he turned his back on the pious assembly and, lifting the flask to his lips, contemplated the bright clear sky for a moment with particular attentiveness.

"Hey," said Roberts, as he pulled down on the bottom of the vessel, "just don't choke yourself – do you plan to take up residence in there? Had you paid a little bit better attention, Rowson's moral – 'do unto others as you would have others do unto you,' – would've been of great use to you."

"Oh, your moral be hanged," said Wilson angrily, as he stretched himself out under the spruce beneath which he had been sitting and gazed up at its thick branches, "there is endless moralizing and 'getting on the right path' in our settlement already; it doesn't suit me anymore at all. What hearty fellows once were among us – men who couldn't suffer a hat on their heads or shoes on their feet, who slept out of doors in storms and driving snow, and knew as little of Sunday as a deer or a bear. Now, a man must keep not just Sunday, but rather Wednesday and Saturday too, and celebrate them with prayer, and why? Because a slick-haired, mealy-mouthed – well, yes, he'll be your son-in-law, Roberts – I didn't think of that –"

"Fire away!" cried the old man, "don't mind me – maybe I think exactly like you – so pull the trigger!"

"Well, yes – you probably already know what I really want to say. I don't like this everlasting 'pointing the way' to heaven; who the devil can get his bearings that way? As for such preaching, I always think of the new settler from up there, the German, who came here three months ago. He wanted to go down from his house to Kellweser's the nearest way, and had old Curtis describe it to him exactly. He told him, and quite rightly, that he must first keep straight west through the canebrake until he came to the holly thickets in the open woods, then fall off a little bit to the north, cross the deep slew there where a lot of dry cypresses are standing – then go straight north to the little lake, and

from there on, leaving the lake on the left, strike out again in an almost easterly direction, otherwise he'd come out on the county road too high. That was
clear enough, and having heard it, a fellow would think it'd be right impossible
that a man with such instructions and five sound senses could get lost. But
Recken[1] was barely in the thickets when he began to go around in circles, and
in the evening, when I went up there to get a turkey, I heard him call for help
just after my shot. Later I tried it myself several times and sent people that way
and, sure enough, try as they might, they always came out at the wrong end.
And now they want to cut a road through there, so that someday they'll finally
learn how to walk straight."

"There's some similarity there," laughed Bahrens, "but I just don't believe
that fellow over there, who rolls his eyes around his pale face so piously and
devoutly, could ever describe the way correctly. But be that as it may; I don't
like him."

"My wife has taken a shine to him," said Roberts. "Just yesterday evening
she declared that he's a saint, that she can really feel her heart becoming pious
and good as soon as he comes through the door."

"God's mercy on us!" cried Bahrens, in shock – "next he'll get a pair of wings
and fly up on a tree branch and eat manna."

"But just look at how the vultures race over us this afternoon," said Wilson,
"that's already the twenty-third that I've counted since I've been lying here."

"The preacher seems to be finished," said the peddler, who had been listening silently to the conversation for a few minutes, "that's the final hymn – I
know it."

"So you're musical too, Hartford?" laughed Bahrens.

"And why not?" replied the other, somewhat piqued – "I play the violin and
know some excellent pieces on the flute. If you don't want to believe it, I have
them with me," and with these words he thrust his hand into his deep coat
pocket, and was just about to make good on his threat when Roberts, alarmed,
caught his arm and cried out:

"For God's sake, man, keep that frightful instrument in your bag. What
do you think the pious congregation over there would say if we start playing
music here. One time last year we had such a joke with Wells down there, who
now of course lives withdrawn and never goes nowhere, unless he's called to
a log-rolling or something of that sort. Not long ago he was staying with me
when he found a bee tree right by the river; he had to have an axe, but he didn't
want to go home just for that, and so I went out into the woods with him, but
I'd never seen such a bee tree before in my life. – That one and one other –"

"Yes, but –," the peddler interrupted him, who was yet unaware of Roberts'
wont. "You wanted to say something about music –"

"Oh, why'd you stop him?" Bahrens laughed. "He was taking off, and it wouldn't have been very long before he'd find himself back in New Orleans or New York."

"How so?" said Roberts – "well, that's just more pure nonsense, I was thinking neither of New Orleans nor of New York, I wanted to tell you about Wells, whose neighbor had brought with him this long pointy thing with holes in it, much like a flute. But he put his mouth on the end, not on the side. Well, he was staying overnight up at Smith's, and in the evening he takes the thing out, as he'd been asked to do. – He'd come straight down from Fort Gibson[2] and was unaware of our customs yet, and he'd also, I believe, lived an ungodly long time on the Indian border and loved to tell stories of how they'd had never-ending struggle and strife with the Choctaws, who had just then been brought from Georgia to the west. By the by, I myself felt sorry for the poor devils, since they'd been shamefully cheated out of their land by that time; but then the bigwigs from Washington and New York came –"

"Hurrah!" shouted Bahrens, who had just been waiting for the keyword, though with the most serious face in the world. "Didn't I –"

"Hey, don't shout so!" said Wilson. "They're all looking over here. But thank God, it's over; Rowson made it quite short for once today."

"He looks sick enough too," Roberts interjected, "I was right surprised when I met him a while ago down there at the corner of the field."

"At the corner of the field? I thought he came from above, down from the northern settlements," Wilson said.

"Well, he could have done that too," Bahrens replied, "if he kept to the right three miles from here to avoid the swampy patches, he must have come out again about at the corner of the field; I rode that way once myself. But it's dryer along the hills."

Meanwhile, the gathering had indeed broken up, and all were now moving casually among one another. But Madame Bahrens came straightaway to the very sprightly little group, grabbed her "old man," as she called him, by a button, and then very earnestly impressed something on him for about a quarter of an hour, while Wilson poked Roberts in the ribs and asked him whether he might be familiar with similar negotiations.

"Children, it's getting late," at last said Smith, who visited prayer meetings zealously and was considered to be a very pious man, "in fact, the sun's already gone down, and I still have several miles to cover. – Wilson, perhaps you'll accompany me?"

"No, it seems I won't," the other responded, "I've promised Bahrens I'd ride home with him – he's eager to tell me something that happened to him last week."

"Well then, good luck to you," Mullins laughed, "just let us know it too, when it's over."

"So you can gossip about it all over the place, right?" said Bahrens. "I've gotten careful about my stories, since – God have mercy on us – what a sight the man is!"

This last exclamation referred to a young man who at this moment stepped out of the thicket and approached them, but whose face was so ghostly pale and terror-stricken, and whose wide-open and lusterless eyes stared around so fearfully, that several of the women fell back in genuine horror, and Wilson sprang up and cried out:

"Halway – what the devil – have you lost your mind, running around in broad daylight like a corpse and frightening people? – What's happened?"

"Something dreadful!" moaned the young man, as he sank down exhaustedly on a tree trunk. – "Dreadful!" he repeated in a hollow voice. "Over there in the old log hut –"

"Well, what's there?" asked ten people at once.

"Just let me catch my breath first; over there in the old log hut – lies – I shudder when I think of it – lies the body of the Indian woman."

"Alapaha's?" cried the crowd, horrified. "Assowaum's wife? Terrible! Dreadful! Ghastly!" everyone screamed in confusion. "How did you find her? How did she die? What does she look like? Who is her murderer?" Thus, with the speed of thought, a thousand similar questions crossed each other.

"I don't know!" said Halway – "just give me some time first to pull myself together. – I ran the whole way from that horrible place in an almost incredibly short time. – Fear gave me wings –"

"But so just tell us – what happened then?"

"Just a moment – just a moment – well, listen then. For the last week I've been at the mouth of the river and was hunting there but left there the day before yesterday to bring back the dried skins of what I'd killed. Yesterday I thought that I could get to Tanner's house, but it was getting dark and I had to spend the night on the river bank, in thick cane. How many evenings I've spent outdoors in the woods alone, how many tempests, how many thunderstorms I've endured and never known any fear, but yesterday a few icy shivers ran through my body, and I stirred up my fire again, since I really wanted it as big as I needed it. I must have had an inkling of what was happening near me. But, in any event, everything else remained quiet; my dog barked just once, and it seemed to me as if I'd heard a horse snort, but that must have been a mistake, since the canebrake there is impassable and the river runs very deep just at that spot."

"Well, Hoswells had already promised me earlier to lend me his canoe, but first thing in the morning I saw bees at work and tried until almost mid-day to find the tree, and then when I didn't have any luck I looked around for the canoe, although with no better result. I crawled around every bend but couldn't discover anything but a neckerchief with provisions that a hunter must have hung up in the bushes and forgot, and at last I went up the road to swim across the river there."

"From there on it was my plan to travel upstream about another two miles to the left to get hold of another canoe that I knew was there. But I couldn't help noticing the peculiar flight of the vultures, which all seemed to alight not very far below the road. Also, two very fresh wolf tracks ran over the road in the same direction, and I decided, since I had nothing in particular to lose, to go and see just what sort of game lay there, or whether a bear maybe had slaughtered a hog, or maybe even a panther a horse. – Almighty God, I wasn't prepared for *that* sight!"

"When I reached the spot where the little hut stands, all overgrown with thick underbrush, I thought surely a hog had fallen into the claws of a hungry bear, all the more so since that morning I had noticed the tracks of one of them on the riverbank. But it puzzled me that none of the vultures dared come down; they all sat on the branches of the trees all around the hut and flapped their wings greedily as I came near them."

"And the wolves?"

"I didn't look for their tracks – I knew now that the carcass must be in the hut, and walked in, still not thinking about a human body; but – spare me a description, it was the body of the Indian woman, I recognized that before I fled – then I flew in a mad rush to the next house where, however, a little Negro girl told me that no one was home, but that everyone had gone to the prayer meeting here, and then I raced on as if an angry enemy were after me, on and on, to find human beings at least."

"But tell us about it then –"

"Nothing – nothing at all – you must see it yourself, and right away; the body mustn't by any means stay there tonight. The wolves that shied away today from going in a building where people once lived will, once it gets dark again, and that's not long from now, get up their courage and tear the body to shreds."

"But where is Assowaum?" asked Roberts. "Could he already be on the trail of the killer?"

"Would he have left his squaw behind unburied?" Bahrens interjected. "No – never!"

"It's not possible that Assowaum himself –," said Smith, looking around timidly, – "he was always opposed to her going the whites' prayer meetings, and has had some harsh words to say about her conversion to Christianity."

"I'd sooner believe that it was her own mother that killed her rather than Assowaum!" Roberts exclaimed vehemently, "I know how much he loved her.

Anyway, we must go, time flies, and it's no small distance to the place. Do you have pine in the house?"

"Enough," said Mullins, "and it could be split in a minute. I wanted to take it with me on Monday evening to the salt lick, but it's needed more for this – we can set out at once. Where's Mr. Rowson?"

"Here!" said the preacher, who until now, noticed by no one, had been leaning on a tree trunk. "We must go this instant and investigate the dreadful affair."

"Great God, Mr. Rowson," said Madame Roberts – "you really must stay here – you're sick – seriously sick and look as pale as death."

"But I really believe it's my duty," said the preacher, "even though I have a painful headache –"

"No, we won't allow it, no matter what," cried Mrs. Mullins – "and the sight wouldn't be good for you."

"But still, I don't know – my dear Sister Mullins –"

"Just stay here," Roberts now stepped into the conversation – "you really do seem unwell, and we don't require you for the sad task that we have in view *today*. Tomorrow, for the burial, is something else; then, if you feel strong enough in the meantime, we'll accept your help."

The preacher nodded his head silently in a half gesture of thanks and was about to turn to walk toward the house when his betrothed stepped into his path, stuck out her hand with a half shy, half friendly, look and softly whispered: "Good night, Mr. Rowson – go to bed and awake in the morning hale and hearty again – good night."

They were but soft loving words that came to him from the mouth of the sweet girl, but they gripped him like an icy fist in his inmost being, and terrified – devastated, he was about to shrink back from the touch of the innocent young girl. Then his eyes met the stares the bystanders fixed on him, his former strength of spirit awoke, he drew the blushing girl to him, pressed a soft kiss on her forehead, laid his hand in a blessing upon her locks, and then strode with firm steps to the house to take to the bed that, though it had been hurriedly prepared for him, was warm and soft.

"What an angel!" murmured Mrs. Smith, as she folded her hands, tilted her head to one side, and looked after him pensively.

"Like a saint," said Mrs. Pelter, who stood next to her and had heard her words – "the good soul grew pale as death when he heard them tell of the corpse, and fairly began to tremble. Oh, such a spirit –"

"Marion should thank her loving Lord God on her knees for giving her such a pearl," said Mrs. Smith.

"So when will the wedding be?" asked Mrs. Pelter.

"Well, it won't be *much* longer," opined Mrs. Smith, "since already just to-day – but they're already setting out, in fact. Are we women going with them?"

"No, that wouldn't work," said Mrs. Bahrens, "and my old man probably wouldn't like to see it either. I'm riding home; but tomorrow we'll all get together again for the funeral."

"Surely," replied Mrs. Smith, as she led her horse to a tree trunk lying nearby and, with its help, climbed into her saddle. Most of the others now followed her example, and a short time after the men burst out of the clearing on their fleet ponies and the departing sun sank down behind the row of hills in the west, the feminine portion of the congregation also left. That did not occur, however, without their having delivered further hearty regards and get-well wishes for their spiritual shepherd to the bustling hostess of the home, who in turn firmly promised to convey all of them, and to care for the invalid as she would for one of her own children.

Notes

1. That is, the new German settler.

2. Fort Gibson, established in 1824, located in what is now Muskogee County (Oklahoma), on the Grand River just above its confluence with the Arkansas River.

Chapter 16
The Deathwatch.

From Mullins' house to the old hut it might be about four miles in a straight line, but the men had put the distance behind them in an extraordinarily short time, and it was not quite dark yet when they reached the little "dead clearing," as such spots were called in the local tongue. Here Roberts stopped, tethered his horse – an example followed by all of his companions – and struck a fire. There were sixteen men, but none among them spoke a word; silently they gathered wood and kindled a bright flame, silently they bound together long stakes of split pine with thin strips of hickory bark – silently they lit these in the fire, and, led by Roberts and Wilson, entered the place of horror with pounding hearts.

The first two stepped nearly to the middle of the cabin, and almost up to the body of the unfortunate woman who had fallen here by a murderer's hand, while the others gently pressed forward and began to form a circle around the victim, so that the red glow of the pine torches held high above their heads cast a horrible illumination over all.

"She's been murdered!" Roberts said softly at last, and then softly the lips of the others echoed it:

"Murdered!"

The frightful fact could no longer be in doubt; the gash on her head, administered by a heavy American Bowie knife, alone would have been enough to kill her with a single blow, without the three stab wounds from the same broad and dangerous weapon that opened the red gates to the source of life. Further evidence that the first wound was the fatal one was supplied by the fact that her mantle of soft dressed skins was splattered with blood on one side only, and blood was not found anywhere else in the hut. After the first blow she must have remained there motionless, and died.

"Does anyone here have any suspicion in what manner, and at whose hand, this unfortunate one met her untimely end?" Roberts asked now. No one answered – at last Bahrens said:

"It's impossible to see into men's hearts, what is brooding in there. But this Indian woman seemed to me so fine and good, to be so pleasant and friendly,

that I can't understand how or in what way she could've made an enemy in
the settlement. I don't know anyone that I'd consider capable of carrying out
such a horror."

"Nor I – nor any of us," was the deeply resounding response.

"Who saw the deceased last?" Wilson asked now.

"I met them both, Alapaha and Assowaum, yesterday afternoon on the
other side of the river," replied Pelter; "they seemed friendly toward each other,
but who can fathom what an Indian's got in mind!"

"Assowaum is innocent," cried Roberts vehemently, "I'd answer for him
with my life!"

"*Why?*" then asked, from the door of the hut, the full resonant voice of the
chief, who at this moment appeared in the gathering, followed by Brown. Unsuspecting, he stepped toward the center as the men gave way to him on both
sides, half in awe and half in pity, so that he did not notice the horrible sight
until he stood close by the body of his wife.

"Wah!" he cried, and started up from the ground like a deer that is shot.
"What is this?"

"Alapaha!" cried Brown, horrified, who had followed him – "Alapaha! –
Great God! Murdered!"

"Murdered?" repeated the Indian in a wild and hollow tone, while his eyes
threatened to start from their sockets and his right hand involuntarily tore the
sharp scalping knife from his belt, as if it must find the heart of the treacherous being who had killed his wife. "Who says *murdered?*"

"Does that look like guilt, you men of Arkansas?" cried Roberts, as he laid
his hand on the shoulder of the savage and looked inquiringly at his friends.

"No – by God no! The poor Indian! Terrible! Who was the killer?" sounded
various cries from the farmers' lips, as Assowaum stared blankly at each man
in the circle who uttered a word, and for a moment really seemed to have
lost all awareness of his circumstances. Then Brown stepped close to Roberts,
pointed to the body, and said, in a soft voice, the least syllable of which could
nevertheless be easily understood:

"This is the second victim within a week that's fallen at the hand of a murderer; rumor laid the blood-guilt of the first one at *my* door; I've come here to
refute the accusation – to prove my innocence. My heart is innocent of such a
horrible crime, but the murderer lives among us."

"A few days ago it was my intention to leave this state and go to Texas; it
still is, but now not until the hand that caused that wound is found out, until
my name stands before the world clear and innocent once more. But it's not
my plans alone that have changed; I've changed my thinking as well."

"You know, men of Arkansas, many of you at least who are better acquainted with me, that until now I've been opposed to the aims and meth-

ods of the Regulators; I considered their illegality fully sufficient grounds to condemn them – I no longer think so. Here at our feet lies a murdered being who, harmless and innocent, insulted or caused grief to no one; who here has not been delighted by her unpretentious and amiable character, who has not been touched by her firmly held and faithful piety, whereby she renounced the faith of her tribe? She is dead – and the laws could not protect her; she is dead – and the laws are too powerless to find and punish her murderer. But here I raise my hand aloft and swear by the almighty God that I will not stay or stop until her blood, like that of the unfortunate one, is avenged; that I will not stay or stop until we find the brood of vipers that has crept in among us and crush their heads. Men of Arkansas, will you stand by me with your hands and with your hearts?"

"Yes!" echoed the hushed and gloomy reply throughout the lowly hut. "Yes! So help us God!"

"Then let us first of all carry the body to the nearest house; early tomorrow morning someone must get the preacher there – he'll be found in the settlement, surely. Then we'll bury the poor woman."

Several of the young men began to carry out this instruction, cutting poles to fashion a crude stretcher. Then Assowaum, who until now had been silently standing by the body, his gaze fixed on the features of his dead wife, stepped forward, gently with his arms pushed those next to him out of the way, and made a gesture as if he would ask them to leave the house.

"What are you going to do, Assowaum?" asked Brown.

"Leave me alone!" breathed the warrior, as he shoved the knife that he had held gleaming in his hand from the first instant back into its sheath. "Leave me alone with Alapaha – just this night."

"But shouldn't we–"

A disapproving gesture by the Indian forced them to obey his wishes. Silently they stepped back, and then softly conferred with one another outside the entrance to the hut as to what they should do.

"Wouldn't it be better if we camped outdoors here?" suggested Bahrens, when they had reached a fairly open but somewhat distant place. "Assowaum may keep the deathwatch, and then first thing in the morning we'll be on the spot."

"That's true," said Brown, "but Assowaum told me on the way that my uncle is ill, and that he had sent Alapaha to him with provisions. But the unfortunate woman was murdered, so the poor man lies alone and helpless in his cabin; I *must* be there early tomorrow morning at the latest."

"How'd it be, then," said Wilson, "if we go back to Mullins' now to first see how Rowson's doing, and whether he's in a condition to officiate at the solemn ceremony tomorrow, and then come back here before daybreak with some provisions for the Indian? Then we'll take Alapaha in the canoe to her own cabin, which lies close by our house. It'll also be the Indian's wish to have his squaw buried near his wigwam."

"But in this raging water only four people at most can sit in the canoe," said Roberts.

"No more should travel in it, by any means," replied Brown. "From Mullins' to Harper's, if you strike from Heinze's in a straight line through the woods, it's barely six miles, so only a little farther than from here; so Wilson and I will take on the removal of the Indian and the body, and the rest of you follow meanwhile with the minister by the land route; then we'll meet at my uncle's at pretty much the same time."

"Good," said Bahrens – "I agree with all that. But shouldn't we now, before we leave this place again, try to find traces of the murderers?"

"That'd be useless," interjected Roberts, "the ground here inside is too hard and dry to distinguish anything, and outside the rain that poured down in sheets after midnight has rubbed out everything. No, the murderer is safe from all pursuit for the moment, but whoever it is, he won't escape our avenging arm, and then neither a preacher's pious, hidebound admonitions nor a governor's empty threats will keep us from stepping in and punishing whoever would violate what's most sacred to us."

"I'd like to go in to Assowaum once more," said Brown hesitantly.

"Don't disturb him anymore this evening," Roberts asked him – "as an Indian he has his own views and feelings, and I hardly think that the sight of a white man would be welcome to him, even if it were a friend."

After this, the men lit once more their pine torches, which had been for the most part extinguished, mounted their horses, and rode slowly back toward Mullins' house. – But the desolate log house, tranquil and silent, enclosed the two beings who, if not quite friendless, still lived as strangers among a people that had destroyed their race, from the midst of which a murderer's hand had crushed its last delicate blossom.

The clear dark sky sparkled in all its midnight glory, rustling winds played with the towering tops of the enormous trees and beat the vast garlanded vines against the slender thrusting trunks in measured rhythms; the river raged foaming and roaring close by the half-fallen hut, and it was almost as if it licked greedily toward the bloody corpse, longing to carry it away in its arms, a toy for its still wilder accomplice, the wide and mighty Arkansas.

In the room within, though, paying no attention to the rustling of the tree tops or the mumbling roar of the agitated water, sat the Indian at his dead wife's feet, just as the men had left him, still gazing silently and pensively at her pain-twisted, bloody, but still so beautiful face. The fire was fairly burnt out, and only now and then a red gleam rose up out of it before its glow was extinguished, making the succeeding darkness all the more striking and gloomy. Then suddenly, as if stung by a viper, the red son of the forest sprang up – his eyes almost burst from their sockets; with trembling hands he threw what dry kindling he could find nearby on the nearly dead embers, stirred these into a new flame again with quivering haste, then turned feverishly to the corpse and studied her features with anguished care.

Alas! The uncertain flickering light had deceived him; it seemed to him as if the rigid features had come to life again, the pale lips had opened. He could not yet force himself to believe that the wife of his heart, his Alapaha, should lie here dead – dead at his feet; and to every ray of hope his sinking, grief-filled soul clung with the strength of despair. Alapaha, the flower of the prairies, was really dead – his loving gaze met only a corpse stripped of its soul and feeling, and sadly the burning kindling slipped from his weakened, powerless grasp.[1]

The momentary gleam of hope had, however, at least roused him from his dreamy lethargy; he brushed from his forehead the long and disheveled hair that streamed around his temples, glanced in near disbelief around the narrow room for a few seconds, and collapsed again with a shudder only after he met the fixed, ghostly stare of his beloved.

The wolves, which the previous night had not dared enter a structure built by human hands, now emboldened by hunger, came nearer to the place that held their ghastly prey. If the scent of numerous fresh tracks kept them back, their fear was increased by the presence of a living being, so that they soon drew themselves up in wide circles around the dwelling of the dead, and plaintively howled the fearful melodies of their funeral chant. Assowaum barely heeded them; he knew these hyenas of the forest but feared them not, and was concerned only with the former object of his love – now, of his pain. Once more he stoked the fire, the bright flame of which illuminated the walls of the hut as if it were daylight, and then paced, peering around and searching for clues and evidence of the crime that had been committed.

The hut, built many years before by a new settler who soon afterwards abandoned it again, had been used in the meantime, though very rarely, by hunters as a camping spot in stormy weather, and was thus completely neglected and ruined. The former owner likely had cultivated a small piece of land close by and grew corn on it, but now the field was overtaken by a vigorous growth of underwood with its closely branching roots, and even within the hut, isolated young shoots betrayed the rich vegetative power of the soil that here, cut off from rain and sunshine alike and nourished only by the moisture of the river flowing past, had pushed up several young oak and hickory saplings on the same spot where not so long ago people had dwelt under a sheltering roof. Near one of these shoots lay the corpse, and Assowaum now sought vainly for clues that might reveal the murderer to him. The ground was too hard to preserve the traces of human footprints in clear outline, and whatever might still have been revealed, the men had trampled. Only there, close by the little frame on which Alapaha had dried the venison killed by her husband – in the scattered ashes – he discovered, not yet disturbed by the others, the partial footprint of a man.

Assowaum regarded it long and carefully, but it was only the front part of the foot, and he could not determine the whole length. Then again, it came from the same sort of boot that Brown wore; it could be the young man's track that he had just now left in the hut. Even so, Assowaum measured the toe on the handle of his tomahawk and looked thoughtfully at the trampled ashes for several minutes more.

But such a clue was insufficient, and he walked around some more, looking for some object left behind by the murderer, and found – his beloved's bloodied tomahawk, which appeared to have been hurled into the corner of the hut by a rough hand, and there had so far escaped his eagle eye.

For the first time, a proud smile of triumph flashed across the features of the savage warrior when he noticed the traces of blood on his wife's light but sharp weapon: Alapaha had died a death worthy of an Indian woman, and the fiend who had destroyed her had first been bloodied by her hand. But this also brought to mind, with renewed intensity, the memory that his wife was dead, and, tightly clasping the tomahawk with his iron fingers, the savage warrior raised himself high, and looked around with flashing eyes as if to catch sight of the murderer and smash him to the ground with a cry of revenge on his lips.

Alas, too late! Where was this rescuing hand in the hour of need? Where was this strong heart in the moment of danger? Far – far from here, and the poor creature had to fall and bleed to death helpless and unprotected. Assowaum wildly ground his teeth together in impotent rage, as if this thought had just flashed through his burning brain. But at last the cool, calm deliberation of the Indian won out. Once more he searched through every nook, every corner of the little room, then left the hut and outside investigated every shrub and every visible patch of moss – in vain. The pouring rain had blotted out everything; but, between the river and the hut, which the rising flood had indeed already reached, his attention was caught by some birch branches, from which the leaves appeared to have been stripped violently. But still, as already said, the rising river had washed out the tracks under these, and the Indian turned back to the hut without having reached his object.

Here, he now prepared the deathbed for his murdered spouse; he spread out her blanket and laid her rigid limbs on it, he fetched water from the river and washed her bloody face and hair clean of the red, clotted life fluid, then he pushed his own blanket under her head so that she would rest soundly and softly as before in the old – beautiful days, and tried to fold her hands upon the heart that had loved him so faithfully and dearly. But her right hand remained tightly clinched, and he was about to give up the effort to loosen her death-stiffened fingers by force, when he felt something strange in them; he renewed his efforts, and in the corpse's grasp he found a dark horn button that she had seized and held onto in her death struggle.

But what was he to do with such a clue? How could it put him on the murderer's trail? Assowaum shook his head sadly, yet thrust his find into the ball-pouch at his side, and sat himself down again quietly at his wife's feet, as if she only slumbered and he would want to watch over her sleep.

He sat thus, motionless, for many hours; the fire fell in on itself, flickered and flared up several times, and died out at last; a thick darkness filled the small room – outside in the woods, the wolves shied away timidly from the human's presence, no sound interrupted the solemn quiet save the rippling and gurgling of the river. Even the owl shunned the gruesome place, and only far, far away, cooed its mournful cry to its companion, whom she then followed with soft silent strokes of its wings into the more hospitable hills. – All was silent, and still the dark figure squatted before the lifeless body, until outside the fresh morning breeze shook the dew from the bushes, a bright streak in the east announced the approaching day, and the night birds with loud and melancholy calls took leave of the retreating darkness.

Voices now sounded outside the hut, and Brown, accompanied by Wilson, once more entered the quiet chamber of sorrow. But the Indian appeared not to notice him; his eyes, which had not for a moment turned away from Alapaha's face, still lingered on the precious features, and only when his friend touched him with a gentle finger on his shoulder did he look up, as if awakened from a deep dream.

"Come, Assowaum!" Brown said then, as he held out to him a friendly hand. "Be a man – shake off this sorrow that threatens to consume you, and let us get to work, first to bury your wife, and then – *avenge her!*"

The Indian had listened impassively to the white man's words until the last reached his ear.

"*Avenge her!*" he cried, as he sprang up with flashing eyes – "Yes – avenge her – come, my brother – the sight of this corpse unmans me – come!" With this, he took his wife's small tomahawk and stuck it in his belt, but then with firm steps helped the two men carry the body to the rocking boat that swung at its vine tether on the waves that broke over the submerged trees.

Wilson now offered him some food he had brought along for him – but he refused it all, silently took his customary place in the canoe, and steered it; paddled by the strong arms of the two men, it shot forth with lightning speed over the boiling torrent, floating surely and smoothly downstream to Harper's house, about ten miles distant.

Note

1. The coming-to-life of a dead person is a key scene in *Wild Sports,* where FG's companion Erskwine ("Erskine" in the English translation), mauled by a bear, briefly appears to come alive again as FG is keeping watch next to his dead body.

Chapter 17
The Burial of the Indian Woman.

Harper's log cabin stood not quite a hundred paces from the bank of the Fourche La Fave, in the shade of young, slender hickory and mulberry trees; the two men, however, had only a short time before begun to make the land near the house arable, and fallen trunks still lay in complete and wild disorder on the northern side of the building, some hewn and some yet untouched. Around the house, however, many conveniences had been installed that were seldom found in the homes of ordinary farmers. Not only was a small window hewn out, but it was even furnished with real panes of glass; despite the proximity of the river, a well had been dug from which to obtain fresh healthy drinking water; and a well-filled "corncrib,"[1] as the repository for corn was called, revealed that the men, if they were not yet themselves growing grains, nevertheless suffered no want as a result, and had provided well for themselves. Chickens and ducks, indeed even a flock of proud turkeys, encircled the door, scratching and clucking and apparently waiting longingly for feed, while two strong brown horses, obviously brought up in the north, stood at the empty trough and rubbed at it with their noses, as if they were impatient and restless at not finding the usual number of corncobs in their usual place.

In the open space before the dwelling, the men who had gathered at Mullins' the evening before had just now assembled, and Roberts was particularly struck by the still, strange loneliness of the place. He rode quickly up to the open door of the house, jumped from his horse, stepped inside, and here found his worst fears confirmed. On a hard crude bed, the blanket thrown from him in the heat of a blazing fever, lay the otherwise so cheerful and friendly old man, who could hardly approach a single house in the neighborhood without being greeted by a hearty handshake and a friendly laugh, but who was now alone and helpless, without a soul to assist him, someone who could have handed him just a glass of water to cool his burning lips.

Shocked, Roberts and Bahrens stepped to the bed of the sufferer and took his hand, but he no longer recognized them, and, in wild and crazed visions of hunts and hikes, raved about his brother who loved another man's bride, and about his nephew who had slain his enemy and had now appeared before him covered in his victim's blood. At this moment Rowson, who had regained all of his steadiness and calm, stepped into the humble chamber and to the bed of the invalid, who at the sight of him rose up and cried out:

"Go away – go away – wash your hands – they're caked with blood – wipe off the blade, it could give you away – ha – your bullet hits home, what a hole it tears – the wound will be hard to heal – right through the brain."

Rowson paled and, shuddering, took a step backward, but Roberts, without turning his gaze from the face of the sick man, said softly: "He's dreaming about his nephew – he thinks he's guilty, and fears for his life."

"Wild fantasies," gently whispered the preacher, as he quickly pulled himself together and bent over the invalid.

"Mister Harper!" he then called to him kindly, as he laid his cold fingers on the other's burning forehead, "come to yourself, friends are nearby –" But he had not quite finished speaking when the sufferer rose up from his bed with a cry of agony.

"Water! Water!" he screamed, "the evil fiend stretches out his claws toward me. – It wasn't me who killed him, no, *who* – no, yes – but it was me – I'm the one – take – me – I struck the – blow," he whispered faintly, and then collapsed unconscious.

"He's really sick," said Bahrens sympathetically, "stay a little with him, and I'll get him a drink of water to slake his fever thirst. The livestock outside also must be fed; I can't bear to see them all running around here so hungry and abandoned."

Without another word Bahrens instantly set out to do what he said, and even before the men had come aground at the landing with their sad cargo, he had, assisted by Roberts, cooled the temples of the invalid with cold compresses, straightened up his bed, prepared a refreshing drink for him, taken care of the animals, swept and tidied the house, and put everything else in a little more comfortable and civilized order again. Meanwhile Rowson sat beside Roberts at the sick man's bed and handed him what he desired, until at last, after several hours of wild feverish dreams, he fell into a slumber brought on more by exhaustion than peace of mind.

Shortly afterward the canoe landed, and Brown and Wilson, followed by the Indian, carried the body up onto the riverbank and laid it down at the mossy foot of a mighty oak.

"Where should we dig the grave?" then asked Wilson, going up to Brown. But the Indian silently took the speaker's hand and led him about a hundred paces away from Brown's dwelling to a spot close to his own wigwam built of wide pieces of bark and undressed skins, to an old Indian burial mound, such as are found in great numbers in Arkansas, and said: "Let the Flower of the Prairies rest with the children of the Natchez. In old times, hate and discord inflamed the hearts of the Lenni Lenape[2] against their red brothers in the south. The Great Spirit has punished them for this – their ashes rest peacefully beside one another."

The men now dug out the earth at the indicated place with brisk fervor until they considered the grave sufficiently deep, and were about to lay the body in a casket that had been crudely nailed together the previous night, and that they had brought with them to the place. But in this they were interrupted by the Indian, who now brought out of his wigwam a number of fine dressed skins in which he wrapped his wife's body, and then with the help of Brown, whom Bahrens had driven out of the room so that he would not further disturb his uncle's brief restorative slumber, he laid his young wife into her last, quiet home.

Mullins now approached, hammer and nails in hand, to fasten down the lid. But the savage refused this as well, and wound his leather trapping thong around the casket, which he then removed again as the earth received its red child.

Upon this, Rowson stepped to the open tomb, and Assowaum had already made a gesture as if he would rebuff the white man's Christian ceremony when his gaze fell on the cross that the other held in his hand, and to which the dead woman had prayed with such reverence. He buried his face in his hands, knelt down next to the grave, and now for the first time a river of sorrow, long held back and manfully mastered, broke forth. His breast heaved convulsively, and tears seeped out between his dark fingers in great crystal-clear drops and trickled down into the piled-up earth that in a few minutes would cover the being for whom he had abandoned tribe and friends, home and parents, and had become a lonely wanderer among an alien people.

Meanwhile the Methodist minister began, in a soft and trembling voice, his funeral sermon over the remains of one who had been shamefully murdered by his own hand. He praised her virtue and piety; he lauded the zeal with which she had clung to the true God and believed in Him; he extolled her constancy and love for her husband and chief, and then beseeched heaven, toward which he did not dare to lift his fearful and criminal glance, for "mercy for the departed and – forgiveness for the hand that, perhaps in anger, shed innocent blood."

But he had not quite ended his prayer when a strange, savage fire seemed to flash through the Indian. Slowly he took his hands from his eyes, and as his stern, penetrating gaze met that of the minister, and the latter, secretly shuddering, fell silent before the dark burning eyes of the warrior, the chief proudly straightened himself up; he grasped with his right hand his wife's tomahawk, which he still carried in his belt, and, stretching out his left hand toward the Methodist, spoke in a loud, sonorous voice:

"Alapaha is dead – her spirit has gone to the blessed fields of the *white* man; her heart had turned from the Great Spirit, whose vengeance has now caught up with her; but why does the pale man ask *his* god for mercy on a woman who forgot *everything*, to belong only to *him*? – who renounced the faith of her people and prayed to the white god? She needs no mercy – you have often told me that your god is just, and Assowaum's wife should not have to beg once for mercy from a god from whom she can demand justice. If your god is just, he must reward the unhappy one, who forgot what was once dear and holy to her, because of him."

Rowson was about to interrupt him, but he was held back once more by the gaze quietly fixed on him by the savage, who in a voice steadily louder and more forcefully resounding continued:

"But your lips also beg forgiveness for the murderer. He dipped his venomous hands in the innocent heart's blood of the Flower of the Prairies; who here did not know her and – did not love her? No! No forgiveness – a *curse* upon the killer – Assowaum will find him – his life has from now on but *one purpose: to punish the murderer*. Whether he is covered with white or red earth, the Great Spirit will welcome him with open arms and a smiling face."

Rowson, who, with a mighty effort of body and will, had constrained himself to endure the dark, menacing gaze of the warrior, now almost silently raised his hands, as if deep in quiet prayer, and after a long and reverent pause said:

"Forgive him, Lord, forgive this unfortunate man, who, overwhelmed by bitter sorrow, has spoken words of wrath and hate that are not pleasing in your sight. Forgive him, Lord – forgive us all who stand here indignant at a deed that was, after all, decreed by your inscrutable wisdom. – Forgive us, that we too perhaps nurture thoughts of anger and revenge, and enlighten us by your radiance that we may come to know that only in your grace, in your peace, lies the salvation that makes us good and God fearing people, and strengthens us to lift up our eyes to you, the Almighty, with pure hearts. Amen!"

"Amen," whispered the bystanders in reply; only Assowaum remained standing in gloomy silence, his right hand always on the tomahawk, until the men took hold of the casket and carried it and placed it in the narrow tomb. Then even his pride was broken, and he sank down before the grave with his hands pressed to his face; by the time he rose up again, the little mound had been rounded, and on its top end, Rowson placed the black cross.

The ceremony was ended, and the neighbors retired to their dwellings; only Bahrens and Wilson stayed with Brown in their friend's little cabin to care for him in his illness, to the best of their abilities. Brown, however, went up to Rowson before he departed, thanked him for his kindly effort to help bury the body of the unfortunate woman, especially when he himself was sick and weary, and invited him, in case he did not wish to return right away, to consider the house as his own. But Rowson kindly declined the offer, since he had so many preparations to make for the altered life shortly in store for him that he could not think of idly wasting whole days, and with an amicable blessing on his lips and deep humility and piety in his glance, he took leave of the young man, who looked after him for a long while, deep in dark broodings. – *That* was the man who had robbed him of all earthly happiness, or anyway had made it impossible for him to attain it. *That* was the man to whom his beloved had sacrificed heart and hand, to whom she must belong from now until the time that death's iron grip would break the bonds that, tied by God Himself, must be unbreakable in *life*.

"Farewell," he whispered softly, "farewell, you beautiful dream that I dreamed once in my crazy, youthful fantasies – farewell, you picture of domestic happiness that I see all around me with Tantalus-like torments, but that remains always withheld from my longing lips. – Farewell, you lovely, pure being, and God ease your sorrow! Forget the unfortunate whose baleful fate threw him into your path to shatter your – his peace. – Farewell!"

"Farewell," whispered Assowaum, who had stepped to his side and heard the last words. – "Farewell – a wonderful word to call out to a dead woman!"

"A dead woman?" asked Brown, starting with alarm.

"Did you not speak with Alapaha?"

"I spoke with a dead woman," whispered Brown, burying his face in his hands, "she is dead – dead – dead!"

"Dead!" moaned Assowaum in a dull echo. "Murdered, but I must find the murderer. – The spirit bird[3] will whisper it in my ear in dreams each night; I will lie next to her grave until I hear his voice. – Will my white brother stand by me for the sake of the dead one? Will he lend his muscle to the arm of his friend before he goes to another land, to fight for the freedom of a strange people?"

Brown silently extended his hand to him, and then walked slowly back to the bed of his sick uncle, while the Indian, conquering his sorrow for the moment, set about with lively diligence to build a roof for the grave from heavy pieces of bark, to keep the rain off it. The sun had already begun to slope once more toward its setting when he completed his wife's final dwelling place, and now in the upper part of it, where the head of the corpse rested, he cut a small opening with his tomahawk.

Brown, meanwhile, could not bear to stay long at the bed of the invalid, to whom he could be no further use for the moment anyway, and he returned to Assowaum to provide some drink and food for him. Just as he came up to him, the Indian was busy hewing out the opening in the roof.

"So now you're destroying again what you've built?" Brown asked him.

"I am not destroying it," said the savage, "but the spirit must have a way out, so that it may leave the body and return to it."

"The spirit doesn't come back, my poor friend," the young man sadly rejoined, "it's gone up there, where the blessed dwell. – It won't miss the earth."

"There are *two* spirits," whispered the Indian softly; "two spirits there are," he repeated more fervently, when he saw that the white man shook his head in disbelief. "Does not Assowaum's spirit fly in dreams back to the hunting grounds of his people? Does it not see there the wigwam before whose door he played his earliest childhood games? Does it not follow the elk through dark ravines as it breaks its way, snorting and crashing, through the thick woods? Does it not see there his father, who with a strong hand helps the weak boy bend the bow? Yes – it is far – far away in distant lands, and still Assowaum lives – he lies on his bed and breathes. Could he breathe if he had just *one* spirit, and this lingered in the land of his people, while he lived among the huts of the whites by the rushing water?* No – the red man has two spirits."

As night fell, Assowaum took the food that Brown had brought him, placed it next to the opening at the head of the grave, and then lit a small fire before it that he tended carefully while he – as thicker and thicker darkness descended on the slumbering earth – sang, in a soft plaintive voice, the dreary and dreadful death song of his people:

> Oh where – oh where
> Do you linger, darling? See, there blossom
> Here in the valley
> All the flowers, all – just you are gone.
> Oh where – oh where
> Sounds the voice that I loved?
> Hark, there resound
> A thousand voices, a thousand – just you are gone.
>
> Over there – over there
> In the top of that oak tree
> Sits the bird
> And he sings the spirit's loud lament.
> Over there – over there
> Is your spirit; oh will I never
> Here in the valley
> Hear again your lovely voice?

---

* FG's note: "Arkansas" (that is, the Arkansas River).

Below – below,
Right on the ground I lie listening
Here in the valley,
And I hear your voice in the grave
Below – below,
Your soft – soft laments;
And they call,
Urging me to revenge – Love, I obey!

Notes

1. "Corncrib" is misspelled "corncrip" in FG's original.

2. The Lenni Lenape or Delaware (with all their related Algonquian tribes, including the "Mohicans") were the models for James Fenimore Cooper's noble Indians. The Natchez lived near the present-day city of the same name in southwestern Mississippi. The conflict asserted by FG between the Natchez and Delaware, the southern boundary of whose original domain was Delaware Bay, is not historical.

3. "The spirit bird": compare with earlier reference to the "ghost-bird" (see note 1, chapter 11).

Chapter 18

Roberts' Adventure on the Panther Hunt. – The Water Party.

Two full weeks had elapsed since the scenes described in the previous chapter, but all efforts to track down the criminal had been fruitless, and in vain Brown, whose uncle had nearly recovered by this time, had searched and worked with tireless zeal to find a trace of the murderer.

Assowaum himself could not be persuaded to leave his wife's grave for several days after her burial. But then he suddenly disappeared, and even Brown did not know where he had gone.

But the settlers were not at all discouraged by these unsuccessful efforts, and saw in them only a so much more compelling proof of the need to band together to protect their rights, since in this case too the courts could not have unearthed a thing, and the murderer seemed, for now at least, to be secure and undetected. Convinced of the necessity of taking a serious step, the majority of the farmers had joined the association that called itself the "Regulators," and a general meeting, that promised to be very well attended, was set for the following day – a Saturday. There even more serious steps were to be agreed on, particularly with regard to suspicious individuals residing in the neighborhood, but who could not be proved to have actually committed crimes and made to appear before their court. Possibly they could tie together threads in the case that would put them on the culprits' trail – if only that of the horse thieves at first, among whom they hoped, and not without reason, to discover the murderer of the two victims.

The warm sunshine rested genially on the green leafy canopy of the forest. – A quiet stillness reigned over the magnificent natural world, not the slightest breeze stirred; but deep, deep within the dark thicket below, there where the Fourche La Fave forced its current through pathless canebrakes and darkly shadowed overhanging swamp trees, the hunt was going full blast, and now the muted baying, now the sharp yapping of the hounds rang out.

"Yoo-hoo – yoo-hoo – you dogs – whoo-pee!" cried Roberts, as he hurtled along on a foaming steed across a broad, swampy patch and spurred the animal, already inflamed by the joyous zeal of the hunt, to even greater efforts through loud yells and powerful jabs from his heels, so that it lashed out wildly and leapt forward into a maze of thickly grown vines. The pack was out ahead, and the scattered hunters each rushed after them in whatever manner their horses could carry them, or as the course they happened to follow would permit, each encouraging the dogs with piercing hunting screams as soon as he could only hope that they could hear him.

"Whoopee!" shrieked Roberts once more, as, his rifle in his left hand, his right armed with his heavy hunting knife to chop through the climbers and vines as necessary, he flew over a huge fallen cypress, at the same time with a mighty blow slicing through a cable-like green thorn liana that had grown together with another and threatened to impede his progress. In doing so, however, he had overlooked another vine that was flimsier but no less tenacious, and before he could raise his hand for another blow, or rein in his pony wildly thundering toward it, the animal slid just under it, and the next moment Roberts lay with rifle and knife next to the trunk that he had just leapt over with such a bold move.

"The plague!" he murmured, as he prepared to work his way out of the viscous mud in which he had just landed with his shoulders. "Here, pony! Come – come on – pony![1] The devil take the beast, I think he wants to go hunting all on his own!" – And he had a point; the intelligent animal, which Roberts had ridden in all his hunts, took too great an interest in the chase himself than to wait on his master and thus be deprived of a having a wonderful time. Like a tempest gone wild he thus followed the pack, liberated from his heavy rider, and in a few seconds he was no more heard or seen.

"It's gone, for a fact!" said the old hunter, grumbling, after he had looked around and listened attentively for several minutes. "Not a trace to be seen – now I'm as good as stranded. – Well, then, I'd really like for them – but wait, the hunt's turned around toward the hills; so it's not at all impossible that the panther, if he doesn't escape to the Petit Jean, will turn down here to the low ground once more, and in that case his favorite spot is the cane brake over there across the river. Wait, my boy, maybe I'll be at the harvest after all, despite my old bones. – Patience, patience – I've found myself in worse fixes before." Roberts' thoughts now apparently led him back again to the Revolutionary War. He smiled to himself with great self-satisfaction, and proceeded toward the nearby river, since he had, during the preceding soliloquy, cleaned the mud off his rifle and poured in fresh powder, and stuck his knife in its sheath again.

Here, however, a new difficulty presented itself to the man lifted from his saddle: namely, how to get across. In vain he sought for some distance up and down to find a shallow spot somewhere that he could use. Then he saw, close by the steep bank, a rotting tree trunk that it seemed a bear had been working on very recently, stripping off several pieces. But now, unfortunately, the dogs had found a warm panther trail, and it would have been impossible to distract them from it even if Roberts had entertained such a thought. But, in fact, he never thought of it at all. Only a few days before, a panther had torn apart one of his foals, and the next night a large fully-grown work horse, upon whose neck it had sprung from out of a tree; in any event, the most important thing to do was to take this creature out of circulation.

But the old hunter also knew how reluctant the panther would be, if it actually sought out again its recently abandoned hiding place, to swim across the river a second time. It was, therefore, all the more necessary to get to the other bank quickly. Moreover, the howling of the pack had become more audible again from across the way, and the hunt could turn in that direction any moment. So Roberts rolled and lifted the aforementioned piece of rotted timber to the edge of the steep bank, threw it down, and then, holding onto the roots of the reeds and cane, climbed down to the water himself; he laid his rifle on the timber, and was just about to begin his crossing when he heard the barking and yelping of the dogs very close by. It was quite easy to see them as they rushed to the water again, and then suddenly broke out in such a wild and frantic howling that Roberts could only think that the panther was treed and had therefore, for the moment, escaped the teeth of its pursuers.

But now there was no more time to lose. He shoved the timber into the stream, and had just reached the deeper water and was about in the middle of the river, when, on the river bank lying opposite, the bushes rustled, the dry cane snapped, and at almost the same time a dark form appeared on the outermost edge of the riverbank, and with the speed of thought threw itself into the current, which closed over it.

It was the panther, and it went under so close to the hunter that he was showered with the splashing water. The small, agitated waves rocked his crude raft as the head of the predator reemerged and the animal headed for the other bank. But by now Roberts had recovered his full composure and presence of mind, which had abandoned him in the first instant of the unforeseen surprise. The lock on his rifle had fortunately remained dry; he quickly drew back the hammer and, with his left arm resting on the timber while he slowly treaded water with his feet, he aimed, in this by no means comfortable position, at the panther, which just now emerged, sleek and dripping water. Struck by the bullet, it jerked upward and slid back into the stream; Roberts was about to let out a shout of triumph, but he slightly miscalculated the equilibrium of the raft, and in the same instant he disappeared with gun and powder horn into the murky current, as the wounded animal roused itself again and, with hurried leaps, fled up the steep slope.

Just as Roberts came back to the surface again, sputtering and splashing, the dogs, which until now had been howling on the trail they had lost, reached exactly the place from which the panther had leapt away. But as little inclined as they had otherwise been to take to the water, now they willingly followed their agile leader when they noticed the dark figure in the water, which they at that moment took for the adversary they were chasing. Roberts' situation at this instant was by no means enviable, for if the hounds, whimpering with excitement and making for their supposed foe with all their might, had reached him while he was still in deep water, the pack would have jumped on him and suffocated him before he would have been in a position to convince them of their error. Being where he was, however, he noticed the danger he faced while there was enough time to swim to the bank, still holding hard and fast to the heavy rifle in his left hand, and no sooner had he reached a place where he could feel the ground than the hounds surrounded him, and Poppy himself went for him. But he quickly raised himself to his full height, shoved the one nearest away from him with his rifle butt, and angrily shouted in a furious voice at the shocked dogs looking up at him:

"Back, you beasts – you damned curs, you – back – you, Poppy, you useless scoundrel – would you bite your own master? Back there, you rogue – get on the *right* trail and go to the devil – *you, Poppy!*" This last exclamation was again addressed, however crudely, to his own dog, which now recognized its master and joyfully tried to swim up to him. But Roberts, whose misgivings persisted, did not entirely trust the truce, took a defensive step backward, fell into a somewhat deeper hole, and, of course, instantly disappeared once more under the water, just as Bahrens appeared on the bank. The latter quickly raised his rifle up to fire upon the panther, for he too believed that he was dealing with none other than the predator they were pursuing. But this time it was the dogs that protected the hunter from his companion's bullet, for in order to avoid shooting one of them, he held his fire, and quickly afterward, to his no small astonishment, recognized his friend. But Roberts never once suspected this new danger, only sputtered out the water he had swallowed as soon as he reached firm ground, and then, cursing, put the dogs on the trail of the animal he had shot. The pack had hardly scented the fresh blood, however, when they stormed after the prey in a wild uproar and cornered it not long afterward while still in the valley.

"Hello, Roberts!" Bahrens now called out from the bank. "What the devil are you doing there in the Fourche La Fave?"

"I'm playing crawfish!" cried the other, still vexed at his less than comfortable situation, as he climbed out of the water and scrambled up onto the slippery river bank. His jest, though, was to prove true, for twice more before he could reach a secure elevation, he slipped and went backward again much faster than he had struggled to ascend, each time to the delight of his friend, who was holding his sides with laughter. Finally his perseverance prevailed; arriving at the top, he grabbed a young tree trunk, swung himself up, and vanished into the thicket without honoring his jubilant friend with so much as a glance.

The latter then hastened at once to his horse, which he had left a short distance away when he heard the hounds in the water; he mounted again and galloped toward the ford which was located farther upriver. But he came to the scene of battle too late, for while he was still in the canebrake he heard the sharp crack of a rifle, and immediately afterward the whining of the dogs, which were crowding eagerly under a tree. The panther was still hanging on above them when he stepped into the small, open patch in which the entire hunt was now concentrated. Claws sunk deep in an oak branch, it clung to the safety of the wood with muscles fully tensed; but soon a convulsive jerk of the freely swaying body gave proof that the badly wounded animal was in its death struggle. Its paws opened, and it plunged into the midst of the wildly rejoicing pack, right onto one of the young dogs whose backbone it broke in the fall, and which then sought to crawl out from under the heavy body, whining and howling.

At first it was hardly possible to pull the poor, crippled animal out from among the raging dogs that were tearing the dead panther apart. But finally the combined strength of the two men managed it, and Cook, one of whose hounds it was, and who clearly saw that nothing more could be done for the poor creature, held the muzzle of his rifle to its forehead and with a bullet put an end to its suffering.

"Well, that's now the seventh dog I've seen die that way," said Bahrens angrily, as he struck his rifle butt on the ground, "but the dumb brutes can't be pulled away when a beast like that's sitting above. Then, before they know it, down it comes and wipes out a couple of them with its great, clumsy bones."

"A bear I shot last year," said Roberts, his teeth chattering from the frost, "knocked two dead this way and broke a third's left hind leg. I had to use my knife on him."

"Hello, Roberts," laughed Bahrens, "you look lovely; we'd better make a fire. But, Cook, where'd you come from? I haven't seen you for a couple of weeks, since that time you went on that useless chase after the wrong horses. Did you shoot the beast?"

"Yes," replied Cook, who had just cleaned out and loaded his rifle again, "I was over there at Harper's and heard the hounds so close by that it was impossible for me to stay sitting still in the house."

"Are we indeed very near Harper's, then?" asked Roberts – "this area here seems somewhat familiar to me. It's right over there, isn't it, behind those cypresses?"

"Hardly five hundred paces from here," Cook replied to him; "we'd best go to the house right away; Mr. Roberts can dry out there, and there'll still be time to skin the beast."

"I wish I knew where my horse was," said Roberts anxiously, "at least that the bridle hasn't gotten hung up in the bush somewhere. I made a knot in it, of course, and it can't hang down very far, but still it's possible."

"Don't worry," said Bahrens, "here comes Mullins and he's bringing it with him. – Where was the horse, Mullins?"

"It was standing there, where the panther probably crossed the river for the first time, grazing; the bank was likely too steep for him," cried Mullins, who at this moment arrived with the missing animal; "but hello, that's a big fellow. It doesn't surprise me that he could knock down that good-sized horse."

It was indeed an unusually large panther, which they had been chasing after since daybreak before they could get it up the tree. And probably it would not have been cornered yet were it not for Roberts' bullet, which had pained and weakened it. It was now about to be lifted onto Cook's horse; but though Cook assured them that the horse had already carried more than ten bears without betraying the slightest indication of fear, nevertheless it was not to be coaxed under any circumstances to allow the dead panther within even five feet of it. In vain they rubbed the blood of the slaughtered animal on its muzzle – it was not the blood from which it shrank, it was the sharp and to him terrifying scent, and the men finally realized that they would have to skin the panther then and there, and take with them only the hide. But only with real difficulty could they get even this on the back of one of the horses, which constantly shied with its head thrown back, and tried to escape the unwelcome load by every imaginable antic.

Soon, however, they arrived at Harper's dwelling, tethered their animals to the surrounding bushes there, and walked in.

Note

1. In FG's original text, the command appears as "Kob-Kob" – perhaps an (untranslatable) reference to the sound the rider makes.

BRUIN AT BAY.

Figure 19.1. "Bruin at Bay." Lithograph after a crayon drawing by Harrison Weir (1824–1906). From Friedrich Gerstäcker, *Wild Sports in the Far West, Translated from the German* (Boston: Crosby, Nichols and Company, 1861). Image courtesy of the translators.

Chapter 19

Harper's Dwelling. – Cook's Account of the Pursuit of the Horse Thieves. – Harper's and Bahrens' Wonderful Tales.

But the place seemed not quite as friendly and comfortable as before, when Harper was still healthy and conducted his little bachelor household with good humor. To be sure, he had fairly recovered his health in the last week, but the weakness that was one of the inevitable consequences of a fever remained, and was still easy to discern in all of his efforts; indeed, even his face – normally so full of a zest for life, healthful and ruddy – had taken on a quite ugly ashen color, and his cheekbones jutted out from it, as if they themselves, amazed at such a transformation, wanted to look around the rest of the face.[1]

But the neighbors did not forsake him in his time of need; all were good to him and took turns with Brown at his bedside as long as he was forced to lie there, and often spent days there to distract him and cheer him up.

Bahrens especially had taken a particular liking to him and had become a frequent and very welcome guest in the cabin of the two men.

Harper was resting on a crudely constructed bed, on his mattress stuffed with Spanish moss, and his eyes, if they did not still glow with their old fire, gleamed with something like their accustomed friendliness at the sight of his treasured guests. Greeting them heartily, he stretched forth his rather emaciated and pallid hand to the new arrivals, especially Roberts and Bahrens.

"Welcome, all of you! Welcome, Roberts, you're an old devil indeed; so, it takes wild beasts to get you to come see me; not bad, eh? But God bless me, how you look! As if you've been hauled out of the water, indeed. Hey, Bill, give Roberts some other clothes to wear, won't you, he'll catch his death from it."

"Thank you, thank you," said the other, as the young man brought him a warm dry outfit and helped him out of one set of clothes and into another, "thank you very much; – but, Brown – I have a particular bone to pick with you; my old woman's pretty cross with you, that you make yourself so scarce nowadays. Ever since that panther business, when Marion was with you, where you must've shot the beast pretty good, since I heard that Cook's oldest boy found it two days later, the skeleton at least, and a part of the skin, the buzzards had otherwise –"

Brown would have quietly let him go on talking, but Cook grabbed him by an arm and cried:

"Hello there – now we're off again, headed straight east like the mail – so – sit down there by the fire, and you, Harper, likewise kindly come closer to the chimney, since even though we've stopped up the cracks pretty well, there's still enough of a draft that you could get chilled again. The damned wind whistles right through."

"Do you perhaps have a wash basin here?" asked Roberts; "in climbing out of the river I stuck my hands so damnably deep in the mud –"

"Oh, Cook, be so good as to give him the iron dishwashing pan – the one without a handle – you know the one."

"Do I know it?" laughed the young farmer, as he used a long-handled gourd to slop water out of a bucket standing before the door of the cabin into the requested vessel. "Naturally I know your pots and pans here, maybe better than you yourself just now. It doesn't take long for a fellow to get to know them."

"No towel?" asked Roberts.

"Well, you surely have a neckerchief with you, no?" said Cook.

"Yes – but it's gotten all wet."

"Oh, well then, take mine here."

"You must tell me about the hunt!" cried Harper. "That's a remarkably big panther skin – won't you spread it out, Cook? There're probably still some cane stalks outside, in front of the door. – Just hang it on the little maple tree on the right here – but up high – the damned dogs pulled down and ate the last deerskin that I had to work so hard for – the beasts!"

Roberts now had to tell what happened to him; meanwhile Cook stretched the skin out and made it secure, but in the process had plenty to do to prevent the narrator from embarking on all sorts of detours and multiple repetitions.

"Say, now, Roberts," he cried at last, when the other had finished, "did you go on so when you courted your current wife? – So help me, I'd have lost patience if I'd been in her place."

"Leaving that aside for now, Cook," said Roberts, "today's the first time I've seen you or even a single one of those that set off on the wrong trail of the horse thieves a couple of weeks ago; what happened there, really?"

"Yes, he hasn't told me about that yet either," cried Harper, "and yet he's here a couple of hours a day."

"You were sick," replied Cook, "why should I torment you then with that boring story; well, the matter is very simple. We found the tracks that led through the river and followed them, since we naturally took them for the right ones and had not come across any others anywhere. Besides, Husfield claimed, before we rode down into the river, that he could swear that they were his own horses. But he must've been mistaken. We didn't look long on the other bank; we threw the torches away and then thundered after the supposed thieves as fast as our already pretty tired nags could race."

"We stopped only once the first night to let our horses rest and ourselves to eat a bit, and there we heard that a man with horses had come by and was riding pretty hard. Naturally, the farmer had only heard the clatter of the horse hooves and hadn't seen the animals themselves but assured us that we'd catch up with him soon, if that's what we intended, since they'd just passed by there hardly half an hour earlier. 'My poor horses,' Husfield moaned at that point, 'how that dog will wear them out now, but God have mercy on him if I catch up with him, for here on *this* rope' – he was carrying a rope with him – 'he'll thrash out his black soul!' It was easy for him to swear vengeance. At daybreak, as we were following tracks clear as day and galloping down a little slope with the reins dropped, suddenly we came upon the man with the horses sitting quietly under a tree, but when he noticed our approach, he didn't make the least effort to flee. I looked at Husfield in astonishment, but he stared wide-eyed over at the horses, and finally cried out as he reined in his own horse: – 'Hell and damnation, those aren't mine!' He was absolutely right; there were a couple of whites there that none of us knew, and the stranger rode his own horse and was none other than that fellow Johnson, who's been hanging around the Fourche La Fave for some time and, as far as I know, is making a living as a hunter."

"Husfield was furious, especially since, as he later confessed to me, he had a particular loathing for the slovenly fellow and expected the worst of him. But there was nothing at all to be done in this case. We rode over to the horses, but Johnson gave us very curt answers and replied to a question about what he planned to do with the horses, 'hopefully he could do what he wanted with his own animals.'"

"Husfield gnashed his teeth with rage, and though I straightaway tried to bring him back to his senses, he was too agitated, and it didn't take long for the two men to be trading hostile words with each other. Of course, Johnson remained very cold-blooded and calm through it all, though he kept his right hand buried beneath his vest the whole time, where naturally he had stuck his pistols and knife."

"Husfield swore the most fearful oaths at last, that he'd lynch him the instant he found him on his own land, and Johnson laughed at that and replied that sometime soon he'd enjoy the pleasure of visiting him. Finally I got them away from each other. But now it was futile to find any further tracks; the rain in the night had washed everything away, and we had to give up the chase. Meanwhile, Husfield held hard and fast that the animals were still in the settlement, and we searched out every corner of the bottom land where a horse could've possibly got into, but to no avail. They're gone, but *how* is a puzzle to me."

"And *where to*, I suppose?" said Bahrens.

"Well, that less so, since probably to Texas. I must just go to Texas myself sometime, to get to know the folks there. Even if you don't find any *humans* you know there, you're sure to find some familiar horses."

"It was also the same evening on which the Indian woman was murdered, wasn't it? You didn't hear anything from that quarter, then?" asked Roberts. "You must have passed very close by the place."

"I think – yes, at least it seems to me someone mentioned that he heard a cry. That was right when we came to the ford, and it would've probably been the poor woman; the distance between the hut and the road isn't considerable at all. Don't you know, then, Brown, where the Indian is?"

"No," he answered, "four days after his squaw's burial, in which time he kept a small fire burning at her grave and constantly put fresh food near it, he left the area, or at least he hasn't let himself be seen again by any of us. Still, I expect him to come back any day, for I don't believe, and never will, that he'd leave the country *before* fulfilling his oath of vengeance."

"But where could he be roving about?"

"Don't worry about that," said Bahrens – "he creeps around and spies; who knows how soon he'll come back, and where he's found a nest. You Regulators could wish for no better ally than that same Indian."

"Is it true, Brown, that they've chosen you as leader in Heathcott's place?" asked Roberts.

"Husfield and me," replied the young man, "he on the Petit Jean, me on the Fourche La Fave; but I'll resign my office as soon as my vow is fulfilled and the murderers of young Heathcott, and that of the Indian woman, are discovered and punished. But I hear that Mr. Rowson's going to preach very zealously against the union of the Regulators as something not only illegal but even unchristian too."

"He traveled a week or so ago," said Roberts, "as I hear, to the Mississippi and to Memphis, to make various purchases there, but must return again this week. As far as I know, he wants to buy Atkins' land, which is very good soil, if there weren't so much swampland –"

"Atkins will sell?" asked Mullins. "I haven't heard a word about that. So he already has a buyer?"

"Rowson seems to like the land," said Roberts, "and I have nothing against it, and at least Marion won't be so far away then. And, we'll build the new meeting house there on the road to the Left Hand Fork, since the logs for that were cut last Christmas, and I should gather them together –"

"Gentlemen, move your seats here to the table and kindly take whatever we have," intervened Brown, who meanwhile had been preparing the simple meal with Cook's help.

"What do you say we taste a piece of panther meat?" laughed Roberts.

"Thank you kindly," said Bahrens, "thank you, I tried it once, and it was so disgusting it nearly made me sick to death."

"Where was that?" cried Harper, who had just guided his cup of tea to his mouth and now paused in expectation.

"Where was that? Well, out there in the woods, where else?" replied Bahrens – "it was on the Ouachita, and we'd been hunting the whole day until late in the evening, when I returned without so much as a claw to the place we'd arranged –"

"You had been stretching your legs, I suppose?" asked Roberts, winking aside to Harper.

"Oh go to the devil!" said the other, as he continued his tale – "returned to the campsite we'd arranged to meet at. Things were going pretty lively there. A heap of bones lay by the fire, and right next to it, over a short lopped off branch from a little low wild plum tree, hung a skinned fawn, a young one, the others said, which would taste delicious; the feet, head, and one of the haunches were missing, though, and when I asked after them, they told me they'd eaten the haunch and fed the rest to the dogs. Well, I don't waste any time when it comes to venison; I cut myself off a healthy piece, and roasted and devoured it all by myself, since the rascals claimed they'd had enough."

"I was right in the middle of my meal when my dog, who was hungry too and had been sniffing all around, comes along and brings something he's carrying in his mouth right up close to me, as if to say: 'You, look here, see what they've shot,' and what was it? The head of a young panther. The bite I was chewing got stuck in my throat, and I looked up in shock at the grinning rascals who were sitting all around me. But when they couldn't hold it in any longer and burst out in roaring laughter, I decided to lie, and make them believe that panther meat was one of my favorite dishes. I choked down the bite that was stuck and wouldn't budge, cut me off another piece, and asked them with the plainest expression in the world, why they hadn't told me right away that it was panther meat, that then it would've tasted twice as good. – In Tennessee once I'd lived for a whole month on nothing but panther meat, only sometimes on Sunday I'd eat a wildcat."

"Meanwhile they stood with their traps open in astonishment, and one of them, a young fellow of sixteen, sat right across from me and watched, chewing along with me in his mind and making the most horrible faces, since my mouthful was apparently disgusting to him. But the bite I had in my own mouth wouldn't go down; the more I worked on it with my teeth, the more it swelled up – I forced myself to it for a while, but finally I couldn't hold out any longer, jumped up and – well, you don't need to know the rest now. – Listen, Brown, the turkey's delicious – have you shot many this spring?"

"It's going all right," said the young man, still smiling at what he had just heard, "moreover, they're very fat this year and have an excellent taste."

"Have you ever eaten a rattlesnake?" asked Mullins.

"No, thank you," said Harper, whom the tea had perked up a bit, and who today for the first time in a long while felt well and cheerful again, "thank you kindly – the creatures have good looking meat, as tender as chicken, but they reek so deadly."

"Only the body," interjected Mullins, "the tail's a delicacy."

"Doesn't the poison hurt anything?" asked Bahrens, surprised.

"Not if you swallow it," said Brown, "anyway, there's no poison in the flesh, just the smell is deadly, otherwise it's harmless, and I know one person who's eaten a sizeable piece of the 'horned snake,' which, as you know, is said to be the most poisonous, without it harming him in the least."[2]

"Is it *ever* poisonous!" cried Harper. "I saw a horned snake like that once sliding up and down a great oak and was just about to shoot it. Then it got mad and ran around and bit one of the little shoots that grow here and there at the base of the trunk in springtime; right after that it stayed quiet for a moment, and I sliced off its head with a bullet. But the oak still died the same month; the little stalk where it'd been bitten turned completely black, and even the little creepers that trailed up it wilted and fell off."

"That's nothing at all," said Bahrens, turning around to Harper, "you know what sort of place Poinsett County is, and especially with regard to poisonous snakes; there can hardly be more in the Mississippi bottom lands. There you'll find the 'horned snake' sometimes, though luckily only seldom. Two years ago a German and his family moved in there (now he's gone again, that is to say, he died, and his family couldn't stand the climate), and at the time he arrived a relation or an acquaintance, or I don't know what, lived with him and was supposed to do the drudge work around the house. But during the week, he always had a fever, and he looked wonderfully curious when he came into the open on Sundays all spruced up good and proper. Then he wore a bright yellow- and red-striped vest – a frightful felt hat, short black and very tight-fitting pantaloons (it would have been better for his legs if those had been a bit wider) and a blue cloth jacket down to the –"

"But what does the look of his jacket matter to us?" said Harper, becoming impatient.

"More than you think," Bahrens nodded his head significantly, and then, without letting himself be further distracted, continued, "down to the ankles, with a very narrow collar and very large white linen pockets which always hung open, and into which our dear youth often shoved squashed peaches and little bits of watermelon and other similar produce. A special decoration was the very large brass buttons on it –"

"But what do these buttons matter to us?" cried Harper again.

"A lot – a whole lot!" nodded Bahrens with great significance. "But listen. So this young man goes one Sunday, a great black bound Bible under his arm, over to a neighbor's, where one of these inevitable prayer meetings was to be held, when he found, close by the narrow footpath that he was following, one of those little green parakeets or parrots that appeared to have just fallen from a bough. He bent down to pick it up, but unfortunately he hadn't seen the 'horned snake' whose prey he so rashly intended to snatch, and which now shot out of the golden leaves under which it had lain hidden and bit the unfortunate man right through the coat in the arm, just under the elbow."

"Naturally, he died within a few minutes, and his kinsman, who was coming along behind him with his wife, found him dead on the path. To be sure, he went for help right away, but it was too late; they carried him to the house on a hurriedly constructed stretcher, there got him out of his coat, and quickly found the small but already blackened wound. The dead can't be awakened, so, since it was very warm, the poor devil was buried that same evening in a coffin that was quickly hammered together, and the blue coat remained hanging on a nail next to the door."

"But what happened to that snake-bitten coat? When the Germans got up the next morning, the sleeve with the poison in it had taken on clear bright stripes; toward noon, the seams turned all light blue, and some pieces came apart, with the right sleeve turning a lovely black color with a slightly reddish shine; through the afternoon the buttons came off and fell, one by one, in gruesome intervals, to the floor; the buttonholes gave way, the pockets and the lining swelled up, and toward evening the loop ripped, the coat fell down and – began to reek."

"But, Bahrens!" shouted Harper, appalled.

"Began to reek, I say – they had to carry it out and bury it," continued Bahrens, without letting himself be distracted.

"Naah, now I've heard everything," cried Harper, setting his cup down and jumping up, "the coat –"

– "literally croaked," said the old hunter with the greatest equanimity, as he took a piece of tobacco from his pocket and cut off a large slice with a table knife, which he then very deliberately shoved into his mouth.

Roars of laughter followed this conclusion, and Bahrens was fairly offended that they did not allow his story more credibility. He remained stiff and somber on his sawn-off tree stump that passed for a chair in that place, sitting and drumming with his fingers on the wooden table cloth.[3]

"Folks, we really must go home," admonished Roberts, when the uproar had died down a little. "I must, at least," he continued, as he saw that only Mullins indicated a readiness to accompany him, "or my old woman will grumble. Besides, Rowson is supposed to get there this evening, and several things concerning his upcoming wedding are yet to be arranged. – Won't you do me the favor of riding with me, Brown? There'll be many things to write in that regard, and though I in my youth, when we had five writing lessons a week – for which the teacher –"

"It's really not possible for me today, my dear Mr. Roberts," said Brown, somewhat embarrassed, "anyway, the Regulators from the Fourche La Fave are going to gather tomorrow at Bowitt's."

"I thought the meeting was at Smith's?"

"Mr. Rowson's been convincing him so long that such an association is sinful that he's pulled out," Brown smiled. "But there's no harm; Bowitt lives not far from him, at a place that's almost the same distance from all of us, and he is himself a zealous advocate for our cause."

"So no one's been able to learn any more details at all about Heathcott's murder?"

"Not the slightest – you know that right after the deed suspicion rested almost entirely on me. I was even supposed to be arrested a few days after Alapaha's murder, but that never happened since there was no evidence. Moreover, the tracks were made by boots, and I could prove through Hoswells that I was wearing moccasins that morning. But all suspicion ended there, since the only one in the whole neighborhood who wears shoes like that is Mr. Rowson, and no one would like to try to accuse him."

Roberts looked up at him, dismayed. – "Yet," he then said to himself, half-audibly – "the dead man *would have* tried it; he could never bear the secretive preacher –"

"Unfortunately it's rained some nearly every morning this whole spring," Brown continued – "and so every track's been rubbed out. – The little knife that we found by the body wasn't known to anyone either –"

"A penknife!" murmured Roberts to himself.

"Anyway, we haven't given up all hope. Even if we seem idle now, we've been active enough, and now suspicion's being cast here and there on people that I'd never suspected before."

"What's happened with the man whose tracks were picked up by the pursuit?"

"Johnson?" said Cook; "they say he's been seen here again, but whether he's staying or passing through, I don't know."

"Listen, Brown, you could at least do me a favor when you ride up into the settlement," said Roberts, "when do you start?"

"In about a half hour; I'm thinking of overnighting at Wilson's."

"Oh, fine! Then you'll go past Atkins' place early tomorrow morning in any event, so it would be a kindness to me if you'd ask him to stay at home next Monday, since that's when I'll ride over with Rowson to take a look at the farm. Can I count on it?"

Brown gave him his word that he would not forget; Roberts then put his now dried clothes back on, and quickly left the cabin to ride home with Mullins.

Notes

1. The description of Harper's illness is reminiscent of FG's description of his own bouts of fever or "ague" in *WS*, 145, 166–67, 188–89.

2. It is not clear what animal, if any, FG's "horned snake" represents.

3. "Wooden table cloth": the point is that there is no table cloth.

Chapter 20

Rowson at Roberts'. – Assowaum.

Almost three weeks had passed since that evening on which Brown took leave of Marion. At that time, he had sworn to himself that he would never again seek her out – and he had kept his oath firmly and faithfully. But what he had suffered in this time, how he had struggled with himself, only he knew; his face had become pale, his eyes had lost their brilliance and their former liveliness. Nothing had the power to keep him any longer in a place where only too soon he must himself witness the sacrifice of a person by whose side he could have found heaven. But before he went, he would at least see his good name established in the eyes of the world, so that no blemish clung to him, no poisonous tongue could taint him with slanderous gossip. Marion did not consider him capable of such a crime, of that he was convinced, but neither must his friends in Arkansas, and as beloved as he might be to them, many even now still considered him the true culprit. Yes, they excused him for it, found the murder to be completely justifiable as legitimate self-defense, and only shrugged their shoulders when talk came to the money. – "It could not have done the dead man much good if he'd taken the money with him into the stream."

So the real culprit must be discovered and punished, the Indian woman avenged; then he would leave a region in which for him, from now on, there could be nothing but sorrow and pain.

And what did Marion feel in the meanwhile for the friend that she knew to be so near, and yet again so far? The heart of a woman is strong, and it must be a great sorrow that breaks it; but Marion felt that she was doing her duty, and in *that* thought she found solace for the otherwise too bitter and crushing sadness. Rowson had her word; true, she gave it when she did not yet know *that* man at whose first appearance she would first discover what love really is, but it was given freely, without constraint or cajoling – she dare not go back on it. And could she have answered before God for breaking the heart of a man, and this her betrothed, to make another happy? Had not Rowson just recently said to her, in his smooth sonorous voice, that he could find his earthly bliss only in *her*, that her face was to him what air and sunshine are to a plant, that her mere presence casts a calm and holy glow through his whole soul, and that he should despair were she ever to turn from him?

Oh, the poor girl moistened her pillow that night with fiery, fiery tears. – No man saw them, but in fervent prayer came comfort and solace to her tortured and trembling heart, and the next morning found her strong and composed.

*   *   *

It was again a Friday, exactly fourteen days since that terrible evening on which the poor Indian woman fell victim to her cowardly murderer; the sun still stood above the May-green shimmering tops of the magnificent clumps of trees that pressed tightly and densely together at the edge of a small field, as if they were now firmly determined to stand forcefully and in concert against the further advance of the audacious hand of man. Solemnly indeed they extended their great powerful arms over and across one another and braided with the winding vines a mighty web that would bind them together forever and always. To this end, they now shook their shaggy heads shrewdly and slyly in the gentle south wind, and perky little squirrels playfully and jocosely carried their messages back and forth. Poor woods – you will not escape the axe that slowly but surely eats its way into your ranks. Your trunks will fall, and then too liana and vines will twine themselves tightly around you in close and loving embrace, and not abandon the fallen; it is hopeless – they can die with him, but they cannot save him.

Meanwhile, outside and inside old Roberts' farmhouse there reigned brisk and joyous activity. The fair young woman stood with a small basket on her arm in the middle of a fluttering and cackling flock of chickens, ducks, and geese, and strewed golden kernels of corn widely about the tidy yard; but outside, at the low fence, a whole pack of grunting and clamoring piglets stormed up and down, vainly seeking in their mad haste an opening by which to take part in the bountiful meal. The mother sat nearby and watched the lively hustle and bustle with a smile, when Marion suddenly let out a soft cry and dropped the empty basket that she was just on the point of carrying back to the house.

At the fence stood Rowson, who waved a greeting to her with a friendly and smiling expression. He had finished his business and had come to take his bride home.

"What's the matter with you?" cried the matron at first, but at the same time noticed the long and eagerly awaited visitor and said – extending a friendly hand to him: "Well, this is nice, Mr. Rowson – very nice of you, that you are finally here again. We have very eagerly awaited you."

"Marion too?" asked the preacher, smiling and stepping over the low fence as he took the hand of the blushing maiden and gently pressed it: "Marion too?"

"I am very happy to see you once more healthy and well," whispered the young maiden, "of course, you know that you are always welcome here."

"In your *house* – but also in your *heart*, Marion?" asked Rowson urgently – the girl trembled and was silent. "Marion," continued the Methodist after a long pause – "the blessing of heaven was upon me in my recent journey. I am now wealthy enough that I can establish a home for myself here in our humble circumstances. Marion, will you be mine, will you next Sunday, on the Lord's day, become my wife?"

"Yes," said the mother, touched, as she drew the shaking, speechless child to her breast – "yes, reverend sir – she has already confessed to me that she thinks well of you, and the rest will come along; you will surely make her happy."

"Whatever is in my power, in the power of a poor, sinful man," said the Methodist, as he lifted his eyes piously toward heaven, "I will do. I believe I know too that Marion is firmly persuaded of this; may I at least hope so?"

Silently, the lovely girl stretched her hand across to him, which he pressed to his lips while she sobbed loudly on her mother's breast.

"Hello, Rowson!" said old Roberts, who at this moment appeared at the fence. "You've kept your word fully. Well, how stands the business?"

"Outstanding, Mr. Roberts!" replied the Methodist joyfully. "Even better than I had expected, and now I come to you to request your blessing on my union with your daughter, to take place next Sunday, in fact."

"But isn't this too unexpected and soon for the girl?" asked Roberts, as he handed over his horse to a Negro lad and, climbing over the fence, walked up to them.

"She's agreed to it," said the mother, "and why do we need grand preparations here in the woods? But how is your house, Mr. Rowson?"

"I intended to invite the two of you at the same time," said the preacher, "to take a look at it early tomorrow, if you will grant me a couple of hours' time. It's small and cramped, to be sure, but I will probably come to an agreement with Atkins this week and buy his place; after that, we will have more room to move."

"But, as for that, wouldn't it be better then," suggested Roberts, "to delay the wedding until that happens? You may be spared many inconveniences by putting it off, and – surely the girl would prefer to move straight into a little farm than just a log cabin."

"That certainly cannot be denied," replied Rowson, "but then it's unclear *when* Atkins will move out; four, indeed maybe even eight weeks could pass by, and, my dear Mr. Roberts, you cannot blame me if I now, after removing so many obstacles, long to call Marion my own."

"Well, in God's name," said the old man, "take her off and be happy together."

"Thank you my deepest thanks to you!" cried Rowson, emotionally seizing his hand. "Marion will never regret having entrusted her future fate to my hands. But now farewell, my *dear parents,* if I may call you so, and soon –"

"But wouldn't you like to spend this evening with us?" asked Mrs. Roberts. "You've been gone so long, and it really isn't right by half to leave the bride alone all the time."

"The time is short, my good Mrs. Roberts," sighed Rowson, "and here in our settlement, where neighbors live so far apart from one another, only a few errands will make the day pass exceptionally quickly. But I hope to have everything finished by tomorrow evening, and then at least to be able to spend the final hours before the happy day in your company, and that of my bride."

"Good – good, Mr. Rowson," said the old man, "that's quite all right. You've been away from your home for a week now, so there's naturally much be organized; so tomorrow evening we'll see you again – by the way – it's still settled that we go to Atkins' together on Monday, right?"

"Certainly," said the preacher.

"Well, good," continued Roberts, "I've already asked Brown this evening to tell him that we're coming; he'll go by there early tomorrow morning to attend the meeting of the Regulators that's to be held at Bowitt's."

"I was told the Regulators had disbanded," said Rowson somewhat more keenly than conformed with his usual calm and collected demeanor. "On my journey I heard it's all decided."

"Not at all, it's just now really getting started. I believe they have, as I heard today, suspicions about several people in the neighborhood, and they'll probably consult with one another tomorrow about what to do now, as the times are singularly dangerous –"

"Would it not be possible to attend this meeting?" interrupted Rowson.

"Why not," laughed Roberts, "but then you'll have to become a Regulator, and to my knowledge you've argued mighty hard against them until now."

"The Regulators need a man," said Rowson, quickly collecting himself, "who will occasionally rein in their too passionate zeal and hold them back from excesses, like the one in White County[1] for example. In this sense, I would not find it incompatible with my position to attach myself to them."

Roberts looked searchingly into his eyes, and Rowson, reddening slightly, continued: "Do you think I have changed my mind in so short a time? No, truly not, I still consider the Regulators' meeting to be wrong, because it's illegal –"

"But – ?" asked Roberts, as the other hesitated.

"Why, you know what he's saying!" cried Mrs. Roberts, half angrily. "The good Mr. Rowson is absolutely right. The young folk rampage about all day, crazy and wild – now, I'm not at all saying they mean any wickedness by it, but they believe they're doing justice, and then maybe sometimes do the greatest, most blatant injustice, and I, in Mr. Rowson's place –"

"No one would be accepted into the group," said Roberts, steadily watching the preacher, who meanwhile looked down several times, though finally he met the other's eyes firmly, "who would not also take an *active* part. I don't think they would suffer an advisor, even if they needed one."

"It's worth a try!" cried Rowson, who had now fully regained his presence of mind. "Tomorrow, if it's at all possible, I'll go by there, and I won't leave until they *send me away*; in that event, I will have done my duty – God himself requires no more."

"Fine," said Roberts, shaking his hand trustingly, "well said. It makes me happy when I see a man remain true to his principles."

"Who is their leader now?"

"Brown – at least for the Fourche La Fave."

"Then *he*, at least, *has not* remained true to his principles," rejoined the preacher as he glanced up at the old man; "I still remember quite well the words he uttered here on this same spot about that very alliance."

"That is a different matter," replied the old farmer earnestly. "Brown found himself half *compelled* to take an active part in this alliance, since his own good name was at stake. He was openly accused of murder, and his only goal now is to find out Heathcott's real murderer. To be sure, he had a quarrel with him, for Heathcott was always somewhat rough by nature, and I still very well recall –"

"I thought the main purpose of the Regulators was limited to discovering the horse thieves," said Rowson, paling slightly.

"Only partly, but if you attend the meeting tomorrow you will hear all about that. The aim now, as far as I've found out, is to round up the suspects, and by means of these to get on the right track, even if they are not really the culprits."

"If they could only discover the shameful murderer of the poor Indian," said Mrs. Roberts. "Oh, Mr. Rowson, you wouldn't believe how I have prayed about it! The woman was so pious and good and clung to you with such reverence. Ah, how often have I seen her weep during your sermons, as if her heart would break – and now to have to die so young, and in such a way."

"Yes, it's terrible!" said Rowson, himself deeply shaken, though of course for another reason. "But, my friends – I really must go, so good night for now. – Good night, Marion; where is the girl?"

"Marion – child! – come out here!" cried the mother. "Mr. Rowson wants to say good night to you."

"Let her go, worthy friend," said the Methodist, interposing, "her heart is full, and she wants to converse with her God. Tomorrow I hope to find her happy and cheerful."

With that, he waved to them both another hearty farewell, mounted his little pony, and trotted off into the now darkening woods.

"Mother, what's really going on with the girl?" asked Roberts when the preacher was gone. "She seems so strange to me. I hope it's not because she's being *forced* to marry that man?"

"Foolish man, who would force her then?" smiled the matron. "She's only half a child still, and thus acts fearful and giddy; and it may be hard enough, perhaps, for her to leave her parents. Now, at *that* man's side –"

"Yes, very well," said Roberts, unbuckling his spurs and hanging them outside the house under a little awning next to the saddle and bridle, "very well, I have heard that often already –"

"You've no fondness for the pious man –"

"No – no fondness; I don't understand why our child should be so much happier all of a sudden with him than with any other man. A fine, true lad with a good heart, and who – was a bit more of a *man*, would have been to me, frankly speaking, just as welcome, perhaps even more welcome, but – as God wills. You women have agreed to it, and I have no more to do with it than to say 'yes.' He has taken a first step toward starting a small farm, and with that an industrious man in Arkansas won't fail."

Rowson's ingenuous demeanor had completely won the old man to him again, for having such a good and true heart, he did not readily believe anything evil about others, so why believe it about the one person in the whole settlement known to be pious and god-fearing? If indeed a dark thought occasionally crossed his mind, either he was not entirely clear about it himself, or he discarded it instantly again as mad and mistaken.

But what, meanwhile, were the preacher's feelings as he rode slowly and thoughtfully along through the shadow-darkened woods? Far enough from the house that he could not be seen or observed from there, he got off his horse, took it by the bridle, and walked solemnly and immersed in thought along the narrow trail that snaked its way through the woods, avoiding all hindrances such as large trees and swampy places. At last he stopped and stood, and said very softly, looking down at the ground before him:

"It's getting almost too hot for me here in Arkansas; the devil might have his fun and by some accident – there are some strange examples of it – bring things to light that wouldn't be at all beneficial to my good name in these parts. I must go away – and that as soon as possible – Atkins may sell his farm as his likes, I'll not chain myself here so that afterwards, when all the others have covered their backs, I'll be abandoned to the wrath of those yelping hounds[2] all alone. No! – It's true the Indian's disappeared," he continued after a while, "and without him it'll be hard for them to – anything at all – I really don't know, even with *his* help, how it's possible, the penknife –"

The horse pricked up its ears, and the Indian stood beside him.

"Good day,[3] Mr. Rowson," he said softly, as he stepped out of the thicket and walked over to him with a slight nod.

"Assowaum!" cried Rowson, as he felt his face turning deathly pale. "Assowaum – where – where were you so long? – We've missed you in the settlement."

"The pale man too has been away," replied the Indian, his eyes fixed firmly on the preacher, "Assowaum returns to the grave of his wife."

"And – you've still not discovered anything about the murderer?"

"No!" said the savage in a barely audible voice. "Not yet – the Great Spirit has kept the sacred bird from whispering the name of the murderer in my ear. So Assowaum has spoken with the spirit of his people in a place that has not yet been desecrated by a single white foot. Now he waits for the voice of his Manitou."

"May he be favorable to you," said the preacher, completely forgetting his earlier abhorrence of the Indian's idolatry. But the latter waved and walked on; the Methodist swung himself into his saddle and, when a bend in the road had concealed him from the red man's eyes, flew along the path, drilling his heels into his pony, his long brown hair fluttering in the fresh evening breeze; and the steed, unaccustomed to such handling, foamed and snorted as it rushed through the flat valley with its impatient rider.

Notes

1. "Excesses, like the one in White County": FG is perhaps drawing on the same incident described in the Foreword (see note 3).

2. FG uses the English word "hounds" in the original text.

3. "Good day" is English in FG's original.

Chapter 21

Wilson's Confessions. –
The Beautiful Washerwoman. –
An Arkansas Cradle. – The Retreat.

Roberts had not been long gone from Harper's cabin when Brown similarly prepared to ride up to Bowitt's, at whose house the meeting of the Regulators was to be held the next morning. Cook accompanied him a part of the way, but then rode off to the left to spend the night in his own house and follow at daybreak, while Bahrens had promised to stay with the convalescent. Harper, though, swore by all that is high and holy that this would be the last day that he would be locked up in that accursed house.

"I must feel leaf and moss under my feet once more," he cried out, "must once more see the roof of green leaves over me; until then, I won't get well." So it was arranged that he would ride with them the next day to Bahrens' house and spend a week there. But as the trip would be too much for a man weakened by fever to make all at once, the men were planning to spend the first night at Roberts', who had long ago invited them.

Meanwhile, Brown trotted on his fiery little pony along the narrow path that was barely recognizable under the leaves and marked only by pieces of bark peeled from the trees. In about an hour and a half he reached Wilson's little farm and found the owner just on the point of mounting his own horse.

"Hello, Wilson, where are we going? To the Regulators' meeting too?" called Brown to him in a friendly tone.

"Yes!" said the young man, though he noticeably reddened at this, and tightened the girth-strap with an altogether desperate fervor. This was, however, already stretched to the breaking point, and only caused the horse to start with great impatience and pointedly gasp for air several times.

"What are you doing there, Wilson?" laughed Brown, watching this – "You're strangling the life out of the poor beast's body. – Are you planning to run a race, that you look after the tackle so?"

"No, not exactly that," murmured the other, "which way are you riding?"

"I was going to your place – and you?"

"Me? I planned to go to Atkins'–"

"Well, that's good, then I'll come to see you another time and I'll also spend the night at Atkins'. – Besides, I have to deliver a message from Roberts there."

Wilson was about to object, but Brown did not notice it, or perhaps ignored it, since he just called quickly to his friend to mount, and then turned his horse's head toward the newly designated resting place.

Wilson was soon at his side, and finally asked, apparently only to break the silence:

"So you have an errand from Roberts – for Rowson, I suppose? He does want to buy Atkins' farm, they say – if Atkins really moves away, of course."

"Isn't that settled yet, then?"

"Who knows? The old man's as dark and secret as the grave. He hasn't said a thing to me about it."

"Why would he say anything to anybody?" asked Brown, smiling, as Wilson, all at once and without warning, started whistling a song and beating his leggings with his riding crop, which he had broken from a bush. He seemed unwilling to give an answer to this question until Brown repeated it, but then he reined in his horse, stretched his hand out to the young man as the latter likewise halted beside him, and said with a hearty tone and look:

"You should learn my whole history, Brown; it's told in a few words, and – you mean well – maybe you could give me some advice."

"Well, let's hear it," replied his friend, "maybe, and maybe not – it's not often that I'm asked for advice, and – in matters of the heart, to boot," smiling when he saw how the blood rose to Wilson's cheeks and temples.

"Yes – you're right," he whispered at last, "it's a matter of the heart, but – not a happy one. Do you know the Atkins household?"

"I've never been there."

"He has a child, an adopted orphan, a girl – oh, you would laugh at me were I to talk about her as my heart would compel me to do. – Yes, I know, you're holding it in for my sake, but inside you're making fun of me just the same. Well, I'll spare you a full description; I have loved the girl now for a year, since the time she moved with Atkins to the Fourche La Fave, and her father – won't give her to me. He's only her foster father, to be sure, but he's raised her and made a fine girl of her – no thanks to his wife, by any means. But now he wants to push a man on her that she doesn't like and whom she won't take under any circumstances – but – he torments her nevertheless."

"That's bad, sure enough" said Brown – "how old is she?"

"Ah, unfortunately, just seventeen," sighed Wilson, "if she were twenty-one, we wouldn't have to ask the old man."

"Does she love you deeply?"

"She's told me so more than a thousand times."

"Well, so what's the big problem? Surely time will soften the hearts of the parents," Brown assured him.

"Yes, if we only had time!" Wilson cried out impatiently; "Rowson gets married tomorrow, and then Ellen is to go over and help the young folks keep house."

"Tomorrow?" gasped Brown, going pale.

"Yes – in the afternoon," Wilson continued, without noticing. "Then if Atkins has sold out, he'll go to Texas, and – the girl will have to go too!"

"Well, so you go with him," said Brown, who was hardly listening to what the other said.

"That won't work," he replied – "I have my old mother who lives in Tennessee, not far from Memphis, and I have to go get her first in any case. She lives now among strangers, and I can't let her die there."

"Then there's very little I can do for you," sighed Brown, somewhat distracted, "I don't know Atkins at all, having only seen him once, and it's highly unlikely that he'd give the slightest weight to my pleadings."

"So you shouldn't try with Atkins, but rather with someone very different."

"And with whom?"

"With Mrs. Rowson. – You're well known to Roberts, and Marion holds you in high regard, that I know. If you approach her very nicely for me, she would surely do it for a favor to you."

"Madame Rowson," said Brown softly, as if lost in deep thought. – "Madame Rowson – can *she* help?"

"Oh, she has a lot of influence with Atkins," Wilson assured him. "When Atkins' wife lay dangerously ill so long last summer, she and Ellen watched by her bed for whole weeks together. – They would do anything for *her*, she's such a good girl –"

"Yes – yes!" Brown sighed deeply.

"Really, you believe that too?"

"What?"

"That she would do any kindness for you."

"My dear Wilson," said Brown, half turning from his companion – "in this matter, surely you could have turned to a better person than to me. Rowson himself perhaps would be a more useful advocate."

"Yes," said Wilson, half angrily, "I know that; but I'll be damned if I can stand the man. The whole neighborhood likes him, the women at least, who are hellbent on him, but I, I don't know, it's always uncomfortable for me when I am supposed to be friendly with him. And his circumstances seem mighty strange too. A year ago he comes here, says himself that he's poor, doesn't do a bit of work, just preaches and doesn't get a cent from anyone for it, but he always has money – drifts all over the county for twelve months in such a fashion, and *suddenly* marries the most beautiful girl on the Fourche La Fave (Ellen excepted, since, I don't know, I still like her better). I myself don't have anything else against Rowson, can't have anything against him – what does it matter to me that he's cowardly, but – I wouldn't like to ask him for a favor even if my whole life's happiness was at stake."

"Have patience, Wilson," Brown assured him, "if the girl loves you and the other man doesn't have her word, everything will come out all right. You have many friends here and you're young and hardworking – what more could you want?"

"I want the *girl,* Brown," said Wilson ingenuously, "and you can preach as beautifully as you like, you look to me like you bear the most awful sorrow in the world yourself and couldn't confide a word of it to anyone. No, I can't keep it so quiet. My fate must be decided before Atkins goes away, and if none of you will or can help me, well, the devil take me if I don't steal her away – and she'll go with me, that I know."

"Have you already asked Atkins to put a stop to it?"

"Yes, and she – the old lady – an angry and bitter woman, threatened to throw me out the door, if I let myself be seen there one more time."

"And you mean to go there now?"

"Of course – but not to the house," Wilson laughed – "I haven't been dropped on my head, you know. No, Ellen is doing the washing today down at the creek, in the bushes there, a couple hundred paces away from the house, and since that's almost the only time I can have a little word with her, I mean at least to put every minute to good use. After that, when she's finished with her work, I'll ride back over to Bowitt's; the weather is nice and warm."

"Can't I get to see your darling just once, so that at least I know what kind of taste you have?" Brown said with a smile.

"Why not?" cried Wilson gleefully, "you'll like her, and I don't need to be ashamed of her; but come, then, we're not very far from the place and we have to turn off to the right here or they'll see us from the house. – Stop – leave your horse here, since we can't ride through the slew, and there's just an old withered cypress lying over it for a bridge. As for my pony, I'll take him down into the cane thicket – that's his usual place."

"So," he said, as he now came bounding back again and ran on ahead of his friend over the narrow bridge – "so – here she is, but softly, we want to surprise her."

The men walked on tiptoe to a little open spot in the woods, right in a bend of the creek whose waters led through a thousand turnings to the not very distant Fourche La Fave, and stood still there, genuinely surprised by the charming spectacle that offered itself to them. Now Wilson cast a triumphant look at his friend, as if he wanted to say: Do you see how right I am? Is that a creature for Texas, and shall I let this fair flower be snatched from me?

Near the gravelly creek bank, supported by two low wooden cradles, hung a great black kettle over a small, crackling fire; several small benches stood around it in a half-circle and held in separate piles the various sorts of washing, colored and white; in front of a plank braced as a table stood Ellen, Wilson's fair love, beating with her broad washing bat the separate pieces of household linen that she took one after the other from the bucket standing near her, and accompanying the rhythmic blows of the beater with her silver-clear ringing voice. But that was not her only occupation. Close by, mounted between two slender hickory trunks, and rocked by the gentle south wind, hung a small hammock braided from pawpaw bark, in which a red-cheeked infant had been quietly and peacefully slumbering until this moment. But now it opened its great dark eyes, cast a glance upward, and then, instead of giving a friendly smile at the magnificent natural scene around it, twisted its sweet little face into a countenance so dreadfully sour that it gave every indication that approaching storms and screams of woe were to be feared. But Ellen had not left the little sleeper out of sight and had no sooner noticed the awakening of this short-tempered budding citizen of the world than she quickly let her beater fall, set the hammock into a somewhat livelier motion, and in a soft caressing voice warbled a lullaby to the child, which was instantly calmed by her presence. The men listened silently. Ellen, unaware of their presence, and half bending down to the now smiling child as if she would kiss it, half teasingly pulling back from it, began to sing:

> The playful wind
> Swings so gently
> In webbing so safe
> The smiling child.
>
> He shoos the flies
> And fans you, dear,
> And steals lots of kisses,
> The mischievous thief.
>
> He kisses your temples,
> The small cheeks so round,
> He kisses your locks,
> Your bright rosy mouth.

He plucks from the branches
What spring gave to them,
And casts on your cradle
The blossoms far down.

So slumber, my darling,
Your sentry, the wind,
Your genial guardian,
He rocks the small child.

He rocks you so gently,
What more could you want? –
With teasing caresses
Now forward, now back. –[1]

"Oh God!" she suddenly cried out in alarm, as Wilson softly approached her during the final verse and laid his hand on her hip. – "Oh, you wicked man, how you frightened me!"

"Don't be angry about it, my dear girl," whispered Wilson, pressing a kiss on her lips that she only feebly resisted, "but look, I've brought a friend here to see you – who –"

Ellen turned swiftly around in alarm. But as her gaze met that of the kindly smiling young stranger, who definitely must have seen the kiss, her neck and face colored as if from a shower of purple, and she turned her feet as if to flee. But Wilson grabbed her by the hand just in time and asked pleadingly:

"Ellen – he's really a good friend, and he knows that we love each other; besides," he went on teasingly, "the little miss can't run off under any circumstances and leave behind her entrusted ward. So – since the little rogue in the hammock indicates no particular desire to wander off, you'd best stay here. – Am I right or wrong?"

"Wrong," whispered the girl, smiling, as she, still flooded by the deepest blush, bowed to the stranger – "wrong, you know you must always be wrong."

"A fine law," said Wilson to Brown with mock seriousness – "a really fine law. Those of our Regulators are nothing in comparison."

"The hateful Regulators –," cried Ellen.

"Wait there," Wilson interrupted her, laughing – "not so fast, miss, here stand two of them."

"You're a –"

"Stop a little[2] – here's our captain, and I –"

"Oh, you're not a Regulator, are you?" the beautiful girl said to Brown, half anxiously, half cajolingly. "I don't believe it."

"Do you have such a terrible idea of these men?" Brown smiled.

"Oh, yes – mother and father have told me horrible things about them: how they pull innocent men out of their beds at night, just when one of them is mad at someone, and then they tie them to a tree and whip them so long they die. Father swore to shoot anyone who comes across his threshold at night with a hostile purpose."

"They aren't as bad as your father seems to think," Brown suggested, "and even if –"

"Well, but, I'd like to put in a word as well," cried Wilson, stepping between them. "I really didn't come here to listen to a disquisition about the Regulators. Ellen, have you spoken with your mother again?"

"Yes," said the poor girl, dropping her head sadly – "but she believes –"

"You don't need to be shy in front of Mr. Brown, he knows everything," assured Wilson when he noticed how his betrothed threw a nervous sidelong glance at the other.

"Oh, it doesn't help anything at all to keep it quiet," sighed the poor girl. "All of Arkansas will probably soon know that I'm to marry that brute Cotton."

"Cotton?" Brown asked, astonished.

"Yes – unfortunately. – Of course, my mother's strictly forbidden me to mention his name to anyone, but why not? – I'd rather die than marry the man."

"And you won't marry him," said Wilson defiantly – "I'll be da –, well, all right, I can't do that," he interrupted himself when his sweetheart cast a chastising glance at him. "But I know what I'll do; as soon as we've discovered the band of thieves that pursue their shameful business in our neighborhood here, and if Atkins still won't bend, well, all right, then – in the name of whoever will take my soul – that's not swearing – if I don't have the last laugh and run off with you."

"And that is what the gentleman calls 'the last laugh'?" said Ellen with a smile at once very affectionate and yet also quite wistful.

"You know very well what I mean," Wilson pleaded – "but what's with you, Brown – you look so thoughtlessly or thoughtfully, whatever you want to call it, up at the treetops."

"Have you seen the man you call *Cotton* recently?" Brown asked, turning now to the young girl without heeding Wilson's remark.

"Yes," she said, "he came back about four days ago, from the Mississippi I think, where he had gone almost two weeks ago. But he comes only in the evenings, and I can't stand his sneaky ugly self; – do you know him?"

"I think so, but I don't really know; does he come – but what's with Wilson?"

Brown had every reason to regard the latter with concern, since he suddenly glided into the thicket like a snake and in a few seconds had disappeared without a trace. The reason for this strange retreat did not, however, remain a puzzle very long, for almost at the same time there appeared on the path leading to the house the stately and still youthful figure of Mrs. Atkins, whose bright shimmering dress had warned Wilson just in time, and he now left it to his friend to deal with the approaching enemy.

"Hello there, Miss!" she cried, advancing with formidable strides and head flung high. "Hello there – keeping company with a man? I've not heard a single blow for the past quarter-hour; is the wash going to do itself?"

"The child –," sputtered Ellen.

"Fiddlesticks – the child – that's lying there as quietly as a ladybug in its nest; foolish excuses –"

"I must ask you to forgive the young lady on my account," interrupted Brown, stepping toward the fuming woman with a friendly greeting, "I come on an errand from Messrs. Roberts and Rowson, and in fact intended to spend the night in your home."

"Well, to be sure, this isn't the open highway," said Mrs. Atkins, though already clearly mollified.

"Indeed not," Brown smiled, now merely endeavoring to spare the poor trembling girl any harsh words, "but I came through the woods a ways and didn't know whether I should ride above or below the slew to get to the house the quickest, so I first went over the trunk lying across it in order to reconnoiter and found the young lady here, whom I've naturally distracted from her work for a few minutes with my questions."

"Young lady – '*young lady*' my foot, just don't put any nonsense in her head. But my husband is up in the house; so tell me where your horse is, I'll send the boy after it!"

"Right there, where the cypress is lying across the slew," replied Brown, who was now eager to take the angry woman back to the house with him in order to leave Wilson plenty of room to maneuver.

"Good, so come on," said Madame Atkins – "and you, missy, stick to it and get busy. Not half of the washing is beaten yet – it's a disgrace, and you've been at it for two hours already! See that you're done before it gets dark! And what's the little one doing?" she said, changing her formerly rough tone to one of genuine maternal tenderness as she bent over the child's hanging cradle, who kicked toward the familiar figure with a beckoning gleeful smile – "that makes the child happy, doesn't it, swinging – swinging the whole day long, and then it doesn't sleep at night, and Ellen must walk about with him until daybreak – the little mischief; but of course – you're waiting; so, Ellen, see that you're busy!"

And with these words she threw one more cheerful kiss to the baby and then once more walked, followed by Brown, to the not very distant dwelling.

Notes

1. The song in the orginal rhymes abcb.
2. "Stop a little" is English in the original text.

SUNK LANDS LOOKING NORTH FROM THE DEEP LANDING.

Figure 22.1. "Sunk Lands Looking North from the Deep Landing." Lithograph after a drawing by David Dale Owen. From David Dale Owen, *Second Report of a Geological Reconnoissance of the Middle and Southern Counties of Arkansas, Made during the Years 1859 and 1860* (Philadelphia: C. Sherman & Sons, 1860). Image courtesy of University of Arkansas Fayetteville Special Collections.

Chapter 22

Atkins' Dwelling. – The Strange Visit. – The Password.

Atkins' dwelling differed significantly, and indeed much to its advantage, from most of the log huts of the settlement, although it too was actually made only of tree trunks. But these, hewn both inside and outside, formed two perfectly identical houses one and a half stories high that were connected in the middle by a space open to the north and south, with the whole structure under a single roof. The farmer had been unusually industrious with the interior as well, and the clean planed-down boards, with which he had very carefully blocked up each opening, were here and there covered with a few enormous advertisements for traveling groups of circus riders, wax figure galleries, and menagerie stalls. One of these last, on bright gold paper, especially distinguished itself; it displayed a man with unusually tight trousers and two enormous feathers on his beret who lay in the arms of a lion and appeared to be whispering something in its ear with utter casualness. Others heralded similar things, and in any event at some point had been brought as curiosities by the owner of the dwelling from Little Rock, the capital of the state.

One of the two buildings that were completely alike each other was used only as a bedroom. Five beds, with a number of mattresses and quilts that perhaps could have served as pallets for another dozen guests, filled its space, while on the walls hung the women's wardrobe and – in a very special corner – the master's Sunday best. But guests were only ushered into this room in the evening, at bedtime, when the various beds were all prepared and awaiting the tired limbs of the outsiders. By day it remained a firmly sealed sanctuary to any eyes not belonging to the household. Even Atkins dared not enter it without the permission of his wife, who carried the key with her.

Brown was now ushered into the living- and state-room, and there he found his host, who balanced on the back legs of a chair while he whistled a song and whittled on a small piece of cedar wood with a half-broken penknife. – The guest's entry disturbed his meditations, but he had hardly cast a glance at the door and recognized the newcomer when, visibly growing pale, he sprang up from his seat and looked wildly at the cornice above the door where a long rifle lay on two pegs; he did not relax until he saw that the guest had walked into his house alone, and with a purpose that was in no way hostile.

Brown was himself disturbed by the farmer's incomprehensible alarm, but he ignored it as much as possible and said, as he went up to him and extended his hand in a friendly and open way: "Mr. Atkins, I'm very sorry indeed if I've disturbed you at all."

"Oh – not at – not bit, not at all," stammered the farmer, still not quite composed, "it was only – it should have too –"

"Of course, I'm an infrequent guest in these parts," Brown smiled, "and though I'm at home on the Fourche La Fave, *here* I'm a stranger. Still, the times in which we live might have made my disturbance, if indeed I've caused such a one –"

"But my dear Mr. Brown," interrupted Atkins, who now had regained his full composure, "don't even mention such a thing; true, you're a rare visitor, but no less welcome for all that, and this may be the start of a right regular and long-lasting acquaintance."

"I hope so," said Brown, shaking the proffered hand, "and it's possible that we'll continue the friendship founded here in a foreign land. At least, I've heard that you're thinking of emigrating to Texas –"

"Yes – but you too? If I'm not mistaken; that is, I was told last week that you – you had actually joined the Regulators – were even to become their leader."

"Yes and no," Brown smiled, "I've really joined them and for the moment I've become their leader, if there's anything to *lead*, but only conditionally – that is, until the time the two murders that happened here recently are solved and punished. Then I'll resign my post and leave the state to become a citizen of the Republic of Texas."

"But the horse thieves!" interjected Atkins.

"Concern me only insofar as I also suspect the murderer is among them. Naturally, as long as I'm their leader, I'll go after them zealously should we come upon their tracks. But it looks like they're too carefully concealed, so we'll have to leave it mainly to luck. Now I've got just *one* goal, to track down those *murderers,* and the Lord have mercy on them if we unmask them. From *men* they have *no* hope of mercy."

"It's strange too," said Atkins thoughtfully, "that suspicion hasn't landed on a single soul in both cases. – Yes – I know – *you* were accused of the first deed, though quite a few disputed it from the start; you had the women on your side especially, and then your conduct with Heathcott that morning, from what I've been able to learn about it, gave no reason to think that you would have shied away from standing up to him in an open and manly fight. So *you* didn't need to take such a way out. Someone must have robbed him just for his money, that's what I had thought from the start, and who knows who all he had dealings with and who knew the secret of the sum he carried with him, apart from those living here on the Fourche La Fave."

"So you don't think any of our people are guilty?"

"Frankly speaking, no, for even those," he added a bit more softly, and almost as if he were talking to himself, "who maybe in other matters are not particular about being honest, I don't think, where human life is concerned, are capable of committing such a cold-blooded murder."

"I hope so," Brown sighed, as he braced his hand on the upper beam of the fireplace and laid his forehead against it – "I hope so; in any event, I expect the Indian back any day, and he surely won't return without news."

"Not without news – indeed?" said Atkins; "sure, the Indian is very clever, but he still didn't know what to make of the hoof prints that time –"

"Because he never looked into them," replied Brown. "His wife's death had shaken him so that I genuinely feared for his life. Anyway, he came a day too late as well, since the thieves had already fled, and the rain had washed out the tracks in the meantime."

"A cursed thing, the rain," smiled the farmer, rubbing his hands softly and smugly behind his guest's back, "it's washed out many a track before, and helped such miscreants to get away. They stole a couple of fine horses from me last year too."

"You should have acted more forcefully against these fellows long ago; they have grown too bold and will end by carrying off your animals before your very eyes. It's even said there's a horse-trafficker living somewhere along the river who keeps a safe place to hold stolen horses."

"Who says that?" asked Atkins, starting up quickly.

"It was mentioned at our last meeting," responded Brown, without observing the movement or changing his position; "and as for that, it was said that if the thefts don't let up, a thorough search should be carried out to see if anything might be found."

"Not everyone will submit to a house search," replied Atkins angrily. "We're in a free country here, and if I don't want someone on my property then I simply say to him: 'March!', and if he doesn't go, then I take my rifle from the hooks."

"Well, you see, Mr. Atkins," Brown responded, turning around to him in a friendly way, "that's exactly the reason why we Regulators have come together. In this matter the laws of Arkansas are too weak. A man against whom no hard evidence exists, even if he's the worst of villains, can sit on his farm and keep calm and undisturbed. He has the right to shoot down anyone who wants to force his way onto his property – that's all right! But this sort of thing encourages crime in a way that the general population can't stand. Who can be sure his property is secure when a robber maybe only needs to lead it home in rainy weather that washes away the tracks to be sure he's out of all danger, and especially when such a fellow is not subject to the people's rising up against him en masse to drag him out of his hideout and – whip him."

"But what do we have laws for?" asked Atkins morosely, "what for, if they're too weak?"

"They're not too weak," replied Brown, "but they can't be enforced. Let's suppose a case where a criminal is caught by the sheriff and sentenced by the court; where's he put until he can be delivered to the state prison? In one of those little log cabins built for this purpose, from which his friends can free him the first night."

Atkins cracked a smile.

"I've been told," continued Brown without noticing it, "you've had a few examples of it right here in this county. Even in the best case, he actually gets to the penitentiary in Little Rock and the state has him under lock and key, but that's barely for one, at the most two weeks, since even a few of the escaped criminals themselves have said that the prison is so badly built that the sheriff couldn't lock them up nearly as fast as they could get back out again. So how does it help us if we obey the laws, deliver the convicts, and then, when we think they're safe and harmless behind bars, find them among us again and busy with our property after just a couple of weeks?"

"Ah, yes," smiled Atkins, "it's not an easy matter. I know that Cotton –"

"Where's Cotton now?" Brown asked quickly.

"Cotton?" repeated Atkins, quickly composed and, as it appeared, quite be-wildered – "Cotton? Dear God, who knows where he's hiding now. I heard not long ago that even the sheriff's looking for him. But why do you ask?"

"They say he's been seen in these parts," replied Brown, who did not want to quote Ellen's statement and cause the poor girl any trouble, but who now became suspicious for the first time on account of his host's lies. "They say he's even been seen on this road."

"Yes, that's very easily possible," Atkins said with a smile, "many ride along this road without even stopping in to talk with me. But people gossip a lot."

"I'm actually here today on an errand from Messrs. Roberts and Rowson," said Brown, who wished to take the conversation in another direction. "Mr. Roberts in particular – ah, here comes my horse," he interrupted himself, as the mulatto rode the brown horse up to the door and jumped out of the saddle.

"Please – stay here," Atkins said, stopping him as he saw that his guest was about to go outside, "Dan *will* take care of that. – Take the horse to the stall, feed it well, and after that put the tack here between the houses," he called to the latter, "and when you're finished with that, then –"; with these words he walked out to him and completed his sentence in a softer voice, so that Brown could not understand anything more of it. But the mulatto nodded his head very significantly, as if he had grasped it all fully, led the horse out, and was not seen again that evening.

"You were going to say something to me about an errand?" Atkins now asked his guest as he returned to the house.

"Yes," the latter answered, as if awakening from a daydream, "Mr. Roberts will be coming with – with his son-in-law to visit you Monday morning or noontime to take a look at the house and fields, and begs your leave to wait on him if he should perhaps arrive a little late."

"Good – very good!" replied Atkins cordially. "I think we can make a deal with each other. The two of them are a couple of gallant fellows who won't press a poor devil eager to emigrate. The wedding is set for tomorrow, eh?"

"Yes," replied Brown with a low voice, "I believe – tomorrow."

"You'll be at the ceremony too, I take it?"

"Who – me? No – I think not. – Our meeting will probably last late into the evening, and then I'm staying at Bowitt's."

"Which meeting?"

"The Regulators'; we gather tomorrow at Bowitt's."

"Meeting tomorrow? Well, that must've been put together mighty secretly, I haven't heard a peep about it."

"Naturally only those who are Regulators would be summoned," continued Brown, who at this moment believed that he had found an opportunity to put in a good word for poor Wilson, "but I'm surprised that Wilson hasn't said anything about it to you. – He was responsible for spreading the word in these parts – it wasn't to be kept secret, by any means."

"Mr. Wilson hasn't been in my house for a long time," replied Atkins, to whom the mention of this name seemed to be unpleasant, "that's probably the reason the matter's unknown to me. But it's all the same to me; I'm no Regulator, and so I have no interest in the meeting. Such companies are likewise supposed to be forming in Texas, indeed."[1]

"Yes," said Brown, unwilling after all to give up his assault so quickly, "but what I'd also wanted to say is that Wilson seems, indeed, to want to settle here in the region for good. I scarcely believe that you could wish for a better neighbor."

"You forget that I can hardly still count myself part of this region," replied Atkins. – "But here comes my old woman with the things for the table already – the days are still mighty short. By the by, Mr. Brown, how's your uncle then? We've all been mighty sorry that the fever took such a powerful hold on the poor man. But the cursed fever spares no one, and it hits the healthiest ones the hardest."

Brown well saw that, for the present at least, any further insinuation would be in vain; especially since Mrs. Atkins was there now, and soon Ellen too would return to the house with the child. Admittedly, he would have liked to chat a bit with the beautiful girl, but he was also afraid that by doing so he would subject her to unpleasant words; in any event, a friendly and grateful stolen glance cast his way told him clearly enough that she and Wilson recognized his earlier kindness in taking the foster-mother away with him and – what was even better – had made good use of the opportunity.

The conversation now turned to the customary subjects – to pastures; hunting; surveys of the lands in the neighborhood, and the disputes of adjacent residents often linked with this; a murder that occurred about five days earlier on the other bank of the Arkansas, where a cattle dealer had been shot and robbed of his wallet, which had contained about a thousand dollars, without the murderer being discovered; then to the current legislation, the election of the sheriff, the governor, etc., until the brightly colored Yankee clock adorning the mantelpiece struck eight. But now the infant, who had been sleeping softly in its hammock that had been hung up in the house, began to stir and cry. Ellen took it out of its little bed and walked with him back and forth in the room, but it cried ever more insistently and would not let itself be comforted, and in scarcely a quarter hour became so sick that the women, worried to death, ran to and fro to fetch every possible remedy they could scrape up in the house.

But it was all in vain; the child cried harder every instant, and now in mortal terror the mother sent out for help. A young American[2] had been charged to hew out a large and very roomy canoe for Atkins over the past few days and was still staying in the house. He and the mulatto were now sent off in various directions to any neighboring or distant farmer's wives who knew anything about children's illnesses to make them acquainted with the poor tot's condition, and to summon them to come as fast as their horses could carry them.

The mother, meanwhile, behaved like a half-crazy person. She ran about the house as if robbed of her wits, all the while making the bitterest accusations against Ellen, that she had neglected the child and would have been happy to get rid of it herself just to be free of worrying about its care.

To no avail, the girl protested her innocence and invoked the love that she had always shown for the little screamer; it was all in vain, and with the harshest, most unjust accusations the woman ordered her to be still and "quiet as a mouse," if she did not want to discover how obstinate *servants* were treated.

Brown was indignant at this, and resolved from now on to try everything within his power to support his friend and to liberate the maid from such mistreatment, though at this moment he knew only too well that any objection would not just be useless, but would have still more unpleasant consequences for the poor girl.

The confusion had now reached its highest stage. The poor little creature seemed to get sicker with every passing moment; Ellen, with quietly tearful eyes full of fear, tried to minister to the dear little one, and the mother, no longer heeding the stranger's presence in the slightest, ran up and down the room and cried, all the while wringing her hands, that this was heaven's punishment for all her sins and weaknesses visited on her now through the poor innocent child. Then suddenly, from outside, a strange man's voice sought entrance, and the dogs, awakened by this, struck up a loud baying and howling. The wind that had blown but gently from the south the whole day had shifted; coming from the northwest, it churned the boughs and branches of the mighty trunks in a mad tangle, and when the door was opened, blew out the light standing on the table. The fire in the hearth had meanwhile burned down somewhat as well, and the house suddenly lay in a deep nighttime darkness.

"Hello in there – can I overnight here?" the voice cried then for the second time – "the devil take the dogs – would you shut up!"

"Quiet, Hector – quiet, Deik – down with you, you rascals – can't you let a man get a word in?" angrily shouted Atkins at the dogs, stepping to the door – then turned to the stranger: "Get off! My boy'll take care of the horse."

"Do the dogs bite?" asked the other, cautiously obeying the invitation and feeling his way over the fence.

"No," said Atkins, "not if I'm with them. But come here and don't fall over the wood there – wait – the steel grinder's there – don't bump into it – so – three steps, the bottom one wobbles a bit. Oh, Ellen, just light the lantern again!"

Ellen had meanwhile been busily engaged in bringing a few pine chips for a fire. Soon the room was sufficiently illuminated that they could at least see the man, who at this moment came into the room, laid aside his old riding cloak and otter skin cap, and with a friendly greeting to the family at the hearth, stepped into the bright glow of the fire, now once more flaming high. He was a small stocky man with lively grey eyes, long straight blond hair, and lots of freckles, clothed in a cotton hunting shirt and gaiters of the same material, while an old and well-worn saddlebag that he carried over his arm and now laid down next to the hearth, appeared to contain all that he needed for a ride through the woods in so wild a region. Indeed, as he approached the two men, his glance shifted restlessly from one to the other, and he seemed to be asking himself which of them he should address as the landlord of the house.

Madame Atkins, by the by, may have been less pleased with the new guest, who promised only more upset and commotion, for she now took the little suffering creature on her arm with a rather sullen look, wrapped it in a blanket, and called to Ellen to follow her with a light and kindling into the other houoo, whoro a fire would be lit on the hearth at once. Ellen quickly complied with the command, and there was every likelihood that Madame would not be seen again this evening.

"Terrible wind outside," said the stranger after a pause, during which he had stared down in front of him while he apparently came to an agreement with himself as to the identity of the landlord; "it blows as if it wanted to rip up the oaks by the roots."

"Yes, it's a little rough out there," opined Atkins, casting an inquisitive glance at his guest. "Have you come a long way?"

"No, not so far – from the Mississippi."

"Going farther westward?"

"Yes – to Fort Gibson – how far is it yet to the Fourche La Fave?"

"I live on the river," said Atkins, and as he did so met the gaze of the stranger. Brown, spurred to action by the restlessness of the child and the entrance of the newcomer, had meanwhile taken his seat at the fire again, and entertained himself with the long fire stick that leaned in the corner of the hearth, occasionally poking it here and there into the coals to destroy a figure that had formed itself in the embers, or to fashion a new one.

"You've ridden along the bank of the river for several miles," he said, now involving himself in the conversation, "but you couldn't see it, since the reeds are probably a quarter mile wide and very thick."

"Yes, I thought that the river must be close. – Nice cane that – it must make fine fodder. – The pasturage is likely good here?"

"Very good," answered Atkins, and again he locked eyes with the stranger, who, careful to keep Brown in sight from the corner of his eye, looked up at him. But Brown stopped in the middle of what he was doing and, deep in thought, left the stick in the fire, where it began to burn brightly. He looked thoughtfully into the fireplace, as if he wanted to recall to his mind something or other that had halfway slipped away from him.

"I've ridden hard," the stranger now broke the short silence, "and the wind's made me thirsty; might I ask you for a swig of water?"

"Well, of course," replied Atkins, and rushed quickly to the bucket to serve the guest what he required. But Brown, gripped by a sudden thought, looked at the stranger and found his gaze firmly fastened on him; he turned instantly to Atkins, though, took the gourd bottle from his hand, and took a long, long drink.

"As soon as I heard this gentleman here ask for water I realized that I'm thirsty too," said Brown, now once more fully composed; meanwhile, he recalled with perfect clarity the conversation in the eerie cabin on the Arkansas, and resolved in no way to let the two men see that they had somehow drawn his suspicion, or that he had any idea of their connection.

"Wait, gentlemen," cried Atkins now – "There you are, drinking the cold stuff all by itself with such a storm outside; how about we pour a little drop of whiskey first? Let that clear the way, and the water can't do any harm afterward."

"That'll profit all three of us," grinned the stranger, while the landlord went to a small sideboard and instantly brought from it a jug and three tin cups.

"Here, Mr. Brown – pour it yourself," he said to the latter, holding out the jug for him – "oh – properly, that's hardly even a drop – that's right. – The more unfriendly the storm is outside, the friendlier we must see it kept inside. – And now, you sir, just what's your name? Mine's Atkins, and that man there is Brown!"

"My name is *Jones*," replied the guest. "John Jones – easy to remember, right? – now, to a better acquaintance, Mr. Atkins – to a better acquaintance, Mr. Brown!" And he lifted the cup to his lips with a friendly glance up at the men. But a half scornful, half fearful smile flitted across Atkins' features as the man who called himself Jones raised a glass "to a better acquaintance" with the Regulator. But he dared not betray what he thought with a single expression or a single look, and contented himself merely to touch the cups of the other two as he said, from the bottom of his soul: "That we may always remain very good friends!"

Ellen, meanwhile, had spread several covers and mattresses on the floor and began to arrange a bed out of them, though she replied to Atkins' question about the state of the sick child's health, saying that it seemed to be in terrible pain, though none of them knew what ailed it.

"Can you get away from caring for it for maybe a quarter hour?" asked the father.

"I hardly know – Madame –"

"Very well – just put the pots on the fire," Atkins interrupted – "you must make something quick for supper for Mr. Jones here. I'll tell my wife about it in the meantime."

With these words he left the room, and Ellen swiftly made all the necessary preparations for the simple table of the western farmer, which consisted of nothing more than warm cornbread, fried bacon, hot coffee, and some butter, cheese, and honey. The two men meanwhile sat quietly on the hearth, and Brown watched the slim figure of the pretty girl, who with bustling haste and skillful hand took care of everything necessary, while Jones, as though deep in thought, worked the long stick around in the fire and knocked glowing coals off the large logs. He only interrupted this labor at last to cast a glance, with a somewhat impatient expression, at the clock standing over the hearth, and then at the door through which he expected Atkins to come back.

The latter finally appeared, and at the same time the supper for the belated guest was ready. But Ellen had still more cooking to do, for just then several horses again stopped outside the door; women's voices were audible, and the sharp tones of Mrs. Atkins sounded shrilly across to her to set out the coffee and to keep ready a considerable pot.

Brown still sat thinking next to the hearth, his head leaning on the side beams; but Atkins lit a second light and said to him cordially:

"Mr. Brown, you seem worn out, here's your light, and if you want to lie down, I'll show you your bed."

"Oh, please, don't make a special fuss on my account!" cried the young man, who saw the beds that Ellen brought in lying rolled together in the corner – "I can wait, and I'm not at all sleepy."

"We have a bed above here," Atkins replied to him, "there you can lie undisturbed, and early tomorrow morning, as early as you please, you can take off for Bowitt's. Anyway, we here below will get little rest, since I just now heard several women neighbors coming in. – The child must be sicker than I thought to start with."

"Looks like you have lady visitors?"

"Unfortunately," sighed the farmer with undisguised dismay, "and may the dear Lord grant that the poor little tyke soon recovers again, otherwise they'll *blather* it to death – so if –"

"Well, in that case I think it's better that I retire," the young man said with a smile; "so good night, gentlemen – will Mr. Jones come up later as well?"

"There's only one bed up there; I guess I'll have to request that Mr. Jones sleep down here –"

"Oh, for God's sake don't make a fuss on my account!" cried the latter, holding his cup toward Ellen, who filled it again from the big heavy tin can. "Good night, then! If you don't get away too early tomorrow, perhaps I'll have the pleasure of your company on the road – of course, I don't know which direction –"

"Upriver. – No, I won't ride so very early," replied Brown; "until morning, then."

With this he also nodded a friendly good night to the maiden, and in the next instant disappeared into the upper part of the house – which, in truth, was formed just by laying boards crossways over the beams. Atkins returned soon afterwards with the light, and he and the stranger observed the deepest silence as long as Ellen was still in the room, partly preparing a bed for the guest, partly putting away the dishes and tablecloth again. Finally, though, she had finished everything; she put the light on the table, took with her the coffee pot and a basket full of cups, and withdrew with a soft "good night" which neither of the men heard, or at least neither acknowledged.

She had hardly left the room when Atkins stood up, snuffed out the light so that the room was but barely illuminated by the crackling logs, and beckoned to the guest to follow him.

"Someone sent you to me?" he whispered then, after he had led the other far enough from the house so that nothing could be heard from there.

"Yes," replied the stranger – "Your name?"

"Atkins."

"Good – I bring horses."

"Where are they?"

"In the bend of the creek."

"Right in the water?"

"Well, of course."

"But how did you know the place? Have you been in these parts before?"

"I should think so," the other said with a smile. "I made the first axe cut here, and Brogan bought the place from me, which *you* then purchased from him."

"So, you yourself placed that secret –"

"All right," Jones interrupted him warily, "what's the use of saying things that somebody else here in the dark might possibly hear. I've never spoken of such matters. Is the gate still in the upper fence corner?"

"Yes indeed; where the creek flows by it."

"Good, then make arrangements to stable the animals; I'll fetch them in the meantime."

"And you don't need any help?"

"None, until we have them inside the fence," and with these words the laconic speaker turned away from his host and in a few seconds had disappeared in the dark. Atkins, however, returned to the house, then went around it and walked diagonally across the small open space to a kind of courtyard in which six or eight horses were running about freely. He climbed over the fence that ran around it, and then likewise was lost in the gloomy raven-black night.

Brown found his suspicions confirmed when he saw through the gaps in the wall the two men quietly leave the house together, and for a long time was undecided whether he should follow them and catch them in the act, or let them quietly complete their nocturnal deeds. But what could he do, alone and defenseless, facing men surely prepared and armed for any surprise? He would only warn them that they were discovered and squelch any further unraveling of the crimes themselves. Thus he remained silent, lying outstretched on his bed, and ruminated on the incidents and singular circumstances of the past day.

Ellen, the innocent child, was in no way privy to the outrageous deeds; otherwise she would not have so ingenuously betrayed Cotton's sojourns and visits, since the sheriff had been on his trail for several weeks. But where did this Cotton live? Where was the cabin or thicket that could conceal a criminal for so many days without the neighbors having at least noticed some slight trace of him? It must be near here, since the man would hardly dare to undertake a long march, especially by day. So where was his hideout? Who lived here in the neighborhood? Wilson? It wasn't with him – Pelter? He belonged to the Regulators alongside him – Johnson? This would be more likely – and here a new source of suspicion presented itself. The pursuers had overtaken Johnson's horses that night; Husfield swore he knew the tracks, and that he had seen their prints again on the north bank; on the other bank they had only followed these horses and found unfamiliar animals that had by no means stamped their hoofs on the opposite bank; Curtis, Cook, and Husfield, had, at least, pledged their salvation on the certainty that they had nowhere seen the large hoofs of one of the horses the previous day.

Johnson and Cotton – there had to be an understanding governing these two; but they could not have carried out all this alone; who were the others, and were they linked in some way to the killings?

At last his head ached from much musing, his thoughts grew confused. The various figures and places that he had seen became blurred in weird and jumbled images; he dreamed at last that he was transformed into the preacher Rowson, and Marion bent down over him and kissed him and called him by the tenderest names while his heart bled, since he owed all this to the likeness of his rival. Finally, these troubled dreams left him as well; his spirit, like his body, yielded to the strain he had borne, and he slept peacefully and soundly.

Notes

1. Roughly contemporary with the events of the novel (1839–44), and just over the state line from Arkansas, the Regulator-Moderator War broke out over cattle thefts in Shelby County, Texas. The "Regulators" were formed to get illegal activities under control, while the "Moderators," in turn, were formed to combat the excesses of the Regulators. Bloody fighting erupted across Shelby and adjacent counties until Sam Houston, president of the Republic of Texas, sent troops to put an end to the hostilities.

2. "A young American": another lapse in FG's point of view (see note 6, chapter 14).

Chapter 23

A Gang of Criminals. –
Unexpected Guests. – The New Scheme.

We must return once more to the twilight hour of this same evening, and specifically to a small but comfortable log cabin that lay in the thick woods and was not connected to the other various residents of the county by any road, or at least one that was easily recognized. Johnson dwelt here and had purchased the place from a hunter about a year before for twenty dollars cash money, a woolen blanket, and a Bowie knife. Later, indeed, he had made a start toward a small field, but he quite soon abandoned this again; then he merely fenced in a small barnyard to keep the wild swine and cows roaming about from his door, or to prevent a horse that he wished to keep nearby from seeking the open range. Since, moreover, he was rarely to be met with in his cabin, which itself lay well out of the way and completely isolated, as has already been said, so it was not often that a settler, or at most a hunter, strayed into this region. Thus the owner had seen his wish fulfilled: to be able to live alone and undisturbed.

The only person with whom he kept any social relations in this neighborhood was Atkins, whose mulatto, who had been initiated into his master's secret, often carried messages back and forth. But now the cabin, otherwise so lonesome, appeared to be not at all empty and desolate, since a bright and warming fire crackled in the fireplace, over which a great iron pot hung from a fixed rod laid across it. Sitting in front of the flame, on low armchairs and chairs, sat Cotton and Johnson, engaged in earnest conversation and both waiting with apparent eagerness for the kettle or pot hanging before them to boil.

"Listen, Johnson – bubbles are rising now," at last said Cotton, rough and impatient – "move along so I can get my drink; I have to hurry, or I might not find Atkins still at home."

"Wait a few seconds, the drink will go flat if the water doesn't boil right," replied his companion – "but wait – it's starting now; now hand your cup here, I won't hold you up any longer."

"Damn it, that's hot!" cursed the other, as he impatiently brought the iron cup to his lips – "it doesn't cool off at all in these confounded dishes."

"Well, that can't be helped," Johnson said with a laugh, "We don't know glass and porcelain here – who the devil is coming there?"

"Where?" cried Cotton, and sprang with a single leap halfway up the little ladder that provided a connection between the upper part of the house and the lower.

"Oh, stay here," said Johnson, who had stepped close to one of the gaps and looked through it, "it's Dan – Atkins' mulatto."

"Now what the devil does he want?" cried Cotton with surprise as he came back and took his seat again. "No bad news hopefully?"

"Here he is and can speak for himself," said Johnson, opening the door and admitting the faithful yellow. "Well, Dan, what do you have to say?"

"Massa Cotton's to stay here," answered the other, baring his teeth and taking off his hat, "Massa Brown's at his place and is going to sleep there."

"Brown? What in the name of the devil leads him up here?" cried Cotton angrily – "I had something very important to talk with Atkins about this very day."

"Has a Regulator meeting tomorrow at Bowitt's," said the mulatto, as he spat his old chewing tobacco into the fireplace and with considerable familiarity cut off a small new plug from the piece that lay next to a knife on the small four-cornered table, close by a bed against the wall.

"Regulator meeting – plague on it!" said Cotton, gritting his teeth. "If I could do as I liked, I'd make those fellows dance lively tomorrow. – But wait, your time is coming, and if we can't let all of you have it, it'll be much easier when we're dealing with individuals."

"Does your master have anything else for us?" asked Johnson.

"No, Massa – nothing more; he'll come over here himself tomorrow morning."

"Then tell him we'll wait for him – do you hear? Well, why do you stand there and stare?"

"Massa," said the mulatto, and his ivory teeth became visible from one earlobe to the other – "there's an empty cup standing there."

"Ah – the flunky's thirsty," Johnson laughed. "Well, here – drink and go to the devil!"

"Thank you, Massa," said Dan; he poured the hot drink down his cunning throat in one gulp, nodded a curt farewell to the two men, and in the next instant again broke into a full run through the thick sassafras that surrounded the place, in order to get back to the house as fast as he could.

"Well," grumbled Cotton, as he settled back comfortably in the seat that he just relinquished, "this evening, at least, I can make myself easy and don't need to rush around. But this Brown – Regulators – poison and rattlesnakes take the fellows, if they –"

His speech was cut short at this point by the distinct clatter of a horse, and with a single bound he once more stood on the ladder, though this time with a full cup in his hand, in order to escape the notice of any unwelcome eye. But once more his caution was unnecessary, since Johnson, who had been looking out, cried out in astonishment, "Rowson!" Even before Cotton could return to the fire and Johnson could pull the peg from the door, that worthy man was already rattling the very poorly secured gate and demanding entrance.

"Hell and damnation, don't leave a fellow waiting out here for an hour!" he cried out impatiently when Johnson could not pull back the wooden linchpin fast enough.

"Hello there," Cotton said with a laugh as the door came unfastened, "that has a Christian ring – you're mighty quick to condemn. What if we'd had strangers with us here by chance, eh? Wouldn't the respectable Methodist have put on quite a show with his mouth full of curses?"

"The plague take 'em all!" snapped the preacher, "pretty soon it won't matter whether folks here think I pray or curse. – I've got to leave."

"What!" cried Johnson, springing up from the chair onto which he had just settled down, "Leave? Have they found out that –"

"Nonsense," said the preacher, annoyed, "best guard your tongue, nothing's discovered yet, though it could be at any moment. The Indian is back."

"If only his Nannabozho[1] had carried him off along the way," said Cotton resentfully, "the redskin's a thorn in my side, and I'd give anything if I could get him out of the way."

"Well, the Indian can't work miracles," Johnson laughed scornfully as he filled his cup anew and handed another across to Rowson, who emptied it with a single gulp. – "The tracks were wiped out long ago, and without them the copper-colored wretch can't get started."

"That's not all," fumed the Methodist, "the devil has taken possession of the rabble around here, and the old Regulator demon is haunting them once more. There's a big meeting tomorrow, and *there live some suspects in the area here that they want to seize* and, of course, want to *interrogate in great detail.* How do you like that?"

"Great thunder!" cried Johnson. "Then a change of scenery will be beneficial for me too. They'll come to *this* nest first; but I don't know, what *you* have to be afraid of in all this? Nobody's cast the least suspicion on you."

"It's the Indian that makes me worry," Rowson said, gritting his teeth; "if only I knew how to get rid of the scalp-locked scoundrel."

"That'll be tough," said Cotton thoughtfully, "but it's possible –"

"And then put the county into even more of an uproar, right? No, enough blood has been spilled here, and the best thing would be that we take to our heels as fast as possible. The storm over our heads can break any day."

"It would just have to be done carefully," continued Cotton, without heeding Rowson's objection. "Everyone around here says that the Indian killed a chief of his tribe and then fled; nothing would be more natural than that a relative of the one killed might follow him out of there to make him atone for the blood guilt. But to carry out something like that for sure, he'd naturally have used nothing other than a *poisoned* arrow, and a fellow can't have lived in Texas and the Arkansas Territory for years without that fellow being able to make up an arrow like that."

"Do you know how to make the poison?" Rowson asked quickly.

"Ah, what good will that do you?" cried Johnson, interrupting them angrily, "the Indian's still just *one* person we can easily keep away from us; the danger lies deeper. If these Regulators dogs really got on the right track and caught one of us who's got his mouth instead of his heart in the right place, then the devil will be our godfather. No, in this case Rowson's right; then it would be better if we all found ourselves on the other side of Uncle Sam's borderline; but we can wait and see. There're still some among us who are *free* of suspicion, like for instance you, Rowson, and even Atkins – you must join the meeting, and if you hear anything there that seems suspicious to you, well, saddle up fast and ride hard. We can find another Arkansas anywhere."

"I'd doubt that," said Rowson, "and anyway talk is cheap for you single people; you throw your rifle on your shoulder, and the instant you throw your right leg over the saddle, you're free men – but I –"

"You're still single," Johnson interjected.

"Yes – today still – but tomorrow evening no more."

"You see the matter too darkly, Rowson," Cotton said with a laugh – "goddamn me, if I had such a reputation as you here in the neighborhood, and stood in such good stead with the ladies, ten horses couldn't drag me out of Yell County. Besides, *if* you're so nervous, why are you getting married then? Just put off the business again. It'll be really tough anyway if we come to your place afterwards and have to be careful with every word that crosses the tongue."

"I can't back out again without raising suspicion," said the minister, as he paced intensely up and down the room, "if I'd just known all that this morning – it would've still been possible to at least put off the thing, but – plague and poison – once I'm married, my wife will have to follow me wherever I go, and that can be arranged in short order. A letter from my old aunt in Memphis who wants to see me once more before she dies should be a sufficient excuse, and once I'm gone they can slander me all they want. It's up to me to see that they don't find me again. – But the Indian; the confounded redskin scares me –"

"Ah, well," grumbled Cotton, "if he should ever get *too* dangerous, then we can always get him out of the way fast. But now, as you very rightly observed, it would only make for more bad blood among the settlers, who anyway are already more watchful than they really need to be because of the *last* blood spilled; but be prepared –"

"Just leave the confounded Indian out of the game," snapped Johnson – "the Regulators are what we have to fear; that's where the pressure on us is coming from, so *that's* the direction in which we have to act. Can *you* attend the meeting, Rowson?"

"Yes – I hope so," answered the latter, "at least so far, they couldn't have any serious reason to object to my presence. I'm planning to go there, in any case."

"Good – then for now there's no real reason that we should worry. It'll be easy for you to get to know about any important business, and we won't have to fear being surprised anymore."

"I can do that, but *now* I can't risk buying Atkins' house and land," said Rowson, "the devil may take his turn, and then I'd be damnably tied down."

"As for that, it comes down to how your cash box stands," answered Johnson – "if the two hundred dollars that he's charging for it is *not* too near and dear to your heart, then by buying it you can keep a lot of people quiet who might otherwise cast suspicion on you around here. But if that's –"

"Yes, you're right!" said Rowson with quick decision, "I'll buy the place, in fact I'll do it first thing Monday; moreover, from this day forward, I'm saying that I *won't* be part of any new undertakings. I want to try one time, at least, to live as an honest man and sleep peacefully."

"It's about time," said Cotton with a scornful laugh; "but I'd still advise Mr. Preacher to take his young wife to the island – that would be a grand place for a missionary."

Rowson turned away glowering, but Johnson took up the conversation and said to Rowson:

"Since Cotton's just mentioned the *island,* I think it's high time to make me better acquainted with circumstances there. Though I know it lies in the Mississippi, and where, I know nothing more about it, in spite of the fact that I've delivered horses there twice myself. The rogues that took them always did it so secretly that I couldn't get anything out of them."

"So it went with me this time," said Cotton, cursing, "if the Regulators had been on our heels, God strike me, they'd have nabbed us, since I'll be damned if those fellows would take us in their boat. We had to turn over the horses, and Weston and I camped on the riverbank until they came back again about two hours later and brought us the money. Weston nearly died of curiosity."

"Hey, listen up," whispered Rowson softly, as if he were afraid of being heard by someone nearby, "no one for sure can hear us from outside?"

"No," said Johnson – "you can speak safely – though I really wish that Cotton had his dog here and hadn't left him at Atkins'."

"He's better off there," Cotton maintained – "but hurry up – time's passing, and I'm tired."

"Well, all right," said Rowson, "I don't see why you shouldn't learn the *whole* secret when you already know enough to betray it. You know about the island – or at least the way to it – but farther down lies a second with lots of splendid hiding places in case the residents of the upper one should ever be attacked or surprised. A good swimmer could easily reach the lower one, especially at night. The people occupying that region used to be under the command of Morrel, who's now become a cobbler, I think, or something like that, in the Philadelphia penitentiary; in any case, they've taught him a trade. At present, the leader of the islanders is a certain – but the name isn't important – I had to swear to keep quiet about it."

"So it's a well-organized band of thieves then?" asked Cotton.

"Yes – better than any that ever existed, and almost completely safe from discovery, since those they're connected with can only benefit from the band's existence, and never by betraying it."

"And how do they carry on their business, so their neighbors are never bothered, or even suspect their existence?"

"The same way the fox does it," Rowson said with a laugh, "only when faced with the direst necessity will he steal a hen from the farmyards next to his abode; we're like him in that regard."

"Leave off your moralizing remarks, if you please," grumbled Cotton – "get to the point – to the point."

"Well, all right then, the point. – They have very little to do with the states they live between, except with the one to the east, as their connections stretch well into Mississippi; for that reason, they need our horses, since they have to be mighty careful in the densely populated areas on that side. All their wealth, though, comes down from upriver. In every big city – that is, on the Mississippi as well as on the Ohio, on the Wabash, the Illinois, yes even on the Missouri – they have their agents, young lads from Kentucky and Illinois for the most part, and these spy around to see which boats are going down the river and what they're loaded with. If it's something that they wish to have, or that they think they can sell quickly and profitably in the southern cities, then they look for a position as pilot, and if that doesn't work, as a common rower, so they can guide the boat straight and proper up to their island and there, by cunning or force, let it run ashore. Naturally this has to happen at night, when only one boatman at the most is on deck. A sign beforehand announces the arrival of a new boat, and the crew – bites the dust."

"Hell and brimstone!" cried Cotton. "Then I don't have to wonder any more where all the bodies in the Mississippi come from; at the beginning of February I was in Natchez when, one time, seven came down together, and every single one without the slightest wound. At the time we thought their boat had capsized."

"Yes, they know how to arrange it cleverly," said Rowson – "but the business is too bloody for me; I want nothing to do with it."

"No, nor I," said Cotton shuddering – "God have mercy on us, that's called running the thing like a butcher's trade! What if there are women in the boats?"

"Young women will be kept on the island, although inside and under guard to be sure, since every member is allowed to have *one* wife."

"So they don't get them out of the way?" asked Johnson.

"That I don't know, and it doesn't concern me," Rowson replied, "but that's exactly the island's greatest safeguard, that all of us can regard it as our place of last refuge. If we're in extreme danger, we'll be taken in there and protected too, that you can be sure of."

"I saw that this last time!" cried Cotton. "I could've perished on the bank, not one of those scoundrels would've lifted a hand."

"Because you didn't know the right sign," Rowson said with a laugh. "Do you think they take everyone across who stands on the landing and yells and waves?"

"But what's the distress signal?"

"Run between the two popcorn trees standing on the bank four times, back and forth – at night of course, with a burning stick of wood – and mind how fast armed men in a boat are at hand."

"Four times, then?" Cotton said thoughtfully – "well, who knows how soon we'll all make use of those fellows' hospitality."

"But step once onto the island," – Rowson warned him – "and you'll belong to them forever –"

"Were you ever on it?" asked the hunter slyly.

"No – not yet," replied the Methodist, breaking off suddenly, "but where's Weston – wouldn't it be better that he's also aware of the danger that's threatening us?"

"Atkins's sent him to the upper settlement," Johnson interjected. "He was supposed to get back to his house tomorrow and then come to mine."

"As for me," said Cotton yawning – "I'm tired and I'm going to sleep. Is there anything still in the pot, Johnson?"

"No, you have what's left there in your cup."

"Well, good night then; whoever wakes up first in the morning, wake the others." With that he shoved into place a few deerskins that lay in the corner, drew an old woolen blanket over his shoulders, threw himself on the hard bed, and was, in just a few minutes, fast asleep.

Johnson and Rowson sat silently beside one another, staring into the coals; each seemed still to have something on his mind, but neither wanted to begin, and several times already the Methodist had jumped up, walked up and down the room, and then stopped again by the fireplace. Finally, Johnson broke the silence and said softly:

"Are you afraid they've discovered us?"

"No," answered the preacher in the same carefully subdued tone. "No, but I'm afraid that it *will* happen."

"How's that possible? –"

"Possible? Rather ask how it's possible that it hasn't happened yet."

"You're a fool and see ghosts everywhere."

"Such foolishness never brought anyone harm," answered the preacher bleakly – "I'm afraid the Indian's become suspicious. The look he threw at me today makes me almost certain."

"Of course, you've got a *particular* reason to be afraid of the Indian," Johnson whispered softly.

"And who told you? –"

"Psst," his friend quieted him – "that one there – but calm down, maybe it's actually better for you that I know about it. Anyway, it was necessary, and I'd have handled it the same. Were you careful to destroy all the evidence?"

"The question's unnecessary. – I washed my clothes the same night, though it was hard enough for me to manage with the wound in my arm. I cut out the hole the little witch made in my sleeve with her tomahawk and put another patch there, and I buried my knife for a full week. But despite all this, an indescribable dread grips me when I think back to that evening, and – I don't know – I almost feel as if I halfway regretted –"

"Oh, nonsense," said Johnson scornfully – "but what about the other one – have you found the little knife again?"

"No," whispered Rowson, much more softly than before, "it's in Roberts' hands – I've seen it myself; he asked me if I knew it. – Johnson, I still don't quite understand how I didn't give myself away *that* instant."

"People say that a rich fellow on the Arkansas River had over a thousand dollars taken from him," said the other now, as he cast a sharp side-glance at his friend – "in fact, you were in the area at that time – did you hear anything about it?"

"Oh, a plague on your foolish gossip!" said Rowson with a curse. – "How should I know about every murder that's committed in the state? Mind your own business and leave me out of the game. And are you sure that Weston can keep his mouth shut? We shouldn't have sent him to the island."

"I believe he's trustworthy," answered Johnson thoughtfully – "and, by the by, one can't see into a man's heart. – So you're really getting married tomorrow?"

"Yes – not exactly under the most favorable circumstances, indeed; but it's the best I can do. – If things become known, well, then the devil may have the whole business; in that case, it would be the smallest of sins to think last of my wife."

"With *those* principles, the marriage won't be much of a hindrance to you," laughed his friend. – "So the girl doesn't matter to you?"

"Do you think that I'd have risked everything to win her if I *didn't* love her?" asked the preacher quickly; "it's a wild and raging passion that draws me to the innocent creature, and I positively feel that this very love is the worst sin that I've committed in my life."

"And still, you can already think about leaving her again?"

"Show me how it's possible to escape and take her with me *against* her will, and you'll find me ready body and soul – but it can't be done. Every stranger she spoke to would afford her protection, and we can't expose ourselves to that. No – if I *could* still back out – maybe I'd do it – maybe not; but it can't be done any more, so she may share my fate as long as possible. – After all, she'll be *mine!*"

"So have you taken any precautions at home in case an escape should be necessary?"

"I should think you've known me long enough for that," said the priest. "There's a small canoe carefully hidden in the little canebrake right below the house; a small suitcase with all the necessary supplies for a journey has been packed and standing ready since that night the Indian woman discovered us, and my weapons are always in order and near at hand – you know the secret passage yourself –"

"How many can the canoe carry?"

"Four, five if necessary – it's big enough and splendidly built; with three oars we could reach the Arkansas in six hours."

"That's carefully arranged – though I hope that we don't have to use it. If we can throw the Regulators off our trail this time, then we're safe. But good night – you lie on the mattress there – meanwhile I'll see to your horse one more time."

Rowson, who was very tired, gladly accepted the invitation, and for a short while no sound was heard other than the deep breathing of the sleepers. Then suddenly there resounded through the silent night the loud shrill cry of an owl; then again, and now a final time. Johnson stood up and climbed over those sleeping in the middle of room to get to the door.

"Well, what are you creeping around here for?" asked Rowson, whose arm he had stepped on.

"Did you hear the owl?" said the other softly.

"Well, bless God, you really want to shoot owls?" grumbled the weary man. "You don't have any chickens here, remember? –"

"Psst!" exclaimed Johnson, as the same sound was heard again, this time indeed in four distinct calls – "it's Atkins – by all that lives! What's bringing him down here in night and fog? – closer now!" he then called out, stepping to the door – "closer now – we're all friends here."

"Good evening, Johnson," said the broad-shouldered farmer, as he climbed over the small fence and approached the door – "we're late guests, aren't we?"

"*We*? – whom do you bring then?"

"A friend who delivered *merchandise*; he'd really like to meet you. But who exactly is in the house with you?"

"Cotton and Rowson."

"Rowson?" asked the stranger wrapped in his dark cloak, now stepping forward quickly – "Rowson? well, well, I hadn't thought that I'd find an old acquaintance this evening!"

"Old acquaintance?" grumbled Rowson from inside by the fireplace, where he was just then trying to stir up a new glow in the half-extinguished coals – "old acquaintance? Who might that be?"

"So you know Rowson?"

"I should think so!" laughed the little man – "is he still preaching?"

"He can best answer that himself," said the Methodist in not exactly the friendliest tone, as he stepped forward with a flickering splint of pinewood held high. But after an initial and nearly incredulous glare, he had hardly recognized the stranger, who now stepped openly into the light, when he extended his hand joyfully and cried out jubilantly:

"Well, as I live, Hokker! – so what brings you to Arkansas once more? Did it get too warm for you in Missouri? Well, you're heartily welcome among us, old boy – just come in, the wind here's blowing the torches out!"

"We can't stay long," said Atkins, "since we've just stolen away quietly from home. Should –"

"Oh, don't make such a fuss," Cotton cried out from within the house, – "time passes no more slowly *outside* the door than here inside, and the damned cold comes in through the open door." Nothing could be said to that, and the men followed Rowson, who lighted the way to the fireplace that he had barely left, and where the empty drinking vessels still lay scattered around in disorder.

"Do you have a drink left?" asked Atkins, as he tipped the great iron pot halfway over to let the light shine inside it – "not a drop more left in there, as I live!"

"Be patient for another quarter hour," said Johnson, "and it won't be lacking."

"No," Atkins interjected, "we really must be going again –"

"Well, first just say what you have to say," his host interrupted him, "while the water boils. *That* at least needn't delay you."

"Well, Hokker, how's it look in Missouri?" asked Rowson, roughly shaking his hand again.

"First of all, no more *Hokker*," laughed the stranger – "my name is Jones – J. Jones, if anyone should ask."

"All right, all right," Rowson grinned, "it's pretty much the same – but what brings you here?"

The stranger, who, as the conversation quickly revealed, was a rather intimate friend of Rowson's in earlier times, now told him and his comrades that he had left Missouri because of "certain misunderstandings" and had taken up residence in Franklin and Crawford counties, in the western parts of the state.[2] There alone was it really possible, as he put it, to maintain "trading connections" with the Indians as well as the whites. Presently "company business" had compelled him to visit Yell County, since because of "envious men" his former favorite path down the Arkansas had become dangerous, and he now intended to stay at least a few days in the area. On the one hand, he wanted to "let his trail get cold," and on the other he wished, given his *present* circumstances, to better acquaint himself with *this* stretch of land, for which he still had a special fondness from earlier times, and of which in "very recent times" he had heard so much that was praiseworthy.

Rowson had listened to his old friend's words with particular interest and frequent approving nods of the head. But now, as the other finished and Johnson again filled the cups with the freshly brewed, sweet, and powerfully fragrant drink, he jumped up, thrust his hand over toward Jones, and cried out:

"Do you want to be one of us? If you want to play your part at once in the comedy that we're putting on here, just shake on it! You can start work first thing in the morning."

"Actually, that started a long time ago," said the stranger with a smile, "and as far as *comedy* is concerned, for some time I've even been used to advantage in *plays of intrigue*, as they say at the theatre in Little Rock. I didn't squander the time I spent in New Orleans, by any means. But all right, it's a *deal*; if I'm up to the thing, and perhaps in the process can still be useful to us upstate as well, then you've found your man in me. Only I still don't rightly know *how*."

"You're going to discover that right now," said Rowson, gleefully rubbing his hands as he took his seat again while half emptying the cup that Johnson handed him. – "Tomorrow there's a Regulators meeting."

"Well, if that's the whole of the joyful message you wish to bring me," Jones said laughing, "then you could have saved yourself the trouble and effort. That would be a reason instead for me to continue on my journey quicker than I'd planned."

"No, you can't do that," cried Rowson, "you must attend the meeting!"

"I? That's the last thing I need!" cried Jones, astonished.

"Yes, you!" continued Rowson, without allowing himself to be interrupted. "None of the current settlers here know you; those who lived in the area when you built Atkins' house are long since dead or have moved away. At first I was going to attend the proceedings myself, but for me the thing has several catches. In the first place, it would barely allow me the time I need tomorrow, though I would have had to make it work if you hadn't come. But then, too, there are some here on the river who don't much like me and would, I'm quite convinced, shy away from saying much in my presence. But early tomorrow I'll introduce you to young Brown (I must get there before you set out) as a 'Regulator from Missouri,' indeed, who has come here to Arkansas to form an alliance with the local Regulators so that the two states might combine their forces in this regard. Such an approach is the best chance to control the dreadful state of affairs that, with respect to horse flesh, threatens to ruin the honest and hard-working farming folk of the Backwoods."[3]

"Splendid! Priceless!" Atkins rejoiced – "that's a really capital plan."

"But I don't know if I have enough time," said Jones thoughtfully, as he tapped the empty tin cup on the seat in front of him.

"Have time!" replied Rowson. "You can't use your time any better, surely, than to uncover their plans and then thwart those that, if carried out, might make an alliance between you and your friends an impossibility, or at least might make it so dangerous that no sensible fellow would risk his neck to carry out such a thing."

"That's certainly true," said Jones reflectively, while he held his cup close to the kettle for a refill, "certainly true – but – would Brown believe me? True, I didn't mention anything about it to him this evening."

"Sure, because you didn't know that he was a Regulator, and you're not going to blab such news to every stranger."

"Certainly – not bad – but will the rest of the Regulators –"

"There's no difficulty there," said Johnson, "as for that, I've already heard them say that they want to establish connections with the bordering counties, so such an offer will be exactly what they're hoping for."

"A spy – a real, genuine spy!" said the Missourian to himself with a quiet laugh, "and pitched into the middle of the Regulators like a violet in a bouquet of roses; a very amusing adventure!"

"And you'll take it on?" asked Rowson.

"Understood," continued the little man with a grin, all the while still talking to himself, – "I'll send them off in different directions – I'll be the one to win a good name here, and if we ever want to carry out a proper heist, well, then we'll send the whole lot of them into the wild blue yonder and – ha, ha, ha – we'll have clear sailing. What an inspired idea, that!"

"And so you won't go to the meeting tomorrow, Rowson?" asked Cotton.

"No, now it's not necessary," replied the other.

"But how will we discover what they've decided?"

"If anything important is in the works," said Rowson thoughtfully, "then Jones, who will get back to Atkins' toward evening anyway, can send our friend's mulatto over this way and give you fellows the news. I myself, though, must settle some important business early tomorrow morning, and spend tomorrow evening at Roberts'; but early Sunday, at nine o'clock, I'll be at the cross oak – you know the tree, Atkins, into which a persimmon branch has fallen so that it looks like a cross. Well, all right, I'll wait at that spot, and you send the mulatto to me there; it's all the same whatever else happens, since it's possible that I'll have a message for you all myself, and I won't have time to ride the whole distance."

"Then that's settled," said Atkins, "come then, Jones, so that we won't be missed at all at home. The devil's loose at my house this evening; my child is sick, and Betsy's sent out the mulatto and my white worker in every direction under heaven to bring help. Three old women from the neighborhood had already arrived before we left the place, and I'm fairly certain that tomorrow we'll have the whole house full. That's happened to me before."

"But don't let Brown go before I get there," cautioned Rowson once more.

"No – don't worry, but don't come a bit too late, since even if I can postpone breakfast a half hour or so, I can't do it for *too* long."

The men now softly called good night to one another; Atkins and Jones jumped over the fence and disappeared into the darkness lying beyond, and the rest sought anew their beds that they might recover the sleep they had lost by the late and unexpected visit. But as he wrapped himself again in his blanket, Cotton still grumbled: "Anybody who disturbs me a second time today, I'll wring his neck – that's for sure" – and the next moment his frightful snores proved how tired he was and how much he needed rest.

Notes

1. Nanabozho or Mamabozho (also "Nanabush") is an Ojibwe trickster figure. FG could have adopted the unconventional spelling "Nannabozho" from a book by Charles Fenno Hoffman, *Wild Scenes in the Forest and Prairie*, published in London in 1839, which FG much later translated as *Wilde Scenen in Wald und Prairie, mit Skizzen amerikanischen Lebens* (1860) but might

have already known about much earlier. Hoffman is the only writer we have found to have adopted this spelling.

2. Franklin County was carved in 1837 from a portion of Crawford County and lies about a hundred miles west of the Fourche La Fave region.

3. "Backwoods" is English in the original text.

Chapter 24

The Pioneer Family. –
The New Regulator Sets a Trap for Himself

The wild west wind that had raged during the previous night, with a last desperate exertion of force before the break of dawn, gathered together yet another armful of dark, threatening clouds that he emptied out upon the earth in swiftly flying showers. But then, exhausted and weak, he made way for the triumphant day; and as the sun with its first rays kissed the distant hilltops and a few tall pines here and there in the valley, there lay a calm and stillness, so much the more sacred for the storm that had passed over it, on the now gently rustling and whispering woods.

The early-rising roosters had already stopped crowing and strutted around the small barnyards of the various farms with important looks and heads held high, flushed with the pleasant sense of having fulfilled their duty, and having made known to their comrades nearby that they still rejoiced in life. All the while, they cast wistful looks at the just opened door of the dwelling to see if a friendly soul might not soon appear with an armful of corn and feed the horses that for a quarter of an hour already had been trotting restlessly and neighing impatiently at the fence. Naturally, they were hoping that they might be freely or accidentally given their mite of grain as well. The geese cackled, the dogs barked, and from the clay chimneys of the little dwellings clear blue smoke rose up straight as a candle and homely, only to nestle in the spruces adorned with millions of sparkling diamonds, and even the clay-yellow river that rolled along under the overhanging masses of reeds and river willows seemed to murmur more sprightly and joyfully in the all-invigorating sunlight.

Fully in harmony with the pleasant morning, a solitary rider, who had left the settlements far behind, trotted through the woods on his lean and sturdy pony, humming a cheerful song.

It was an old acquaintance of ours, Cook, who had started off from his house early this morning with an empty stomach, in order to reach the meeting place as quickly as possible. Now he occasionally urged his animal to a brisker pace so as not to arrive too late for breakfast at the next house, which was still about three miles distant.

But however casually he had pursued his course to this point, he suddenly gripped in amazement the reins of his swiftly arrested pony and listened up ahead. – What was that? – The horse seemed no less surprised than his master; it pricked up its ears and listened carefully to a sound surely not to be expected at such a place.

Indeed, there was not a single house to be found within an area of three full miles, and yet, here in the middle of the woods, right behind a thicket of holly and sassafras bushes, a rooster crowed – a very lively rooster, in very good voice – and Cook looked around himself bewildered and disconcerted.

"Surely I haven't gotten lost?" he mumbled softly to himself. – "Ah, God forbid; without a doubt, I know every deer and cow path in the woods – new settlers? that's not exactly likely in this place; but hello – aren't those wheel marks here next to the path? The rain's pretty much washed it out; but yes, sure enough, they've run over the bush there, and here they've grazed an oak, – emigrants, then; in that case, a fellow will learn something new"; and with a slight pressure of his thighs he conveyed to his pony his desire to catch up with the strangers. The latter did not, indeed, need to be persuaded for long, since a dim presentiment of various gleaming golden corn cobs, delivered in a wooden bucket, rose up in its inmost soul (and why should a pony, so completely dependent on itself and its own inner resources in the pathless forests, *not* have a soul?). Neighing loudly, it made its rider aware – by means of a sideways leap, a well-timed kick with both rear legs, and other noises – of the joyful willingness with which it sped toward these new acquaintances.

In a few minutes the rider had left behind the little rise that separated him from the strangers, and now saw before him one of those camps of emigrants that are often met with, especially in Arkansas and on the way to the West or to Texas.

Two large wagons with white linen stretched over them formed the center-point of the group, around which stood tethered several teams of bulls, each bound together two-and-two by a great wooden yoke. A small white-headed lad, about eight or nine years old, stood by them and shoved a single broken-off corncob into the mouth of each, one by one. But the animals, their great soft eyes fixed dully and drowsily on the next piece coming their way, chewed and swallowed with complete calm whatever they actually got, and then, as if to plead with or admonish him, licked their young feeder's sleeve and hand with their long rough tongues, hoping to alert him that they were now receptive to, and ready for, a new load. Five horses, bells around their necks and forefeet tied together – "hobbled," in the local language[1] – grazed in the lush canebrake very close by. The emigrants themselves had apparently spent the night inside the wagon, since the place revealed no tent or shelter where a person could have slept in the rain. But just now they were in the process of arranging themselves around a table laid on the ground, while outspread woolen blankets formed the seats. The cheerful rooster, whose bright call had first betrayed the presence of the new arrivals, now sounded for the second time his cry of warning or welcome.

Other than the aforementioned eight-year-old lad, the little family consisted of the husband, his wife, two grown daughters, and two young fellows of eighteen and twenty-two years of age. They were now sitting down, much after the Turkish manner, around the meal awaiting them.

"Come, Ben," cried the father, – "the animals have enough; they were standing in the reeds the whole night, to be sure; they won't eat a bite more. – Quiet, you dogs; what do the beasts already smell again after they yapped and barked the whole night because it occurred to some miserable panther to howl nearby. – Down with you!" –

Despite this friendly encouragement, the dogs thus addressed, which were securely tied under the wagon, were not at all inclined to obey the admonition. They only barked more furiously toward the road from which Cook now trotted over and approached the group.

"Good morning to you all," he cried in a friendly way, as he jumped from the saddle hardly ten paces from them and threw the reins over the neck of the little snorting horse; "good morning, how's it taste?"

"We'll see," cried the farmer in his direction, – "come – lie down with us and eat, if you haven't yet had breakfast. – Here, Anna – a cup for the gentleman – dig in – help yourself!"

"Many thanks," said Cook, who had no trouble at all complying with the hearty invitation, "that suits me splendidly; mind you, I hadn't hoped to find such good company and such a splendid breakfast here in the middle of the woods, but" – with that he looked around at his horse which, wisely enough, did not wish to forego any advantage by pointless browsing, and looked, frowning and with ears pricked, intently over to where Ben was still rustling the corn.

"Bring an armful of corn here, Ben," cried the farmer, without allowing his guest to finish speaking – "you can put it in the iron pot standing there next to the wagon. The pony probably won't care what sort of ware it eats from."

With a gentle half-suppressed whinny, the pony gave his full assent to this proposal, and straightaway with very busy jaws did full honor to the meal that was set before him.

"And where did you come from, sir?" asked Cook at last, after the collected members of the little circle had put to the most practical use a pause of about a quarter of an hour.

"From Tennessee, from Wolf River."[2]

"And where to?"

"To Franklin County, at the foot of the Ozark Mountains."

"Already picked out a spot?"

"Nothing in particular yet, but we'll find one soon, surely. I have a brother living there."

"Ah-ha! – there's capital land here too –"

"Yes – I know that well, but the people on the Fourche La Fave are said to love horseflesh too much."

"Ho ho," laughed Cook, "have the Arkansas River people already put a bug in your ear? It's not that bad. Still – truth to tell, it's bad enough; I'm just on the way to a Regulators' meeting, but I hope we'll now put an end to that dreadful state of affairs. Then Arkansas won't any longer be mentioned only when someone's talking about bands of robbers and thieves."

"Arkansas in general?" the farmer asked with a laugh, "yes! – in the United States overall, in Tennessee and farther south, north, and east, they know *Arkansas* only in *that* regard. But once you come across the Mississippi, into the state itself, then *Fourche La Fave* is the word. – You have an outstanding reputation in the area."

"That may be," said Cook, "but it's still not as bad as it's made out, and even if there are a few good for nothing fellows in the region, then the d – yes, well, I was about to say – we'll push them out all right. I wish you could attend our meeting today. – Anyway, it's Saturday, and tomorrow you'll hardly journey any farther."

"Tomorrow?" asked the farmer. "Because it's Sunday? That makes no difference. My old woman is sensible enough there, and none of the Methodists skulking around here have yet been able to make the girls nervous and fearful about the hellfire to come. This fine weather must be used, and since I'd very much like to seed a few fields with corn this year, if it's at all possible, you'll understand that I have no time to waste –"

"No, certainly not. But I think it might interest you to get to know our Regulators' laws."

"It certainly would," said the Tennessean. "So you would really carry out lynch law? I've heard about it at home, but I never yet believed it."

"Yes, it's necessary," replied Cook, "here in our state we're not yet equipped, first, to put criminals in front of a court, and then to keep them in secure custody. Everything is still too new here. But no state needs it quite like Arkansas, so something *must* be done if we aren't to destroy ourselves or, as you yourself said, acquire such a reputation in the rest of the states that nobody else will move here, and our land, if not worthless, will never increase in value."

"Yes, yes," said the Tennessean – "quite right; *we* did the same thing five years ago, at a time when a not inconsiderable band of thugs had also formed in the 'district.' But a few arm-lengths of hemp and a suitably serious view of the matter soon crushed the rascals. It's also a bit uneasy over on the Arkansas; as we came up the river early this week, a farmer living there who had been in the 'Indian Nation'[3] to buy hogs was foully murdered by a scoundrel on his way back."

"I heard about it," said Cook, shuddering, "no one's discovered the culprit?"

"No," said the old man, angrily striking his fist on the tablecloth in front of him, such that the board lying underneath flicked a small glass salt shaker high in the air, "no – and I only wish that the greasy scoundrel would come as near to me as that time when I stood behind a tree with my rifle, or even on the open prairie; I'll be damned if I wouldn't let the daylight through his skull!"

"So you know him?"

"No – I don't know him, but I saw him; at least, it couldn't be anyone else. Our wagon, you see, was going along the road, and I and Ned there, my oldest, had gone a little off to the side with our rifles. We thought we'd maybe shoot a deer, since we'd noticed a whole lot of their tracks on the path. At the top of a little lake, Ned had taken one side and I the other, when I noticed a narrow path that came out of the thicket and seemed to lead to the road that we had just left, along which the wagon was coming maybe half a mile behind us. Then I heard something rustling in the bushes and, thinking it was a deer or a flock of turkey hens, stepped behind a tree. But it was two riders, both clad in the usual blue woolen outfit, with one of them wearing a broad-brimmed black hat. They spoke very earnestly with one another and rode on past me without noticing me; I said nothing to them either, since I didn't want to make any unnecessary noise and chase away any game that might be grazing nearby."

"I may have slowly meandered another hundred paces farther, and meanwhile the strangers had disappeared in the bushes behind me, when suddenly, in that same direction, I heard a shot. Well, at first I thought that Ned hadn't been able to get around the lake up there on account of the waters and was following me, and just happened to have an opportunity to shoot, since neither of the two men carried a rifle. So I let out my hunting cry to see if he'd come upon something or other; but my boy answered me right away from the side of the lake lying directly opposite. Well, naturally I didn't suspect anything except that there was yet a third hunter in the area, and not worrying myself any more about him, I continued quietly on my way.

"That was already late in the afternoon, and on that still same evening people passed by us on the road where we were camped who told us of a murder that had occurred. The dead man had been shot through the head. Of the riders, though, neither came past our wagon.

"When I heard this, I instantly got on my black horse (at this point the women were screaming pretty badly, since they were starting to get scared) and galloped as fast as the animal could go to where the body was supposed to lie, in a farmhouse not very far away from where the murder had happened. Just as I suspected, it was one of those that I had seen riding together that very day, and in fact the older one; so the fellow with the broad brimmed hat must be the murderer. I described him as well as I could, but no one present would identify him, indeed didn't even remember coming across him. Though I still stayed two full days more in the neighborhood, the culprit had disappeared without a trace; and according to the reckoning of people who knew exactly how many hogs the murdered man had taken away with him, and their going price among the Indians, he must have had about a thousand dollars on him. Likewise, naturally, nothing more was seen of them."

"Yes, yes," said Cook, "similar things have occurred here as well, almost even worse than open robbery and murder. – Well, let's hope, at least, that we strike the head of the snake that's nested in *this* region. Those over there across the Arkansas may see how to manage things on their side. – But which way do you mean to take?"

"I don't know exactly; the road runs along this side?"

"Yes – on both sides; but the one on the other side might be the most advisable for you, since farther above, where the left-hand fork[4] comes in, the passage through the river is very difficult, especially with wagons."

"So what's the best way for me to get over? how far is it yet to the next house?"

"Well, the next house is Wilson's," said Cook, "the second, about another half mile farther, Atkins'. But you could go across at the former; there's a right good ferryboat there, and a wide easy way down to the river."

"Is the ferryman's name Wilson?"

"No, he only lives there; the ferryman's called Curneales."

"All right, then, I thank you for the advice and I'll follow it; but if you're ever in my neighborhood, well, just ask for old Stevenson and seek me out. You'll be heartily welcome!"

"Thank you, thank you!" said Cook, who meanwhile had stood up and saddled and bridled his horse again; "anyway, it's time that I make my horse step lively, or I'll arrive too late; I still have several miles to travel. So Godspeed!"

With a hearty farewell and a handshake, the young farmer then took leave of each member of the family, including Ben, who had fed his horse so well, and soon afterward trotted off, singing and chatting with his equally satisfied pony, toward his intended destination.

After a hard ride of about an hour he reached Atkins' door, where, to his astonishment, he found Brown still. He had supposed him to have long been at the meeting place, or at least on the way there, and now found him still here, standing quite calmly next to the saddled horses. Moreover, Brown was very intently conversing with the stranger who had come the previous evening, and whom Rowson, who just then arrived, introduced as an old friend.

"Hello, Cook!" the leader of the Regulators called to him brightly, "it's wonderful that you've come; now we can ride together."

"Good morning – good morning!" was his answer, "but I thought you were long underway."

"That's *my* fault," said Atkins, reaching his hand out to Cook, "or my wife's fault really, she dawdled over breakfast an unforgivably long time this morning. But the sick child might have slowed her down perhaps –"

"I would have ridden out long ago," said Brown, "but Mr. Atkins –"

"But not without having a bite to eat?" interrupted the latter. "That I'd have never allowed, no; besides, you still have enough time and now we've gained new company by it."

"Nothing's lost by it yet," said Brown, shaking the hand of his friend Cook, who was standing next to him, "but, Mr. Rowson," he then turned to the other, who had just handed over his horse to the mulatto, "don't you want to come with us? I thought, when I saw you, that that was your purpose in being here."

"I would have very gladly attended this meeting," replied the Methodist, "if some important business this very day had not kept me from it. Tomorrow I celebrate the union with my bride, and, as the gentlemen will probably understand, such circumstances can give rise to unavoidable errands."

"Certainly," replied Brown in a nearly flat tone – "and this gentleman is, as you said, also a Regulator? He didn't say a word about it yesterday evening."

"You'll find that very understandable," Mr. Jones said with a smile, "when you consider that I found myself among *complete* strangers."

"Certainly a most commendable precaution. – You wanted to go to Fort Gibson, right?"

"That was my intention, and still is. But since I've found here, quite accidentally and unexpectedly, an old friend in Mr. Rowson, I think I'll pass a few days in the neighborhood. I'd be very pleased if I could attend today's meeting of the Regulators; it might be possible to unite this group with ours in the north, and with a common goal in view we could then achieve far sooner and much more easily what both parties are now working toward separately."

"You're right there, no doubt," replied Brown, looking him steadily in the eye, "and so you wish *me* to introduce you to the Regulators?"

"That's my wish, and I'd be much obliged to you –"

"I myself would be very thankful to you on my friend's behalf," Rowson interrupted him at that point, "and then if he can't find accommodation with me just now, on account of the present change in my household, perhaps Mr. Atkins would be so good as to put him up again tomorrow night. Then later we can come to an agreement with one another."

"Don't worry about that," said Brown with a smile, "I have no doubt that Mr. Jones will stay with us here for some time. Only, whether he likes the Fourche La Fave is another question."

"I'm easily contented," responded Jones to the young man in a very friendly manner, "but wouldn't we like to start? It's getting late."

"Mr. Jones' horse!" cried Atkins to the mulatto, who stood in the door and stared over at the men.

"Listen, Brown, I don't like his looks a bit," whispered Cook to his friend as he bent down to him.

"When we get to Bowitt's I need to have a few words with you alone," the other whispered back.

"Is something –"

"Psst – just be quiet – it'll wait until we're up there."

Jones, meanwhile, had also mounted up, and Brown was swinging himself into the saddle when the mulatto led out another two horses, one of which was fitted with a sidesaddle.

"May God bless me," cried Cook – "another sidesaddle; I was quite astonished when I counted them hanging up there in the passageway; seven of them, and this here is the eighth; what's going on then?"

"It's one of my wife's visitors," said Atkins, "a sick call, on account of the child. But this one here belongs to Ellen – she's supposed to go over to Roberts'."

At that moment the door opened, and Ellen came out of the house with a sun hat and a shawl. She carried a small bundle in her hand, which the mulatto took from her outside, and as she turned her little head shaded by the deep bonnet toward Brown, he could not fail to see that her eyes were red with crying. But she quickly turned away, climbed into the saddle with the help of a smoothly hewn tree stump placed there for this purpose, and immediately galloped off down the road, followed by the colored man.

"What's the matter with the girl?" Brown sympathetically asked the master of the house, who gazed after her shaking his head – "it seemed to me as if her eyes were filled with tears."

" – Eh – nonsense," said the other – "she doesn't want to leave the sick child – she said she'd never see it again, and so – my wife probably had a little set-to with her – the old lady grumbles sometimes, but she doesn't mean any harm. – The silly thing's taken it to heart. Well, she'll grow reasonable yet, once she gets a proper husband."

"Oh come, Brown – damn it, stop dilly-dallying. – Time's passing!" cried Cook impatiently.

"Yes, yes," replied the other, "I just need to have a few words with Mr. Rowson; a question –"

"He's gone into the house; you can speak with him tomorrow or this evening, surely; it'll be noon before we know it, and the folks up above have surely been waiting on us for the last four hours."

"All right, then, until we meet again!" said the young man, as he waved once more to those who remained behind; then, followed by the others, he trotted quickly along the path that led into the woods.

Notes

1. FG uses the German "gehobbelt," the past participle of "hobbeln," a verb (not in *DWB*) evidently formed after the English "hobble," which had found its way into the German language at around this time. The German writer of western novels and Gerstäcker-admirer Karl May, in his first novella written expressly for young readers, "Der Sohn des Bärenjägers" ("The Son of the Bear-Hunter," 1887), enthusiastically embraces the term, introducing his readers to "Hobble-Frank," named after his characteristic limp, and offers the following explanation: "an expression used by trappers, [which] means tying the front legs of horses together in such a manner that they can only take small steps . . . a practice to be adopted only in conditions of absolute safety."

2. The Wolf River flows for about a hundred miles through western Tennessee and northern Mississippi before joining the Mississippi River.

3. "District" and "Indian Nation" in this paragraph are given in English in the original text.

4. "Left-hand fork" is in English in the original text.

Chapter 25

Harper and Marion. –
Ellen's Arrival at Roberts'.

The bright morning sun shone peacefully and pleasantly on Roberts' cozy home. The pines and oaks that bordered the field and the farmyard had not yet lost their adornment of pearly dew, though now they cast it down to the fragrant earth in soft glittering showers, and in doing so waved and nodded with their branches, as if to say: "Go – go – you cannot truly leave us, you glittering dewdrops, and as soon as it grows dark, you will secretly climb up again in damp mists, force yourself upon us once more and gather yourselves here above to renew your proud, flamboyant, lovely glory. – Go – go – you will come again, even if we shake you off another thousand times."

Four large stately turkey hens, nurtured from eggs found throughout the forest, strutted and gobbled proudly about the open spot that surrounded the house, and seemed, through a grand unfurling of their splendor and beauty, to seek first to earn the kernels of corn that Marion brought them in a little basket before they condescended to receive the morning gift. In the little, low hickory bushes that were left in the neighborhood of the house on account of their shade, blue jays shrieked and fire-red cardinals twittered, and here and there a frisky silver-grey squirrel glided down a random tree trunk. From there it jumped swiftly onto the fence, ran along this, carefully following its zig-zag course, and then, startled by some fowl or other rustling in the leaves, swung itself again with a flying leap onto the tree standing nearest to it, until it knew itself to be safe. But it did not take long before it looked cautiously around the slender trunk from above, the little head very shrewdly and cleverly turning to the side, and little ears pricked far forward as it listened below, in order to see what might have caused the suspicious rustling.

The two women were alone. Almost before daybreak, Roberts had set out into the woods with his hounds in order to look after his herds there, but he had promised to be back again before midday, and Madame Roberts now went about her housework in a wonderfully bustling manner involving every pot and pan in the house. Indeed, even the smokehouse had been ransacked and some very mysteriously wrapped and stored tins and glasses pulled out of

It, which contained in part sour pickles and honey, in part various forest fruits preserved in a fine and delicate manner, and which today were brought forth for a feast as magnificent as it was rare.

Marion had been entrusted with the task of baking bread, and kneaded the delicate white flour with her even more delicate fine hands into small flat "biscuits."[1] Later these would be baked in the high iron pan with a lid, but for now they lay spread out in long equal rows on the table, and were only pricked with a fork to allow easy access to air and to raise them a bit.

The two women were, quite in the customary fashion of American women of the backwoods, clad in outfits they had woven themselves, but the material was of the best and most excellent sort, and the colors and patterns chosen were most tasteful and meaningful. In this effort, Mrs. Roberts sought to be outdone by "not a single person in Arkansas and in no other state either," as she herself put it, although she admitted, happily and not without almost as much pride, that her daughter was *almost* her equal in skill.

Marion had parted and pulled back her full auburn hair, fastening it in a simple and smooth knot. The only ornaments that she wore were two small half-opened white roses, and, sweet and delicate like her swelling lips, the soft maidenly red of the budding blossoms glowed and wafted from their barely opened crowns. She had finished her work, and now gazed down the road silently and pensively, hands folded before her, her little head leaned as if weary upon the brightly scoured doorpost.

"Hasn't he come yet?" the mother asked, as she held a just-opened stone jar to her nose with the look of a connoisseur.

"Who?" said Marion, jumping up startled and turning quickly to her mother.

"Who?" continued the other, without noting her behavior. "Who? foolish girl – Sam – whom you yourself sent down after Mr. Harper to have him invited today. Though he doesn't at all deserve our dispatching people into the world in search of him. – He surely could have let himself be seen again once in all this time."

"He was sick, of course –"

"Well, his fine nephew then, who's gone over to the Regulators now. – You were sick *too*, and it would have been no more than polite to ask how you're getting on. He's always been kindly received here and doesn't have a thing in God's wide world to do at home –"

"He was caring for his uncle," Marion said quietly.

"Oh sure – I knew you'd probably take his side ever since the business with the –"

"Mother!" the deeply blushing girl interjected, more softly than before, and with a gentle reproach in her tone.

"Well, sure – he rendered you a great service that time, that's right," murmured the old lady, "but still nothing more than anyone else would have done in his place, and – but I won't say a thing against him, child," she then nattered on busily, as she was carrying the containers no longer needed back to their proper and designated places – "I have nothing against him in any way. – He's certainly a nice young man, but precisely because of that I'm quite angry at him, that he doesn't come here sometimes. Of course the business with Heathcott –"

"But Mother!" cried the daughter in a tone full of reproach.

"I know what you're going to say," she continued, without allowing herself to be distracted – "I know what you're going to say; but why, then, has he not shown himself here since that time, if he has such a thoroughly good, clear conscience? – Mr. Rowson lately allowed that I was quite right about that."

"And Mr. Rowson, of all people, has every reason to defend Mr. Brown, whenever it is in his power to do so," cried Marion, turning to her mother more fervently than before. "That is something that does not please me about him."

"But he has defended him," she retorted, "he's defended him bravely; but what can he do about it, when our friend can't shake off suspicion completely?"

Marion turned to the side in order to conceal an unbidden tear that stole into her eye. But now her mother had quite enough to do, bringing in various pieces of meat that she still had to prepare before twelve o'clock. In doing so, she happened at one point to go to the small window cut into the logs that, contrary indeed to the Arkansas custom, was provided with a pane of glass, and to her horror suddenly discovered three horsemen approaching along the road. It was the anticipated Harper with his neighbor Bahrens, and behind them her own Negro boy.

"Good gracious!"[2] cried out Madame Roberts in terror, "here comes Mr. Harper already, and I'm not finished. – Oh, that rascal of a youngster should have told them: not before twelve."

"Oh, never mind, Mother," said Marion with a smile, gently wiping the moist tell-tale spot from her cheek with her finger – "those two men are not so particular, they're good friends of Father; Sam must have met them when they were already on the way."

And, besides, there was nothing more to do about it; Mrs. Roberts merely arranged with the utmost dispatch her, as she believed, somewhat displaced bonnet before the small mirror, smoothed her apron, and then went kindly and heartily, if also with a face slightly flushed from her work, to meet the two guests.

"Welcome, Mr. Harper, welcome as if raised from the dead!" she said, reaching her hand to him. – "Just come in, gentlemen, my old man will be home again straightaway, he just wants to look after a couple of cows who haven't come home for milking for a long while. – Just come on, Mr. Bahrens, even if I'm not entirely organized yet."

"Madame Roberts," said the other, laughing, "I'm intruding on you without an invitation today, but I only learned that you had guests when I was already on the way."

"I thought you were at the Regulators meeting," answered Mrs. Roberts, "otherwise, I'd have already sent over there for you long ago – but just come in, we can't arrange everything outside the door."

The two men accepted the invitation, and Harper, though still very pale and feeble to be sure, having recovered all his former jovial disposition which had justly gained him so many friends in the settlement, was first of all made to sit down and partake of a cup of a reinvigorating drink prepared especially for him out of honey and fruits, and then to relate how it went with him in his illness, who all had cared for him, what he had taken for remedies, and how he had gotten better again. He complied with all this with the most amiable willingness in the world, and particularly extolled his nephew and his three neighbors, Wilson, Cook, and Roberts, who had rendered him great service. "Even Bahrens," he continued, extending his hand over to him, "left his corn-field and came over to my place for a few days. They all love me; what more can I ask here in the woods?"

The conversation now turned to the subjects that lay closest to them, that is, all possible manner of vegetables and other edibles that were either already bubbling on the fire or stood piled up on a small side table awaiting further use. Meanwhile, Mrs. Roberts selected a sharp knife and declared her intention to go into the garden to collect some greens.

Bahrens, who had already shared with her some exceptionally marvelous incidents involving fabulously large asparagus and fairy-tale cabbage heads, insisted on accompanying her, and Harper stayed back in the house alone with the maiden.

All morning Marion had been longing for a few minutes alone with Harper to speak about her distant friend. He was, indeed, the only one to whom she *could* speak. But as soon as this wish was fulfilled, it seemed as if all her heart's blood flowed up to her face and temples. Her tongue stuck to her palate, and she could bring forth no sound. Harper too was silent, though both surely thought of the *one* subject; both were fearful of touching on something so distressing for both of them, but did not have the heart to strike up another trivial conversation. Then Harper finally broke the silence that was growing painful, and said, reaching his hand across to the young girl with a sorrowful but kind expression:

"How are you, Marion? Well, I hope, indeed? That's good. – Be a good, strong child – I'm glad – heartily glad, to find you so well and – and content. – Mr. Rowson," he then continued, as Marion silently extended her hand – "Mr. Rowson is a very decent man, and will surely make you as happy a girl as you deserve to be. – The – the boy[3] is as changeable as the wind, and, you see, it is perhaps better so –"

"He's now with the Regulators," he further told her, understanding her questioning glance, "but only wants to see whether or not the real murderers can be found out. – Plague and poison! – it would be a delight to see the fellows hang."

"And he is not guilty – is he?" asked the girl with a pleading look.

"Guilty?" Harper said, jumping up from his chair – "Guilty? Is there still someone who thinks him guilty? – No, not *you*," he said then, lovingly stroking her white hand, which he had not let go of again, "certainly not you, but other people shouldn't any more either. I myself believed it once, I admit; I knew his blood was quick to fire up. But the stolen money immediately made me hesitate, and just after that it was discovered that he was wearing his moccasins that day, and both tracks were from boots or shoes. No – he's not guilty of this bloody deed, but I hope that some lucky coincidence or other will someday reveal the true culprit."

"The Regulators indeed are, as you say, meeting for that reason," softly replied the maiden.

"Ah, but they too are only human," averred old Harper, shaking his head – "they're not even Indians. Now, if Assowaum were with us; but the rascal has very secretly – very Indian-like slunk away, and nothing more has been heard from him. Of course, Bill still maintains that he'll come back again."

"Mr. Rowson recently declared here that the Indian's secret removal very much speaks against him," said Marion.

"Oh – Mr. Rowson should be a bit more sparing with his suspicion," cried the old man, somewhat irritated. – "It's not nice to charge a man with such a horrible thing, even if it's just an Indian. Besides, it wasn't he; I'd joyfully pledge my neck on it."

"Is Mr. Brown still going to Texas?" whispered Marion tremblingly.

"Yes," Harper confirmed, suddenly sad and dejected again. "I can't talk him out of the crazy idea, and I believe if they found the murderer today he'd go away tomorrow. – Has he already bought the horse from your father?"

"That's what made me ask," said Marion – "I heard my father say this morning that he had to catch the bay for Mr. Brown that usually grazes up in the valley. It gives me endless woe to be the cause that's driving him – away from *you* –"

"It has to be this way, dear Marion," the old man comforted her, as he stood up and kissed her forehead – "and – perhaps it's best that it happened this way and not otherwise; who can know? So take heart, my dear girl, and turn a brave face to the world." With this, he lifted her chin with a gentle hand and tried to look cheerfully and blithely into her eyes, but his voice quavered, and he had to struggle mightily not to become infected himself, at last, by her sorrow.

Just at the right time, Mrs. Roberts and Bahrens now came back out of the garden, the former laughing indeed, though with a certain pious indignation on her features, since Mr. Bahrens had related things that "could not be true, of course, as much as she wished to rely on his word." Bahrens, however, stood fast by what he said, and then called to Harper to bear witness to things that he claimed that he had already shared with him.

They were still in the midst of this half-serious, half-playful dispute when two horses stopped in front of the house and Ellen entered, followed by the young mulatto.

The girls had known each other for some time and exchanged warm greetings, and Mrs. Roberts also welcomed the young orphan with genuine kindness, since Rowson had told her (in this case the truth, for once) not only that she was sweet and good, but also that her step-mother, Mrs. Atkins, really treated her more like a slave than a child in her family, even if an adopted one.

Harper was still a stranger to Ellen, though Bahrens had seen her often. After the first greetings, she shyly asked her new mistress, or rather friend, whether she had arrived soon enough, since she had been delayed a bit at home.

"Soon enough, dear child," Madame Roberts interrupted her, – "soon enough; first thing in the morning we'll ride over to your new home. There will probably be a number of things still lacking there, since one can't really expect that a bachelor will have fully stocked his household. Later we visit the judge, where Mr. Rowson will preach in the afternoon, and then he'll join the young people together. In the evening we'll bring them home, and you, dear child, will stay with our Negro boy, whom you may keep with you for a while until you are all settled in."

These matters were soon brought in order, and now the much weightier one of the midday meal moved to the fore. But neither Rowson nor Roberts came, and the matron had already begun to grow very impatient. Bahrens had just, after repeated prompting, been obliged to blow a second time on his long straight tin horn, the sound of which was borne far out into the woods, when it was finally answered by Roberts' hunting call, though still far off; soon the dogs, joyous heralds, came whooping and yapping along the country road. A few minutes later both Roberts and Rowson trotted up together with somewhat greater haste than was customary, likely because they wanted to show their respect for the urgent summons and not leave the women waiting any longer.

Notes

1. FG uses the English word "biscuits."
2. "Good gracious" is in English in the original text.
3. "The boy" apparently refers to Brown.

Chapter 26

The Regulators' Meeting. – Jones Finds Himself in a Most Unpleasant Position. – Cunning versus Cunning.

At Bowitt's house on the same morning had assembled not only a goodly number of the neighboring farmers and hunters, but even those living at a greater distance. But none were allowed to enter the house itself. There, indeed, two corpulent Negresses, borrowed from a nearby mill owned by a prosperous man from Little Rock, bustled about and worked to prepare breakfast for quite a few who had already traveled a long stretch of road, and in the meantime also made the necessary preparations for the midday meal. At the same time, there hung in front of the house, and mounted on two low supports over a blazing fire, a not unsubstantial kettle to keep boiling water ready, so that now and then the chilly morning air might be tempered and made more agreeable with a hot invigorating drink.

But despite the fact that the cup that usually brought life and happiness to the "men of Arkansas" frequently went around the circle, today an almost solemn seriousness seemed to have shackled the tongues of most of them. Under a tree thick with leaves, which had shielded the foliage strewn beneath it from the falling rain the previous year, the Regulators stood with grim attentiveness and firm resolution on their dark suntanned faces, and gathered closely around a single man, who with lively gestures and an easy tongue seemed to share with them something apparently very interesting.

He was one of those mixed individuals, belonging to no particular state, half-white and half-Indian, whose almost too dark color not infrequently raised suspicions of a low ancestry among the Americans. In the backwoods, this sort of person was called Canadian French, half-Indian, or, even more likely, by the nickname "Gumbos."*[1] This brown individual, who was rather a strong and sturdy fellow, now related to his listeners with lively gesticulations

---

* FG's note: "Gumbo, a favorite dish of the Creoles born in the southern states of French parents, and used there as a nickname for all those of French descent."

how he had followed the trail of stolen horses out of the Cherokee Nation, but that about five miles from this place he had lost the tracks, and was already on his way home again. Then he had heard of the "Regulator Meeting"[2] and had now ridden here to bring these animals to the attention of the Regulators, at least, and to leave behind a precise description of them, even if, at this point, they never came back.

The Canadian, for he called Canada his home, was a small heavy-set man with long black glossy hair, dark fiery eyes, blindingly white teeth, and very prominent Indian cheekbones, as well as a somewhat wide, flat nose and large nostrils. The color of his face was, to be sure, barely darker than that of the men standing around him; but his clothing was fully Indian, and the very belt that he wore was wrought of pearls embroidered on red wool, and richly ornamented with panther fangs and bear claws.

The Regulators speculated back and forth as to how strangely most of the tracks led into the neighborhood and then, almost miraculously, disappeared, when Brown, Jones, and Cook rode up and were welcomed with friendly greetings by those gathered in front of the cabin. Almost at the same time, Husfield also arrived from the other direction, and first of all refreshed himself with breakfast, since he had already, as he declared, ridden fifteen miles on an empty stomach.

As soon as he had finished this, he approached those friends who arrived most recently, for whose benefit the Canadian repeated his story. Then Jones edged into the conversation and asked the half-Indian whether a white horse with black hind legs had not been among those missing.

With gleefully astonished enthusiasm, the stranger affirmed it.

"Then I've seen them," said Jones, striking his right fist into his open left hand, "then, goddamn me, I've seen them."

"But where?" the pursuer asked quickly and fiercely.

"About fifteen miles from here; just late yesterday evening and up on the mountain ridge that separates the waters of the Maumelle from this river."

"And which road did they take?" asked the former zealously – "were they on the open road or –"

"They crossed the road just as I came up the steep mountain from the other side," replied Jones.

"And how many men were with them?"

"Only one that I could see."

"That's them," cried the half-savage jubilantly – "a farmer on the border also saw them, only the man couldn't describe them since he was too far away. But roughly where will I find the tracks?"

"Surely the rain and wind have erased them," Jones said thoughtfully – "but if you get up the mountain (the last house that you pass from here is Greathouse's) and ride about four or five miles from there without coming across the tracks, then my opinion is that you'd best ride right across to the Arkansas. It flows not very far from there, and in the log cabin standing on the river bank you'll surely get news about the stolen horses."

"Then I don't want to waste any more time, at least, so that I don't lose these tracks, even if they're very cold," cried the stranger – "thank you all for the guidance – good bye, gentlemen!" And without much further ado the Canadian was about to hasten to his pony and set off after the thieves. But Brown seized him by the sleeve of his leather hunting shirt, and when the thus detained man looked at him with surprise, he said in a friendly tone:

"Grant us about another half hour. The trail thus described is, as you must realize, really very uncertain and time-consuming, and we can't possibly reach it in such little time as we have. Anyway, your horse seems exhausted and needs rest. So if you're still thinking about setting off after them in an hour, then you can take mine; it's in fresher condition and will soon make up the lost time for you. We can trade again on your way back."

"But if, meanwhile, the fellow should find a boat that'll take him off?" said Jones.

"It won't happen that fast, since steamboats still aren't very frequent on the Arkansas. So you'll stay here a little and then take my horse?"

The half-Indian, now once more full of hope, nodded his head with great satisfaction, though he was almost happier to acquiesce to Bowitt's gesture inviting him to the laden table than he was to Brown's advice. While at first he seemed to display a certain reticence, he soon confessed that not a morsel had passed his lips since the previous morning, and now, to the horror of the Negresses, quite tore into the food and drink.

"Gentlemen," Brown then spoke to the assembly when the half-Indian had withdrawn, "first of all, at Mr. Rowson's suggestion, I have introduced to you a stranger who wishes to be inducted among us as a *Regulator from Missouri.* He hopes through this to establish a *connection* between us and the northern states, but first and foremost he wishes to visit our assembly and get to know the *spirit* that drives it. Isn't that right, Mr. Jones?"

The man so questioned merely bowed obligingly.

"Since he has already begun this work," Brown continued, "by putting a man needing assistance on the right path to get his lost property back again, I don't believe that any further recommendation is required for him to join our assembly, which otherwise is actually secret, or at least closed – don't you think so too?"

"That's plenty," the men cried, almost with one voice, and Husfield stepped forward and expressed to the stranger his particular joy in being soon united in such a fashion with the brother state.

"What did you want to say to me then, Brown?" Cook now asked, once he had gone a few steps aside with the latter.

"Don't move from the newcomer's side," Brown whispered quickly, "he belongs to the gang – psst – not a word more – tell Wilson, and you both watch him – do you have your Terzerol? (Cook affirmed it) – good – I only wish those Negroes there were out of the way; I don't trust the rascals, and they could give the alarm –"

"So is that also a lie about the horses he saw?" asked Cook quickly.

"Psst – he's looking this way," whispered Brown – "he mustn't notice yet – take Wilson to help you, and then we have to get dinner over with quickly so that the Negroes go away."

The men then separated for a short time, but when Jones shortly afterwards was collared by the Canadian again and questioned about several details, Cook once more stepped up to the young leader and said softly:

"We can't get rid of the Negroes, they're staying here the whole day. What we have to do, it must be done soon. But I'll take care that the black scoundrels don't get away and spread rumors."

"Have you told Wilson?" asked Brown.

"Yes – don't worry, he won't come away – that'll be a capital joke. But the meeting should get started."

At this moment, Husfield approached Brown and asked him whether they shouldn't begin, since many of those attending perhaps wished to return home again the same day. Brown said not a word in reply to this but led him away a few paces away from the others, and then briefly and with as few words as possible told him his suspicion.

"And what do you want to do?" asked Husfield quickly.

"More of that later," Brown whispered – "only, the Negroes make me nervous. Who knows if we undertake something here whether they won't –"

"A plague on it! You're right," Husfield interrupted him – "besides, it looked to me as if the stranger nodded very furtively to one Negro[3] – treachery could ruin everything for us here – but wait – let me take care of it – Bowitt will stand for us and he knows his people; I'll inform him of it. Meanwhile, put off your decision until you see me enter the circle and take off my hat – go! Jones is coming; it might not be to his liking if the two of us are whispering together secretly."

With this, Husfield straightaway lost himself among the others, and Brown, as the elected head of this county, called the men to him and opened the meeting. As he did so, in true Arkansas fashion, he stepped up onto the stump of a felled tree in order to stand somewhat higher, as much to be able to see them all as to be seen by all. By way of introduction, he spoke of the purpose that had brought them together here, and of the *lawfulness* of the meeting itself, though he asked in closing whether they were also firmly and earnestly resolved to carry out with a bold and united front the *unlawful* part of their union, the exercise of so-called *Lynch Law*, and, if the majority of the Regulators should find it necessary, to punish, even with death itself, *those* who deserved to be sentenced to such a punishment. A loud, thundering *"yes"* gave proof that all of this was spoken from the soul of each, and that they were firmly resolved to venture life and limb in doing what they had begun and undertaken.

In the meantime, Brown noticed that Bowitt had spoken for a while with two young fellows, and these now separated themselves from the others. Then, one of them took his position just opposite the house door, and there seated himself on a block of wood and began to examine the lock of his rifle very intently, while the other one, holding the saddled pony by the bridle, approached the first and struck up a casual conversation.

"Well, Massa," said one of the Negro women to the two men, just as she took a basket full of wood chips from a young black boy about twelve years of age, and dumped them near the door of the cabin, "don't you want to listen to the meeting?"

"Still too young, Lyddy," said one of them with a laugh, "and not handsome enough. – Only handsome folks are allowed to be present."

"Oh, golly,"[4] said the black woman. "That's crazy, Massa – Massa Hokker there –"

"Who, Lyddy?"

"Oh – Massa – Massa Hostler there," cried the black woman, obviously becoming embarrassed. "Massa Hostler isn't very handsome either; what's Massa doing with the gun? – Is everything all right?"

"You don't understand, Lyddy," said the young fellow. "When an army camps anywhere, sentries are then posted –"

"Oh, golly – golly!" shouted the black with a laugh, such that her eyes, like two great white balls, nearly popped out of their sockets, and a double row of teeth became visible of which a shark need not be ashamed. "Sentinels in front of the kitchen door! – oh, golly – golly!"

The young people laughed as well, and joked and played with the two Negresses, who meanwhile were washing the dishes inside the little building and kept watch on the new provisions of food placed next to the fire. Still, they took turns stepping to the door, and seemed to take a special interest in the proceedings being held not very far off from them.

"So we are gathered here today, my friends," continued Brown, now straightening himself up and looking around the circle, "in order to put an end to the horse thieves' mischief, which has brought us discredit in every state of the union. But while we can act forcefully and decisively against open enemies, and those strangers who assail us from outside, we can't do so with those who creep in among us as friends and comrades, who flatter us and press our hands heartily by day, while at night they consort with a brood of robbers from other places."

"But how to discover these, I hear you ask, how expose them, when they are wily and cunning and know how to evade the searching eye of justice? That is difficult indeed, but there above us lives a God who sometimes, when they least suspect it, delivers sinners into the hands of the avengers."

At this instant, Husfield stepped forward, took off his hat, and wiped his forehead.

"Call it accident or fate," Brown continued, meeting his gaze – "that just now made *me* privy to such a secret; but privy I *became,* and *now,* comrades, I hope that we've found the trail on which the she-wolf sneaks out nightly and secures her prey."

"Where? – what's found? – what have you discovered, Brown? who is it? here in the settlement? someone on the Fourche La Fave?" sounded the voices in wild confusion, and Jones, who until now very calmly and complacently leaned on a tree, turned his head slightly and almost imperceptibly toward the cabin. He wanted to see whether, in the worst instance, he had a clear retreat to his horse, which was tied not far from him and somewhat separated from the others. But as he turned his head, he met the eye of Cook, who stood very near and slightly behind him, and who whispered to him softly and in a friendly tone:

"You couldn't have come here at a more favorable time, don't you think? Those in Missouri will be astonished when they hear it."

"Yes – very favorable," said Jones – "very favorable, I – am extremely curious," (he turned his head to the other side and saw Wilson there, apparently indifferent, leaning on a tree), "yes, really extremely curious who is meant by it. It's a pity that I don't know the folks myself."

"Oh, maybe you'll get to know them," replied Cook – "but just listen!"

"Directly, my friends," Brown reassured the impatient men, "you'll find out everything, just have a little bit of patience. In point of fact, an accident, if we want to call it thus for the moment, some weeks ago brought me – how, I'll tell another time – into possession of a code which at the time, to be sure, I didn't know how to make use of, but that a short time ago became clear and unmistakable to me. It was an arrangement of two gentlemen to recognize and communicate with a third party through certain words and expressions, even if they were otherwise complete strangers to one another."

"Anything I can help you with?" Cook asked Jones, who at this moment tried to pass by him to get to the outer edge of the circle.

"Only a glass of water," the other whispered back, "I'll be back here in a moment –"

"Lyddy, a glass of water for Mr. Jones!" Cook cried suddenly in a loud voice, so that everyone looked around at them in bewilderment. Brown paused for a few seconds in his speech and smiled, while Jones grew deathly pale. But the black woman, who had already long awaited an opportunity to draw nearer to the men, and especially to the spot where Jones stood, grabbed a cup of the desired drink with all haste and waddled, as fast as her exceptionally corpulent figure would allow, to the tree by which he stood.

He thanked her and took the cup and drank, but at the same time whispered a few words to the black woman, and then remained standing outside the circle while Wilson also stepped forward, asked the Negress for a second drink, and positioned himself next to the stranger, on the opposite side from Cook.

Brown had cast a quick glance at the events just described, and after the short pause that it caused, he continued again in a loud voice:

"A question about the Fourche La Fave, a question about the pasture in this area, and a request for a drink of water were the cues, and where do you think the traitor among us has lain in wait?"

At this moment Lyddy came out of the kitchen with a small basket full of corn and went to the stranger's pony, whose bridle, as Cook confirmed with a quick glance, she put in order. Meanwhile, everyone in the assembly listened in breathless silence for the report that would reveal to them those who had dwelt among them as traitors and villains for so long, unsuspected and silent.

"Gentlemen," then said the leader of the Regulators, raising his voice after a short still pause, "yesterday evening I was in the house of our old neighbor *Atkins,* and he is the traitor."

"Strange story, that," whispered Cook, resting his arm familiarly on Jones' shoulder, who looked him in the eye with a fixed gaze and ashen cheeks – "very strange story, that!"

Jones felt that he was betrayed; felt that the gaze of the Regulators' leader was locked on him, even though he did not look him in the eye himself. – He knew now that there was no other help for him than quick flight, and that he must clear a way for his exit however he could. Thus, quietly but quickly getting his right hand beneath his vest, he seized the Bowie knife he kept hidden there, and threw one more inquiring glance over at the Negress, who had just finished her preparations.

All of this, so long here in the telling, in truth had taken only a few seconds to occur, while a murmur of astonishment and confusion ran through the assembly as Brown finished speaking.

"But the knave," Brown now continued with raised voice, as he stretched out his arm toward the stranger, "who, with his thievish tricks, slipped into our midst, into our settlement, under the cloak of night, yes, as a 'Regulator from Missouri' no less – is *that one!*"

All turned, shocked and indignant, toward the one indicated; but Jones had anticipated this moment of astonishment. With a swift snatch he jerked the broad razor-sharp knife from its sheath and, in order to carve out a path for himself, brandished it about in the air so that those standing nearby, who had no inkling of such an outcome, recoiled in terror. But Wilson, who from Jones' first gesture had divined his intention, knew what he sought with his hand under his vest and fully grasped his plan. Hardly had the broad steel flashed in the hand of the unmasked traitor than he seized him by the arm with a quick and certain grasp, and in the next moment the spy lay under his knee, knocked down by the powerful fist of the backwoodsman, and he squirmed in vain against the strength that held him immobilized and bound as if in an iron vice.

A wild astonishment, a strange and almost sense-disorienting surprise seemed, in the first instant, to have rendered the assembled men helpless and impotent as they almost unknowingly jostled each other in confusion, and stood stunned by the unimagined, not yet comprehensible event. But this almost magical paralysis lasted only a few seconds before rapid activity soon summoned all their powers.

"Stop the Negro!" shouted Brown, who, as soon as he saw the enemy captured, cast his eagle's glance across the open clearing and just caught a glimpse of the bright jacket of the Negro boy gliding snake-like into the thick bushes. Probably he intended to flee and warn the criminal's comrades. But the shout was unnecessary. One of the young men posted as a sentry had suspected the fellow from the start and did not let him out of his sight, and as soon as he made a move to reach the thicket he swung himself into the saddle of his little plucky pony. Driven with whip and spur, it flew away with him like a whirlwind over the tree trunks lying in the path, and in a few seconds he had overtaken the Negro.

The latter, when he saw himself pursued in such a manner, made no further effort at flight, but rather pressed himself to the earth and asked in a pleading voice that nothing be done to him, that he surely would not run away, that he would not take a step from the house.

The two fat Negresses themselves acted as if they had suffered a stroke, though naturally they did not try to set foot outside the house, since flight on their part was impossible. The little building with the three blacks inside was now surrounded by several sentries, who nevertheless spoke kindly to their temporary prisoners and, while they were at it, took pains to remind them for God's sake not to neglect the midday meal.

Jones, meanwhile, was bound and led into the circle of men, where, though with downcast eyes, he nevertheless remained stubborn and stiff-necked and would not answer a single question.

"Lay the hickory across him!" several voices then cried out. "Damn the dog – tie him to a dogwood and let him peel the bark!† – hang him up by the hands and set the dogs on him!" – All of these friendly suggestions were addressed to the victim, who stood among them pale and bound, but with teeth clenched tightly and desperately together. He seemed to expect the worst, but now that it had finally come crashing down on him, not to fear it in the least.

Incidentally, several of the ferocious backwoodsmen already wanted to put their threats into practice, and one in particular stripped off with great zeal the stringy bark of a pawpaw tree in order to bind the prisoner to the aforementioned tree. But Brown fended them off and said calmly:

"Stop – leave the man in peace. As long as we have the chance to attain our goal without such means, it's always better. We still have Atkins, who in any case knows more about these present matters than this fellow, since I'm firmly convinced that the evening of the day before yesterday he and Atkins were complete strangers."

"Then it's also a lie that he's seen my horses, and he wanted to send me on a wild ride in the Maumelle Mountains!" now cried the half-Indian, stepping forward angrily. But Brown held him back and said:

"He's seen your horses in any event, since I don't doubt for an instant that he's the same one who brought them here –"

"Ah, so he shall –"

"Stop!" Brown continued, grabbing the angry man by the shoulder – "they're here; Atkins can't have sent them on yet, even if he'd intended to do so the next night –"

"Then we should go there at once!" cried Husfield – "if we find the animals at his place, well, surely, the proof is plain to see."

"I'm afraid *not*," said Brown – "this morning I was in his farmyard and studied its whole layout. If he has the horses in his custody, they're by no means *inside his fences*; so there must be a place somewhere behind the field or the stock pen (probably down below, in the bottom land overgrown with

---

† FG's note: "The dogwood tree – a species of Cornelian cherry, but with bitter inedible berries, has a rather easily peeled bark, and, since it grows in tremendous quantities in Arkansas, and seldom gets larger than four to five inches in diameter, it came to be used very often by the Regulators and by slave overseers too, who would bind the hands of white criminals, or in the latter case slaves, to it, such that under the pain of the chastisement they turned about and in doing so completely rubbed off the bark from the soft trunks. Thus the commonly used expression in Arkansas of 'letting someone peel the dogwood bark' instead of lashing him."

rcedo) where the animals are kept fenced in by the thick cane itself, or maybe by shrewdly felled trees in a kind of natural enclosure."

"But then the only entrance is anyway from his land," cried Cook impatiently.

"Of course," Brown responded, "at least, I can't think of any other way, but that doesn't matter. He can't be made answerable for that in court. What runs *free* in the woods – since *outside* the fence is freedom –"

"Oh, damn the courts," said Smeiers, now coming forward and morosely shifting his cap; "we haven't come together here in order to ask what the *courts* would say about it – damn them! I say again. We're after our own justice, and when *we* are convinced that it's justice, well, that other nonsense won't matter to us. For this reason, and with this in mind, we've made you our leader; if that's not all right with you, well, say so, and someone else will take over."

Brown wanted to reply to this, but Husfield interrupted him, asked to say a word, and then turned toward the assembly as a whole, but especially to the one who had spoken last, and who seemed now to have the greater part of the Regulators on his side.

"Gentlemen," he said, "I believe that you all know me, and not one among you will think that my zeal to serve a good cause is weaker than his, but – Mr. Brown is right. It's not enough for us to know now whether Atkins, as an accomplice of horse thieves, *did* conceal and store horses, but rather whether he's *still* doing it and in what manner it's done.

"That he must have help with it is as clear as day – tie up the young fellow there if he puts one more foot outside the cabin," he now interrupted himself and pointed over toward the young Negro, who, apparently quite embarrassed, at this moment slid swiftly back into the doorway – "keep a better watch on the boy, or he could ruin the whole plan for us."

The guards had been listening too intently to his speech, and now, ashamed of their negligence, stepped once more to the door. But Husfield continued: "Since I've heard everywhere that Atkins seldom or never leaves his house, then he must have people at hand who take care of such little matters for him. To be sure, these can't live far off from him."

"Johnson has a cabin only a short distance away from his house," said Wilson.

"Damn the scoundrel," Husfield exclaimed, his previous composure completely forgotten with this discovery, "so *that* dog's in cahoots with him too, and the show with the horses that time was a fake. A plague on him – but wait –" he then continued thoughtfully – "here, too, cunning and calm will have a more sustained effect than mad ranting and raw uncalculating force. So again, I cast my vote for Mr. Brown's suggestion that we think the thing over first before we act rashly and maybe foolishly. We still have several hours' time before we'll be forced to decide something; perhaps Mr. Brown will now be so good as to make us acquainted with the plan that he's drawn up."

"Gladly," said the young man, climbing up again onto his earlier speaker's platform – "it's easily told, and will be just as easily understood. We know the magic formula that secures us entry to the secret place where our neighbor keeps the stolen goods. But it's not yet known *that* we know it; that's still our secret. So my proposal is this: this evening send a man to Atkins that he doesn't know, with several unfamiliar horses; maybe this Canadian here is just the right one."

The one so indicated shook his head.

"No – damn it," he then said – "I was there already – this morning at day-break – he probably didn't see my horse standing outside, but I myself – lots of women in there –"

"That is unfortunate. Well, then we'll find another who must stop at his place, give the password, bring up the horses tied outside according to his instructions, and get the animals to the spot from which they'll be led to the appointed hideaway. Meanwhile, we'll lie in ambush nearby and pounce on the battleground only after a prearranged signal."

"That's all very well and good," said Wilson, "but where will we find some-one before evening whom Atkins *doesn't* know; since Atkins knows almost every man in the whole of Arkansas."

"So what were you doing at Atkins'?" Husfield asked the Canadian.

"What was I doing? I was asking about horses," replied the latter.

"And he answered?"

"He hadn't seen any."

"That, at least, was nothing but a plain lie. It'll certainly be hard to find a man – he knows you too, Kefner?"

"I should think so," laughed the latter – "for five years!"

"And you, Jankins?"

"Oh, as well as his neighbor."

"And you, Williams?"

"He knows them all, Mr. Brown," said the last one addressed, "so we'll have to go farther afield. Unless on the road, maybe, we –"

"Wait!" cried Cook – "I have it – a capital idea – the old man won't mind a day or two, we can supply him corn and provisions enough."

"Who then?" several asked.

"Didn't you see a wagon cross over on your ferry this morning, Wilson?" Cook now asked the latter.

"I've been here since yesterday evening," said the one addressed, slightly reddening, "but how should that be of use to us?"

"They can hardly be more than, say, two miles distant from us here in a straight line, on the opposite side of the river," replied Cook, "an old Tennessean with his two boys driving the wagon. One of these, the younger one or the father himself, must stand with us. Atkins *doesn't* know *them*, and if everything's set about cleverly the old fox might walk into the trap."

"But who will ride across?" asked Wilson, "and how can we find them?"

"Oh, nothing's easier than that," Cook directed him – "you cross the river right here, cut straight through the bottom land, go left past the little lake, and just look for the wagon tracks when you get to the road. If the emigrants have already passed by, which I hardly believe, then you're sure to catch up with them in a very short time, and if they've not yet passed that spot, well, so much the better, then you'll merely ride to meet them."

"In that case it would be much better," said Brown, "if you went yourself, Cook. As I understand it, you've already made acquaintance with the old man, and precisely for that reason it might be easier for you to win him to our plea."

"All right," Cook replied decisively, "I don't mind. – It's all the same to me, and where I can help, I'm glad to do it. Besides, it truly won't be difficult to make the old warhorse join in with our plan. I'd bet my life that he comes himself."

"Well, that would settle it," Curtis said with a laugh, rubbing his hands happily – "lizards and earthworms, now I do believe that we'll get on the trail of these damned highwaymen, who are so generous with hot lead and cold steel, and then God have mercy on them. – They'll get a taste of hemp until they've had enough. But in the meantime, what do we do with the prisoners? I don't trust the Negro. The black rascal has already tried to slip away a couple of times, and I don't doubt in the least that after that he would have burned a path straight over to Atkins'."

"We have to tie him up," said Brown, "since we mustn't expose ourselves now to the danger of betrayal."

"The Negresses too?" asked Wilson.

"The boy, at least," said Husfield, "one guard will suffice for the two women, and if the youngster makes the slightest attempt to flee, then we'll tie him to a dogwood and let him dance. Where's the pawpaw bark?"

"Better take a rope," objected Bowitt, "there's some lying under the bed in the corner. So is Jones well secured too?" With these words he walked up to the prisoners and was about to look after his bonds, when the Missourian, who in some way inexplicable to all had worked his hands free, jumped away from the tree to which he had been fastened, and with winged feet tried to race toward the woods. But he did not get far. When he made his first leap in front of Bowitt, who fell back more surprised than frightened, Wilson was standing hardly ten paces distant from him, and caught him after a short footrace. But the one caught was so enraged by this that he engaged his much stronger opponent and, in a great desperate rage, sought to wound him with his fists and teeth.

In truth, Wilson required all of his skill to evade the savage bites of the infuriated man, but finally a powerful blow from his fist threw the raging fellow to the ground. He was then firmly bound by his hands and feet and carried into the house, which, surrounded by four guards posted with loaded rifles, left no further danger to be feared from that quarter.

Meanwhile, Cook saddled his little pony, and soon thereafter the two trotted to the river in order to seek out once more his acquaintance of that morning. Brown and Husfield, for their part, posted sentinels in all directions in order to sever connections with the other settlements, and to prevent the possibility of Atkins being warned; the other Regulators, meanwhile, took care that the mid-day meal was prepared, and that all else that was necessary was arranged. In the shade of the solitary groups of trees left standing in the clearing, they then settled down together, in part to talk about their plan for the evening, in part to rest and, with the setting of the sun, to be refreshed and fortified for new exertions.

Notes

1. We have not found another use of "gumbo" for people. According to the *Oxford English Dictionary*, the phrase emerges around 1838 as a term for the patois spoken by blacks or Creoles in the French West Indies, Louisiana, and Mauritius.
2. FG uses the English phrase "Regulator Meeting" in the original text.
3. In the original, FG uses the slur "nigger" (the only occurrence in the entire novel).
4. FG writes "Oh, Golly" in the original.

Chapter 27

The Return from the Meeting.

In the wild and still sparsely developed woods of the West, where the scattered and solitary residences of farmers often lie separated by great and impassable distances from one another, the inhabitants all feel and understand more so than elsewhere the value of neighborliness. It consists, though, not merely in maintaining friendly relations among themselves, but in lending a hand and helping and supporting each other when necessary, and when the strength of one person no longer suffices. This applies to plowing the first field, rolling together the immense trunks that must be burned in order to clear a fruitful strip for corn, raising houses, or carving out a canoe. The simple request need only be issued, and they arrive with ax or plow and work into the late evening harder and more strenuously than they perhaps would do for themselves a single day in the whole year.

If the men come happily and willingly to complete tasks that could also, without great danger, be left undone for a little while longer, how much more ready to help are the women where illness is involved and they are called together for counsel and help, though this happens seldom enough. Not one – at least none who is able to leave the house at all – will wait for a second messenger to come, but gathering together all possible remedies with haste, the women will mount their horses and rush to the place where they are urgently needed, as joyfully and willingly as if they were attending a celebration or enjoying a day of merriment.

Madame Atkins was not, to be sure, particularly well liked at all in the whole neighborhood, since, for one thing, she visited almost no one and came very seldom to a prayer meeting of the pious, which was particularly held against her. But then too, she was never seen at a single "quilting frolic" or a "log-rolling party,"[1] which her husband seldom failed to attend, and in doing so she must have deeply alienated the fair ladies of Arkansas. For these reasons, they were all the more struck that she had now sent round, and indeed with such a pressing request for help, her nocturnal summons. This would not have been done without real danger, and only a very few could resist the desire to help a child. The old grudge was no more thought of, and before the oun otood at midday eleven women, most of them married and elderly, had arrived with every conceivable powder and elixir, but above all with an almost unbelievable quantity of calomel, in order "to save the sweet life of the poor little mite."

Indeed, the sick child found itself in a genuinely mournful and even dangerous state; a burning fever raged through its tiny veins, and, moreover, it must be suffering inwardly with quite severe pains since it could hardly be comforted and screamed and whimpered almost without cease. The mother paced up and down the room in despair, and now abandoned the infant wholly to the hands of strangers, among whom the Widow Fulweal especially had acquired a reputation as a sort of doctor in matters of childhood illness. As Madame Mullins told Madame Atkins in complete confidence, she had, in fact, already cured three children of maladies which not another person (that is to say, backwoodsmen) could. Of course, the other five who had died under her hand had been afflicted by incurable ailments, as she (Madame Mullins) had seen with her own eyes in three cases, and she (Madame Mullins) had not exactly been born yesterday, when it came to children and their illnesses.

Besides Madame Fulweal and Madame Mullins, there were to be found among the ladies on hand – at least, the ones that were known – Mesdames Bowitt, Smith, Pelter, Hostler, and Kowles, plus two Misses Heifer at the rather dangerous age of twenty-five ("*recently at least,*" as they themselves confessed when pushed to the limit), and still several other farm women, some from the southern and some from the northern bank of the Fourche La Fave.

These had taken full possession of the Atkins' so-called "sleeping house." Mrs. Fulweal, moreover, seemed to wield in that small circle a certain force of authority which by no means would have otherwise belonged to her in the settlement, but that here, because of her aforementioned expertise, was freely acknowledged.

But now, with midday already long passed, and while the women were still occupied with alleviating the distresses of the little sufferer – some putting cold compresses on its temples, some putting warm ones on its belly, and filling it with enough medicinal paste,[2] teas, and calomel powder to slay six less hardy urban children – three members of the Regulators rode at a slow pace along the road that led from Bowitt's house to Atkins', and remained stopped from time to time, as if they were waiting for someone who must soon overtake them. Finally, just as they had reached a little rise, a rider became visible on the heights lying opposite; he came blasting from there at a full gallop and waved with his hat from a distance as soon as he saw the men, as if he wanted them to wait for him.

It was Cook, whose little pony seemed fairly bathed in sweat, and who with flushed face at last reined in alongside the three friends, Brown, Curtis, and Wilson.

"A plague on it," he cried out as he approached them, threw his hat on his head and drove it down to his eyes with a mighty blow, "so why did you race off as if you'd missed something amazing? – just see how my horse looks. – I'll ask for a new one from the assembly."

"We were going to wait for you on this rise, Cook," said Curtis, "since we –"

"And wasn't it just as possible to start out together and ride from Bowitt's house like sensible Christians? Do you think the Tennessean sat there on the road, all saddled and bridled, until I came?"

"Well? Did he agree?" Brown asked quickly.

"And if he did *not* agree, eh?" asked Cook, turning around toward him, "then the gentlemen would have taken a lovely ride for nothing."

"But he's coming – right?"

"Well, of course," laughed Wilson – "just look at his face, he can't hide his pleasure, not at all. Just speak out, Cook, time is pressing, and if we stop here too long we can easily raise suspicion."

"And yet we *must* stop here until we've arranged everything among ourselves," said Cook – "why didn't you wait where you were; it serves you exactly right. You think that when you're finished with your lunch, the other men can go hungry until the next meal, right? But now, seriously, Stevenson's coming, and with his eldest son and three of his horses too."

"Not counting the one he's riding?" asked Brown.

"Well, naturally, every horse thief rides the stolen horses," laughed Cook – "Brown, you are very much behind the times. Those are precisely the two main qualifications for a competent horse thief, to be able to hang on the back of a horse for weeks at a stretch, and then to make inhuman treks back again on foot. Every horse of his own that he rides is pure loss. – But what plan have *you* thought out yourself?"

"Hasn't Husfield disclosed it to you?"

"No, he put me off about it, since I would catch up with you. The lazy fellow lay under a tree and seemed to want to get ready for this evening's work."

"But has he told you that he and Curtis must stay overnight at Atkins'?"

"Yes – but nothing more."

"And where is the Tennessean?"

"Up at Bowitt's with his son. The old man was all fire and flame when I told him of our plan and wanted to take all the youngsters with him right away. But when the women heard about the robbing riff-raff in the neighborhood, there was quite a rumpus, and suddenly no one was allowed to leave. But the old Tennessean kept his head above water and finally agreed that the two youngest could stay behind to protect the family. Then, in order to calm the women, they were outfitted with knives and pistols, at which point Ben, the smallest, received a special warning to 'not hurt himself,' and off we trotted as fast as the horses could go. Now for your plan."

"It's simply the following," replied Brown. "The Tennessean – what's his name?"

"Stevenson."

"So, Stevenson stays until nearly evening at Bowitt's, in order to arrive at Atkins' place about an hour after it gets dark. – You two – Cook and Curtis – accompany us to Atkins' and make some excuse to stop off there. We two, Wilson and I, will ride by."

"Then why did you come down here with us now? Surely you could have stayed just as long at Bowitt's," said Cook.

"So that Atkins couldn't possibly become suspicious," responded Wilson. – "But if he sees us riding calmly by here toward the house, he'll naturally think that everything is in order and won't look into it any further. Since Brown is the leader on the Fourche La Fave, he'll have to consider it obvious that this ride home means that the meeting is adjourned. "

"But where will you stay in the meantime?"

"We'll ride to Wilson's house – leave our horses there and return again on foot."

"Listen – just look out for Curneales – I don't trust him farther than the end of my rifle!" warned Cook.

"Just as little do we," replied Wilson; "but in order to throw him off the trail we'll shoulder our rifles and go toward the salt lick that lies south of my house. From there, if we get started right at twilight, we could still get to the spot at the right time."

"And where are you going to keep yourself hidden?"

"Wilson here, who's been in Atkins' house often before, believes that he can tell with reasonable precision where the secret gate is to be found. But be that as it may, the hiding place *must* lie in the cane brake that runs down behind Atkins' house to the Fourche La Fave; there's no other place there, and Hecker told me recently that it's impossible to break through it. He had shot a turkey and, though he'd heard it fall, he couldn't get to it, the toppled and *felled* tree trunks lay helter-skelter there."

"How many men do we muster for the attack?"

"About eighteen – they'll be altogether sufficient."

"And what do we say to him if he asks after Jones?"

"Curtis knows that already, but I can quickly go over it with you again. Husfield has taken Jones with him to the Petit Jean to a Regulators' meeting to be held there tomorrow. That river lies a little closer to the state of Missouri, so it's also more exposed to robberies from there, and he'll find it quite in order for a group of our people to be sent from there to the border."

"Will he believe that?"

"Why not? – He'll think that Jones himself will have persuaded them to do it in order to lead them off the trail of the horse thieves dwelling here. You could also give him to understand that. Once you're in the house and you hear our signal – a sharp whistle – then instantly seize the weapons there, since we don't want to spill blood if it can at all be avoided."

"But the many women who were there this morning?"

"They're in the way, indeed, but that can't be helped. Besides, even if they should all be there, they'll sleep in the other house and can in no way hinder us in carrying out our plan."

"Would a shot not be a better signal?"

"A shot? – in the middle of the night, and not a bit of moonshine? No, I don't think that's a good idea. Why alarm the neighborhood, when it can be done with such ease otherwise?"

"Have you also thought of the mulatto? Naturally, he's in cahoots with his master and if there are actually accomplices nearby he'll get the news to them, whatever it takes."

"We're covering all the roads," said Curtis, "and he'll have to fall into our hands on one of them."

"Wouldn't he favor a path through the woods?"

"In that sort of darkness? No, I hardly think so," replied Brown, "but that can't be helped. Once we've caught the top horse-trafficker in the act, he'll have to name the rogues that helped carry off Husfield's last horses, and we'll definitely find the murderer of the Indian woman among them."

"Come, then," said Cook, "tarrying this long here on the mountain, if someone should happen to see us, could only raise suspicion. By the way, I wish we had the Indian on hand today, he'd render splendid service. I'm about to believe that he's not coming back, however improbable that seemed to me at first. But not the slightest thing has been heard from him for a full nine or ten days now."

"Mullins claimed to have seen him in the woods yesterday," said Curtis, "but it was in a very dense spot and only for a moment. He also told me that he had called to him, that is to say he shouted into the woods in the direction in which he had noticed him, but never caught another glimpse of him."

"He's not gone," Brown asserted, "I'd swear to it. I had to give him my word not to leave this part of the country before Alapaha is avenged; so it's not likely that he meant to desert me."

"Well, we'll see," said Cook, shaking his head; "but if he has it in mind at all to come back, and wishes something to be done in his case, then he would have done much better to stay here and more diligently carry out the investigation on the spot. – But, as I said, we'll see."

The men, meanwhile, continued to pursue their way, and now approached Atkins' residence, which lay at the foot of the upland region. He already stood before the door and appeared to have been waiting for them. Incidentally, when they reached the fence and he did not see the stranger, he came to meet the Regulators at the outermost gate and presumably wanted to ask the question on the tip of his tongue but was actually afraid to utter it.

"How is the child doing, Mr. Atkins?" asked Brown, as he reined in his horse and stopped next to the man as he greeted them.

"Thank you – not especially well, sir – I'm afraid we're going to lose the poor little thing. Well, is the meeting concluded?"

"For the present, yes! – the neighbor women are all still here – right?"

"Almost all, at least eleven; – enough to kill half a dozen children; but my wife wants it so. Well, has anything been decided? – But won't you dismount and rest a little, gentlemen," he interrupted his own question – "you still have plenty of time to get to the next houses – or perhaps stay overnight with me, indeed."

"No, I thank you, Atkins," Brown declined, "at least for myself; Uncle has ridden over to Roberts, so I must look after the house and feed the animals; otherwise, I'd be delighted."

"Listen, Brown – you may ride on alone, then," said Curtis, – "I will stay the night here. I'm not missing anything at home."

"Good – then I'll keep you company – if Atkins really has space for guests and the ladies haven't occupied both rooms," exclaimed Cook.

"Space enough – only dismount, and anyway I'm curious to hear the news from up there. But where have you left my guest from yesterday?"

"He's with Husfield on the Petit Jean, but let's talk about it in the house," replied Cook, as he climbed out of the saddle and then immediately unbuckled it and hung it over the fence. Curtis followed his example, and Brown (Wilson had slowly ridden on ahead during this time) repeated his farewell and trotted off quickly after his friend.

Meanwhile, Atkins led his two guests into the house, where they found another unfamiliar young man by the fireplace. Their host introduced him to them as Mr. Weston, "his nephew," who had come to the Fourche La Fave in order to settle here, and probably would be living with him for some time.

"I must be very much mistaken," said Curtis, "but I believe that I've already seen you once before – or it was someone who looks extraordinarily like you –"

"That's quite possible," Weston smiled, somewhat embarrassed. "It was when I went to Little Rock and stopped off here for a few days. – I think I met you once while I was out hunting –"

"Yes, of course," said Curtis, – "I remember now – it was above here on the river, – where you were camping. So I was right after all."

"You mentioned that Mr. Jones has ridden to the Petit Jean," Atkins interrupted him, "will he likely stay there long?"

"No," responded Curtis, "indeed he charged us to tell you that he will be back by noon the day after tomorrow at the latest."

"Are the Regulators there meeting as well?"

"Early tomorrow, as I understand it. Husfield has taken several from the Fourche La Fave across with him."

"But I thought that suspects were to be identified, taken to prison, and cruelly interrogated?" asked Atkins, and one could see the interest he took in the answer to this question.

"Yes – that was to happen," said Cook casually, as he walked to the fireplace and there turned his boots before the flame in order to dry them, "but we've not been able to quite agree about it. For one thing, there was not enough suspicion placed on any single person, and then it also appears that neither Jones nor Brown quite agree with the punishment."

"Mr. Brown doesn't either?" cried Atkins, astonished.

"No – but next week we hope to carry it through, for something *must* be done," Cook inserted himself into the conversation. – "Otherwise the scallywags will laugh at the Regulators in the end."

"Weston – would you perhaps be so good as to look a little after the horses of the gentlemen here," Atkins now turned to the young man who had stood up and walked to the door. "And take the saddle out there from the fence," he continued, as the other was on his way to swiftly execute his request. – "The cursed cows chewed up another saddle blanket just yesterday – and then just go over to my wife for a little, she has something more to tell you."

Weston nodded to him that he would take care of everything as requested – then carried the saddle onto the porch and went around the house. But here, instead of seeking out the little stable in which the strangers' horses stood, as soon as he could no longer be seen from the house, he sprang over the fence and in the next instant had disappeared into the thick woods lying behind it.

Notes

1. "Quilting frolic" and "log-rolling party" are approximate translations of FG's own coinages "Steppdeckenfrolick" and "Klötzerrollfest."

2. "Latwerge" (the German term used by FG) or "electuary" is a medicated paste prepared with a sweet substance (such as honey or syrup) to make it more palatable (*DWB*). It is applied to the teeth, gums, or tongue.

Chapter 28
The Indian on Johnson's Trail.

"Just where is Weston?" said Cotton, impatiently pacing back and forth in the little cabin that had already served him as a lodging and a place of refuge for several days; "he promised me this morning to bring news right away, and the Regulators surely must have already dispersed by now. They won't sit around up there a whole week. – Brimstone and rattlesnakes – I'm getting uneasy here at the thought of being taken up and lynched; a plague on the dogs! I'll probably have to say adieu to this neighborhood here. To hell with *any* life lived in *such* a manner!"

"We still have time for flight," Johnson answered him, yawning, as he lay outstretched on the only bedstead in the house. "But I'd very much like to take with me the new shipment that Jones has spoken of, and which is to come along next week. Hell's fire – seventeen horses! that will make it worth the trouble of taking to our heels."

"I just don't see how we're going to bring them all away safely," grumbled Cotton. "Besides, the remaining horses that Weston has tracked down will come in at the same time as these; and if they can't keep on *that* trail, they must be blind."

"We won't ride these through the woods," replied Johnson – "Weston has already negotiated with a steamboat captain to take them on board at Fort Gibson."

"Well, but then they'll just get right back on their trail," cried Cotton, halting his march in astonishment. "If they're taken from the Indians and got right on board, why, a child could follow them."

"And what about it?" laughed Johnson; "they can't chase after a steamboat, and we'll ship them out in Little Rock. If they should actually set out afterwards in another boat, assuming that another one is indeed lying there, they'll lose the scent without fail on the broad streets of Little Rock. But be that as it may, we'll have time in any event to reach the Mississippi swamp, and from there the island, and the Fourche La Fave won't see me again after that."

"It will be much regretted," replied Cotton; "but I'll swear, here comes Weston! Well, it's about time – the sun is just setting."

While Cotton was still speaking, the aforementioned sprang over the low fence and in the next instant appeared in the narrow doorway of the lowly cabin.

"Damn it all!" cried Johnson, jumping up from his bed in fright when he glimpsed the deathly pale face of the young man. – "Harbinger of bad news, what brings you? Are the Regulators –"

"No, no," whispered Weston, shaking his head, "we have nothing yet to fear from them."

"Well, what's with you then?" said Cotton angrily, "why, you look as blue in the face as spoiled buttermilk. – Out with it – what is it?"

"The Indian is here," he gasped, throwing himself down, exhausted, on the only chair standing in the room.

"Well, if it's nothing more than that," Johnson scoffed, as he resumed his former place on the bed, "then you could have spared us a fright. Damned foolishness to come tumbling in here thus, as if half a dozen Regulator rascals were yelping at your heels. How did the meeting end? where is Jones?"

"On the Petit Jean with Husfield – tomorrow there's another meeting there – Cook and Curtis are at Atkins' place – nothing has been decided about us yet. That's all well and good – but Johnson, you shouldn't take the Indian so lightly, he's on *your* trail."

"On my trail?" Johnson cried, now somewhat upset again, but still half incredulous. "How should he come onto *my* trail? – after all, Husfield was on it with his whole band and still had to turn back empty handed."

"Did you go along the path that lies between here and Atkins' house this afternoon?" asked Weston.

"Yes – about a half hour ago, and what of it?"

"As I hurried along this same path about half an hour ago," related Weston, "right there where the young gum tree has fallen across the way, and was about to bend around its top, I saw something move on the path. For an instant, I thought it was a bear that had wandered this way, but shortly, and not at all to my pleasant surprise, recognized the Indian, who, bent over with his eyes firmly fixed on the ground, came striding up to and right into me. A meeting seemed unavoidable, and I was just about step out from behind a shrub and speak to him, when, hardly fifteen paces from me, he came to a little moist spot and suddenly stopped there. At first, I couldn't quite make out what he was really after, but soon I found that he was closely examining one of the perfectly imprinted tracks there. He took his tomahawk from his belt and compared the track that he found there with one that he seemed to have marked on it, then all at once straightened himself to his full height, turned his back to me, and swung his weapon with a threatening gesture in the direction of the house here, and then left the path, from which he walked into the woods on the right, straight over the first low hill."

"And the track?" Johnson asked urgently.

"Was yours," said Weston. "As soon as the damned savage had disappeared over the rise, I quickly sprang out from behind my hiding place and looked at the track. – It was your right shoe, all right, as beautifully and cleanly stamped in the soft mud as if a mold had been made especially for your foot."

"So you didn't follow the Indian any further?" asked Cotton, as Johnson paced up and down the room in deep thought, stamped his foot, and furiously ground his teeth.

"I certainly did!" replied Weston, and Johnson, turning quickly toward him, asked:

"What became of him?"

"First of all, I was on pins and needles," said Weston, "since, to speak frankly, I didn't wish the redskin to find me on his own trail. But I couldn't keep myself from climbing up the hill, since I knew that one can look out from there over the whole long ravine, right down to the greenbrier thicket. So I crept as quietly as possible up to the top, since the red-skinned Mr. Scalping Knife could easily be lingering up there somewhere! But he wasn't there, and I was already about to pull back, since I thought that maybe he had turned again toward the Fourche La Fave through one of the side ravines, or had even climbed through the pine thicket to the mountain ridge above. Meanwhile, it had become dusk; then it suddenly seemed to me as if I saw the gleam of a fire down deep in the ravine. All was dark immediately afterward, but after a little while I saw the glow anew, and I now no longer had any doubt that it was the Indian who had lit his fire down there, probably in order to camp there for the night."

"And where is the place?" Johnson asked quickly.

"Do you know the place? Just this side of the greenbrier thicket," Weston explained to him, "there, where the last hurricane toppled a lot of pines down the mountain?"

"Somewhat in the same neighborhood where we shot the wildcat out of the little elm?"

"Just there," Weston cried quickly, "as far as I could tell, he must be camping in exactly that area –"

"Then he won't have chosen any other spot than under the slightly protruding rock, where he's adequately protected from the dew as well as from a thundershower," hissed Johnson through firmly clenched teeth, as he stepped to the corner and seized his rifle.

"What do you intend to do?" asked Cotton, taken aback.

"To put an end to that damned red spy's snooping," he rasped.

"Nonsense, Johnson," Cotton cried angrily – "you'll bring the whole neighborhood down on us. What the hell do you care if the red brute knows the length of your soles or not? As long as one of us presses a *shoe* in the mud, there's no danger, and he can sleuth all he likes. With *horseshoes* it's another matter –"

"You don't understand," Johnson said darkly, "it's not the first measure that the dog's taken of my foot. I know from reliable people that it's already happened on other occasions. Now there's no longer any doubt that he's on the *right* track and – the worst of the thing is – he *knows* it – that's why he must die."

"I'll be damned if I understand you," grumbled Cotton, pushing the logs in the fireplace together with his foot. "Anyway, since the thing isn't *so* pressing, I'd advise you to put it off until –"

"The Regulators have me by the collar and hang me on the nearest oak? Is that right, you wiseacre? No, there's no safety for me as long as the redskin lives, so away with him!"

"I'd like to know what you have against the redskin?" Cotton objected in the same gruff tone. – "When the – the – affair with the squaw occurred, you were still who knows how many miles down the road, so less suspicion can fall on you than on any other human being in the whole of Arkansas. And as for the horses –"

"But I am telling you," cried Johnson, now pushed to the limit – "horses don't have a thing to do with this, and – but how does it help me for you to stir the mess up once more –"

"A – h, s – o," Cotton then said, stopping in amazement, as if a new thought dawned on him, "does the wind blow from that direction? – So in *that* business –"

"Oh, go to hell with your conjectures," Johnson muttered. "If only it were completely dark now, the ground here is burning under my feet."

"Yes, yes," Cotton went on, without acknowledging the coarse remark, "if that's how the matter stands, then of course I'd want to advise a graceful exit myself. But why have you never said a word to me about it? I really wouldn't betray you, after all."

"So what are you actually talking about?" asked Weston now, quite astonished; "I can't make a bit of sense out of your drivel. What does this everlasting mystery-mongering mean?"

"Yes, this would be a good time to tell stories," grumbled Johnson; "no, I'm starting off, I can't stay here any longer."

"Johnson," Cotton then said, "I don't like the rifle. – The bang – you can hear it too far off in the middle of the night, and why the needless noise? I've prepared the arrows that we spoke of recently. Can you manage the bow?"

"Like an Indian," replied Johnson, "to be sure, I lived among the Shawnee for seven years; but to hell with it, – I don't know – a bow always seems a damned uncertain weapon to me – instead of that, give me a bullet anytime –"

"All right, but at least try the arrows once," said Cotton, as he climbed up the short ladder to the room above and soon afterward returned with a bow fashioned from stout hickory and four arrows. "There," he said, "just take a shot; wait, here's a potato that I'll place here in the ashes; now step back, there in the corner – just hit the potato for me."

Johnson smiled and weighed the bow in his hand for a moment, then fitted the arrow to it, took aim for a few seconds, and an instant later the wooden shaft, having bored completely through the target, quivered in the soft earth of the hearth.

"Excellent," Cotton cheered, "a masterful shot; hit the red rascal like that, and he'll go no farther."

"It's still an uncertain shot," said Johnson, still half undecided, though nevertheless excited by the fine shot.

"Uncertain? The poison on this roughly filed point here kills in five minutes," whispered the hunter. "Hit the Indian with it just in the arm, just in a finger, and he wouldn't get to this house again if he ran in a straight line as fast as his legs can carry him."

"The poison kills without fail?"

"As surely as I hope to escape the fangs of the villainous Regulators –"

"Oh, let the poor Indian live," pleaded Weston, "why spill his blood? Surely enough has flowed already. You're beginning to spook me; you talk about a person's life as if it were a deer or a bear."

"Now he's starting to talk nonsense," Johnson said angrily, while he still held the arrow indecisively in his hand. "Mind your own business and leave *us* alone. The Indian dies!"

"Then *I*, at least, will have nothing more to do with it," cried Weston resolutely, "his blood is on you; tomorrow I will return to Missouri. I joined you to trade in horses, but now there's nothing here but blood and always more blood. – It makes me shudder – good night! –"

He stood up and was about to leave the room.

"Stop!" cried Johnson, leaping in front of the door in a manner half dismayed and half menacing, as he held the poisoned arrow toward the young man, though without, as it appeared, thinking about it – "you're going to betray us!"

"Help!" screamed Weston, springing back in terror from the dangerous weapon – "Murder!"

"Plague and death," cried Cotton angrily, as he shoved the wary Johnson back from the door and placed himself between him and the young man, "to hell with these antics now."

"I wasn't even thinking about the poisoned arrows," said Johnson – "but why does Weston want to leave?"

"In part because I'll be missed at Atkins', and then, too, I don't want to be a witness to yet another murder. To think that I'm going to betray you is not only vicious, it's foolish too. I'm too deeply involved myself to have any real hope of a pardon, even if I weren't bound by my oath."

"Do you still remember your oath?" asked Johnson threateningly.

"Yes," breathed Weston softly, shuddering at the same time, "you have nothing to fear from me – but next time be more careful around such weapons and – let him live – Johnson, let him live," he pleaded desperately, gripping the arm of the gloomy man. "Perhaps it will still be safe for us, yes, even *without* his blood. Remember that the poor devil's wife already –"

"I'll be damned if I'll listen to this gibberish any longer," cried Johnson, angrily shaking the young man off him. – "Go – away with you – you can be of no use at all to us here; but, Weston – remember your oath, and don't think that, even if God himself pardons you, you will escape *my* vengeance."

"Save your threats," Weston said earnestly, "I'm no traitor, but I'll have no more association with you from now on. Early tomorrow I'll go back to Missouri – I'm ruined for this sort of trade –"

"Or still too new at it," laughed Cotton; "well, good luck to you, Weston, if this is really what you want, and – with any luck, I'll get up to Missouri sometime in the next couple of years."

"Farewell, Johnson," said Weston, extending his hand to the man, "at least let's have no ill will on parting."

"Farewell," the latter replied, sullen and half-turned aside.

The young man left the house, climbed over the fence, and in the next instant vanished from the sight of the two men gazing after him into the thick bushes surrounding the little house.

"We really shouldn't have let him go," said Johnson, now restlessly pacing up and down the room, "I don't trust the fellow."

"He's trustworthy," Cotton averred – "I know him – *he* won't betray anyone. – But there are other men whom I don't trust."

"You mean Rowson?" said Johnson, stopping before him.

"Yes!"

"He's in it too deep – if everyone were as reliable –"

"Yes, now – but let him get into a jam, let him see the rope on one side and the hope of deliverance on the other, and then watch what he does. Or rather, *don't* watch, since in that case I'd rather rely on my legs than on his honor. I don't trust him."

"It's getting dark," said Johnson, "I'll go, but – I don't know – I'd prefer the rifle –"

"You're a fool," cried Cotton, "hang it all, you'll shoot just as surely with an arrow as with a bullet, and one can keep you from being discovered, while the other is sure to betray you. When they find the body –"

"I'll be long gone from here," laughed Johnson – "do you think, given this Regulator business, that I'd leave my neck in a noose?"

"But the new horses –"

"You may care for them yourself, by tomorrow I will have left for the island – tonight I'll put my few belongings in order, and at daybreak I'll take for myself one of Roberts' horses that are grazing between here and his house. Before they find the Indian, I'll be across over the hill and far away."

"But Rowson."

"May follow, if he sees danger – he knows where I'm going. Do you want to come with me?"

"I've promised Atkins that I would help handle the next shipment, and I'll keep my word, *must* keep it in fact, since my wallet is a pitiful sight. The last round-up brought in damned little. If this one sets me straight, it may be that I go to Texas with Atkins. – So you want to take the rifle after all?"

"Rifle and arrow," said Johnson. "First I'll try the poison, and if I'm not entirely pleased with my shot, then the lead may lend a hand."

"Then you're certain that you can sneak up on him?"

"If he's camped there where I expect he is, yes" – replied Johnson, exchanging his hard shoes for soft, silent moccasins. "There's not a single dry leaf on that rock that can betray me by its rustling."

"Well, if it must be done, then at least be sure to hit him," Cotton cautioned.

"Never fear, once I'm within range of him, he's mine. Besides, the place is remote enough, and he'll have to scream loudly if he wants to attract anyone that way. Where will you stay in the meantime?"

"Here – I'll use the time to whip up a nice stew so that you'll find something warm when you return. So Heathcott –"

"Oh, hold your tongue about ancient history and brew your drink, that's more useful."

"Don't leave me waiting on you too long," the hunter called after him.

"You can believe that I won't sit down by him first," the other said sullenly, threw the door shut behind him, and straightaway glided with soft but hasty steps through the woods to the next mountain crest, from which Weston had glimpsed the Indian's fire.

The night was raven black; not a star lighted a sky obscured by sinister thunderclouds, and the dull unearthly rustling of great treetops announced the coming storm. Far above, on the mountain ridge that separates the waters of the Fourche La Fave and the Maumelle from one another, a lone wolf howled its night song with sharply piercing plaintive cries, and an owl answered scornfully from the dark top of a pine, in which it hoped to find protection from the advancing violence of the storm. Animal and man sought the shelter of a warm chimney or a thick canebrake; only the murderer with his bloody thoughts trod along his dismal path, unmindful of the ever-increasingly powerful and threatening signs of a whirlwind, rifle and bow held with desperate grip in his clenched hand, and the wilder and more savagely the elements raged, so much the bolder and more defiantly flashed his eye. The storm was, indeed, his confederate, and through it he found even greater confidence for his bloody work. That is, if the Indian really were camped at that place, then in such weather he certainly had sought the protection of the overhanging rock guaranteed to shield him fully from the threatening rain as well as against any falling trees, and thus it would not be possible to hear his footsteps or his approach; the roar and bluster in the boughs and branches of the forest would drown out everything else. Vengeance would surely be *his*, just as soon as he found his victim.

Cautiously he followed the course of the little ravine, though he could have chosen a shorter path to the place with which he was well acquainted. But it is difficult at night, and without starlight, to maintain a straight direction through the woods, and even a practiced backwoodsman does not like to attempt it without a pressing need. He had wrapped a woolen cloth thickly around the tips of the poisoned arrows so that he did not wound himself by untimely accident, and, his weapons in his left arm, he walked higher and higher, feeling his way carefully with his right, until he recognized the vicinity of a fallen spruce and knew now where he stood.

Just there the ravine formed a kind of jog, and right above it was the rock under which the Indian had to be lying, diagonally across from anyone approaching from that side. So Johnson decided first of all to reconnoiter, since discovery, given the protection of the wind's steadily increasing howl, was no more to be feared at all. Avoiding, nevertheless, every unnecessary noise, he crept along under the tree trunks that had been toppled cross-wise into the ravine, left his rifle there where he could find it again in an instant, so as not to be hindered by his numerous weapons as he crawled forward, and slithered like a snake toward the edge of the rock that had until now separated him from his victim.

Triumph! His heart beat almost audibly – there – stretched out before the fire lay the red son of the forest, unaware of the danger from poison and lead that threatened him; his weapons rested at his side, and propped up on his right arm, he gazed thoughtfully into the unsteadily flickering flame. Gripping the bow with a firm hand, Johnson heaved himself up and looked keenly across in order to mark the spot to which he should send the deadly arrow, since the distance between him and his victim was scarcely ten paces. But here he found a fresh obstacle. The Indian's outspread blanket, which he had set up to windward in order to be protected against any rain driving in at an angle, concealed the greater portion of his body, so that actually only the front part of his head and his right arm were fully visible, while the rest of his frame lay hidden under the woolen screen. To be sure, Johnson could precisely determine the spot where he must strike the Indian, and had he had his rifle with him instead of the arrow, he would not have hesitated a moment longer; but now the strange thought suddenly arose in him that the wool, though it could not stop the arrow, might yet deflect it or take from the poison all its strength; in short, he was afraid to take such a doubtful shot.

Moreover, there came to him an irrepressible fear before the powerful figure of his enemy, whom he knew to be of the utmost resolution, and who if merely wounded might retain sufficient strength to overtake him and try the sharpness of his tomahawk on his skull.

Besides, the way the blanket was spread required him to creep at most only twenty paces to the right, directly behind a stately elm that stood on the slope of the hill. Then the breast of the encamped warrior would offer him a broad and certain target, and from there his arrow could not fail to do its deadly work.

The first bolt of the fierce storm now flashed and threw its pale and ghostly light across the landscape. As though pleading for help, the colossal arms of the gigantic trees eerily thrashed and waved in the garish light, but the next moment all was wrapped once more in a night so much the more impenetrable. Johnson now raised himself in order to reach the desired location quickly and finish the matter, but from under his right hand, with which he had been holding tightly onto the projecting root of an oak tree, a stone slipped and rolled a few paces down to the bottom of the ravine. He remained lying motionless, nestled close against the ground, so as not to be betrayed to his victim, and then very slowly raised his head to observe the effect that this unusual noise might have produced in the Indian.

The sound had not, in fact, escaped the attentive ear of the savage, and he listened carefully and raised his whole head above the blanket so as to examine the circle of light thrown out by the fire; but Johnson lay in the shadow of the oak that rose somewhat higher up the slope than where he was situated, and Assowaum's gaze passed over him. Then an even more brilliant flash illuminated the ravine, and the murderer flinched in fright. But the bolt seemed quite to have blinded the Indian, since he pressed his hand against his eyes and then sank, apparently reassured, back into his previous posture.

Johnson watched him another moment and then slid snake-like back about five or six paces, where he could not have been seen by his victim even in daylight. Here he clambered up the right side until he was behind the elm, from which he had the enemy's camp right in front of him; having reached the spot, he slowly pulled back his bow, laid the deadly arrow on it, and then quickly but carefully raised himself up for the shot. – Then – almost involuntarily a cry of astonishment and terror escaped him, for – the place by the fire was empty – Assowaum had vanished.

But before he could form a thought, could even move a muscle, he felt a hand on his shoulder, looked – starting back in terror, into the fierce menacing face of his enemy, saw the raised arm of the red warrior – his tomahawk flashed in the glare of the fire burning below and, struck by the flat side of the dangerous weapon, he collapsed, stunned and silent.

Terrible was his awakening. Sulphur-yellow bolts crackled and hissed through the swaying tree tops, loud cracks of thunder crashed down, and the floodgates of heaven seemed opened – all of nature was in an uproar; but bound and gagged so that he could not move a muscle or utter a sound, the captured criminal lay tethered to the root of a hickory tree, abandoned and alone in the riot of the angry elements. In vain he struggled with the strength of despair to break his bonds, or at least to free an arm from the cords that were almost cutting into his tendons. In vain he stretched his limbs, causing the blood to well up under the sharp leather straps that held him entangled; his conqueror understood the art of tying a knot, of making his bonds unbreakable. Feeble and exhausted, he finally was forced to quit his almost insane efforts, and now lay still, panting and quite senseless.

The storm had slackened; but, as with the heaviest of rains, water continued to pour down from the leaves, the wind was chasing the dark cloud masses before it, and the bright disk of the moon cast here and there, through the torn veils of mist, its pale clear silver light on the earth below.

Johnson had just awakened from his second swoon – a feverish chill shook his limbs, and for the first time the terrifying thought now struck him that the Indian had abandoned him here, never to return; that Cotton, awaiting his reappearance in vain, would flee, and he would be forced to slowly starve to death here, if a merciful wolf did not sooner put an end to his miserable existence.

He could already hear their shrill cries from the nearby mountains – they were gathered together after the storm to embark on their collective hunt for prey, and here, precisely here, where he now found himself, he had very often noticed how they crossed the ravine as they moved from the mountains down to the river.

Almighty God, was he to die in such an awful way? – the howling came nearer – the wolf scents its prey from a distance of many miles. Again the wretch strained against his tight bonds, again he ground his teeth on the gag and struggled until the blood threatened to spring from his veins. Despair gave him the strength of a giant, but he could not break the Indian's fetters. – Then suddenly he lay still and rigid, as if hewn from stone – where was his ear directed so anxiously and hopefully? – why did he fix his gaze so hard and fast on that dark strip of woods – down the ravine? There the wolves did not howl; their clamor sounded to him from another direction.

No – it was not the wolves, but he had heard a call, a familiar and friendly call. – It was an imitation of an owl's call, the signal among his confederates – it must be Atkins or Cotton – maybe both. – They had come to rescue him, and here – here he lay, bound and gagged, unable to move a muscle or make a sound in reply in order to indicate the place where he languished. But nearer and nearer came the voice, louder and more urgent grew the summons of the searcher. Now he stepped to the upper end of the ravine – Johnson could clearly distinguish the outline of his form against the darker background; again sounded the call of the owl, louder and more urgent; at first three, now four times; the prisoner wriggled and writhed like a worm – but he was not able to wrench himself from his bonds and his gag.

Finally – finally, the steps resounded nearer; the searcher had crossed through the ravine – he knew the place where the Indian had lain and went around it – now he must pass by his friend – pass very close by. – Again sounded the call, and listening with body bent forward, the hunter harkened for a reply. Johnson tried his utmost at least to make the leaves rustle with his foot – to shake the young tree trunk on which he hung – in vain. The wind still rustled and blew the branches about, and the leaves were wet and soft; his foot, which frantically bore into them, remained inaudible.

Then the figure approached – it was Cotton – Johnson could clearly recognize the hat that he wore on his head – could see the brighter glow of his pallid face as he came directly toward him – another twenty paces in the same direction and he must tread on his body. – There he stopped – again the call sounded, and the searcher turned his gaze everywhere; of course, he did not expect to see his friend, he only listened in the darkness in case he might not hear the answering voice. His eye roamed almost insensibly and without sympathy over the shapes that presented themselves to him; only occasionally he cast a timid, anxious glance down into the ravine, where he likely suspected the Indian's corpse to lie.

Then he turned – he seemed to have altered his plan – listened once more toward the rustling woods to determine whether that cry of the wolves was the anticipated owl call, and then, seeing that he was again mistaken, he slipped quickly and noiselessly into the nearest thicket.

It was over – there was no further prospect of rescue, and, despairing and wretched, the prisoner collapsed. He no longer heeded the howling of the wild benoto; death was a matter of indifference to him, if not desirable even. He cast but a single glance of defiance and powerless rage toward the clear, now bright and golden starry sky spread out above him, and then closed his eyes, as if with this glance he had taken leave of life and of all hope.

Chapter 29
Rowson at Roberts'. –
The Turkey Hunt. – Ellen and Marion.

The midday meal was finished, the dishes washed up and put away, and the friends sat in an intimate circle before the entrance of the little dwelling and chatted of this and that. Rowson had moved his chair next to Madame Roberts and her dear little daughter and held his bride's hand in his own, whereas Harper took a place beside Ellen, and Bahrens next to old Roberts. But whichever various directions the conversation took as it tacked this way and that, it always came back again to the subject of marriage, and Harper had already been asked for the third time why he did not look about a wife who could sweeten his old age.

"And make death easy, eh?" Harper asked, quietly laughing to himself.

"In a certain sense – yes –" said Madame Roberts, "though that might not be the chief purpose, in any case it might be the last. Anyway, I don't quite know what you mean."

"Well, they tell such a story over in Tennessee," said the little man, "really the woman there did it, but – here if I –"

"Out with it," cried Bahrens – "here are two budding ladies who might learn something."

"But whether it would contribute to the usefulness and piety of their husbands –" Harper replied, shaking his head.

"You make me truly curious, Mr. Harper," said Madame Roberts – "should the girls then be permitted –"

"It's a perfectly harmless story, and happened to the judge in Randolph –"

"So it really happened –"

"Oh, of course – the poor man had become quite ill, probably had an inflammation of the chest or something of that sort, and as they continued to doctor him with only calomel and castor oil, he grew weaker and more wretched by the day, so that the doctors (a couple of quacks who were hanging about in the area) gave up and pronounced a death sentence for him. His wife stayed by his side to the end. But the poor devil must have suffered dreadfully, and people said that he couldn't die since he still had something on his conscience. Finally he died – the neighbors were called in, and the next day – it was summer and very warm – her husband was buried.

"His completely inconsolable widow wept and wailed incessantly; finally one of the women in the neighborhood asked her how the poor man had actually died.

"Oh, dear God, good Madame Sewis, said the mourner – you should have seen how the poor soul suffered; he kicked and jerked and writhed and seized the covers with both hands so that I couldn't get them off him by any means, and he probably couldn't have done it himself, since he must have had a cramp, the dear, good man. So I laid my left hand gently on his mouth, and held his nose closed with the thumb and forefinger of my right hand, and with that he went to sleep as gently as a dear angel – it was a real comfort to me to see him die so peacefully after all his suffering."

"Yes, but my God, so she actually smothered him!" Madame Roberts said, rising from her chair with shock.

"Smothered? Oh no," Harper said with a smile, "she just 'eased his death.' True, there was a good deal said about it later in the neighborhood. But the woman moved up to Kentucky the next month, and there the thing stands."

"That is quite horrible!" said Marion, "and you tell this story with that smile on your face?"

"I just thought the cast was rather funny," remarked Harper – "to a certain extent a very true picture of marital tenderness."

"Oh, God," Roberts inserted himself into the conversation – "that's no longer a new thing; the *steam doctors* run things now in Arkansas, like that tall fellow Hartford, the shopkeeper, who was with us here a couple of weeks ago and was present when the body was found, – say, Bahrens, you were one of them too, and isn't it remarkable that they still haven't found out the culprit?"

"Yes – but what were you going to say about Hartford?"

"Yes, right – well, he treats the dead and the dying with steam and calomel. At Locksmith's he put two children under the ground in one week, and day before yesterday, when he was over at Bestvilles', who have only been living on their piece of land a couple of months, the one they bought from Pelter, and which Bestville paid way too much for –"

"In what manner do the steam doctors treat, then?" asked Ellen. "I've very often heard them talked about, and have never yet been able to discover exactly how they carry on their business."

"Oh, the whole thing would be extraordinarily easy and harmless," Bahrens opined, "if they left out the da – all the poisonous stuff out of their medicine. A real steam doctor only cures through sweating, and that they took from the Indians."

"The Indian, that is to say, finds in sweat the greatest healing power and turns to it in every case of sickness. The tribes that live on the river excavate genuine sweat ovens in its banks, which they crawl into, and afterward plunge from there right into the cold water. But if they live on even ground where they can't do that, they make a little low tent out of hides, or, if they trade with the whites, out of woolen blankets, undress themselves, which with an Indian doesn't take long, crawl in, and then have their friends hand in hot stones that have been set aglow in a great fire kindled nearby."

"The tent is pulled down tightly, and onto these stones they pour cold water from a vessel they carry in; this then evaporates and the whole small area is filled with thick steam."

"Many have more cold water poured on them afterward, many do not, but with this the treatment is nevertheless ended – excepting, of course, the absurd dances and magic spells that must always accompany it, but even so do no more harm. Our steam doctors, though, feed their patients with lobelia* and other such hellish plants, make them drinks out of Spanish pepper that are fit to burn the souls out of their bodies, and don't rest until nature finally triumphs or perishes. This I know, they're not coming near *me*."

"I actually believe that Bahrens himself was once a steam doctor. He knows so much about it," Harper said with a smile.

"If you ever have a wife, Harper," Bahrens replied to him, "then you won't need a steam doctor any more – she'll make it hot enough for you."

"As for that I'm safe, I wouldn't know how to come by one. The only way would be to do it as my brother had to, the one who staked himself in a lottery and paid himself out."

"Staked in a lottery, Mr. Harper? himself?"

"Well, the thing was very simple; he made six hundred lottery tickets at ten dollars each for girls and widows under thirty years of age – you should have been on the screening committee – and staked himself *with* the six thousand dollars thus acquired."

"But Mr. Harper –"

"Well, nevertheless he got rid of only five hundred and thirty something, so he kept sixty something and had a strong hope of winning himself again – yes, a fine win that! A young girl, who brought three witnesses that she was only twenty-eight years old, got him, and he is now the happy father of a family. Though here in Arkansas it might be hard to flog six hundred tickets."

"Not if *you* were the jackpot," laughed Marion. – "I am firmly convinced that lady contestants would come from all directions."

---

* FG note: "Lobelia, a species of poisonous plant, often called 'Indian tobacco,' since the savages frequently mixed it with their tobacco."

"And would you also take a ticket?"

"Why not?" Marion said with a smile – "of course, sometimes you win something that you can't use. In that fortunate event I could, indeed, give you to a good friend; to Ellen, for example – that's allowed, right?"

"Eh, why not," said Harper, "and I would have made very few objections."

Meanwhile, Rowson had listened to the conversation and very seldom entered in, though he held an outstretched turkey wing in his hand as a fan, and now and then used it to shoo away the flies and mosquitoes that swarmed around his bride.

Madame Roberts likewise took a fan, since the heat was really oppressive.

"We're going to have a storm," said Roberts, throwing off his coat, "the air is so oddly muggy – I must have a look at the thermometer – by the way, Rowson," he continued as he stood up and went to the door of the house – "do you know those people whose wagon we could still see when you came up to me at the salt lick? A Tennessean – a former neighbor of mine – Stevenson, a splendid old fellow. I was mighty happy to see him again; and Marion, the girls have grown up so, you wouldn't even recognize them again."

"Oh, why didn't they turn into our place?" asked Mrs. Roberts – "one sees old friends so seldom, you know. Do you know the Stevensons too, Mr. Rowson?"

"Not that I remember," replied the latter, "and I usually have a pretty good memory. Stevenson – the *name* is, at least, familiar to me from Tennessee, but hardly the family itself."

"He was over on the Arkansas when the last murder occurred," said Roberts, now returning with the thermometer in his hand, "and saw the murderer – twenty degrees – it's astonishing –"[1]

"That's not possible!" cried Rowson, forgetting himself.

"Oh, yes it is – you see twenty degrees here – and it's all of that," responded Roberts, whose exclamation referred to the degree of heat, and held the thermometer out to him.

"Indeed," replied Rowson, quickly collecting himself. "But how could he do that?"

"Could do what?"

"How could Mr. Stevenson have seen the murderer? It was even said that the man shot himself, since no one else's tracks were discovered."

"Nonsense," said Roberts, shaking his head. "He stood behind a tree where the two men had to pass by him at a distance of only a few paces, and hardly five minutes before the shot landed. He swore to me that he could pick the fellow out of a thousand again. If you had come out on the road just a hundred paces further up, you would have had to pass by his camp; he is a splendid old fellow; he would have delighted you immensely."

"I don't doubt it at all," said Rowson, "but –"

"Well now, tell me, Roberts," Bahrens interrupted him – "how is that thing there that you have in your hand and call a thermometer actually constructed so that you can see by it whether it's hot or cold?"

"Well, the quicksilver *rises* in the heat," replied the one to whom the question was posed, "and the colder it gets, the more it *falls* accordingly!"

"And the weather adjusts itself to that?"

"No, the thermometer adjusts itself to the weather –"

"But didn't you once tell me that it got so beastly cold in the Green Mountains in 1829 just because they didn't have such a thing up there?"

"Ay, heaven help us," Roberts said with a laugh.

"But that was a mighty cold spell!" cried Harper. "That winter I lived on Lake Erie, in Cleveland, and the quicksilver dropped God knows how far below zero. An old Pennsylvanian that I lived with declared that it would have fallen even farther if only the thermometer had been longer."

"Will Mr. Stevenson be stopping in this neighborhood another few days?" asked Rowson, who until now had been looking down at the ground in deep thought.

"No, perish the thought! He said – that's right, you came straight here – no, he's going directly to the region in which he intends to settle, at the foot of the mountains. He did assure me that our land here on the Fourche La Fave pleased him immensely, and he seemed to have no mean desire to stay right here. But his wife and daughters are beastly frightened of horse thieves, since these, as they had heard on the Arkansas, where, if I'm not mistaken, they stopped for two days and bartered for a couple of new steers, since the old ones –"

"Well, the women have nothing to fear on that score," said Bahrens, "we'll soon be done with their company."

"Undoubtedly," Rowson said with a smile, "people make it out to be more dangerous than it really is. The Fourche La Fave has a much worse name than it deserves, and –"

"Hello – what do the dogs have there?" cried Roberts, jumping up – "Poppy's been chasing a scent for a while, and now the pack is running across the field as if the devil were at their heels."

"It's turkeys, Father," said Marion, "Ellen and I walked around down there before dinner and saw a whole flock right by the brook."

"Ay, why didn't you say so sooner?" cried Roberts, starting forth – "I haven't shot a turkey in over a week – are you going with me, Bahrens?"

"Of course," said the latter, fetching his gun, which he always took with him, from the house – "and if I'm not mistaken, the dogs already have them in the trees."

"Yes indeed, I recognize Poppy's voice. But now we must hurry, otherwise they'll be pushed down into the bottom land, and it's hard to come after them there."

Bahrens required no further encouragement, and the two men ran at a swift pace down to the fence of the corn field, where the dogs were racing around wildly among the trees and seemed no longer to know on which of them the fugitive animals sat. But even the hunters looked around for the quarry in vain, since, for a start, the leaves were too thick, and then the wily turkeys compressed themselves so tightly on the limbs that not a single one could be detected.

"It must have been an old gobbler[2]," said Bahrens, "and that's really nothing special to eat now."

"No," said Roberts, "just yesterday I saw four hens together here that could no way breed this year. There's no plumper roast in the world than such a hen at this time of year."

"Well, then we must sit down," replied Bahrens, – "call the dogs. – You stay here, and I'll go over there on that little hill. If we can keep the dogs quiet, then it won't be much longer before the hens report back – they don't like to be still for long."

Roberts, perfectly agreeable with these precautionary measures, called in his dogs, which were made to lie down very near him, and for probably a quarter-hour neither of the men moved a muscle. Finally Bahrens softly but skillfully imitated the call of a hen, and it was not long at all before another answered from a tree directly above Roberts.

At first the dogs looked up at their masters precociously, as if they would say – "well, do you hear it up there?", and then again into the tree, and finally began to grow impatient. But Roberts wanted to wait until Bahrens likewise had a bird to shoot, and only when answers came from several of the various quarters and the other man lifted his rifle did he straighten himself up and take aim at his prey.

Meanwhile, the turkey hen stood up on the branch to which she had been closely clinging and looked all around, her long neck twisting about in every direction, to see if the earlier danger had passed. Then popped Bahrens' rifle, but almost in the same instant Roberts had gotten ready to fire, and in less than a second both birds plunged heavily down from their not inconsiderable height, where they were instantly welcomed by the dogs.

Madame Roberts and Harper had, during the time the two men were gone after the game, tried to strike up a conversation with the Methodist, starting first with one thing and then another. This day, however, Rowson seemed little inclined to detailed responses, and all in all appeared to be dreadfully distracted.

The girls were better entertained in the meanwhile, walking about arm in arm in front of the little dwelling. But they did not speak of their future plans (each miraculously avoided any allusion to herself), rather of their beloved childhood and adolescent years, and recalled to memory all the bygone but still precious gambols and pleasures.

"Ah, dear Ellen," said Marion, as she stopped and gazed into her friend's eyes, sighing, "but those were truly beautiful and blessed times, when we yet did not know what care and sorrow, what grief and pain, are. The passage from this happy era to a riper life is so imperceptible, it comes so gradually, that one doesn't notice it until one has left all those sweet days far, far behind, and when before us an abyss –" she stopped suddenly in mid-flow, as if she were afraid to complete the sentence, and turned her head away so that Ellen could not observe the two clear dewdrops that beaded in her eyes.

"Why are you so sad, Marion?" gently coaxed her friend, "indeed, you are poised to achieve your desires, and I should think that a union with the man whom we love would not permit us to be so sad and melancholy. That one commits oneself to such a step with some trepidation I find quite understandable. Do you have some sorrow?"

"No, dear Ellen," whispered Marion, still turning from her friend a face now damp with tears – "no – I'm just a foolish child and – and really should look to the future with true joy and happy assurance. – But listen – two shots were fired just now – they seem to have found the turkeys. Now there's something more for the two of us to do this evening," she then went on, turning to Ellen with a smile. But in her eyes her friend also observed the traces of tears shed secretly, and so said quickly and anxiously:

"Oh Ellen, dear, good Ellen, what's troubling you then? You see, I'm such a spoiled creature, and always so occupied with myself that I hardly noticed, or at least ignored, how downcast and silent you've seemed for some time. May I know of it?"

"Yes!" said Ellen, smiling through her tears. – "You shall know all – but not today – within a few days only, when you are calmer and unperturbed. Then you shall learn everything; but" – she continued coaxingly – "once I have made you my confidante, then you must also help me – I'll help you in return."

"If only you could – dear Ellen –"

"So something is troubling you, indeed?"

"Mother's calling me, if I'm not mistaken, I'll come back to you directly," said Marion, and flew into the house. But no mother had called, she only wanted to be away from the vicinity of her friend and grapple with the feeling that compelled her with an almost irresistible force to confide to that same friend's heart all – all that tortured and tormented her. She felt that merely the thought of the oh, so ardently beloved man was a sin, and her task from now on was to renounce him and to live entirely in accord with her duty, which must be at the side of her sacred and precious husband.

The men now returned from the hunt laden with their booty, and the conversation again became general in nature. Indeed the girls had plenty to do to pluck the turkeys before they cooled, a task that on this occasion was attended with particular difficulty. Both asserted that no game so fat had passed through their hands in a long time.

But Rowson had, meanwhile, likewise shaken off that which had troubled or disturbed *him* and had entirely regained his earlier composure. He even seemed this evening to wish to lay aside for once that stern, austere character of an orthodox priest, and display himself as lively, indeed even cheerful, and yes, more than anything, to his own advantage in Marion's eyes. Madame Roberts was enraptured, and old Roberts twice took Bahrens aside and gave him to understand in confidence that he believed the preacher to be reborn. In the first place, he had already been in the house about six hours without preaching a single time, and then he had a certain spontaneity and freedom not only in his tone and bearing, but even in his gestures, such as he had never noticed in him before.

"He is an entirely different person this evening," he cried again after a while, rubbing his hands together, "damned if it's not so – and he's remarkably transformed – though much to his advantage, much to his advantage."

But Roberts could not escape the prayers, for before going to bed Rowson first gave another very long, unctuous sermon to which the men had to patiently submit.

The next morning at breakfast the plan for that Sunday's festivities was drafted, and Madame Roberts was all for their leaving together right away, in order to put her future son-in-law's dwelling in good order, eat there at midday, and then in the afternoon ride over to the judge's house, barely a mile from there. Mr. Rowson was in full agreement with her on this but begged the group to tarry just about an hour more, since he first had to ride a short distance, but would be back in a very short time.

"But truly, Mr. Harper and Mr. Bahrens, you will stay today as our guests?" Madame Roberts asked these two. – "No you don't – Madame Bahrens won't be angry," she assured him affably, when Bahrens tried to pose difficulties. "Today we *must* all celebrate together, and I only wish that Mr. Brown were here as well. But of course that can't be helped at this point. So finish up your business as quickly as you can, Mr. Rowson, and when you return you shall find us ready and willing."

Rowson then mounted the horse that the Negro boy led out to him, waved once more a farewell, and trotted off along the narrow country road more quickly than was his usual manner when leaving Roberts' or some other house in the settlement.

Notes

1. FG uses the Celsius scale, of course, though a temperature of 20°C or 68°F is not particularly hot. Weather data for Little Rock around 1840 are not available. The closest reliably documented location for the same period is Fort Gibson, OK (near present-day Muskogee, OK), and weather records collected there show that FG was right on the mark. In May 1840, for example, daily mean temperatures ranged from a low of 55.8 to a high of 73.6°F (information provided by T. R. Paradise, University of Arkansas, Fayetteville).

2. FG misspells English "gobbler" as "Gobler" in the original text and supplies the parenthetical translation "Truthahn" (turkey), which we have omitted.

D.D. Owen del.

MAGAZINE MOUNTAIN FROM STONE POINT IN THE GRAND PRAIRIE OF FRANKLIN COUNTY
SAND-STONES, SHALES & THIN COAL OF THE MILLSTONE GRIT.

Figure 30.1 "Magazine Mountain from Stone Point in the Grand Prairie of Franklin County. Sand-Stones, Shales & Thin Coal of the Millstone Grit." Lithograph after an original drawing by David Dale Owen. From David Dale Owen, *Second Report of a Geological Reconnoissance of the Middle and Southern Counties of Arkansas, Made during the Years 1859 and 1860* (Philadelphia: C. Sherman & Sons, 1860). Image courtesy of University of Arkansas Fayetteville Special Collections.

Chapter 30
The Ambush.

After Weston left Atkins' dwelling, the two strangers had made themselves as comfortable as the circumstances permitted, then Curtis stepped to the door and looked thoughtfully up at the blue-black cloud masses that were beginning to tower in the west.

"I shouldn't be at all surprised if the storm came this way," said Atkins from his side – "see how those white wispy veils of mist are being pushed ahead. – If we just don't get a hurricane. It looked just like this six years ago on the White River, and afterwards all hell broke loose."

"You were on the White River six years ago?" Cook asked him.

"Yes – and lived about two miles below the road that leads from Memphis to Batesville."

"That must have been about the time when they hanged that Witchalt who had killed his father, right?"

"Later," remarked Atkins, "I came about four weeks after he was hanged."

"Those White River boys practice harsh justice," Cook laughed – "that horse thief – but now what was his name – they let him dangle too."

"I can't blame them for that," cried Curtis – "no honest fellow can have mercy on a horse thief – that is to say, if he has horses himself, isn't that right, Atkins?"

"Yours is a mighty self-serving justice," – the latter replied evasively – "but – you're getting hungry, aren't you? I'll –"

"Thank you – thank you," cried Curtis, staying him – "we ate heartily at mid-day and can easily wait until the proper time – don't go to any bother. – Besides, your wife will not be keen on serving any unscheduled meals today."

"No, certainly not," said Atkins, "for the state of things over there is enough to make you go deaf and blind."

"Is the child still no better then?"

"Unfortunately not – but how could it be otherwise? It's already bad enough when a sick person falls into the clutches of *one* doctor, but now there are eleven of them over there; and I now rely so firmly on my child's constitution that I truly believe that they *can't* kill it, otherwise it would have been long dead. – But I'd better fetch a light, it's beginning to get dark. Thunder, how the wind outside is whistling now, we're having a remarkably stormy spring this year."

With these words he left the room, and the two Regulators found themselves in full possession of it.

"Listen, Curtis," Cook said to his friend after a short pause, "I'm truly sorry about Atkins, that he's one of those scoundrels."

"Speak quietly," cautioned Curtis, "who the devil knows whether someone's lying hidden up above. – Yes, I am sorry too, incidentally; on the whole, he's a right decent fellow otherwise, and I've always liked him well enough. It's true that he has a rather shady look, but that probably comes from 'peeking around the corner' so often."

"I'm curious what they'll do with him," Cook continued thoughtfully – "I really hope that they don't hang him – listen, Curtis – I wouldn't like to be to blamed for his death; he deserves punishment, and I understand quite well that we *must* put an end to this dreadful state of affairs, but to hang – no – not for the sake of his wife and child."

"Well, that would be a neat means of defense," Curtis said with a laugh. "Sure, then all the rogues would need to do is marry in order to be safe from the rope – that shouldn't be considered a hindrance – but I would feel sorry for him too. No, we don't want to hang him, only –"

"Quiet, he's coming," Cook interrupted him, and their unsuspecting host stepped into the room with a light molded out of wax and deer fat, set it on the table, and lit it with stick of pine.

"The wind's whistling out there as if it would blow away the roof from over our heads," he said, stirring up the coals in the chimney a little; "if the wind doesn't divide and disperse it, we're certain to have the storm here in ten minutes."

"Bad for those who are outside today," said Curtis, "even the livestock strangely crowded against the house toward evening."

"Were there many people from the Petit Jean at the meeting?" asked Atkins.

"Not especially," said Cook – "most of them probably counted on it being closer to them tomorrow. Only one stranger, who was looking for his stolen horse."

"A half-Indian –" replied Atkins – "yes, he was at my place too and inquired about them. But unfortunately I couldn't give him any information."

"You *really* haven't seen his horses?" Cook asked, fixing a sharp gaze on him.

"No – how should I?" replied Atkins, without meeting his look. – "Anyway, I haven't gone beyond my fence in the last two weeks, and then the horse thieves are not likely to drive the stolen animals past house fronts."

"Hardly," said Curtis with a smile – "but now what are the dogs doing – they're making an unusual racket, indeed."

"Perhaps another of the Regulators who's been driven in here by the approaching storm," said Cook.

"Probably –" replied Atkins – "still, I'll just have a look – quiet there – you beasts! – quiet!"

With these words he walked to the door, and Curtis whispered to Cook: "That's Stevenson, you'll see. He's chosen a bad time, though; at any rate, we'll have to wait until the storm passes over. By the by, those fellows in the cane brake will have a fine time, while we'll be most comfortable here."

"How far is it yet to the Fourche La Fave?" a voice outside then shouted over the clamor of the dogs.

"Plague and poison," murmured Atkins to himself, and jumped down off the steps toward the fence – "it would be awfully damned fast if that's the second lot arriving already – Jones told me it would take another week –"

"It flows right near here," he then said out loud to the man, who, thickly wrapped in a broad rain cape, sat on his horse.

"Who are you – sir?[1] – My name is Atkins."

"Do you have good pasture here?" was the low answer.

"Where do you come from?" whispered Atkins just as softly – "speak –"

"I would like a drink of water."

"Hell and damnation! Jones told me it would be another week –"

"Let's get the horses to safety quickly," whispered the stranger – "my boy is with them, and there's a frightful storm in the offing."

"Getting wet won't hurt them –" replied Atkins – "I have strangers in the house and can't go now –"

"But the rain would wash away the tracks so neatly," the other objected.

"That's certainly true – but – how many do you have?"

"Three."

"Only three? Jones told me about seven."

"The others come tomorrow evening – we dared not make the tracks too broad."

"Is that the boy that I'm to keep here to move the animals onward?"

"The boy? Yes, right – yes – he knows all about it."

"Does he also know the way to the Mississippi?"

"We've just come –" the old man misspoke, but fortunately he had realized his mistake in time, and continued after a short cough – "from the west, to be sure, but the boy has been *in that area* often before. But get going – big drops are beginning to fall."

"Good – just wait a moment then, and I'll tell those inside there that you'll look after your horse yourself or something like that – hello – who's that there?"

A man approached the fence, and immediately revealed himself to be Weston.

"Ah – you've come at the right time, Weston," cried Atkins. – "Here is a stranger with horses – you know what to do – go with him around the back and get them to safety. I can't very well leave the two Regulators alone!"

"You have Regulators in there?" asked the rider, apparently shocked.

"They're only guests who are spending the night," Atkins reassured him – "but you really must wait until the storm has passed, it's about to cut loose. If the horses are standing in the brook, there's no harm done; they'll not find the tracks."

"In the brook?" said the stranger, "but they're not standing in the brook. I have them up at the corner of the field."

"Ay, the devil take you then; why didn't you take them to the old place?"

"It's the first time I've been here."

"Well then, we had better take them in right away," Atkins cried angrily – "since I really wouldn't want hoof prints up at the corner of the field tomorrow morning – the half-Indian is still in the area. So go with him to the rear door, Weston, I'll step into the house for a moment first and come to you directly."

"Excuse me, gentlemen," he said to the two Regulators as he came back into the room and pulling the door closed behind him; "a stranger has arrived who seems to be quite particular and wants to put his horse up himself. He'll come in presently. But, hallo – here comes the storm – well, that's no mean uproar, to be sure. – The lighting flashes so that a man can barely get his eyesight back afterward."

"Strange how bright it is," said Curtis, looking through a small window hewn into the wall, – "with such a lighting flash one can survey the whole field with a single glance."

"Won't you sit by the chimney, gentlemen?" remarked Atkins, somewhat anxious, – "there's a draft there, and it's more comfortable here."

"Why not?" cried Cook – pulling up his chair and sitting down with his feet thrust under the chimney mantel – "come, Curtis – let the storm growl out there and thank God that your own skin is dry."

"For that I *am* truly grateful," said Curtis with a laugh, as he took a bottle out of his saddle bag, "and so that you see how much I appreciate it, let's first straightaway – Jesus, what a thunderclap! – drink to being frightened! Where are *you* going, Atkins?"

"I must go over to my wife for a moment; women are frightened to death when they're alone thus. I'll be right back."

He slipped quickly out the door and pushed it back into the lock – that is, to the wooden handle that served as a lock, and for a few seconds the two

Regulators sat silent and motionless on their chairs. But then Cook sprang up and whispered softly:

"Curtis – my heart's starting to beat strangely – what a night this is – the lightning fairly reeks of sulphur. Well, those out there in the canebrake will be well and truly soaked."

"There's nothing to be done about it," replied Curtis, looking all around the room – "so, there are two rifles – one over each door – that's prudent. It would be best to render them harmless. We won't need them, and Atkins could do some damage with them after all." With that, he climbed onto a chair and first took down one and then the other on the opposite side. "In fact, both are loaded; – puh – there's dust on this one here. Now, I think, let's blow a little of the powder out of the pan. He won't have time for a new load. Are there other weapons besides?"

"I don't see any more," said Cook, looking all over the room – "if there are more, they must be hidden –"

"Search the bed first – underneath – is nothing there?"

"No – I don't feel anything – but – yes, here – two pistols, in fact. Oh, not bad, very close at hand if a man had the need. Just wait, you rascal, we'll spoil *that* sport for you too – so – you're fixed as well. Now I'd like to see which of the four rifles goes off first."

"Better take care with the pistols, sometimes they'll still fire anyway, and a single spark –"

"I've spit a little tobacco juice in it – better do that with the rifles as well; – and when he snaps the trigger, nothing will catch."

"I shouldn't be surprised at all if the storm rips the roof off the house – did you hear the tree fall just now? Thunderation, it's beginning to feel eerie to me; I rather wish that we had waited for a quieter time."

"My heart is beating like a forging hammer," said Cook – pacing rapidly up and down the room – "we won't hear the whistle at all over the ruckus outside."

"That won't make much difference; we dare not leave our posts, of course – but – I wish that I could see something. It's awkward to be groping around in such confusion and uncertainty when one knows that a gang of hardy fellows is meanwhile waiting in ambush outside. To me, it's just like when you're camping in the woods at night and hear something rustling, and don't know where or what it is."

"Or in a wide cave with a pine torch, and you hear a bear whimpering and can't figure out which side he's hiding on. I – that must have struck, lighting and thunder were almost one and the same – I was once in that situation –"

"Did you hear anything?"

"No – but what should one hear over that bluster outside. – I'm only sorry for poor Stevenson and his boy – well, they'll remember Arkansas –"

"Is the Canadian with them in the canebrake then, or have they posted him in the woods?"

"Ay, heaven forbid – he's with the attackers, and an able fellow he is for that. – Listen – wasn't that something?"

"I didn't hear anything. – But what will the women over there say about it?"

"I'm sorry that the child has to be sick just now."

"There's nothing to be done about it, why – by God, that was the whistle – now, Cook, look lively – the dance is starting –"

*   *   *

"Come quickly," whispered Atkins to his men waiting outside the fence – "once we have this behind us it'll be all the better, since that *storm* will wash out every track – but God punish my soul if it's not too bad to be out in such a rain. Jones definitely told me that you wouldn't come for a week –"

"Oh, damn it, save your chatter until we're dry," grumbled the old man, pretending to be peeved – "is this weather for conversation? I have nothing to do with it other than to deliver the animals, and I wish to God that I'd left it to someone else. Baring one's back to such a rainstorm could be the death of a man."

"Where are the horses?"

"Up there in the corner somewhere – my boy is with them, that is, if the poor chap hasn't been washed away." With these words, he stuck his finger between his teeth and whistled softly but sharply.

"What the devil are you doing?" asked Atkins, alarmed.

"Did you hear it? Over there, he answered," said the old man, "he lives still, to be sure. Where's the entrance?"

"Right up there – you're not far from it, but when you come back, just ride in the creek bed about a hundred paces farther up. See, there!"

"See? Now I ask you how anyone can *see* in such weather, for God's sake, truly *see*; not a hand in front of your face, except when it flashes. But there's the boy – hey, Ned – come here; are you still alive?"

"Yes, father," whispered the young man – "but it's terrible weather. It frightens me."

"Nonsense – you'll be dry again soon – come, follow us. Have the animals stood quietly?"

"Pretty much – only the black one shied at the lighting."

"Naturally, what beast would stand for it quietly – but what are you doing? Are you taking down the fence?"

"Yes," said Atkins, – "I deliberately have no gate up here – just placed feed troughs in the corner. There are too many spies in the neighborhood, and anything slightly out of the ordinary immediately raises suspicion. – So – come on in here – watch yourself, there are still felled trees lying there. Ah – that flash came at the right time!"

"So is the place where you left the horses far from here?"

"Not a hundred paces more – a plague on it, that was a blow! – just leave the fence down until we come back; none of the beasts will run off – they're all standing under the shed – so – just follow me – this is the place."

At that moment a dazzling bolt of lightning illuminated the whole of the surrounding area, and Stevenson saw that they stood by a fence over which gnawed-off cane hung from the other side.

"Wait a moment," Atkins then said quickly, "I'll just shove away the fence rails and the tree trunks below – that'll give clearance right away. – All right, now down below with the animals, no one will look for them there, and then into the house – a warm drink – hell's fire, what are you doing – betrayal! –"

And he had good reason to be surprised, since hardly was the entrance to the secret hiding place opened when Stevenson gave out a shrill and resounding whistle. In the next instant a dazzling bolt illuminated the spot with the light of day. Atkins, half-blinded by the glare, saw a mass of dark figures rush by, and as the thunder boomed in mighty blows, smashing and cracking along the firmament, he felt the powerful Tennessean stretch his hand out toward him and try to seize him by the collar.

Now, however, came the darkness, in which intimate familiarity with the terrain was a great advantage, for like a snake he slipped away from under the menacing fist. Stevenson instead grabbed his son, who had leapt forward at the same moment to stop the crook; but a second flash revealed to them the fleeing figure of the horse trafficker, and Weston, whom the initial surprise had almost paralyzed, also flew to the spot where they had only just now entered the enclosure.

Even so, the place was guarded, and he[2] had almost leapt into the hands of two other men that he was running toward, when another flash revealed to him his new danger. He quickly turned around and tried to escape over the fence. Even here he heard the sounds of pursuit, and now realized that this was no sudden, chance discovery, but rather a planned assault; he saw that every avenue of escape was cut off and that his only remaining hope was to find, by passing through the house, or between the house and smokehouse, that the narrow space almost always occupied by the dogs was still free. From there he could possibly gain the woods, and thus at least a moment of safety.

But just as he jumped on the porch[3] and tried to pass between the buildings, he heard, in the room to his right, a wild wrestling and swearing – before him the loud voices of the enemies closing on him, behind him the pursuers – so now, in anguish and despair, he plunged into the chamber full of women, who with a collective cry of terror got up from their seats.

Notes

1. "Sir" is in English in the original text.
2. "He": the would-be escapee here is Weston.
3. "Porch" is in English in the original.

Chapter 31

The Company of Ladies. –
Account of Various Children's Illnesses,
Related for the Consolation
of the Mother. – The Surprise.

"Oh, Madame Mullins, I would ask you to pour me another cup of coffee," said the widow Fulweal, as she once more took the anguished and groaning child from the hammock and walked up and down the room with it. "How his little head burns," she then cried, holding the tiny one so close to the light that it drew back its small feverish face in fear, and was on the verge of breaking out anew in cries of distress.

"Sshhh – baby,* sshhh – don't cry – what lungs the child has, and already that's the third dose of calomel that I've given him now this blessed day. Sshhh, baby – Sshhh."

"Yes," said the elder Miss[1] Heifer, as she filled her short little tobacco pipe with glowing ashes and drew the smoke in between her words in order to kindle the tobacco, "yes – the little mite – has already – made all our – arms – lame today. – Poor little thing – that –"

"Do you have any more tobacco, Miss Heifer?" asked Madame Fulweal now, while she stepped to the chimney and pulled from the cracks in the crossbeams an identical pipe kept there – "I've been able to smoke just twice all day, and can't bear to chew it. Oh, Madame Mullins, please take the baby for a little while."

"Why don't you chew gum wax, then?"[†] asked Mrs. Smith.

---

* FG transliterates the word as "Bäbie" and adds a note: "Small child – an infant."

† FG's note: "A highly disgusting custom in the American West, and especially in Arkansas, of chewing a wax or resin that flows out of the so-called gum tree, and that has a curiously sharp but not at all pleasant taste. The backwoods people, but especially the women and children, chew this so-called gum wax until they are tired of it, and then give it to another member of the family who, without the slightest abashment or the least aversion, continues the work already begun."

"Yes, I got myself some wax the day before yesterday morning," said the young widow, "but Betsy wouldn't give it back to me when I rode away. Oh God, how that child cries — wouldn't you like to drink a cup of coffee too, Mrs. Atkins? It would do you good."

"I thank you, I thank you," said the latter, fearfully approaching the child and laying her ice-cold hand on its hot forehead — "merciful heaven, it's growing ever sicker — it's sure to die on me tonight."

"Oh no, surely not," Mrs. Smith consoled her — "Don't you believe it, Madame Atkins — as I've seen very different children — Preston's baby, that had the dark red spots on its little cheeks much worse than your little one here — coughed much more too, and still lived another five days."

"But it died?" timidly asked the mother.

"Yes — unfortunately, we did everything we could, of course, for the poor mite — Madame Fulweal there knows it. — It got red pepper tea until it threw it right up again, the poor little thing, its stomach was so weak, and the mustard plaster on its back turned the whole of its little skin as red as fire. — But it still died."

"And what an angel the child was," threw in Mrs. Fulweal, who had now gotten her pipe to light and had once more taken the child on her arm — "a true cherub — it swallowed down the calomel and the oil as if had been syrup. But it fell asleep so gently too — it was a real joy to see it."

"Stewart's baby was also a sweet little thing, before it died," said Mrs. Smith, "it had a cough just like this one here — remarkable, how fast it happens. In the morning it was still pink and healthy, and by evening it was pale and gone — the poor little sweetheart!"

"Why, then, is the child getting all these little bruises?" said Madame Bowitt, bending down to him.

"Where? Where?" cried the mother in terror — "What's with these bruises? Are they dangerous? Oh God, the child is dying on me!"

"Nonsense," said Mrs. Fulweal — "bruises — I should like to know where these bruises are. What does Madame Bowitt know, then, about children's illnesses; the third of hers that died was barely six months old, and all three were sick less than a week."

"The bruises, as a visiting doctor once assured me — are a very bad sign," chirped the youngest Miss Heifer — "Brother George's girl got them, and it didn't miss dying by much that very night; but it nevertheless lived on until the next morning."

"Then is the child truly getting bruises?" wailed Mrs. Atkins in deathly agony — "is it already so far advanced, then? Must it then really die?"

"Oh, heaven protect us," said Mrs. Hostler, "look — it's not that dangerous — bruises mean nothing. — If it just didn't have a whistling when it coughed; my poor little girl that died last month wheezed just the same."

The mother sat on the only bed in desolate sorrow and wrung her hands.

"Ladies!"[2] Mrs. Knowles began. Until this moment, she had silently smoked her pipe, but now she knocked the ashes out upon the hearthstone that supported the single immense log in front of the fireplace. – "I really don't understand why you're tormenting the poor mother so. – Lord Jesus, the lightning – it's really affecting me! – Neither bruises nor coughing and wheezing are such sure –"

She had to stop talking, since the rolling thunder overwhelmed even the cries of the child for perhaps a full minute – "sure signs," she continued her speech at last, as the storm died down – "that one can always count on them to mean nothing but death. Heavens, I myself know of two cases where both children survived, that is to say, one went blind and the other was bitten by a mad dog, but the bruises weren't to blame for that. Why be alarmed when there's no danger yet?"

"So you believe that my child can recover?"

"Well, why not? It's taken enough medicine to make six children well, and if it didn't look so yellow in the eyes –"

"Yellow in the eyes?" asked the newly agitated mother, as she raced to the child with a light – "And what does that mean? Madame Fulweal – *you* have much experience; do you believe that –" she dared not finish the sentence, but rather buried her face in her hands and softly lisped: "I deserve this – on account of Ellen – deserve it by my knowledge –" She started up, terrified that someone had heard the treacherous words, only to sink back down again into her former position.

Then the dreadful stroke of lightning already mentioned twice crashed over the treetops into the roaring and quivering woods, and the women were driven back as one before the angry storm god who was shaking the foundations of the earth. A deathly silence reigned for several seconds, but then the youngest Miss Heifer whispered softly to Madame Mullins, sitting next to her:

"Exactly such weather as that time when Houston's first little child died – exactly such thunder."

"We haven't had a storm like this one for a long time," groaned Mrs. Fulweal, and lit her pipe for the fifteenth time, "it's almost enough to make you nervous and fearful in your own home. How must worse it must be for those outside!"

"What did your youngest actually die of that time, Madame Mullins?" asked the elder Heifer, as she moved her chair over to the latter. "We were told that it was smallpox, and we were all not a little concerned, as you can imagine –"

"The Lord bless you, dearest Miss Heifer – the smallpox – no, how can people talk such silly stuff – smallpox! The sweet little thing had nothing more than mild dysentery, and I still don't know where it could have gotten it. The whole time he hadn't eaten anything more than a couple of green peaches and plums that children always eat in the summer, and surely they weren't to blame."

"Then were any of you there when Mrs. Carlton's Anna died?" asked Mrs. Fulweal.

"I was there," said Mrs. Smith – "and I don't want to say anything bad behind Mrs. Carlton's back, but this much I know, you ought to have a cup of coffee when you sit up the whole night – and a little tobacco wouldn't have hurt her either –"

"Wasn't that the time the doctor from Little Rock was up here, Mrs. Fulweal?" asked Mrs. Curneales. "Couldn't he help him?"

"The doctor? Well, I would just like to know why he should be cleverer than those of us up here," remarked Mrs. Fulweal, tossing her head to the side contemptuously – "particularly where children's illnesses are concerned. – He comes with a few scraps of Latin and gives the matter another name and that's all – comes out with words that would twist any honest person's tongue in his mouth, and – my, what lightning this evening – and they die afterward anyway."

"The little mite," she continued, quite in her element now as she saw the others listening to her with rapt attention – "I had half-saved the little mite already; of course, it was still very sickly, and its little legs were growing cold, and it wouldn't keep down anything that we gave it, it threw up the best calomel again – it couldn't stand the smell of 'Indian physic'[3] or the sight of lobelia, but otherwise it was already well on the road to recovery. But the doctor hadn't yet been in the house for half an hour when it lay over on its side, kicked with its little legs once more, gasped for breath, and was gone. To me, such a doctor should – but what's going on?" Mrs. Atkins jumped up and listened attentively to something outside.

"What was it? – Did you see anything?" asked the speaker in alarm.

"No – I saw nothing – but – did you hear that whistle? – out there in the yard?"

"Yes – I thought so," said Mrs. Mullins. "But the storm blusters so loudly that you can't distinguish anything clearly."

"Didn't someone call out there?" asked Mrs. Atkins – pale and frightened, with her ear to a chink in the cabin wall.

"Oh, God protect us," mumbled Mrs. Fulweal, "who would be out in such a storm – well – what I meant to say was – should such a doctor come across my threshold with his little bit of this and his little bit of – Jesus in heaven!"

But her outcry this time was due to no mere fantasy, and all the women jumped up with her, horrified and alarmed, as the door flew open and through it dashed young Weston – mortal dread and anguish on his face, with wet hair flying and eyes bulging – while in a voice choked with terror he cried:

"Hide me, or I'm lost!" Then, only half consciously, yet with part of his instinct intact, leaping in a single bound to the safest and best concealed corner of the room, he collapsed behind the bed, which largely filled that one corner.

"For God's sake – Weston – what's happened?" gasped Mrs. Atkins in mortal dread. But the other had no time to answer, for at this moment the dark figure of the half-Indian sprang into the open doorframe, and with a harsh voice cried out:

"He must be in here – where is he?"

"Where is who?" said Madame Fulweal, who, being intimate with Cotton and Weston, halfway understood what was happening, and so was the first to recover her presence of mind. "Where is who? Is this any way to enter the houses of strangers, and what's more, a room where there are ladies and sick people? – where is who? why does the gentleman stand there and stare – the wind's blowing out the light – over there is where people live!" And without allowing another word from the Canadian, who was surprised and bewildered by this defiant behavior, she pushed him back from the door and threw it shut.

"So!" she said, as she shot the little iron bolt – a true article of luxury in Arkansas – that was mounted on the door – "now let's take a look at our prisoner."

But meanwhile the other women, Mrs. Atkins excepted, had also regained their senses and tongues, and now began such a confusion of shouts and questions that even the sick child, alarmed and frightened, lifted its little head. At the outbreak of the disturbance it had been laid again in its hammock and remained, for a moment, silent with fright. But then it threw itself back on its pillow again and raised such a bloody racket that Mrs. Fulweal asked as a special grace from heaven to see this tireless child silenced for once.

"What's going on here? who is this man? what's he been up to? whose dark face was that? where did this wet fellow come from all of a sudden? and should they hide him, or would he be asked after again?" All of this whirred and swam in a genuine chaos of confusing voices, so that each lady could barely hear the questions that she herself posed. Then someone took hold of the handle, and straightaway there was a rap upon the door.

"Who's still out there so late, and what do you want?" asked the widow Fulweal, once more appointing herself official spokesperson, a role the others were pleased to leave to her. "Don't you know that a sick child is lying here?"

"Ladies – you will permit me a question," said a voice that Mrs. Atkins recognized with trepidation as Brown's – "has a young man fled into this room?"

Mrs. Fulweal looked around the circle of her fellow conspirators before she answered. But pity for his suffering had already won over their soft feminine hearts in Weston's favor, and whatever he had done (they were, in any event, united in their firm resolve to discover *that*), they did not intend to turn him over. A general nod of the head answered her look, and widow Fulweal, as interpreter for the fortress, undertook its defense. But in order not to speak a positive lie, she considered it expedient to act insulted and aggrieved, and so cried out in her rather sharp and cutting voice, full of disgust and indignation:

"Well, now I'm wondering what else you're still looking for here? But, really, this is no time for foolish pranks, here in the middle of the night and in such a storm.   We're on the point of going to sleep, and wish to be undisturbed – good night, sir!"[4]

With that, the negotiation was broken off, and the questioner seemed satisfied. He had, at least, given up any further effort to discover any details of the matter, and had left the door. Mrs. Fulweal now listened at the door for several minutes along with all the others, hearts pounding and anxiously beating. But no further sound could be heard – all was as still and quiet as the grave, and the widow was about to creep on tiptoe to the still motionless fugitive cowering behind the bed, when her attention, along with that of the other assembled women, was drawn to Mrs. Atkins. For she was frantically holding on to the back of her chair, and apparently was doing everything in her power not to yield to the emotions that pressed upon her. After a short struggle, though, she lost consciousness, and would have tumbled to the floor had not the women caught her in their arms.

The full horror of her situation had overwhelmed her in that moment that she recognized the voice of the leader of the Regulators, and fearing the worst, since she knew that her husband deserved the worst, her body, already weakened by nocturnal vigils and dread, cracked under the combination of anxiety and fear.

In the other room, meanwhile, events no less frantic and turbulent were taking place. Hardly had Curtis called out a warning to his friend and the two men taken their posts at the two separate doors than a step was heard on the hollow plank floor of the porch connecting the two houses, and almost in the same instant Atkins, with wild flashing eyes and flying hair, came crashing in. He was certain that the men were part of the conspiracy, but he also knew that he was hopelessly lost in the woods without weapons, and that he must now procure some, even if he should endanger his own life in doing so. So counting mainly on an initial surprise, he tore open the door and sprang into the room.

But here he saw quickly enough that his rifles were under the control of his enemies; the bed, though, was nevertheless unoccupied, and with a cry of triumph he flung himself to it, tore the pistols from it, and, pointing the cocked weapons at Cook, rushed back toward the door, which the latter had blocked. Perhaps he intended only to make him yield, but when the Regulator calmly maintained his position, he pulled the trigger, instinctively sacrificing another's life for his own.

A terrible – fearful sound it is for one who has bet his whole hope of life, everything he has, on you, a powerless gunlock, when you strike against the steel with a feeble, dull blow; – the limp hand sinks, and is no longer able to hold the treacherous weapon. – Gone – that was the last hope – gone.

Atkins looked wildly at the door through which he had entered, but at that same moment his pursuers burst in; Cook and Curtis threw themselves upon him and tied his now unresisting limbs with solid ropes.

"Where's the other one," asked Brown, pushing back the door – "has any-one kept track of him?"

"He ran over there to the house," replied the Canadian. "I saw it with my own eyes – but they don't want to give him up."

"Then I'll see for myself whether they'll refuse me entrance as well," replied the leader of the Regulators, and walked over to the door lying opposite. But we know the result, and without any more time and effort to lose, he imme-diately hit upon the surest measures to seize the fugitive as soon as he tried to flee into the woods.

"Gentlemen," he said, turning to his friends with this purpose, – "this fellow must not escape us; he definitely belongs to the gang, and who knows whether he was one of the murderers, or to what extent he was involved in the crimes that have occurred here. – So we must surround the house, but quietly, so that we give him the idea that the way is clear. Have they caught the mulatto?"

"No," said Bowitt – "the rascal must have slipped through the thickest part of the woods, otherwise he couldn't have escaped us."

"That's bad – that's bad!" Brown muttered – "he'll sound the alarm; but we can't help that. We've disturbed these rascals' nest, their safe hiding place; from now on we must rely on our good luck. So, gentlemen, to your posts – the rain has eased up, and the wind outside will soon dry us off again. Take the prisoner to the fire, Cook – he's wet too."

"All right," said Cook – carrying out the order with Curtis' help, "but then let the two of us who are dry join the outposts, and Stevenson and his boy may guard the prisoner by the fire. We already owe them a great debt, and really don't want to see them sick."

"No more than fair," replied Brown; "but where are they hiding?"

At that moment, the two Stevensons walked through the door and were soon made familiar with their new, more comfortable, or at least drier, assign-ment. The other men then repaired to their posts, and Brown, who had spoken quietly with the elder Stevenson about some matter or other, was about to follow them when he stepped back from the door in something like shock, since there stood, with wet hair hanging down, with fiercely glowing gaze and a proud, grim countenance – the Indian.

"Assowaum!" cried Brown in joyful surprise – "have you finally come? We've been doing your work in the meanwhile."

"It is good – but – why are you holding *him* there?" said the Indian softly, his hand, in which he held a bow and several arrows – rising toward Atkins.

"He was the horse trafficker for the band; but you shall learn everything. – Have you just now returned?"

"No – I have a prisoner."

"Whom? And where?"

"Johnson – out there in the woods."

"Do you know that he's guilty?"

"He thought a panther was on his trail and feared his fangs. Do you know these weapons? The arrows are poisoned. With them he crept into Assowaum's camp and tried to kill him."

"A plague on him! – You tied him up, right?"

"Yes."

"And he can't escape?"

Assowaum smiled and whispered softly: "He whom Assowaum binds, he does not move."

"But where were you so long? There were some here who claimed that you had fled."

"You were not among them," replied the savage. "But does my brother believe that I have been idle during this time? – I know the murderers of Heathcott."

"You know them? – Who, who was it? Speak!" cried Brown, wild with joy.

"Johnson and – Rowson!" said the Indian softly.

"Rowson – almighty God – that's not possible!" Brown shouted, horrified – "That's – that would be horrible – Rowson a – murderer."

"Johnson and Rowson," Assowaum repeated just as calmly, but just as firmly, as before. "The pale man also had a part in the horse rustling."

"Man, are you sure of this?" groaned Brown, still not able to grasp the terrible thought, to realize that Marion was in the hands of a traitor; "do you really have proof for such a horrific charge?"

"The pale man was with the horse stealers, I know it, and next to the white man's blood stood his foot."

"Righteous God – Assowaum – do you know *whom* you accuse?"

"The Methodist," said the Indian darkly. "Perhaps he also crushed the Flower of the Prairies; though until now Assowaum has circled the camp in vain. But he killed the white man; for four days I have known it."

"And why have you kept silent?"

"If the white men found the criminal guilty of one murder," Assowaum said with a wild, almost spectral smile, "they do not take notice of the others – they hang him, and Assowaum would see his personal revenge in the hands of others. But Assowaum is a man – he will avenge himself!"

"But where do you have your prisoner?"

"Out there in the woods; he thought to find a chief sleeping. Has my brother ever seen a panther who closes his eyes?"

"So we will – what's that? That's already the third time an owl's call has sounded from over there, and always in a different direction – could it be a signal?"

The Indian listened – once again the monotone call of the night bird that shuns men and daylight rang out – three times – with slow measured pauses –

and three times, with the same timing, the red son of the forests answered it. But at this point, the call from over in the thicket fell silent and was not heard again.

"It was an owl," said Brown, still listening into the quiet night.

"Maybe," replied the Indian thoughtfully – "and then maybe not. – That man there will probably recognize the signal."

Atkins, to whom this designation pertained, had been casting nervous stolen glances toward the door, and, when Assowaum answered the call, shot up as though terrified. But now, when all was silent and the beguiling imitation call was not answered, a vicious and scornful smile flitted across his dark features, and without betraying any further sign of interest, he crouched down again in front of the warming embers. But he answered not a single one of the questions that Brown directed to him, and, with angry contempt, he turned his back on him, as well as on the man who had first betrayed him and was now his jailer.

The Indian had, meanwhile, again left the cabin in the company of several Regulators, and a deep silence reigned for probably half an hour, when all of a sudden a wild cry of terror was heard from the far section of the fence, there where it butted up against the woods. Promptly thereafter, Wilson and Bowitt brought in the prisoner Weston, who had stepped into the trap and attempted his escape.

Not long afterward, Assowaum also appeared with two of the Regulators, who hustled Johnson into the room, pale and with eyes timidly downcast, where he was suddenly faced with his most bitter enemy, the fierce Husfield.

"So, then – sir?" asked the latter, regarding him from head to foot with astonishment – "you're with the band after all, and, it appears, in a very desperate situation? Who found the man?"

"The Indian," said Cook, pointing to him.

"Ha, Assowaum!" cried Husfield, seeing the other for the first time – "it's good that you're here again, and even more so that you've brought with you such evidence of your goodwill. I'll be damned – Assowaum, if I know how best to show you my deep appreciation – a plague on it – five hundred dollars wouldn't be as welcome to me. There, there, have my silver-plated rifle – I know that yours is no good anymore – she's always misfiring, and you've wanted a good weapon for yourself for a long time. – Take her, may she give you as good service as she's given me. And you, fellow –" turning then to the trembling criminal – "this time you shall not escape your punishment. The last time we saw each other, you were damned insolent; maybe now the boot's on the other foot. Just look how the villain trembles and shakes; his knees can barely hold him up any longer."

"Poison and death on you!" the prisoner cursed, now defiantly gathering himself for the first time. "You can bind me here – and – lynch me – damn it, but you don't have to mock me. You dogs – all pouncing on one man."

Husfield was about to explode, but Brown checked him and said:

"Let him talk. – He may boast and swear, but we have a right to hold him prisoner; our warrant for that is the Indian, whom he would have furtively ambushed and murdered. That's the first charge; the rest will come later. As soon as we have his comrades, the court, and by that I mean *our* justice – will decide the rest. Now, above all else, we must find out these scoundrels' other den. Who knows the way?"

"I!" said Assowaum; "but does my brother believe that the bear returns to his lair if he scents the tracks of the hunter at its entrance? The owl signal is for those who live here; we did not know how to answer it, and those rascals were warned – the den is empty."

"You may indeed be right, Assowaum," said Brown, "but we must make the attempt, and from there on our next task is to find the – the other whom you consider guilty. There's still time, thank heavens, but I can't imagine such a horrible thing."

"So who is the other man of whom the Indian speaks?" now asked Stevenson.

"You will meet him tomorrow," replied the young leader of the Regulators, staring grimly at the ground – "but – surely, Mr. Stevenson –" he then continued, as if awakened from a dream – "surely you will stay with us until we have brought the matter to an end? You really must see how we here in Arkansas exercise law and justice. –"

"I'll stay here – of course," assured the old farmer, returning the proffered handshake with a hearty grip.

"But then your women must consider my home as their own, at least as long as you're here," said Heinze, also stretching out his hand to the old man. "Cook has told me that they're camped not quite a quarter mile away from my house, and since I have to go up there tomorrow morning anyway, I'll fetch them myself. When do we hold our court?"

"Monday morning."

"And where?"

"In the open woods this time, at the place below Wiswill's mill where the steep rock juts out into the river. Up on the top there's an open space, and we'll convey there all those we've taken prisoner to that point."

"Whom are you looking for still?" asked Husfield.

"Cotton and – Rowson!"

"Rowson? The preacher? The Methodist?" all cried at once in astonishment and surprise.

"The preacher and Methodist," Brown answered softly.

"And who is his accuser?" asked a stunned Mullins.

"Assowaum!" said the leader of the Regulators, pointing to the Indian, whose dark figure leaned quietly against the chimney as he met the looks aimed at him without flinching.

"He has blood on his hand," he said softly at last after a short pause – "he has blood in his tracks, and the waters of the Petit Jean – the waters of the Fourche La Fave, could not wash it away."

"And tomorrow he will take home old Roberts' daughter as his wife," cried Cook, bewildered – "it's not possible, the Indian must be mistaken –"

"The pious Rowson," groaned Mullins, speechless with horror, still half disbelieving it.

"Talk is useless here," said Brown, quickly resolved – "now we must act. If it is mere suspicion that rests on the preacher, then his own good name requires that it be lifted as soon as possible, since no stain may taint a man in his position without calling down upon his guilty head a tenfold doom. But now, above all, we must capture the criminals who are nearby, and are probably already warned. Assowaum can lead us to Johnson's house, and from there we'll start together for Roberts' dwelling, which we must reach while it's still early in the morning."

"It's definitely a mistake," said Mullins, "the Indian is, after all, only human, and –"

"For a week Assowaum followed the tracks, and measured and compared them," replied the savage darkly; "as surely as that storm there shakes the old trees – the pale man is an imposter."

"What good are words!" replied Brown – "he's accused, and –"

"But by whom?" Mullins interrupted him angrily – "the Indian, who never liked him because he converted Alapaha to Christianity, accuses him. – Should we seize and mortally offend a pious and god-fearing man on his word? That can never be. – Bring evidence first, for otherwise I will *not* give my consent to such a rash deed."

"Put him face to face with me," said the Indian, as he proudly straightened up from his relaxed posture, "put him face to face with me, and if his eye can meet mine – then hang me. Are the men satisfied?"

"Yes," said Husfield earnestly. "I don't understand why we should give more credit to the testimony of a white man than to that of a red one. I've never been able to bear the Methodist myself, and I shouldn't wonder a bit if now a wolf is hiding under the lambskin. He's just as good as any other man, and the fact that he preaches earns him, in my eyes at least, no special merit. If he *clears* himself before the court, so much the better for him. But I almost fear that the Indian's evidence is too sure, since he doesn't have the demeanor of a man who is acting on mere suspicion. Lead us on, Brown – each minute that we waste will never come again. Lead us on, and may the guilty man meet damnation and punishment, so that we can secure and protect our righteous justice."

"And what's to happen with these prisoners?" asked Cook, pointing to Atkins, Weston, and Johnson.

"It's best that we take them away tonight," said Brown – "the whole house is full of women, so Mrs. Atkins has help and support. But where to with them?"

"I'll take them," said Wilson – "I'm sure that Curneales won't refuse to take in the Regulators with their prisoners, and then we'll only need to arrange for a secure guard."

"*I will* hold them," cried Curtis. "I'll be sure to find some comrades to help, and my rifle will vouchsafe that they don't escape. But take off, then – it can't be too long before it's morning, and if Cotton is really forewarned, it'll be a hard task to bring him in. All the hounds are at his heels. So now, without further ado, one party go with the prisoners and the other to the hunt."

The steps required for this were performed quickly and noiselessly, in order not to pointlessly unsettle the women further. Within the next quarter of an hour, the three prisoners found themselves conducted by six heavily armed men on the way to their temporary prison. Pelter and Hostler stayed behind in Atkins' house as guards, and the rest, led by Assowaum, started toward the secluded cabin of the gang, in order there to capture, if possible, the man they had sought so long, or at least to obtain new evidence of the guilt of all those that they had brought in and imprisoned to this point.

Midnight lay upon the woods. The mighty tree tops still rustled and roared, and shook cold showers out of their green windswept locks; faint flashes of lightning still streaked across the horizon far to the east, and afterward the distant thunder still rumbled and muttered softly – softly. Then a dark figure quickly and carefully darted over the fence that enclosed Johnson's lowly cabin. It was Cotton – he slid through the open door into the inner room of the cabin, gathered together there the weapons and clothing he owned, hid several other things that he apparently wished to conceal from the eye of the enemy in a hollow tree not far from the cabin, then raked a fire that he had quickly kindled again in the fireplace into a corner of the room and under the bed, cast a fleeting glance of farewell at the room that had so long afforded him protection against his pursuers, muttered one more bitter curse between his thin, pale lips, and then disappeared as quickly and noiselessly as he had come into the thick, impenetrable shadow of the woods.

Notes

1. FG uses "Miß" to represent the English word with German spelling.
2. "Ladies" is in English in the original text.
3. "Indian Physic," also known as Bowman's Root or *Gillenia trifoliatia*, a popular herbal remedy used by Native Americans.
4. "Good night, sir" is English in the original text.

Chapter 32
The Cross Oak.

The cross oak marked a place widely known among the hunters of the Fourche La Fave. It stood not far from the bank of a small lake, on the edge of one of the many sloughs or marshy streams that crisscrossed the bottom land, and close by a thick cane brake that had been burned the previous year through the carelessness of some hunters. Only withered and half-burned cane now surrounded the place, among which the young, spring-green reeds had barely begun to force their way up again in isolated and scattered spots.

But a tall and mighty persimmon, whose top had been split by lightning, had placed one of its boughs in the main fork of the neighboring tree, the oak in question, and in this way had formed a rough but easily discernible cross.

Cotton, like Rowson, knew the place well, and the latter especially had often used this spot for prayer meetings or so-called camp-meetings.[1] Cotton was, by the by, the first to arrive at the place today, and had walked up and down the bank of the slough for about an hour before the time appointed by Rowson. And if he cast impatient glances in the direction from which he expected his friend to come, he also listened nervously and cautiously, now toward one and now toward another direction, as if he feared some surprise or danger, and each falling leaf made him turn his head there swiftly and anxiously.

Then a dry branch broke, and like a snake the hunter glided behind a fallen tree trunk, where he lay as silent and motionless as the timber that concealed him. It was, however, the one so impatiently awaited, and the fugitive quickly burst from his hiding place once more.

"Finally you've come," he cried sullenly – "I've been standing here in mortal agony for an hour, and –"

"You have no reason to complain; I'm here a little before the time still. – It can hardly be eight-thirty, and you know that we were to meet only at nine."

"Yes, perhaps never to see one another again."

"What's happened?" Rowson asked in alarm, since he now noticed for the first time the pale, distraught face of his friend and ally. "You look as if you were bringing news of someone's death. – Are the Regulators –"

"By the devil, I wish it were merely news of someone's death" – muttered the hunter through his clenched teeth; "those Regulator dogs have somehow caught wind of it and stormed Atkins' house."

"By thunder!" Rowson cried fearfully – "and did he confess?"

"I wasn't curious enough to inquire about it," grumbled Cotton. – "And Johnson too must have fallen into the damned Indian's hands, since he went out to do away with him and – hasn't come back himself."

"But how do you know that Atkins –"

"When Johnson didn't come back, I went out to look for him, but found no trace of him; then I slipped over to Atkins' house to tell him of my fear. But there I noticed a commotion about his farm. – The horses were galloping wild and scared around the enclosure, and when I crept to the fence and up to the secret entrance, I found it open. This just raised my suspicions even more; but I still wanted to try to get closer to the house, and gave the agreed signal several times, one after another."

"Well?" Rowson asked, swiftly and tensely.

"For a long time it wasn't answered," continued the hunter, "and, at last, incorrectly – only three times. Then I knew that treachery lurked behind those apparently peaceful walls. For a while now I slipped quietly around the farm, but before long, in spite of all my wariness, I nearly fell into the hands of the rascals that had posted themselves around there. Just as I was about to turn the corner, a gang of dark figures sprang out of the places in which they'd been hiding until then and threw themselves on someone who, judging by his voice, could be none other than Weston. You can imagine that I took to my heels at this point. As fast as my feet could carry me I flew back to Johnson's cabin, hid the things most valuable to us there in the hollow gum tree that lies not far from the house toward the river, took the weapons, and set the nest on fire. After that, finding you was my only hope."

"But what can we do?" asked Rowson, his frightened gaze fixed on his comrade. "What if the prisoners betray us? Where is Jones?"

"Probably also in the hands of the Regulators," Cotton said, gnashing his teeth; "at least I believe so now, since otherwise he would have returned."

"Then we must flee," said Rowson – "there's no other way out. – There's still time."

"But how? they'll give chase and catch up with us."

"We can't go on horseback, of course," replied Rowson. "Now that the yelping dogs are up and ready to go, we might have them on our heels only too soon, and after the rain we left tracks an inch deep. But my boat is safe for us; the river is still pretty high, and since no danger threatens us today from Harper's house either, maybe we can reach the Arkansas undiscovered. After that there will be no further trouble. By tomorrow morning we'll surely be at the mouth of the Bayou Meto,[2] and once there we're saved."

"But your bride, and mine! – Ellen will grieve mightily," the crude hunter laughed scornfully.

"We can't think of them anymore," said Rowson. "Plague and poison, to see the morsel literally snatched away from one's lips so! But my neck is much dearer to me, and I doubt that they would make much fuss about us once we're in their claws. Yes, if we were handed over to a court and properly examined by a judge and lawyers, then I'd go on saying let's wait for it; there will be time for a getaway later. But things being as they are, the devil may trust the scoundrels, I don't. Fortunately, everything's ready, and we can, as soon as we get to the house – but the devil and all, I am about to have visitors. Damn it! I almost forgot about it."

"Visitors?" Cotton cried, astonished. "What does that mean?"

"That I intended to celebrate my wedding today," replied Rowson with a blasphemous curse. "The whole pious assembly is probably already at this moment on the way to my home, and if they get there before us, then we're lost. – But maybe it's not yet too late – maybe I can still meet them on the way, and then I'll think of something to make them wait for a moment yet. We *must* have a little time for our preparations. If we gain but a single hour's head start, then I won't worry any more, then we're saved. So hasten as quickly as you can to my house, I'll get there pretty much the same time you do, though I must first go to Roberts'. My horse is good, and if it just holds out for today, then it may break down when it will."

"But you might get there later nevertheless," said Cotton; "for believe me, I won't stop anywhere along the way."

"Then climb up the ladder meanwhile into the upper part of the house. There's a little suitcase there that's prepared for just such an event and contains all that we'll need on the way."

"And the signal?"

"You'll see me arrive. For several hundred paces the house overlooks the little surrounding forest meadow in which I built."

"But it's really not right to leave our comrades in the lurch like this now," said Cotton thoughtfully. "For who knows if we couldn't be of use to them if we stayed here one more night! There are many among the farmers living here who secretly wish us well and would gladly render us aid; but *they* certainly won't trouble themselves if we take flight at the first shot fired."

"Oh, the devil take your reasonings!" Rowson cried out impatiently. "Do you think I mean to walk in among them now, when maybe Johnson or Weston have confessed, so that I can be straightaway seized and bound as well? No, I'll be damned if I'm going to stick my neck in a noose just to see how a few others are doing whose necks are already in there and whom I cannot help anymore anyway. – I'm going – now *you* may do as you like."

"But you really don't know, do you, whether *your* name will be mentioned at all. Besides, you know our oath."

"Yes indeed – all very well, but the devil may trust the oath, I don't. It wouldn't be the first that a black hickory stick has broken; – and didn't you say yourself that Johnson was afraid that he'd be betrayed by that red dog of a savage? The same thing threatens me, only to a much greater degree. If the Indian hadn't shown up again in our region, then maybe I'd take a chance and stay. But I can't be subjected to the skulking vengeance of such a fellow, and for that reason I'll cut and run. So are you coming with me or not?"

"Well, naturally I'm not going to stick my finger in the fire all alone, that you can believe," the hunter responded sullenly. "To be sure, I don't dare show my visage in Little Rock. – No, *I'm* quite comfortable enough on God's earth, and I have no use for my neck to get caught among the oak branches. So away then – but where will we go?"

"I'm going to the island," said Rowson resolutely, "where are you bound?"

"We'll have time enough on the way later to ponder that," replied the hunter evasively, "the main thing now is to get away from here, since any other place, even the Arkansas penitentiary, is safer for us now than the Fourche La Fave. So follow quickly and don't leave me waiting long. – It'll scare me to sit there alone for as much as an hour; every second I'd be afraid of seeing the house surrounded by Regulators."

"Don't worry – I'll be there fast enough. Hopefully the Roberts haven't started yet, since naturally their presence could seriously inconvenience us. I'll be with you as swiftly as my horse can carry me. Anyway, I'll be damned if I won't be glad when I can throw off this wretched preacher mask. It's become awfully annoying to me, especially in the last couple of weeks."

"I only hope that the Arkansas air better meets with your approval *unmasked* than masked," replied Cotton, as he drew out from under a thick tangle of greenbriers and climbing plants his bundle of clothes wrapped in a woolen blanket, and threw it on his back – "all right – now I'm ready to travel," he continued, casting a nervous glance all around – "so follow quickly – good bye!"

"Good bye!" answered the minister, and looked thoughtfully after him for a short while, until he had completely disappeared behind the thick pawpaw and sassafras scrub. But then he walked quickly to his horse, which awaited him grazing calmly, swung himself into the saddle, dug his heels into the animal's sides, and galloped, as swiftly as the thick underbrush permitted, into the woods toward Roberts' home again.

Notes

1. FG uses the phrase "Camp Meetings" in the original text.

2. Called "Bayou Meter" by FG, Bayou Meto rises just northeast of Little Rock and flows about 150 miles to empty into the Arkansas River near Arkansas Post, the first territorial capital, roughly ninety river miles below Little Rock and thirty miles above the confluence of the Arkansas and the Mississippi. French colonial documents refer to it as Bayou Metre, apparently an allusion to its depth.

Chapter 33

The Criminal Unmasked.

Harper and Bahrens had reluctantly submitted themselves to the invitation. But it had been so heartily offered that the two could hardly refrain from accepting it, and now saddled and bridled their animals in order not to let the party wait for them any later.

Marion carried out with a certain anxious dread all the preparations for the step that would forever take her far away from her parents' house, and so strikingly and intensely was precisely this feeling stamped on her features that Bahrens himself, crude and in such matters careless and unconcerned, noticed it and brought it to Harper's attention. The latter, however, tried to dissuade him from it, and each silently concerned himself with whatever he wished to be concerned.

But Mrs. Roberts had quite a lot to prepare and pack up, and for a long time watched the comings and goings of various persons with obvious impatience. Finally, though, her customary restlessness, which made her want to do everything herself, and wish to look after everything herself, triumphed, and rising from the chair in which she was seated, turned to Marion and Ellen, and said, taking Marion's bonnet[1] from a nail:

"Come, children – get dressed and be gone; this running around here is becoming too much for me. I still have a host of little things to pull together and take along that are absolutely essential for a new household, but can seldom be found in a bachelor's quarters. Meanwhile, as soon as Mr. Rowson comes back, Sam must take the two baskets on his horse, and we three will follow you as quickly as possible. Afterwards you may amuse yourselves as well as you can. Anyway, we won't leave you waiting long."

No one had any objection to this – even Harper bristled only slightly – and soon afterward a small caravan, led by Roberts and Bahrens, was set in motion, while Mrs. Roberts, busier than ever, bustled about among all manner of jugs and little boxes and crates and cases. She brought out quite a number of things that she afterward had to put away as impossible to transport, and had already unpacked the two baskets for the third time only to constantly fill them up again. Then suddenly, while she was still hard at work, the figure of the Indian appeared in the doorway, and the red warrior gazed ahead so gravely and somberly from under the unruly hair streaming across his forehead that the matron actually let out a faint cry of fear, or rather surprise. She almost let fall the earthen vessel full of dried peaches that she carried in her hand.

"Ah, Assowaum," she finally cried with a smile, "I was almost frightened when I saw you standing there so unexpectedly – it was almost like a ghost. You haven't been around for quite some time. How have you been?"

"Has the pale man already led home the brown-eyed girl?" said the Indian, without taking notice of her friendly salutation, and looking around the room with anxious curiosity – "has Assowaum come too late?"

"What's wrong with you, man?" cried the matron, now truly terrified by the savage's darting eyes. "What do you want with Mr. Rowson, whom I know you've always called the pale man?"

"I want nothing from him yet," whispered Assowaum, "not *yet*, but the Regulators are asking after him!"

"What has he to do with the Regulators, he doesn't belong to them one bit – doesn't approve of their meetings at all –"

"That I believe," said the savage with a smile, but the smile that flashed across his dark features was so ghastly that the matron seriously feared that he had become insane over the loss of his squaw. Cautiously she looked around toward the Negro boy, who was just then saddling her own horse outside the door.

Assowaum may have read what was going through her mind, since he ran his hand over his forehead, brushed smooth the hair that had fallen over it, and said softly: "Assowaum is not sick – but he came here to save your daughter. Is it too late?"

"My daughter? Almighty God, what's the matter with her? What does this mysterious talk mean? Tell me the worst – what's happened to my child?"

"Is Marion already the pale man's wife?"

"No – but what has Mr. Rowson –"

"The Regulators are on his trail – he is Heathcott's murderer –"

"Great God!" cried the matron, terrified, and staggered back to her seat as the Indian remained standing, calm and grave, at the door.

"That is slander," she said at last, gathering herself – "a disgraceful, wicked slander. Who is the wretch that accuses him of this?"

"I myself," whispered Assowaum – "I myself," he repeated after a brief – breathless pause. – "He may defend himself, but I fear – that his hands are also tainted with the blood of Alapaha, my wife –"

"Horrible – frightful," moaned the unfortunate woman, "and my child –. But no, it's impossible – it's a mistake – a terrible maddening mistake that will and must be soon cleared up. He'll come out pure and innocent in any court proceeding."

"Onishin," said the Indian – "but where are your people? – where is the old man, where the girl? Where the pale man himself?"

"He must return any moment – Marion and Roberts have ridden ahead to his house; the wedding ceremony is to take place this afternoon at the judge's home. Man – it's not possible, surely – Rowson – that pious, god-fearing man *cannot* be a criminal. – He must have killed the Regulator, who was always abusing and insulting him, in a fit of anger –"

"And whom did he blame for the deed?" the Indian asked gravely; "the pale man had two tongues in his mouth, the one spoke with his god, and the other raged at the criminal. Did he do right, when he knew the blood was on his own hand?"

"I can't believe it – I can't grasp it," wailed the woman, wringing her hands.

"Do you remember the day after Alapaha's murder?" Assowaum said in a suppressed voice, as he took his squaw's small tomahawk from his belt and laid it on the table. "With this weapon," he then continued in a voice that was almost softer, but sounded distinct, hollow, and sepulchral, "with this weapon the Flower of the Prairies defended herself against a cowardly murderer, and on that day Rowson's arm was wounded. This button" – he continued in a whisper, taking the relic from his ball-pouch, "I wriggled out of Alapaha's fingers, clenched desperately in death. It must be Rowson's – Assowaum has spoken to people who say that it is Rowson's button."

"All that is still just uncertain, vague conjecture," cried the matron, rising and looking the red son of the wilderness straight in the eye – "that's still no proof, man. – I tell you, it's not possible – Rowson is innocent!"

"Onishin! then ask the man himself, for here he comes," replied Assowaum calmly. – "Will the pale man grow paler still when the good woman says that he is a murderer?"

Before the matron was able to answer, the savage had picked up the little tomahawk again, and with noiseless step reached a hiding place in the corner by the bed, over which hung a white fly net. Almost in the same instant, the preacher's pony, covered with lather, stopped at the fence. The rider swung himself out of the saddle and immediately afterward stepped across the threshold, where he certainly should have noticed the matron's ashen complexion. But far too occupied with his own danger, he merely asked in a hoarse, almost inaudible voice where his bride was, where the men were; indeed, a curse hung on his lips when Mrs. Roberts, still trembling to be sure, but nevertheless already composed again, answered that they had ridden ahead and expected him and herself to follow shortly. But his old accustomed guardedness checked any harsh word, and he was just about to turn aside in order to catch up with them, if that were still possible. If he could reach his own house early enough, then he could still hope to manage an escape by water that was perhaps already cut off by land. Then Mrs. Roberts called him back and bade him come to her.

He well knew that further dissimulation now was only an unnecessary waste of time, and that he could perhaps miss the moment of opportunity altogether. But then his better nature gained the upper hand with regard to the woman he had deceived so dreadfully, and he decided at least to take his leave of her in peace. With this intention, he walked quickly back to the table on which she leaned, and here he noticed for the first time her completely altered and ashen complexion. But before he could ask a question about this, the matron said in a very serious though still friendly tone:

"Mr. Rowson, will you promise to answer freely and frankly something that I want to ask you?"

"Yes," said the preacher, half dismayed and half embarrassed – "but I must ask you to make it fast, since I – I really must be off again – you know that so many matters of business –"

He did not have the heart to raise his eyes to her; he was frightened by a feeling that he could not even explain to himself, – it seemed to him as if he stood before his judge.

"Mr. Rowson," said the old lady now in a soft but distinct tone – "strange things have been related to me about you this morning."

"About me? by whom?" asked the preacher in alarm, "who was here?"

"They're still mere conjectures," Mrs. Roberts continued calmly – "and, I hope to God, that they shall remain mere conjectures. But it's important that you discover for yourself what is being said about you so that you can vigorously and thoroughly defend yourself against it."

"I truly do not know – these puzzling words – just what has happened?" Rowson stammered, becoming more embarrassed, and already casting a nervous side-glance toward the door, as if he were resolved to cut things short and avoid any further questions by flight. He had, meanwhile, been playing absent-mindedly with a flower that lay on the table against which he was leaning, and now similarly picked up the button that the Indian had left behind there.

"Don't touch that button, sir – for God's sake," cried the matron, overcome by a sudden feeling of shock and fear as she noticed it – "it's –"

"What's the matter with you, Madame Roberts?" asked Rowson, who had swiftly rallied and seemed determined to put an end to this conversation. "You seem out of sorts. What about the button? It's one of mine that probably –"

"Of yours?" the matron screamed in horror, and grabbed the back of her chair – "of yours?"

"What's wrong with you?"

"Assowaum found that button in the hand of his foully murdered wife," now cried the hitherto fearful and feeble woman, almost convulsively sitting up straight and high. "Only Alapaha's murderer could have lost that button –"

The preacher's hand shot almost unconsciously to his side, where he carried the concealed weapon. But as he cast a jittery glance around the room, his eye met that of the Indian, who, his rifle raised, fixed his aim on him and cried out in a booming voice:

"One step, and you are a corpse!"

Rowson considered himself lost. Then Mrs. Roberts noticed the threatening attitude of the savage, and could not but believe that he intended to take revenge right here and now for the innocent blood shed by his wife; she threw herself on him from the side – knocked his death-dealing barrel in the air, and cried out in horror:

"Oh, just not here – just not here before my eyes!"

Rowson saw this move and knew that this was likely the last favorable moment afforded him for escape. So, with the agility of a panther, he sprang out the door before the Indian could shake off the woman, swung himself into his pony's saddle, and in the next second had disappeared into the thicket that bordered both sides of the narrow path.

In furious haste the red warrior stormed after him. But before he could get the fleeing figure of his enemy in his sights, the thickly leafed bushes had already withdrawn the man from his sight, as from his bullet, and the criminal was, for the moment at least, saved. – But he did not evade his pursuer so readily. With two strides Assowaum was at the side of Mrs. Roberts' riding horse which, already saddled and bridled and retained by the Negro, waited near the fence. In a flash, he threw off the sidesaddle, tore the bridle from the hand of the completely bewildered black, swung himself onto the bare back of the animal, and, furiously pounding his heels into its sides, followed the tracks of his victim.

Note

1. FG uses the English word "bonnet."

Chapter 34
The Siege.

"You see perfectly well that I was right after all – this is the house!" said Roberts, as the little caravan crossed the edge of the woodland glade and now stood before a tall fence that surrounded a simple building that, as of this date, would contain Marion's whole world.

"Indeed!" cried Harper, amazed, "but the tree markings pointed us in an entirely different direction. I had in mind that he must live somewhere farther up on the high ground. Now we'll be almost like neighbors, to be sure, since my house lies not at all so very far away from here, down the river."

"Well, Marion, how do you like the place?" asked old Roberts, turning to his daughter – "eh? A bit silent and spooky, don't you think? Yes, that's because of the nearness of the river, as well as the thick sycamores, the dark willows, and the scattered cottonwood trees that are still found here; farther up, though, there are very few of them standing, and Smeirs[1] recently assured me –"

"It's very silent and lonely here indeed," whispered Marion, grasping Ellen's hand as if she were afraid that her voice would disturb the profound silence – "I don't know what makes the place so desolate, so – ghastly."

"Because there's no livestock," said Bahrens. – "That's completely natural. Where no cowbells sound, and chickens and pigs don't race around the barn-yard, where there's not even a few dogs to jump out at you and make such a commotion that a man can't hear his own words, and a flock of geese always begins to cackle at exactly the same time that you're trying to call something out to somebody waiting for us in the house, then it's also not comfortable and cozy there, and to *me* at least would always seem uninviting."

"But why would Mr. Rowson buy livestock?" Harper interjected, "when he might move on again in a week?"

"Oh, fiddlesticks," replied Bahrens. "If I live just three days in a spot, I must have at least a few chickens or pigs around me to pick up the precious grain that otherwise would be wasted. Just see how it looks there in the yard, the corn lies scattered thickly on the ground; ah, if my old woman saw that!"

"It'll be different now," said Roberts with a laugh – "his wife will soon set his mind straight, and it's even possible now that he'll no longer preach twice *every* Sunday or once sometimes on Wednesdays. But the horses' comfort is looked to, that's a fact – troughs enough."

"What's wrong, Ellen?" asked Marion, herself disturbed as her friend uttered a soft, half suppressed cry – "what is it?"

"Oh, nothing," said the maiden with an embarrassed laugh, and with it cast a fleeting but nevertheless anxious sidelong glance up at the house – "nothing – it was just an illusion. But all of a sudden it seemed to me that I saw an eye gleaming between those two open slits up there."

"Where? up there?" Bahrens laughed – "a guest would hardly have taken up quarters there. Whoever would live in this house could find a cozier place – why, the door is open."

"And what a door it is!" said Harper, who now opened the gate and was the first into the house. "Remarkably strong, as if he were guarding who knows what great treasures here. Well – it appears pretty tidy," he then continued, looking all around – "for a bachelor's household, that is, though the women would take exception to several things about it. But that can't be helped; down at our place much remains to be desired too. Of course, when Alapaha was still alive," he then sighed softly to himself, "everything there was always perfectly comfy and neat, – and now –"

"It will be that way again, Harper," Bahrens interrupted him in a friendly tone – "maybe even better. – Brown is bound to marry, and then you won't need to complain any more about a bachelor's household; then the bachelors will be done with housekeeping."

"Come inside here, you girls!" cried Roberts, who had now joined the two men, "inside with you. – Here your reign begins, and Marion may take possession at once."

"So –" he continued, when they had done as he asked, "so – that's all right. – Now come and set things in order here to your heart's content, and meanwhile we'll kindle a fire outside and hang the iron kettle over it. There isn't actually a kitchen in the house that I can see, and my old lady, who can't stay much longer at all, since in such matters –"

"Whoa," cried Bahrens, laughing – "there he goes again! Here's the tinder – but where do we build the fire? A poor place for wood, this – got to carry it fifty paces, at least. So first we'd better fetch a few branches over here – is there no axe on the farm, then? Nice establishment, this!"

"One's leaning in the corner there," said Harper.

"Good, then meanwhile you stay here."

"No, I'll carry wood with you," Roberts insisted, "Harper can build the fire – the wind has surely blown enough dry leaves and brushwood here."

The men now went about their chores laughing and telling stories, and the girls stayed back at the house alone. But they did not change position, and with hands entwined they stared gravely and silently into each other's eyes. Then finally Marion could no longer control her inner feelings, and throwing herself on her friend's breast, relieved her long and terribly oppressed heart in a soothing river of tears.

"Marion, what ails you?" Ellen asked, alarmed. "For God's sake, what's wrong with you? – Some terrible thing or other torments you – I've seen it for a long time – you are not happy."

"No," sobbed the poor girl and wound herself all the more closely around her friend, who tried to loosen her arms so as to look into the eyes of the weeping woman. "No – God knows – I'm not happy, and – never will be!"

"But what's wrong? For Jesus' sake! I've never seen you like this – you're trembling and shaking – Marion, what do you lack?"

"What do I lack?" asked the Methodist's bride, rising wildly and convulsively, – "what do I lack? – everything – everything in the wide world – trust – love – hope – yes, hope itself I lack, and now – now it's too late – too late – I can't turn back now."[2]

"Marion, you frighten me!" whispered her friend softly as she embraced her fitfully – "what do all these puzzling words mean? *Can* you not trust me, or *may* you not?"

"I still *can* and *may*," Marion now said resolutely and brushed her dark locks back from her forehead – "these next few minutes are still mine, I'm still my own mistress; in an hour it may be too late. – Well then, Ellen, hear what until this moment has made me miserable, what from this moment on will poison my whole life – what's the matter? what is it?"

"Just look there," said the girl, astonished, "isn't that Mr. Rowson? – Great God, his horse must be bolting. – Just look how he flies."

"Hello, Rowson!" shouted Bahrens and Roberts from the edge of the woods, just now catching sight of him – "what the devil has happened?"

"Great thunder!" cried Harper and jumped to the side, since the gasping and frothing animal had nearly run him over – "Rowson, have you gone to the devil? What the hell's happened?"

But the latter did not deign to give the men an answer, nor even a glance. He sprang from his horse, tumbled through the narrow fence gate into the house – slammed the door shut, terrifying the two girls, shot two iron bolts to lock it, ripped his rifle down from its pegs and then looked quickly around the room as if he were firmly resolved to shoot down the first person who stood in his way.

"Almighty God – Mr. Rowson," cried Ellen, frightened to death, "what do you mean to do? murder your bride?"

"Cotton!" Rowson cried hoarsely, once he had satisfied himself that there were no men in the cabin, and without bestowing another glance on the girls – "Cotton!"

"Yes," the latter answered sullenly from above – "I'm here, but – look out down there – the Indian's coming. Hell and damnation – he must have been right on your heels?"

"Come down here – fast!" ordered the preacher, as he removed several small plugs from the gaps between the logs, and thus in no time created loopholes and lookouts – "come down here – we'll soon have work to do. – We have unwanted guests."

Like a cat, the hunter slid down the rough logs of the cabin, and now Ellen required Marion's arm to keep her upright when she caught sight of *the* man whom of all people on earth she feared the most, and who now appeared on the scene under such singular and mysterious circumstances.

"What's the meaning of this? – for God's sake, Mr. Rowson, let us out," Marion implored, at this moment for the first time fearing that she was a prisoner, and in the hands of criminals. – "Let me go to my father – what is the meaning of all this?"

"You'll soon find out, little dove," the hunter said with a scornful laugh, as he took the second rifle from over the fireplace – "you'll soon find out. – But, poison and rattlesnakes," he then went on angrily, turning to Rowson – "you've lured me into a fine trap here – fool that I was to crawl up into that hole. I could be sitting calmly in the canoe now and have a sure five miles distance between me and the knaves out there."

"Back off," shouted Rowson through the opening, without making any reply to his companion's reproaches – "get back, or you're dead!" and in the same instant his shot blasted through the opening in the cabin wall, and, throwing the discharged weapon down, he took a single step to the bed, tore the mattresses aside, and brought four more loaded rifles to light.

"Wait, you red beast," he then muttered to himself – "I hope I've put your spying to rest. – Back from the door!" he thundered now rudely to the girls: "this is deadly serious – back, if you value your life!"

"But what do we do with these wenches here?" asked Cotton angrily.

"Hold them as hostages," said the Methodist, "*their* lives are warrants for ours. – If we can just hold out until it gets dark, then we're safe."

"I don't yet see how," answered the hunter morosely, as he now looked around carefully in all directions and then reloaded his rifle from the ball-pouch assigned to him – "they'll light fires all around the house this evening, or even put it to the torch."

"The girls are our safeguard," laughed Rowson, "but, hallo – here comes old Roberts, alone, without a rifle – he wants his child back again. Can't happen, old man." –

The three men, sooner expecting the heavens to fall than what was taking place before their eyes, had observed the Methodist's explosive arrival with astonishment, and at first believed, as did Ellen, that the latter's horse was running away with him. But hardly had the normally so placid preacher disappeared into his house, and before Bahrens and Roberts, the one with an axe and the other with a lopped branch on his shoulder, had yet reached the fence, the sound of thundering hoof beats again was heard behind them. But just as they turned their heads with utter surprise in that direction, the Indian burst forth, his long black hair fluttering in the wind, his rifle in his right hand, the reins held loosely in his left, and bent down almost onto his right knee in order to more clearly discern the tracks that he followed.

"Assowaum!" cried the men, shocked and surprised – "What's happened? What do you want with the preacher? What's he done?"

"I want his blood!" said the Indian through gritted teeth – "his own red blood – the heart from his body!" and throwing himself from the back of his froth-covered animal, he stormed to the fence and clambered up on it. At the same instant, the Methodist's voice sounded, a shot cracked forth from within, and Assowaum fell down from the fence, the top rail of which he had just reached. But before the men could recover from the shock, he jumped up again, flew around the tall enclosure, and stepped behind a thick tree trunk there, from which he could fire at the back side of the cabin and cut off any escape toward the river.

Bahrens and Harper followed him there. But Roberts walked up toward the house, firmly resolved to wrest his child from the hands of the fugitive. He did not yet know, indeed, what the Methodist was accused of, but his puzzling behavior revealed all too clearly that he himself must be conscious of some offense.

"Get back there!" Rowson shouted to him from the house – "back, if your life is dear to you."

"Release my child to me," Roberts called, "let the two girls leave the house. – I swear to you *I* have nothing against you, I don't even understand what all this means; but you've shot at the Indian – blood has flowed, and I will take the women from a place where they don't belong. Give me my child!"

"Get back there," shouted Rowson menacingly, and raised his rifle. But Marion threw herself into his arms and cried beseechingly:

"For God's sake – man – would you murder my father?"

"Get the wenches off my neck, Cotton!" the preacher cried angrily – "just listen how that fool out there rattles the door – a good thing they didn't all try to storm us at the same time or it could have been bad for us. Now, to work – the girls must be tied up – their arms mustn't be in our way – if they don't keep quiet, gag them too. We only have a few minutes to spare, and we must use them!"

"Help! Help!" screamed and pleaded the two maidens as they felt the rude hands of the two men seize and bind them.

"Robber! Scoundrel!" raged old Roberts, and tore at the oaken door with the might of despair. Bahrens too rushed up to help his friend, and Harper himself, as much as he felt weakened by his earlier excitement, grabbed a freshly hewn branch also to lend the father his feeble arm. But before the men had clambered over the fence and reached the door, the weak, trembling limbs of the two unfortunate women were encircled by strong ropes, and Rowson cried out menacingly:

"Open your lips to another cry and I'll shoot the old white-headed fool down like a dog."

"Mercy! Mercy!" whispered Marion softly and tremblingly – "have pity!"

"Fire out there once, Cotton, but don't wound anyone," cried the Methodist to the other man. – With that, he himself stepped with his rifle to one of the rear openings and tried to get another shot at the Indian. But Assowaum had guessed the preacher's plan, and did not intend to recklessly surrender his life. Accordingly, and true to the conduct of war among his tribe, he had withdrawn behind a tree, and from there he could prevent his enemy's escape until the Regulators, who were following on his heels, should arrive. To capture Alapaha's murderer alive and unscathed was now his sole and solitary aim.

Moreover, he did not know that Brown, to whom he was attached with all the faithfulness of his people, loved Marion, even if he had perhaps suspected it. But this could not, in any event, distract him from his fixed purpose. He would and must avenge his wife, even if the whole world perished in the process.

A bullet fired from Cotton's trusty barrel that tore the hat from Bahrens' head made the rest of the men aware of the danger to which they exposed themselves under the fire of an enemy driven to extremes; Roberts himself now restrained his friends from storming the heavy, solid door by force. They were not even armed, and thus could not hope in this manner to effectively assail the panther in his own lair.

"I'll go to meet him alone and unarmed," Roberts said, "he enjoyed much kindness in my house, and won't now dare to refuse to grant my only wish – the return of my child – get away from there," he pleaded once more when he saw that Bahrens hesitated, and cast angry and defiant glances over at the house, "go – I still hope to resolve everything amicably and find a solution to this mystery."

With these words, and as Bahrens and Harper left the inner enclosure, he turned toward the open crevice behind which he supposed the Methodist to be, and was just about to begin his speech when the latter called out scornfully:

"Stop right there, my liege! – I've preached too long myself to still be able to find much pleasure in such sanctimonious drivel. But in order to come to a short and sweet understanding with one another, hear my words, which this time at least are not meant to constitute a sermon, even if today is the Sabbath, the day of the Lord."

"So I haven't been mistaken about you, after all – knave!" growled the old man in bitter rancor while stomping his foot furiously. "Just go on mocking our gullibility for trusting in your slick words. – But woe unto you, if you disturb a hair on the head of one of those girls that unlucky fate has dealt into your hands; for then your flesh will be torn from your limbs piece by piece!"

"What's the use of talking, I –"

"Stop – don't speak yet," cried the old man in great agitation – "look, you have, as it appears, committed some terrible crime, since otherwise I can't explain your behavior, but whatever it is, you still have time to flee, and I myself will help you do it. – Take one of my horses – take money – but give me my child – give me back the two girls. Remember how kindly you were welcomed in our home, remember that today I was going to call you *son* –"

"Take his offer," advised Cotton, "he won't make such an offer again soon – if indeed I'm included. I'll let the girls go free –"

"Hold on there," the Methodist interrupted him swiftly – "are you mad? Do you think that the Indian behind that tree there will abide by what the old greyhead here promises? Show your scalp at any of the open spots and watch how soon his lead will shoot over here. No, those are just promises to lure us into a trap. There's no safety for us before it gets dark."

"But why don't we blaze a trail now by force? Those three men are unarmed, they *can't* stop us."

"And that damned red-skinned rascal behind the pine won't bombard the whole river bank?"

"But how, if the Regulators should come this way?"

"It's a wonder to me that they aren't already here," Rowson said with a scornful laugh – "a plague on them – I defy them all the same!"

"Then I would like to know how you're planning to escape at night if they surround the house?"

"They dare not risk it in the light of watch fires," whispered Rowson, "since we could have them in our sights from here. But if they camp in the dark, then we're saved. A narrow passage that Johnson and I dug with unspeakable effort leads out under these boards to where the canoe lies hidden –"

"And why don't we use it right away? Can a better occasion be found?" Cotton cried angrily.

"Blind fool!" fumed Rowson – "at this moment that villainous redskin stands right on top of the spot where the boat is hidden in the thick cane. But even if he can't see it from up there, it would still be impossible *at this point* to float it without giving ourselves away."

"But the Regulators!"

"Poison and death on them! whatever is in their power, they'll do, but they dare not risk a hostile attack on the house as long as we have these rifles and the girls as hostages."

"Well," Roberts shouted outside – "have you considered my proposal? – I see that there are several of you. – All of you, go – all of you who have sought protection in the house go free from here, there's still time, since the judges aren't here yet. But give me my child again, set the innocent girls at liberty!"

"Hear my answer!" replied Rowson – "my life is ruined, and that Indian is firmly resolved to take it. If you can persuade him to accept your conditions, well, then I'm ready; but if you can't do that, then remember that at the first attempt to storm this house by force, the two girls will die by my hands."

"The Indian must consent!" Roberts cried gleefully – "he can't be allowed – almighty God – it's too late – here come the Regulators!"

He was right – the dull tromp of some twenty horses was soon attended by the rustling and breaking of twigs and dry branches. Assowaum let out his war cry, and immediately afterward the Regulators burst onto the battleground, led by Brown and Husfield.

"Mee-eu wau iauyaumbaun!" rejoiced Assowaum as they surrounded the dwelling, having quickly surveyed the whole situation – "now he's mine – now I have his blood!"

But Rowson appeared fully to realize the danger that threatened him if he fell into the hands of *this* enemy; he feared even the Regulators less than he did the Indian. Thus, when in his moment of joy the Indian allowed just a small portion of his body to be visible behind the tree, a second shot was fired from among the slits in the cabin wall, and the blood from the chief's second flesh wound stained the ground.

Swiftly incensed by this mad, rash attempt to defy even such an enemy, the Regulators sprang from their saddles and were on the point of tearing down the fence, when Roberts threw himself in their path and announced the distress that his child was suffering.

"Great God!" cried Brown – "Marion in the hands of that scoundrel – what's to be done?"

"Attack," shouted Husfield, enraged – "attack and drive the brutes out by force. – Let them dare harm a hair on the girls' heads and we'll burn their limbs from their bodies one by one. – But if they surrender themselves willingly, come what may, then – then they shall just be hanged, pure and simple. Here are the ropes."

"Spare us your charming speeches," laughed Rowson, who had heard these words. – "Whoever comes closer than ten paces from this house is a dead man. There are six of us and we have eighteen rifles. – But should you, in spite of that, value your life so little – fine, I swear by the everlasting God to which you howl and pray each Sunday that the girls will die a shameful death first – I'm not joking!"

"The devil take the swaggering wretch," cried Husfield as he threw down the fence rails, "follow me, comrades, in five minutes the nest is ours!"

"Stop!" shouted Brown, Wilson, and Roberts, springing to interpose themselves – "stop – that would be murder – murder of the innocent girls. These knaves, driven to desperation, are capable of the worst, and other means must be found to compel them than so recklessly sacrificing the lives of those we want to protect."

"Do you call it protecting them if we leave them in the hands of those ruffians another two minutes?"

"Something must be done," shouted Brown – "but without danger to *their* lives – where is the Indian?"

"Allow us a free withdrawal – give us at least twenty-four hours head start, and the girls go free!"

"Good! So be it!" Brown cried quickly.

"Stop, sir!" Husfield interrupted him – "we have the scoundrels who performed such ghastly deeds, we have in our power the murderer of poor Heathcott, whose blood alone demands vengeance, bloody vengeance; we dare not forfeit that so carelessly. The rest of the group has to vote on this matter. Are you willing then, you men, to let the villain slip away, merely because he now threatens to murder a couple of girls that are in his power? Or –"

"No – no – no!" shouted the crowd, excepting Harper, Wilson, Roberts, and Brown.

"Men – you are fathers too – think of your children!" Roberts begged.

"Roberts!" said Stevenson, who until now had been silent, as he stepped forward. "Don't fret – nothing shall nor may happen to your child; but it would be reckless to set these criminals free because of such a threat –"

"Let's storm the lair," several cried – "he knows what awaits him, and will not want to increase his punishment by a new crime –"

"No, you men of Arkansas!" Stevenson said, restraining them – "it's true that I'm a stranger here among you, but grant me a word –"

"Speak, Stevenson!" said Husfield, "you've acted as if you're one of us, and for that you've earned all the rights that we ourselves possess."

"All right then!" said the old man in a subdued voice, "then hear my proposal – but before that, post guards so that none of the scoundrels escape while we're debating here."

"The Indian keeps watch at the river," Brown said, "and two of us are posted on each side toward the woods; we are here – flight is impossible for them."

"So hear my plan," Stevenson continued, "the prisoners know very well indeed that there's no way for them to reach the woods as long as it's daylight, and so they've placed all their hope on the descending darkness. We can achieve nothing by force, as things now stand, since I believe with Roberts and Brown that, driven to extremes, they will dare anything. So that's why we have to resort to a trick. As soon as it's dark, we'll light our camp fires here in front, and the Indian especially must show himself by them so that he can be seen from the house."

"He won't want to expose himself to their bullets for the third time," Cook interjected.

"There's no need," answered the old man – "it's uncertain shooting in the twilight, and then it'll be to their particular advantage to keep *us* quiet – *they* certainly won't break the peace first. Then their only hope is the river or the surrounding woods, since I don't know whether there's a canoe lying about –"

"No, there's none to be seen," said Wilson.

"Good," the old man continued, "then they'll want to swim across the little river all the more, in order to throw us off their tracks. Individual sentries must be hidden at the edge of the woods (but carefully enough that no one can see them from the house), and I'd bet my neck that we'll catch them if they quietly steal off to the river's edge when it gets dark."

"So I shall know my child to be in the hands of the murderers and thieves for that many more hours?" wailed Roberts.

"That will never do," Husfield interjected, "it's almost eleven o'clock and – plague and poison, I can't wait to see the praying scoundrel hang!"

"Well, if that's what we want, Mr. Husfield," said the Tennessean with a laugh, "then I feel exactly the same way. It'll be a long enough wait for me too, but what else can we do? – let the rascals go? You yourself don't want that; we couldn't answer for it to the whole of the United States; and it won't do to expose the poor girls to their rage. – But here comes the Indian inching along – just look how he stays outside the range of their rifles. They must feel a particular malice toward him."

Stevenson was right – Assowaum glided along like a snake behind the fallen tree trunks, blackberry thickets, and dense clumps of trees, and when he saw that there remained just one small open spot in the woods between himself and the men, he flew across it at a swift run and hid his body among the knot of men gathered there. His caution proved to be not at all unnecessary, since hardly had he stepped into the open space than a third rifle bullet showed how closely his every move was followed from the house. But this time he swung his rifle triumphantly, and held the arm struck by the second bullet out to his friend, who instantly tore his scarf from his neck and bound up the bloody though trifling wound.

"So why does the Methodist have such a frightful rage toward you?" Brown now asked him. – "He never fires a piece of lead if he can't aim it at your red skin."

"He knows me!" said the Indian, straightening himself up proudly. "He knows too that he is doomed by my vengeance – he killed Alapaha!"

"What? your wife? the preacher? Rowson? the Indian woman?" the men cried in shocked and bewildered disarray.

"He slayed Alapaha!" the savage repeated tonelessly – "it was *his* blood that stained this tomahawk."

"The fruit is overripe!" cried Husfield. "It seems to me a sin to wait even one more hour."

"Wait," said the Indian, "if you storm the house, then the pale man will die; he knows his fate; he will be brave. But he belongs to the Feathered Arrow and may not die. He is mine! Wait until the sun is in his bed. Assowaum will lead you!"

"Then at least occupy their attention now," said Brown – "the poor girls are sure to despair if they know we're outside here and don't hear us stir. They'll accuse us of being cowards."

"In any event, we can't give the villains too much breathing space," Wilson said – "otherwise, who knows what they'll do out of insolence. If I'm not entirely mistaken, that rogue Cotton is also with them in there, and he's capable of anything."

"Atkins' mulatto escaped us too," said Cook. – "It's possible that he's found refuge there as well."

"Rowson indeed spoke of six," Curtis interjected.

"Swagger!" said Stevenson – "nothing but swagger – he wants to intimidate us. – But is the place where the Indian stood also manned again, then?"

"Your son went in that direction," Husfield said, "he'll look to it."

"Good – then one more time we'll invite the besieged to surrender, and threaten them with an attack, so that we at least hold them in check," said Brown.

"In what?" Bahrens asked, astonished.

"So that we don't leave them too much time for reflection," said the young man with a smile. "Who wants to be the next emissary?"

"I have nothing against it," Bahrens said, "whatever I can do to help lead the villains away from the right path, I'll surely do. But I'd rather go at the scoundrels with rifle and knife – the devil take them, my forefinger's really itching to send a half ounce of lead over there. If only one didn't have to fear hitting one of the girls."

"Hallo, who comes riding there?"

"It's your Negro, Roberts," said Cook, "your wife will be scared to death at home, for as we came by she looked pale as a corpse and merely called to us to save her child."

"Send the boy back to her and say that the girls are safe," Harper begged – "otherwise she'll worry herself to death. – I hope that we've made those words come true before the lad gets there."

"Naturally I can't tell her how things stand," the old man admitted, shaking his head, "she'd be scared to death. What if she also knew that Rowson –"

"She cried: save my child from the hands of the preacher," said Curtis – "*how* she learned about it, I don't know."

"He betrayed himself," Assowaum interposed. "But time is short. The buzzards are prowling up above – they know their prey. We are the buzzards now, we must swarm around the cabin until evening. The pale man aims the barrel of his rifle at Assowaum, just as the turkey eyes the eagle circling over him. But as soon as the whip-poor-will calls for the first time, the sight on his barrel will blur, and he must watch on all sides in case he does not hear the battle cry of the Ojibwe."[3]

Notes

1. "Smeirs": elsewhere in the novel, the name is spelled "Smeiers."
2. Echo of Corinthians 13:1–11.
3. FG uses the alternate nineteenth-century spelling of "Odjibewas" for Ojibwe.

Chapter 35

Ruse and Counter-Ruse. – The Assault. – Indian and Methodist.

"Save your bullets!" Cotton said angrily, as Rowson took aim at the Indian while he slipped away, and at last, when he sprang across the narrow clearing, fired at him – "you might make better use of them. The Indian is no more dangerous to us now than any of the others. If we fell into the hands of the gang, they might have the ropes ready for us before the redskin could say a word about it."

"And if I were a thousand miles from here," the preacher said, grinding his teeth, "I wouldn't think myself safe until I knew that the red scoundrel is under the ground. – The others, I laugh at."

"He's left his post," whispered Cotton; "wouldn't it be possible to get that canoe afloat fast and at least get over to the other bank?"

"Don't be a fool and stop talking nonsense," Rowson grumbled angrily, while he reloaded his discharged rifle and then examined the flash pans of the others. "Would you really, by acting rashly, cut off our last remaining avenue of escape? If we risk pushing out the canoe while it's still daylight, and we're discovered, which is what will undoubtedly happen, then we've lost our craft and we're delivered into their hands with no hope of escape. But if we actually do reach the other bank, then we'll have the whole gang of howling rascals on our trail. Remember that it's rained."

"True! But if they post themselves around us so that we can't even get to it at night, and then starve us out –"

"Starve us out?" Rowson said with a scornful laugh; "who would die first, then, the girls or we?"

"That's right," said Cotton thoughtfully – "they won't dare do that for their sake – but I don't know –"

"So let me tell you," whispered Rowson, drawing him aside so that the two maidens could not hear what was said. "The place where the canoe lies is so hidden and so far from here that they won't think to post a guard back there after it gets dark. I can guess their plan. They hope that we'll try to get to the river bank as soon as it's dark, and that would have to happen if we hadn't, fortunately, the underground passage."

"And what do we do afterwards with the girls? I'll be damned if I don't feel a very particular desire now to take them with us. If we camp out at night, they could cook our meals for us, and – the devil take them – and afterward a man isn't bound by any great marital obligations."

"They must come with us," Rowson whispered still more softly – "if only in order to shield ourselves from the enemy's bullets fired from the bank, should our escape indeed be discovered too soon."

"Good," Cotton said with a grin, rubbing his hands. – "That rogue – that Wilson is also with the Regulators – it would be a particular delight to me to snatch this morsel right out his mouth. But what if they scream?"

"I will take care of that," replied Rowson softly. "Naturally we must gag them, but we don't want them to realize that yet, so for now let's not pay attention to them at all. In the meantime, I'll tell them some lies to keep them quiet until evening."

"So meanwhile, keep a watchful eye on those fellows so that they don't grab our throats by surprise," he then continued loudly, "and when it gets dark we'll break through; we must reach the woods, and then we're saved. But you" – with this he turned to the girls, "keep nice and quiet until then, and when we leave the house, if you'll swear after that not to call out for help until we're gone a full hour, then you'll be returned to your friends this very day."

"We will pray for your successful escape," Ellen cried joyfully – "but keep your promise, and oh – take off these bonds. I give you –"

"Quit the useless chatter, my little dove," said Cotton, keeping watch meanwhile through the various lookout holes – "be glad that your tongues are at liberty, you must make do without your arms until tonight."

"The ropes are hurting me," Ellen pleaded, "you've tied them so tight they're cutting into my flesh –"

"Well, that can be remedied," said Rowson, as he walked over to the girl to loosen the knots a bit. "And how is my little bride?" he continued, turning to Marion, who kept her face turned from him contemptuously, "are you angry, my little-bitty bride?" he said with a smile, and tried to brush her hair caressingly from her forehead.

"Back, traitor!" cried the lovely girl with eyes blazing with fiery anger – "back – or I'll call for help and defy your threats as well as your weapons."

"But, dearest Marion –"

"To your post, Rowson – poison and rattlesnakes!" the hunter cried angrily – "is this any time for such antics? wait until – the Regulator dogs are dispersing out there again," he interrupted himself suddenly. "It almost looks to me like they're going to venture an attack. I'm damned if I don't want to burn one into *Brown's* skin – he's almost within range."

Trembling, Marion leaned against the bed post to which both girls were tied.

"No – save your lead!" said Rowson, "we don't dare stir them up any more for now. But if they come within ten paces and make any suspicious moves, then *fire*! and naturally, in that event, shoot down the leaders first – Brown, Husfield, Wilson, and Cook – those are the most dangerous."

"And the Indian?"

"He's the exception," Rowson cried, "wherever he shows a bit of his red skin, there I'll fire."

"There goes the dog slinking into the bushes again," said Cotton, pointing through the slits in the cabin wall, "just look how he hugs the ground. It's really impossible to get a good sight on him."

"So go ahead and demonstrate your shooting skill that you're always boasting about," Rowson cajoled him, – "send a piece of lead through that Indian devil's ribs there, and I'll give you two hundred dollars."

"Thunder and lightning, Rowson," said the hunter in astonishment, though without turning his eyes from the figure of Assowaum, which was now visible for a few seconds. "You must be damned rich if you can pledge two hundred dollars –"

He brought his rifle quickly to his cheek as if he would fire, but after a while dropped it again – "can pledge two hundred dollars for one shot; but I'll try it – if he steps in front of my barrel –"

Again his barrel jerked up, but this time as well the "Feathered Arrow" reached a sheltered refuge before the other could get a bead on him and pull the trigger.

"A plague on his shadow," cried the hunter, stomping his foot angrily, "I'd just as soon follow a streak of lightning through a hawthorn hedge with my rifle as this Indian. He shoots along the ground like the arrow from which the scoundrel takes his name. Just what does he have in mind? Rowson – watch the villain – or he'll spy out our boat, and then good night, island."

The Indian had, however, no particular purpose in mind and did not suspect that a sturdy canoe lay hidden in the thick cane that lined the bank and hung down over the river. He wanted only to occupy the attention of the besieged, and then, after darkness fell, he planned to creep up on the enemy; several of the Regulators, among them Curtis and Cook, had firmly promised to stand by him. Even if the besieged carried out their threats, and the girls fell first under their blows, what did the Indian care – his squaw had been murdered too; – no one had helped her – the murderer lay hidden in that cabin, and before another sun shone on its roof, that man would have to be either dead or in his grasp.

Thus hour after hour passed; "the great light" had crossed over the meridian and sunk deeper and deeper. – Already the landscape was colored with softer, redder tints, and the distant mountain ridges and the scattered tops of giant pines glowed like fire. Raptors left the shadowy branches in which they had dreamed away the midday heat, and, like sharks in a glass-clear sea, swept across the green billowing ocean of leaves after their prey; here and there a few merry squirrels still sported with mad leaps from limb to limb and, after sending out a vain summons to their fellow playmates, sought the safety of their nests. Rabbits crept out of their hiding places, hollow trees and dark burrows, and pricked up their long ears in great astonishment when they discovered men occupying the place that until now, and as long as they could remember, had served as their undisturbed playground, while high above in the clear, bright-blue sky a small night hawk rocked back and forth, and now and then sent out with short, broken tones the harsh cry peculiar to these creatures.

The evening came on, and with it a deepening of the conflict, since until now the beleaguers had made only steady efforts to occupy the attention of those they had surrounded, sometimes by attacks they threatened, sometimes through sudden movements, now to this and now to that side.

"As soon as the sun is down," whispered Rowson to his companion – "I'll slip down to the boat and reconnoiter. Hopefully the canoe is in good order; it was, at least, yesterday morning, and the river has dropped only a little. Meanwhile, you keep good watch, and when I come back, we'll first get the weapons down below and – then gag the girls – that must be our last load. If they prove themselves too obstinate – well – you have good bones – a blow of the fist will knock them out; but don't hit them so as to kill them."

"Don't worry," laughed Cotton – "a little swoon can't do any harm, at least until we've first got five miles behind us – after that –"

"Speak more softly – your sweetheart, that saucy thing – is perking up her ears mightily. If they make a racket too soon, it'll spoil our fun. But if they scream a little when they're gagged, well, it won't do any harm; maybe the fools will attack then, and while they're banging their skulls on the oaken door, we've meanwhile gotten through the passageway and come out at our landing place."

"Then we must, in any event, get across the river right away," said Cotton – "we can glide along unnoticed in the shadow of the thick cane on the other side – luckily the wenches are both wearing dark skirts. But what will we do with them later?"

"With the girls?" Rowson asked – "nonsense, don't trouble your head about that now; if worse comes to worst, there's room enough on the island or –

under the Mississippi. Anyway, I'll be on my way – so keep a close watch, Cotton – there's still light enough for you to notice if the Regulators should undertake anything in particular."

"Don't worry about me and come back quickly. The ground begins to grow warm under my feet; I wish I had the paddle in hand already. There goes the red rascal slinking away from the river again – should I shoot him?"

"No – now it's too late," Rowson said as he lifted up the boards that concealed the passageway – "you can't hit him any more anyway. This is the worst time of day for shooting with a rifle; but keep an eye on him – see where he stops; I'll be back again shortly."

With these words, he disappeared into the artificial cave, and Cotton shifted with quick steps from one opening to another so as to not allow a single one of the enemy's movements to escape him, and thus avoid a possible surprise here at the last moment.

"Marion," Ellen whispered to her friend while this was going on – "Marion – take courage – I've freed my hand – when Rowson was loosening the knot, the other knave called out a warning to him before he could tighten them again as securely as they were earlier – I'm free."

"Oh, loosen my bonds as well!" her friend pleaded softly – "I'm about to die from fear and pain."

"Quiet – he's coming," whispered back the circumspect Ellen as Cotton approached, though without paying any attention to them, so that he would not leave this side of the cabin unguarded either. Ellen, however, so as to arouse no suspicion, did not alter her position in the slightest, though she cast an anguished glance around to see where the nearest weapon lay, so that, in case of need, she could seize a knife or a rifle, or whatever it might be, with which to defend herself and her friend.

On a chair barely two paces away from her lay a long pistol, and against each wall – she could almost reach the nearest one – leaned a loaded rifle, so as to be instantly ready in all the various directions.

"Loosen my bonds," Marion implored – "I must despair if any longer you –"

"Just wait a few seconds yet," begged Ellen – "look – as soon as Cotton's in that corner again, I'll be able to move and free you; then take the rifle that's standing next to you. Do you know how to handle it?"

"Yes," whispered the maiden – "my father taught me."

"So much the better – afterward we'll throw the bolt and defend the entrance until we get help –"

"But they'll overpower us – Rowson has promised us safety, after all, if we're calm and quiet," Marion said.

"I don't trust him," replied her friend just as softly. – "I heard some things that lead me to suspect treachery. – Now – now look out – as soon as he steps to that corner, I can help you."

Cotton had gone slowly in a circle with his eye on the gaps left open in the wall, and now approached the bed by which the girls were standing, the curtains of which must hide them from his sight when he stepped behind it.

Ellen had waited on this moment – the thick dark-colored mosquito net concealed him – she had already taken a step forward to seize the weapon – when Rowson's head rose up again out of the tunnel, and the next minute stood in the middle of the room and fixed his gaze on the girls, a picture of intense watchfulness.

"Cotton – do you hear nothing?" he asked softly, as the other stepped once again out of the corner.

"Hear? Where?"

"It seemed to me as if someone broke loose a piece of board somewhere – surely no one could have snuck up to the house?"

"He would have to have been mighty clever," muttered Cotton – "the tall fence is still standing, and really it's not so dark that you would miss seeing someone climb over it. And what would it help if someone were really able to do it? Our loopholes are set very strategically, and if –"

"All right," Rowson interrupted him, "ever since it got dark it's seemed mighty eerie to me here – I wish we were on the water."

"Is the boat ready?"

"All set – so now let's go – most of the Regulators are camped there in front, and even if they do, in fact, have hidden lookouts between here and the river, which I don't at all doubt, still we can slip quietly across the Fourche La Fave and make use of the dark shadows over there for a speedy escape."

"But the girls –"

"Must be made silent; now to the boat!"

"And how do we get our weapons and the box down there? If we have to carry the wenches, then –"

"Just crawl on ahead there and take the little case and two rifles with you – you can't miss – the tunnel is straight as a rope, and the canoe lies directly in front of it. – Put the case in it as quietly as possible – and the rifles, and then come straight back. Everything must be completed in ten minutes."

"What are we taking with us for provisions?"

"I've just put them in. They were sitting in the tunnel and now they're in the canoe," Rowson said.

"Mighty fine! – meanwhile, keep a close watch – I'll be right there."

Rowson walked restlessly up and down the room. Outside, not the slightest breeze stirred – not a sound was heard – a deathly silence settled over the landscape, and only a few dark figures moved slowly around the campfires, a full hundred and fifty paces toward the mountains and away from the house.

"What the hell are the scoundrels up to? are they hatching mischief somewhere or other?" he muttered to himself as he stood with folded arms at one of the openings and looked out through it.

He turned his back to the two girls.

Ellen stepped forward silently and took the pistol from the chair, but instantly slipped back to her previous position, since Rowson turned and walked to the other wall of the cabin.

"Just where is Cotton – the devil take him!" he then swore angrily, resuming his previous pacing, "if he's a two-faced –"

He jumped down into the tunnel and listened.

"If I just had a knife to cut your bonds," Ellen whispered into the trembling girl's ear –

"The plank on which I'm standing is moving" – said the other just as softly and fearfully – "what is going on?"

"These must be friends," cried Ellen joyfully in a voice that was barely suppressed.

"What?" Rowson asked, standing up again so that his head was just visible over the floor.

"We are praying," said Ellen.

"To hell with you," the Methodist said crossly, bending down again.

"I was going to shoot him," Ellen said with a shudder, "but my hand is shaking so badly – I wouldn't have hit him."

"There must be someone under the plank here," whispered Marion – "I feel it clearly –"

"Then lift your foot – it's friends," Ellen said, "the river lies on the other side, and the secret passage must lead to it."

"Almighty God – if I only had my hands free!" wailed the maiden.

"A plague on the knave – I don't hear or see anything," Rowson said angrily, jumping up again. "The devil take me if I don't believe that the fellow's playing me false. But then God have mercy on him – I ought to send him –"

At this moment the plank rose straight up, and the Indian's dark threatening eyes flashed forth from the opening.

Rowson had seized a rifle, and was about to climb back down into the passage, when the heavy board from beneath which the "Feathered Arrow" was pushing out moved slightly and scraped a bit to the side – the Methodist turned his head quickly and there, in the uncertain twilight of the cabin, met the gaze of his mortal enemy, who wanted to make use of the cleric's initial surprise and tried to spring swiftly up out of his awkward position.

But as unnerved and startled as the preacher now was in the first instant of his surprise, he nevertheless gathered his wits quickly enough to be dangerous to the Indian, half of whose body was still stuck beneath the plank. That is, he could neither get up nor go back fast enough, and the heavy gun stock that almost certainly would have sent him to follow his wife was already raised, when Ellen, with a courage that was worthy of an Indian chief, leaped forward and fired the weapon at the cleric, just as he was poised for the death blow.

"Hell and damnation!" the latter cried and toppled backward; but Assowaum required no more time than this to emerge from the constricted space that would have become so very dangerous to him. Like the panther of his native woods, he slid up and out of it, and in the next instant sprang with a wild leap at the throat of the murderer, who collapsed helplessly with a cry of fear and despair.

At the same moment, the plank rose again, and Curtis dove forward into the room. Just then, though, Cotton returned to collect the girls, and, seeing the danger his friend was in, promptly decided to come to his aid.

Ellen, meanwhile, had jumped to the door and thrown back the bolts, while the Indian, boldly defying the new threat, tore his tomahawk from his belt, and, without removing his left hand from his victim's throat, swung it toward the enemy who had just appeared.

But the latter quickly grasped how things stood. On one side, Curtis was hurling himself at him; on the other, Brown was storming through the now open door with his Regulators, and Cotton determined shrewdly enough his advantage. With lightning speed he jumped back into the underground passage and, aided by the darkness, fled to the safety of the boat. But Curtis, who saw the fugitive vanish, thought that he had thrown himself to the ground in order to escape the initial encounter, and afterwards perhaps reach the open. With a coarse oath on his lips, he thus leaped toward him, and the next moment tumbled head over heels into the gaping hole.

"Wah!" cried the Indian, as his eyes glistened with wild joy – "want to know who comes back first."

"Torches over here!" Husfield then shouted from the door, "torches here, and surround the house – one of the villains has hidden himself under the floorboards."

Several of the men quickly came forward with pine stakes that had been kept at the ready, and Cook, wrenching the light from the hand of the foremost, followed his friend. Brown, meanwhile, hurried to the side of his beloved, and, trembling with the joy of victory and the passion of love, he barely was capable of cutting the tight bonds of the poor girl with his hunting knife.

But Marion, stunned by the swift reversal of her fate from fear, worry, and deadly danger to security and happiness, sank trembling and swooning into the arms of her beloved.

Wilson and Ellen formed a separate group at the door.

"Here's an underground passage," Curtis shouted up from below – "the others have escaped. – To the river, you men – quickly, and shoot at everything that moves."

The Regulators stormed off, and immediately afterward five or six shots rang out in rapid succession.

"So the scoundrels had a boat after all," said Husfield – "and the Indian and I were convinced that we had left no stone unturned."

"Are you wounded, Curtis?" asked Cook, who had jumped down and was helping the other man to his feet again at the entrance to the tunnel.

"Yes – no – I don't think so – plague and poison – I dove head over heels into that accursed hole, and can thank God that I've gotten out of it all right."

"Hello," Cook said, as he regarded the spot somewhat more closely – "an artfully made promenade here. Well, every old fox digs emergency tunnels for himself so that he can escape if worse comes to worst. The thing was planned cleverly enough, but I think that the Indian arrived a little too soon."

"Where is Rowson?" asked Curtis, who had now recovered enough to be able to clamber up above.

"Here!" answered the Indian, as he took a leather cord from his bullet-pouch and bound the prisoner's feet with it – "who has a scarf?"

"What do you want with a scarf?" asked Cook, who had likewise worked his way back up again.

"The Methodist is wounded," the Indian said softly. – "The young girl there saved the life of the Feathered Arrow and shot the pale man in the shoulder – Inya!* how pale he looks."

"The Indian indeed feels pity," said Stevenson, who had just walked through the door – "yet another new attribute that I'm discovering about him."

"Pity?" asked the Indian wildly, as he drew himself up straight and cast an angry glance at the speaker. – "Who says that Assowaum has pity on the murderer of Alapaha? But he must not die now – not here – not from this wound, that was struck by the hand of a woman. The revenge must be *mine*! Who has a scarf for the shoulder of the pale man?"

"Here's my neckerchief," said Stevenson, handing the requested item to the Indian, "but – what do I see?" he continued, bending over the unconscious body of the preacher with his torch, "I've seen that face somewhere before – the features are familiar to me."

---

* FG's note: "An exclamation of astonishment."

Rowson opened his eyes and looked timidly up at the speaker.

"Heaven and Earth – that's the murderer of the cattle dealer!" the old man then cried, as he jumped up, half in shock and half in fierce anger. – "By the eternal God, that's the face of the blackguard that shot him down so treacherously."

"To hell with you," cried the wounded man, and, grinding his teeth, turned his face to the side.

"Where is Brown?" asked several voices.

"Here," said the latter softly – "can no one fetch some vinegar? Miss Roberts has fainted."

"My child – my dear child!" cried Roberts, kneeling in mortal anguish next to the limp body of the ashen girl.

"Marion – sweetest, dearest Marion," Ellen whispered to her in her ear, when, after the first surprise and agitation had passed, she had withdrawn herself blushing from Wilson's arms.

"Here's some water and whiskey," said young Stevenson, handing across to the leader of the Regulators a tin cup filled with the former and a demijohn filled with the latter. Brown showed himself not at all unskilled at rubbing the forehead, temples, and wrists of his beloved with a zeal that astonished Bahrens, standing close by.

"Harper!" he whispered to his friend – "is Brown a doctor then?"

"No," replied the other man with a smile – "why?"

"Well, because he really knows how to rub a person; my arm would have gone to sleep long ago. – He works it like a steam engine!"

"Father!" then sighed the beautiful girl, opening her large bright eyes – "Father!" but her gaze did not meet her father's, though he held one of her hands fast in his, rather that of her beloved, who bent over her with tender care and watched with serene joy on his face as the dear creature awakened.

"Father!" breathed the maiden, and closed her eyes again, but with such a calm and peaceful smile that it almost seemed that she took the passing scene for a beautiful dream and feared to lose it by an actual awakening.

"Have you not been able to catch up with any more of the fugitives?" at last asked Husfield, who considered it his duty to take on the responsibilities of leadership now that Brown's surgical talent was so much in demand.

"No," replied Hostler – "didn't catch up with them, but I'm pretty sure that our bullets have had an effect. When we came to the river, we saw the dark shadow of a boat glide along the opposite bank, and immediately fired our rifles at it. Right afterward we heard something hit the water and splash around in it; the darkness was too great to be able to see anything more. Anyway, I hope to God that our leaden messengers did their duty and dispatched at least one of them."

"There was only one more with this one here," said Ellen shyly – "Cotton is his name, you all probably know him."

"Cotton! the – plague," Wilson cried – "didn't I know that the brute had crawled into his hole here. I can't believe that he's escaped us!"

"And what shall we do with the preacher?"

"The Regulator court is tomorrow," said Brown – "and there he must be interrogated. – Another four accomplices are awaiting their judgment at the same time. – You know the place. I would be pleased if you would present yourself there as well, Mr. Roberts. – We need mature and experienced people at such serious hearings. – Who's still out there on watch?"

"Only a few," replied Cook, "the Canadian with a couple of our people. Three or four are gone to cut off the fugitive's route, if possible. Just these two stayed in the nest, and there probably weren't any others hiding here."

"So has no one found a trace of the mulatto then?"

"No – nothing significant – though the Indian thought this morning –"

"He is in the mountains," said Assowaum – "I saw his tracks."

"After the rain?"

"He must have been to the house again after the rain; – the bird whose nest is destroyed still flutters about the tree for a while. The yellow one mourned the loss of his bed."

"Where is Wilson?" Brown asked, looking around in search of him.

"He's outside taking care of the horses," said Husfield – "and it will be best for the ladies to get started. But one of us must stay here and search the place carefully tomorrow by daylight."

"Husfield – will you do me that favor?" Brown asked hesitantly, and, as it seemed to the former, reddening somewhat. – "It could, actually, be that I –"

"Most happily," the Regulator interrupted him, laughing – "you simply must not leave your patient, so meanwhile I'll cover your retreat. Tomorrow morning at eleven I'll be at the appointed place. But you need not delay the hearing for me – just go ahead and start."

"We'll deal with Atkins and Jones first," replied Brown – "and we'll probably have to begin early. So follow as quickly as you can."

"Ah, there are the horses," cried Harper – "well, young man – you little rascal, you don't have even one single greeting for your old uncle this evening. He's probably completely vanished from your mind on account of the young lady, eh?"

"Uncle!" Brown cried, and cordially grasped the hand of the friendly old man – "Uncle – I'm very happy."

"How do we transport the prisoner, then?" asked Curtis now – "we don't have a boat."

"The Indian will take care of that," Bahrens said, "he sits right next to him and stares him in the face like a love-struck girl. Brrrr – it makes me shudder when I imagine, hidden behind that gentle gaze, the bloodthirsty feelings flashing through the head and heart of that Indian. Such savages are really horrible folks."

"I wouldn't want to be in the Methodist's skin," muttered Cook, "not for all the treasures of the globe. If the Regulators were to set him free, I believe the Indian would bite his throat and gorge himself on his blood."

"The wound will not permit him to ride," said Stevenson, who meanwhile had examined Rowson's arm – "the bone is shattered."

"Do you think the wound is dangerous?" asked the Indian, as if waking from a dream.

"If he has to ride and he gets a cold, yes," responded Stevenson. – "The night is damp. Throw in a fever and it could kill him."

"I will carry him," said the Indian.

"Whom?" asked Bahrens – "the whole preacher?"

"Yes," replied Assowaum, and threw his woolen blanket around the wounded man.

"Gentlemen," old Roberts now spoke to the rest of the men – "I've heard that some of you will stay here tonight. These I'll expect for breakfast tomorrow, but the others who are starting off with us now, since the prisoner of course likewise must be transported, and my house doesn't lie so far out of the way, because at this point my wife will already have been mighty worried –"

" – so I invite all of you together," Harper continued with a laugh the speech that Roberts had begun – "to stay with me this evening. Even if we'll be a little cramped for space, it can all be easily arranged – we're in Arkansas, after all."

"Bravo!" Roberts said good-naturedly, "spoken from the bottom of my heart. So, gentlemen, since you so kindly have opened your arms to me and mine – that is, Brown to my daughter, and Harper to my speech, let's get going then. Does the Indian really want to carry the unfortunate man?"

Assowaum answered this question with his deed. Despite his own two wounds, he lifted up the heavy body of the cleric with the ease of a feather ball and, without another word, stepped outside and into the narrow road. But Rowson must have been unconscious, for he lay motionless in the arms of his enemy, and his wan countenance, made horrific by the long dark clumps of matted hair fluttering around it, rested on the shoulder of the avenger.

"He won't actually murder him?" Marion whispered nervously to her guide, on whose arm she had leaned until now, and who now helped her into the saddle.

"No, Marion, you needn't fear any further bloodshed this evening," replied the young man. "But tomorrow morning the court of the Regulators will decide about the wretched man, who has taken on himself a terrible blood guilt three times over. The measure of his sins is overflowing."

Marion shuddered deeply. She remembered the frightful danger that she had barely escaped: to fall victim to this monster – but she said not a word.

"And where is our little heroine, our Amazon?" asked Bahrens, looking all around for Ellen – "hail and lightning, where's she hiding then? I declare myself her knight this evening."

"Too late," said Brown with a smile – "too late, sir – the post is taken – Mr. Wilson had the kindness to assume this duty – since no one else signed up for it."

"Too late? indeed?" said Bahrens – "well, it often works that way for me, and I could tell you a delightful story in that regard, if the sight of that Indian out there hadn't frozen the blood in my veins through sheer horror and fright. Does he not carry his victim in his arms as tenderly and carefully as a doting mother her child, and does he think of anything other than that man's blood?"

"It's true," said Roberts, who was riding next to him – "it's somewhat frightening when one considers the deliberate calm with which the red man approaches his vengeance. But the most precious thing he had in the world was taken from him, and if now he seeks to fulfill the oath that he swore on his wife's grave that time – surely you were there as well, Bahrens – ?"

"Yes!" said the latter, starting up from deep thought – "indeed – yes. – By the way, Roberts, don't you have (just between us) a little drop of whiskey in your house? I know your wife can't stand it – but this evening, I believe, I'd be sick if I couldn't get a proper mouthful. I've completely lost my appetite for food."

"Remind me of it again when we get to the house," said Roberts softly, "but – don't let Marion see it. – The women always stick together, and if they did nothing else, well – one time they upended my bottle and let it drain out, and that would be too bad. – It's real Monongahela."

"Do you know, Roberts, how the Methodist up there in the arms of his enemy appears to me?" said Bahrens after a short break.

"Well?"

"The Pawnees have a legend, according to which a roguish Spanish trader, bound to a horse with the body of the wife whose life he had made miserable, races in eternity over the plains, utter despair always ahead of him; – I don't believe that the Methodist – however long he lives – will see anything but the eyes of the Indian fixed upon him."

"Come, Bahrens, let's ride on ahead, calm my wife, and get the quarters ready," said Roberts. – "It's starting to feel eerie to me here too."

The two men galloped on past the rest of the train. But as their torches illuminated for a moment the faces of the Methodist and the Indian, they saw how Assowaum glanced down anxiously at his victim, but then immediately afterward straightened up once more with a triumphant look and quickly strode on again, as if completely unburdened. – The Methodist still lived.

Chapter 36

The Court of the Regulators.

The place chosen for the present court of the Regulators lay somewhat closer to the Fourche La Fave settlements than that chosen previously, and indeed was on a steep hill or "bluff" that rose up with vertical rock walls on the south bank of the river, and that was bordered on both sides, the east and the west, by valley lowland and thick cane brakes.[1]

About a mile further downstream the river was crossed by the road on which the Regulators had once been misled by Rowson's cunning, and the little hut in which Alapaha fell by a murderer's hand lay, as the reader knows, barely half a mile from this in a straight line.

But as quiet and deserted as this rugged hilltop usually was, since not a single house stood for many miles around, at least on *that* side of the river, it now appeared lively and stirring. Under the slender pines and thickly leaved oaks and hickories, around five different fires, were encamped about twenty robust hunters and farmers, shining specimens of the true backwoodsman, some busy preparing their breakfast, some busy eating it, and once again the blue smoke curled boldly and gaily up into the clear morning air as it had in earlier times, when the original tribe, the *Arkansas,*[2] occupied these highlands.

But as common as such camps are in Arkansas, or in the western woodlands of America generally – two particular groups here shared not at all the other men's appearance and free demeanor. They composed, as it were, the background of this picture and camped the farthest away from the steep slope, under two solitary stands of dogwood trees whose white flowering branches overshadowed them as if a roof of flowers. But the central figures little heeded this charming scenery, and gazed down, brooding darkly, upon the gold leaves of the previous year on which they lay outstretched with fettered limbs.

It was the prisoners Atkins, Johnson, Weston, and Jones, watched by two of the backwoodsmen who leaned on their long rifles nearby.

The other group consisted of only two persons – the Methodist and the Indian. – Above these a red fire liana coiled in rich picturesque windings with its funnel-shaped crimson blossoms, among which the white swelling splendor of the spicebushes and the dogwoods formed a wonderfully charming contrast. Beneath the roof of foliage and flowers a carefully gathered bed of leaves, covered with warm blankets, served as a cozy soft resting place for the wounded cleric, and next to it crouched the Indian. But seldom did he turn his attention from the figure outstretched before him, and then only to maintain the fire crackling nearby in order to make the cool morning air more bearable to the suffering prisoner. Next to him sat a cup filled with water, which he several times brought to the burning lips of the man rendered prostrate with wound fever in order to slake his thirst, while he carefully arranged the displaced blankets again so that not a single raw breeze could aggravate his situation or make it intolerable for even a moment.

The barking of several dogs was now heard no great distance away, and shortly thereafter the Regulators who had participated in the ambush of the previous evening came up the hill, with Brown, Roberts, Harper, and a stranger in the lead, and greeted the men already assembled there. Brown then introduced the stranger to the Regulators as a lawyer from Pulaski County, who, happening to be in the area, heard of their court session that day and wished to attend, if they would permit it. With this, Brown, after explaining that Husfield would be able to join them only in about an hour, declared the session open.

First of all, a jury of twelve settlers was now elected, at which point the prisoners were allowed the right to reject those whom they held to be biased in the matter. But not a one made use of this privilege. They knew well enough how clear their guilt was, and, since Husfield was not present, it appeared that even Johnson was indifferent as to which of his enemies were judges or in the audience. He saw only two trusted, friendly faces among the crowd; but these prudently kept themselves well back and seemed not at all inclined to play an active role in this drama. – They were Curneales and Junnegan, who both leaned against a tree and only now and then imparted their observations in low whispers.

"And who will speak for the prisoners?" Brown asked, as two men from the Petit Jean, Stevenson, Curtis, the Canadian, and Cook stepped forward as plaintiffs against the accused.

"With your permission, I will undertake it," said the unfamiliar lawyer, stepping forward – "my name is Wharton, I'm a lawyer in Little Rock, and I don't believe that you'll deny these unfortunate men an advocate."[3]

Several of the Regulators were about to object to this, but Brown took the floor and declared to the stranger how they were prepared to allow him to defend the criminals. But he should remember that those assembled here had established unrestricted Lynch Law, independent of the power of the state, and would remain true to their principles, whatever the consequences might be.

"But defend these people," he then continued, offering his hand to Mr. Wharton in a friendly way; "if there is anything to say in their favor – so much the better. Far be it from us to wish injustice done; but woe also to the guilty. The laws of the state were too weak and powerless to protect us – we stand here now the residents of these magnificent forests, and we will protect ourselves. – But time is passing, and we have a busy and arduous day before us. Let us begin."

The indictments now began; first against Atkins and Weston as the horse traffickers, and against Jones as the thief or conveyor of the stolen horses. But since there were no witnesses to any thefts committed earlier, they confined themselves solely to the case that had occurred and been discovered most recently.

The secret hiding place for the purloined horses was specifically determined and the guilt of the defendant Atkins established beyond any doubt. Indeed, not only had they found the Canadian's horses at his place, but also two other animals that had been led away from a settler on the Fourche La Fave a short time earlier, so that at last he himself was compelled to acknowledge his guilt.

Weston was then led forward, but he steadfastly denied everything, until a man from the Petit Jean thereupon insisted that he be forced to make a confession and be whipped until he admitted his guilt.

Wharton then, of course, objected to this without reservation, and called it "cruel" and "inquisition-like." But it availed him not – the majority voted for "dogwood." Without further ado, the wretched man was tied to one of those trees and whipped with the flexible shoots of a hickory bush until the blood ran from his shoulder and long black welts ran along his sides and even on his breast, since the tip of the elastic wood had lapped around him like a fishbone.

The pain finally forced out of him an admission of his own guilt. But no hellish torment was capable of bringing to his lips the name of a single accomplice, and at last he collapsed unconscious under the lashing.

The Regulators – aroused by the blood and indignant at the criminal's stubborn silence, as they called it, thirsted for his life and cried out tumultuously:

"Hang him – to the oak with him – he's admitted that he stole the horses, why should we delay any longer with him!"

But Brown at this point inserted himself to mediate and declared this to be against the established process of the court. – That is to say, all must be heard first, and after that the jury would have to decide about the life or death of the prisoners.

Jones' guilt was clear and obvious, and only one opinion ruled regarding it; even Wharton could say but little in his defense. But now their concern was to investigate the more serious crime, the murder of Heathcott, and in this matter those coming forward as accusers against Johnson and Rowson were Curtis and the shopkeeper Hartford, who had been sent for at the Indian's request.

Indeed, only a few days before Hartford had received from Rowson, at second hand, one of those banknotes that he himself had previously seen in Heathcott's possession. It was from the state bank of Louisiana and still carried on its reverse a special identifying mark, the name of one of its earlier owners.

The Indian had later compared Johnson's and Rowson's footprints with the marks on his tomahawk and found them to match.

"Moreover, Johnson tried to murder the Indian," said Brown, "we all –"

"Why waste valuable time with more charges?" someone interrupted him from the middle of the crowd. "The rogue deserves hanging on account of the one murder – but if the jury in fact pronounces him not guilty, which I very much doubt, there's still time to try him for the other one."

Wharton was about to step forward and defend the accused; but before he could even begin his speech, the latter started up despite his fettered arms, and cried scornfully:

"Be quiet with your sanctimonious prattle. The scoundrels have already decided to hang me, and it'll be done – the plague on their necks; but at least I won't do them a favor by trembling and groveling. Yes, you *cowards* –, twenty of you pounce on a single man; I *did* shoot the Regulator, and I'll be damned if I couldn't cut the throats of your whole gang with great delight."

"Away with him to the oak – away – hang the rascal!" shouted most of them, and a few had actually already leapt toward the fettered man. But Brown threw himself between them and cried:

"Stop! Order, you men of Arkansas. We must first try the preacher; the sworn jurors will then pronounce the sentence."

"All right, then – Rowson to the front – bring the Methodist up!" roared the crowd, and drew back again, leaving the space in the middle free.

When he heard his name on the lips of the riotous crowd, Rowson rose up in shock and looked pale as a corpse. But he struggled in vain to stand since his bonds held him down, and Assowaum first had to loosen these and then still had to support this man weakened by loss of blood and fear before he could stand up straight. But his limbs failed to do him service; his knees, trembling and quaking, knocked against each other, and he would have sunk to the ground again had his diligent guardian not caught him and held him upright. As soon as he had collected himself for a moment, Assowaum led him before the court of jurymen encamped on the green field.

"Jonathan Rowson," the leader of the Regulators now addressed him gravely and sternly, "you stand before your judges. You have been charged –"

"Stop – stop – no more," the preacher said in a soft whisper, his eyes wandering wildly and fearfully in every direction – "no more. – You don't need to charge me – I'll confess everything – reveal everything – as 'state's evidence' you may not hurt me. That way I shall – I'm under the court's protection – I shall –"

"A plague on your miserable cowardly soul," Johnson cried in disgust – "look everyone, how the yellow-belly shakes."

"If you open your mouth once more without being asked," cried Hostler, who was doing sheriff's duty there, "I'll knock in your skull with this little piece of hickory here – got it?"

Johnson fell silent, grinding his teeth without moving.

"You can't murder me!" cried Rowson, large bright beads of cold sweat collecting on his forehead and temples – "or – at least you have to protect me from this devil here, who watches over my body as if he hoped to get hold of my soul. I'll confess everything – I hereby declare myself as '*state's evidence*.'"

A murmur of contempt ran through the ranks of the Regulators, but Brown took the floor and said, turning to the wretched man, who lifted up his fettered hands toward him beseechingly:

"This remorse comes too late, Rowson, even *this* can't save you. Accused of three murders, not to mention the disgraceful treachery with which you snuck into the families of this peaceful region, your life is forfeited to this court. Do you have anything more to say in your defense?"

"Here comes Husfield with the others," said Cook, "but they're bringing neither of the two fugitives back."

At this moment, Husfield rode quite close by the prisoners, threw to the ground a bundle that he carried in front of him, sprang from his saddle, and left the animal to itself.

"Anything new, Husfield, that could throw light on any of the various charges?" asked Brown.

"Nothing important," replied the Regulator, "incidentally, here's an old coat that looked suspicious to me, since it seemed so carefully washed and well concealed."

"*Wah*," said the Indian, who had stepped forward and pointed to the place from which one of the horn buttons was missing – "Alapaha seized this button in her death struggle, and here – here was the wound."

Without waiting for a reply, he walked to the silent and motionless cleric standing there, took his scalping knife from his belt and slit his left sleeve up to the armpit, where the red, barely-healed scar from the Indian woman's tomahawk was visible. Assowaum quietly pointed to it, and said softly:

"He is the murderer!"

All were silent – it was as if each feared to break the terrible silence, and Rowson's glance flew fearfully from face to face to find just one whose features expressed compassion and mercy. – They all stood there – each one rigid and cold, and their grim severity, their close-knit brows, announced his approaching fate.

"This pocketbook," Brown said at last, "was also found on this miserable man here who, as it appears, heaped crime upon crime to achieve his dark designs. The sum contained in it – eleven hundred dollars – is roughly the same that was said to be carried by the cattle dealer who was slain on the bank of the Arkansas. Mr. Stevenson has recognized Rowson as the same person he saw that day with the murdered man, a few minutes before the deed was done."

"Do you know this penknife – Rowson?" he then asked the pallid murderer in a lower voice – "do you recognize the bloodstains on it?"

Shuddering, Rowson turned aside and groaned, pointing at Johnson:

"That one there advised it – why pin it all on *me* – why put every crime on *my* shoulders?"

"And you confess that you are guilty – guilty of three murders?" Husfield asked him.

"Yes – yes – I'll confess everything – everything – still more – much more horrible things – I'll tell you about the Mississippi –"

"I object to this proceeding," said the newcomer attorney, stepping forward quickly – "you are eliciting from this unfortunate man here an admission of guilt while he still stands in hope of being pardoned and set free as state's evidence. Moreover, you have elicited a confession from young Weston, or whatever his name is, by force and, in a sense, by torture, –"

"Sir," Brown interrupted him calmly – "I told you at the start that you stand before no legally constituted tribunal organized by prearranged rules. That is just what has forced us to stand up for ourselves, since lawyers practice tricks and intrigues before the courts of the state so that the worst criminals evade punishment, perhaps because some triviality is overlooked in the indictment, or a witness is missing, or else a loophole is found by which someone who can pay gets out of his predicament and avoids punishment. We here are an assembly of *Regulators*, and the law that we practice is *Lynch Law*. These men have been charged, and will be punished if found guilty. – If you can prove to us or even give us hope that one of them is *without* guilt, then you may be assured in advance that he shall thence go free and unhindered. – As far as I know, that is the only thing that you have to do in this matter. What has the jury decided about Atkins? –"

"Set me free," shouted Rowson in despair – "set me free – and I'll confess things that –"

"Silence – I'll save you!" whispered the Little Rock lawyer to him.

Amazed and joyous, the wretched man gazed up at him, but he met only a wary look of warning from the other man as he turned from him toward the jury. These consulted with one another a short distance away concerning the fate of the accused.

After a short while, they returned with a unanimous verdict:

"Guilty!"

Atkins sank to his knees with his hands covering his deathly pale features.

"And Weston?" asked Brown.

"Guilty!"

"And Jones?"

"Guilty!"

"And Johnson?"

"Guilty!"

"And Rowson?"

"Guilty!" sounded forth in a horrifying – bone-chilling chorus. Weston sobbed out loud, and Johnson, darting a poisonous look at his judges, gnashed his teeth with rage.

"You have heard it!" said Brown after a long pause, during which Rowson, forgetting everything else around him, merely hung on every movement of the stranger. It was the *last* hope that was left him, and in his mortal agony he looked on the stranger as a saint endowed with supernatural powers.

"The court of the Regulators herewith declares you *guilty* and sentences you to *hang* for your offenses!" said Brown in a firm deep voice.

"Away with them," shouted some member of the crowd – "to the nearest trees – feed the vultures with those dogs!"

"Stop!" cried Brown, intervening, his hand outstretched toward the men pressing forward; – "stop! the court sentenced them, but, men of Arkansas – let's not rage against our fellow men like wild animals. – All should not suffer the same punishment; all are not equally guilty. So, is there none whom you would want to reprieve?"

"Atkins' child died last night," said Wilson, stepping forward – "his wife lies very sick down there – he's wanted to emigrate to Texas – I would think we let him go."

A momentary silence reigned – Atkins looked with vacant – tearless eyes from one to another.

"I vote for *mercy!*" said Brown.

"And I too," Husfield agreed, "in any event, comrades, let's not start our first court with too much blood. I beg for Weston's life too. The poor devil has made known all of the crimes that he has committed; we can't blame him for not wanting to betray his accomplices; I, for my part, find it noble. Shouldn't the thrashing he's received be sufficient punishment?"

"Yes!" said the men after a brief consideration.

"But he must promise to better himself!" cried a delicate voice. – They all laughed and looked around at the speaker.

"Mercy! Mercy!" now pleaded Jones, who probably saw in the general conduct of the Regulators how seriously inclined they were to take drastic measures, and decided to use this first light-hearted moment to his advantage. "Pardon me too – I've lapsed only once – and anyway, I belong to another county."

"That wouldn't help you much," Brown said – "but in this case I vote that we turn over this man, who admittedly belongs to neither Fourche La Fave nor Petit Jean, to the courts in Little Rock; they can decide about him. He won't come back to the Fourche La Fave, of that I think we can be certain."

"Away with him," some of them cried, "give him to the sheriff!"

"It would be a shame about the rope," said Curtis; "but, gentlemen, I still have something to argue against this last judgment. The fellow has infringed on our laws here, and if they stick him in the penitentiary in Little Rock and he breaks out, and it's obvious that he will, he'll laugh at us from here on out."

"By my salvation, no!" anxiously cried Jones, who may have had some forebodings.

"I wouldn't pay much for that," Curtis replied to him. – "No – as to that, I vote that we first make him acquainted with our various types of wood, hickory and dogwood; after that he can go. Then, at least, he'll remember our little river fondly."

"Curtis is right," said Brown – "and my view is that this Jones, if not so bad as Rowson, is nevertheless one of the wiliest villains that can be found. So if it's agreeable to the men of Arkansas, then that Negro there may pay him fifty lashes."

"Gentlemen!" Jones beseeched nervously.

"Fifty is really too few," cried Bowitt, when the others had concurred, "but, in that case, we might choose another man besides the Negro to punish him; I trust that –"

"Stop," the Canadian interrupted him. "I'll give him the blows – I still owe him something –"

"Mercy! Mercy!" pleaded Jones, who well knew *how* this half-savage would work on his back.

"That has been extended to you," said Brown, turning from him – "if you got what you deserve, you'd get the rope – away!"

"And Johnson and Rowson?" then asked Husfield, looking slowly around the circle while the Canadian led the whimpering Jones aside.

"*Death!*" resounded dully and drearily from every lip.

"Sir – if you're going to save me," whispered Rowson, his features white as death, to the stranger, "it's now high time – you don't know the Regulators –"

"Keep silent and depend on me," the lawyer said just as softly and cautiously.

Wilson had, meanwhile, clipped Atkins' bonds and offered him his horse for the ride home. The latter nodded his head gratefully, loosed the bridle from the branch to which it was fastened, and was about to mount. Then he bethought himself again, remained standing for a few seconds bent over the pommel of the saddle, then turned back and quietly extended his hand first to Wilson, then Brown, and then Husfield – pressed theirs heartily – swung himself into the saddle, and thundered off with slack reins toward his dwelling.

Brown looked after him thoughtfully, and then said to Wilson:

"In his case, this has been beneficial – I shouldn't wonder if Atkins became an honest man."

"Save me – or it will be too late," Rowson whispered again in mortal terror – "you've promised – you *must* save me."

"Lead the prisoners to their death!" Brown said in a low but sonorous voice.

"Stop!" cried the lawyer, now stepping into their circle, "stop! in the name of the law! These criminals deserve death – it is true, but I here openly protest against this court's action, which would be just as much a murder as those that these men committed. Hand them over to me and I will be their accuser before the magistrates of the state, but here –"

"Do your duty," Brown reiterated calmly without taking any notice of this interjection, "has one of the prisoners anything more to say?"

"I will reveal everything!" screamed Rowson – "just hear me – I will reveal everything, if you will guarantee my life. – I will toil in prison until the end of my life – but give me my *life* – only my life. I have frightful things to reveal."

"Your life is forfeited," gravely replied the stern judge. – "Prepare yourself for your death!"

"Back!" shrieked the wretched man – as the Regulators stepped up to seize him – "back with you – I have surrendered myself to the law – I –"

"Stop!" whispered the Indian, who thus far had crouched next to the fettered figure of the Methodist like a panther preparing to spring, but now raised himself to his full height and laid his hand on the shoulder of the criminal, who drew back shuddering at his touch. – "This man is mine. *You* have pronounced him guilty – but *I* am his executioner!"

"No – no – no!" screamed the Methodist in deadly terror – "no – anything but that – away – away, you Regulators, away with me – hang me – hang me here on this tree! – no, not here – a little farther off – a hundred paces – a half mile – but don't deliver me into the hands of this devil! – help! – help!"

Without waiting any longer for an answer from the Regulators, Assowaum bound the arms of his victim with leather cords and took the frantic but helpless struggling man in his arms like a child.

"Gentlemen – this is horrible!" said the alien lawyer, shuddering, – "surely you are not going to allow that savage to drag the man into the woods and there torture him to death?"

Not one of the Regulators answered a syllable – all stared silently at the Indian, whose features, unaltered and calm, betrayed not a trace of what was going through his mind. Even Johnson appeared to have forgotten for a moment the danger of his own situation.

"Have pity!" screamed Rowson – "I am subject to Lynch Law – have pity – save me from this fiend who has ahold of me!"

The Indian stepped with him out of the circle and walked away down the narrow footpath that led to the flat land, and from there to the river.

"No – I cannot permit that!" cried the stranger and hurried after the chief, resolved at least to save the miserable man from this danger. But when Assowaum heard footsteps behind him, he turned his face to the lawyer and cried menacingly:

"Follow me on my dark course, and you will never again return to your people – *I know you!*"

"Save me!" Rowson pleaded – "save me – for your soul's salvation, save me!"

Assowaum turned around, and in the next instant had disappeared with his victim into the thicket. But Wharton stood still as if rooted in the earth, and stared, half-dreaming and almost insensible, after the slowly receding figure of the red warrior.

No one else on the hill dared disrupt the solemn stillness. Each remained in his place with deeply felt horror – the men hardly dared to breathe, and only Brown walked softly and silently to the edge of the rock that towered above the river and, his arm slung around a young oak, gazed down onto the riverbed. There, however, the Indian glided away in his canoe with slow, steady paddle strokes, and in the bow of the boat lay the bound figure of the Methodist.

Jones' screams of pain first aroused the men from their torpor; the Canadian, who saw nothing very extraordinary in the chief's work of vengeance, had meanwhile used the interval of silence to tie the small feeble man to a young dogwood tree, and now, with the best will in the world, let the flexible wood dance around his back. He cared little that the latter, writhing under the painful strokes, screamed and wailed, or that he had already received sixty – sixty-one – sixty-two – sixty-three blows.

Brown intervened at last, and freed the beaten man from his enforcer, who did not seem to think twice about abiding by the allotted number of strokes.

"Since he was already at it," as he said frankly enough, "he might just as well take away the fellow's appetite for horseflesh forever."

In the meanwhile another group had led Johnson down to the tree designated for his execution. Bowitt exhorted him to pray once more. But for an answer he spat at him and turned his back on him scornfully. Not a word, neither plea nor complaint, passed his lips; so the Regulators, disgusted by this last display of impudence, threw the noose around his neck without further ado, lifted him up on a horse – the Negro had to climb the tree and tie the rope onto a projecting bough, and Curtis took the bridle off the pony that stood quietly under the burden imposed on it.[4]

Johnson's elbows were bound together across his back, and he sat up high in the saddle; the rope reached straight up. – For as soon as the horse took just one step forward to graze the grass that grew in abundance on the crest of the hill, it would be all over for him.

Still, the pony did not stir or budge, but looked with its large eyes from one to another of the men, as if it knew and understood that every gaze was fixed on him with great anticipation.

"What's the point of these antics," Johnson now cried half angrily – half anxiously, while a cold sweat of fear ran down his forehead – "take the horse away and make an end of it!"

It required only one squeeze of his thighs for the pony to spring forward – but he did not move a limb – nor did the horse that bore him.

Brown swung himself onto his saddle and galloped down the hill. – The others followed him, though a few of them kept an eye on Wharton. Jones likewise stayed behind, but the Canadian was already watching him so that he did not thwart the sentence as pronounced.

The horse of the condemned man still stood motionless, and Johnson looked half defiantly, half despondently over toward them.

"Come," said the half-Indian now to the horse trader – "I know very well what you have in mind, but you won't spoil that man's sport – away with you."

"But, still, to leave him so –"

"Away with you, I say, or – we're alone now –" and with these words he swung one of the sawn-off switches near at hand. The next moment the men left the place, and Johnson sat alone on the animal that remained silent and motionless – under his gallows.

Notes

1. The trial scene described in this chapter is evocative of several similar climactic scenes in Cooper's Leatherstocking novels, especially *The Pioneers*, *The Last of the Mohicans*, and *The Prairie*.

2. That is, the Quapaw. The word Arkansas is rooted in a French rendering of an Illini word for "the people of the south," a reference to the Quapaw.

3. "Wharton" is, in fact, Captain Kelly, the mastermind behind the band of river pirates mentioned by Rowson as the destination of the stolen horses. Kelly is the sinister protagonist of FG's *Flußpiraten des Mississippi*: a more terrifying version of Rowson, who is ridiculed in that novel as a coward. Even more duplicitous than Rowson, Kelly, or "Mr. Dayton" during the day, is a respected justice of the peace and the guardian of the law in Helena, Arkansas. However, unbeknownst to his respectable wife, he moonlights as the leader of a gang of depraved criminals.

4. Johnson's hanging is no doubt inspired by the failed execution of Bob Rock in chapter 11 of Charles Sealsfield's *Kajütenbuch* (1841).

Chapter 37

Roberts' House.

While on the rocky mound of the Fourche La Fave the Lynch Law sentenced and punished its victims, silent mourning reigned in Roberts' house, where until now Marion's mother had lain pale and senseless on her bed. The swarm of Regulators had left with their prisoners, the sun had climbed high above the treetops, and still Mrs. Roberts had given no sign of regaining consciousness. Then suddenly, as old Roberts began to walk up and down the room with a very grave and thoughtful face, and as Marion, quietly weeping, knelt and prayed at her bed, and Ellen, likewise silent and grieving, sat by her side and held the old woman's cold hand in her own, the latter suddenly opened her eyes and gazed up at her Marion as if astonished and amazed – still not entirely clear as to what had actually occurred. But Marion jumped up jubilantly and with a cry of joy threw herself upon the neck of her mother, who had awakened to a new life.

"Child – dear child –" she said softly, "have you been restored to me? Have you come back to us again? Has the – God have mercy on me – my head spins when I think back on that moment – has the wicked foe who appeared to us in the form of that man gained no power over you?"

"No, my little mother – no, sweet, dear little mother," cried the happy girl – "oh, now all is well, since you've once again opened your eyes so clear and bright. Now everything will be all right."

"But – what's going on with me, child? Is it morning or evening? It seems to me as if I've been dreaming a long, long time. Where did all these people come from?"

"Margareth!" then said Roberts, who had approached softly and carefully and sat himself down on a chair next to his wife's bed. – "Margareth – dear – good Margareth, how are you?"

"Roberts here? and Mr. Bahrens and Harper? and Ellen? – Then you didn't really ride away?" asked the old woman, uneasy and astonished; "did I just dream it all then?"

"You shall come to know everything, little mother," Marion urged, stroking her hand pleadingly – "but now, now you really should stay very still and recover first!"

"Recover?" asked the mother, raising herself up in her bed – "recover? I'm strong and well – only my head – my head is a little dizzy. But tell me, oh please, tell me what has happened. Roberts – Bahrens – Harper – what's wrong with the men? they all look so serious."

"Nothing's wrong with them, Mrs. Roberts," Bahrens answered her, as he stepped up and shook her hand – "not in the least – not any more, at any rate. Only so long as you lay there cold and pale as a corpse, everyone in the room was mighty spooked, so it may be that we're still wearing slightly stupid faces. Harper here is half-way a patient himself. But now let's spit it out; it's best that you know it all at once, since anyway it's not terrible, and afterwards your heart and ours will be easy."

Marion was now obliged to tell the tale; from the first moment, how Rowson burst into the house and Cotton climbed down out of his hiding place, how they were tied up and how Ellen freed herself; Assowaum's first appearance, her friend's heroic deed, and the rescue by – the Regulators, invoking the general name by which the fair girl shyly avoided all mention of the man she loved. All this she related to her little mother, who listened with rapt attention and lovingly pressed her hand in her own, still believing that her precious child was in danger, and unwilling to let her go for fear that she might lose her anew.

"So, my dear girl, to you alone I genuinely owe the life of my daughter," she then said, turning to the blushing Ellen and extending her free hand across to her.

"To me? Oh God, no," replied the latter timidly, "my role in the matter is quite trivial – the pistol – I don't know – I think it must have gone off by itself; at least, I've always been afraid of firearms."

"Ellen was truly our saving angel," Marion interrupted her. "The Indian would have been lost if that shot hadn't fired, and after him – maybe the – one who came next. But in any event the wrathful man would have sacrificed us to his revenge. Ellen is surely the heroine of that night."

"But where are the others? Mr. Curtis, Brown, and Wilson?" asked the matron – "they, who along with the Indian ventured their lives for you so boldly and selflessly, they surely deserve the warmest thanks."

Harper coughed significantly at the word "selflessly," and a scarlet blush spread over Marion's countenance.

"The young men are sitting in judgment of the scoundrels," said Roberts, – "and if you hadn't been so very ill, then I too would have been at the Regulator's court today. When such villainous acts occur, the rascals must be shown once and for all that the old spirit is not yet entirely dead in us backwoodsmen. Well – they will also, without those of us who are here, where we have plenty to do –"

"But didn't you say," asked Mrs. Roberts with a shudder – "that this man – this – Rowson –"

"Let that be now, old woman," Roberts interrupted her soothingly, "when you're quite well and strong again, then we'll talk over these events in more detail; by that time we'll also know the outcome of the Regulator's court. But now, young lady, get for us whatever the kitchen and smokehouse have to offer. We celebrate a festival today, a festival of redemption, and indeed a double one, in both a spiritual and a physical sense, for in a physical sense these accursed horse thieves, from whom not a single hoof in the barn was safe anymore – not long ago they tried to steal Hostler's stallion from the middle of his barnyard, and his fence is over eleven feet high. Still, he doesn't have a 'rider'* on it, and I've told him –"

"And spiritually we can thank our Lord God even more yet –" Bahrens interrupted him, as he saw that Roberts was galloping with loose reins toward New York once more – "at least now the preaching will let up a little."

"But, Mr. Bahrens," the matron said in a reproachful tone – "will you cast blame on such a holy matter?"

"No, certainly not," replied the latter, eager to avoid anything that might upset the still not fully recovered woman – "certainly not – but the benefit of it is that we will be very careful in our choice of preacher, and rightly so. A burned child avoids the fire."

"Hallo there!" cried Harper, intervening – "it has been forbidden to touch upon the matter further until we first have a regular meal in our stomachs, and I find that no more than fitting and proper. We've been sitting next to the bed since yesterday evening and going hungry; that's not for me."

"You shall be satisfied at once, good Mr. Harper," said Marion, stretching her delicate hand out to him with a smile – "you mustn't be cross – Mother –"

"Pssh – pssh – no excuses," said the little man with a laugh – "I know all about it – I myself haven't felt hungry until now. But now that it's happened, I'll say so right away, before it's too late, or gets any later; it can't be very far from midday."

"What do you say we ride over to the meeting?" Bahrens asked – "I have a mighty urge to take part in it."

"We'll get there too late," replied Roberts; "the place is pretty far off, so it would better to wait on it. Brown and Wilson have both promised me to come over this evening and tell us the result. It's very accommodating of them."

"*Very!*" cried Harper, and cast a side-glance over at Marion. But the latter appeared to be busy with her mother and to have missed the remark completely, while Ellen likewise was turning away from them. With extraordinary and praiseworthy zeal she blew the nearly extinguished embers in the fireplace into a bright blaze and laid wood upon them in order to cook the belated meal for the men.

---

* FG's note: "A term for the uppermost fence rail, set up high by special supports."

Meanwhile, the evening drew near; Mrs. Roberts had fully recovered once more, and since the weather was mild and warm, everyone sat under the blooming dogwood tree in the little garden. The place was, indeed, particularly pleasant, not only on account of the numerous shade trees, but also because of Marion's careful hands which had made a home here for several wild woodland flowers that delighted the eyes with their luminous colors.

But as often as they might turn the conversation to more distant and indifferent subjects, their eyes again and again flew toward the direction from which they expected their friends, and again and again the probable result of those grave proceedings formed the axis around which revolved their suppositions and observations.

"They probably won't punish him so severely," said Mrs. Roberts at last after a short pause, during which they had stared thoughtfully at the ground – "if the wound was so bad, that's surely punishment enough –"

"For such crimes?" asked her spouse, sternly and reproachfully. Shuddering, the matron buried her face in her hands.

"The Indian took pity on him," whispered Marion demurely – "he cared for him with a tenderness of which I had not thought him capable –"

"The Indian?" the old lady asked, looking up at her daughter with astonishment – "the Indian cared for – his wife's murderer?" she then repeated, still incredulous and amazed.

"Yes – as we take care of the cattle that we're going to slaughter," Bahrens said with a slight shudder; "to me the Indian never seemed so frightful as in this loving care – I just can't get rid of his image."

"And you – poor – poor child," the mother said now, turning lovingly to the maiden sitting next to her; "who can ever make you amends for this terrible deception?"

"*Brown!* truly – there he comes running," cried old Roberts, while Marion, shocked at first, looked up at him and then, trembling and blushing, buried her face in her mother's chest.

"And there's Wilson too," Harper cried – "well, now we'll discover how it's all turned out."

"They look serious and solemn," said Bahrens.

"A serious and solemn business it was, too, that they've concluded," replied Roberts; "but a fine and noble right they've exercised at the same time, the right of self-protection – of self-defense, and that we'll preserve in Arkansas as long as we still have marrow in our bones and blood in our veins."

At this moment the two men raced up, threw themselves off their horses, jumped over the fence, and greeted their friends with warm words and handshakes.

Chapter 38
The Revenge of the "Feathered Arrow."

Gently and silently, a small slender canoe, guided by a sure hand, glided under the overhanging swaying reeds and the fluttering, waving willows bending down to the green bed of the happily babbling stream. Not a sound was heard as the paddle was lifted, lightning-quick, from the water after each stroke; not a sound was heard as it was dipped just as quickly back into the flood. A stag that had come down to the water drank on calmly; barely fifty paces away the dark shadow glided by, silent and ghostly – he saw it not; only when the canoe had disappeared in the distance, melting into the reeds and bushes through which it shot, did the skittish creature lift his beautiful head. He snorted, stamped his foreleg on the gravelly bank on which he stood, and trotted slowly and proudly back into the thicket from which he had barely emerged. A telltale breeze had carried to him the scent of his enemy.

Gently and silently the canoe glided onward, and only the swirling air bubbles that frothed and boiled to the surface with each powerful stroke of the paddle revealed the path that it took, as they sprang up in small isolated eddies, only to dissolve and disappear into the current that had produced them.

The Indian steered the canoe, and in the bow lay, bound and senseless from fear and exhaustion, the Methodist.

The prow of the small slender vessel was now pointed across the river; a few minutes later it ran up on the smooth pebbles of the shallow bank and stopped. Rowson opened his eyes and looked around, but shuddered when he recognized the place where he had, that night, murdered the wife of the man whose prisoner he now was, and from whose vengeance no God could protect him.

The boat landed, and Assowaum sprang to the shore, winding the grapevine that served him for an anchor rope around a small birch that stood there. He then returned to his craft, and slowly and carefully lifted his prisoner from it.

"What do you mean to do, Assowaum?" he pleaded in a hoarse and faltering voice. – No answer was given him. – "Only speak! – in the name of all the saints, speak!" cried the perjured preacher in despair – "speak, and let me know the worst!" Silently his executioner carried him up the bank and into the hut, the scene of his crime.

Rowson turned his face in terror from the place that he knew only too well and closed his eyes. Assowaum calmly laid him in the middle of the hut, right next to a small hickory sapling that had sprung up there. Not a sound broke the deathly silence, save the heavy breathing of the unfortunate one. It was just the spot where Alapaha's body had lain. The Methodist could no longer bear the tormenting suspense; he glanced up, and saw the Indian crouching very close to him, as though ready to leap, watching his slightest movements keenly and carefully, but otherwise stock-still and seemingly lost in contemplation of his victim. A triumphant smile passed over his dark features as he studied the look of anguish and terror on his victim's face. He now rose silently, took from his belt a catch rope, and tied his already bound prisoner, carefully and firmly, to the tough young tree against which he lay.

In vain the unfortunate man offered him treasures and wealth; in vain he told him of gold that he had buried, all of which he would give to him, his enemy, if he would set him free, or at the very least end his agony with a blow from his tomahawk. Silent, as though he did not understand the words that the other breathed passionately into his ear, the "Feathered Arrow" finished his vengeful task. The Indian left him for a few moments – helpless, bound by hand and foot, and held fast to the floor by the young tree – and returned with some dried leaves and brushwood.

Now, for the first time, a dark foreboding shot through the mind of the miserable man. – He knew the customs of the savage races of the West, knew their merciless cruelty, and a wild and shrill shriek of agony and terror broke from his breast, while he struggled furiously against his bonds, all in vain. The Indian did not hinder him – a gag would have prevented any further cries of pain, but no, every sound was music to his ear. Laughing, he bent down, and blew the smoking leaves into flame. This done, he brought a bundle of resinous pine sticks that he had quickly split, and from the circle of flames that formed around the walls of the hut, a ribbon of fire rose whose fiery tongues licked greedily at the dry limbs.

Louder and still louder echoed the piercing cries for help through the silent woods, but the Indian only more intently fed the flames so that it could not be extinguished on any side. The victim was quickly engulfed, as though in a broad sea of fire.

Only now, as the heat became unbearable, and his skin was blistered in many places, did he leave the brightly glowing room and, once outside, swinging his tomahawk and chanting in loud and jubilant tones, began his song of victory and triumph.

Ghastly were the preacher's howls and screams of torment – ghastly was the crackling and flashing of the anguished flames of the brushwood whose smoke rose sluggishly through the green canopy of leaves and forced its way into the clear, bright spring air. But here it stayed; the yellow-green cloud lay like an eerie and somber veil over the sea of leaves from which it had barely risen.

Wilder and more horrible grew the cries for help from the sufferer, and louder and more jubilant sounded the joyful song of the Ojibwe, so that a wolf jumped from his hidden lair nearby and fled in fear, looking for a quieter and cozier bed.

Finally, the rafters of the decaying roof collapsed – throwing up a great shower of sparks – *one* frenzied cry of pain broke from the rising tongues of flame – a black cloud rolled heavily from the fire and – it was all over.

The blood-red sun sank behind the distant mountain ridges; but near the scene of the fire stood the red warrior, brandishing his weapon and chanting his monotonous wild song of revenge and victory:

> Alapaha!
> From the grave, from the gloomy
>> Grave, rise,
> Hurry, hurry as in earlier days
>> To me, beloved,
> For your blood, it is atoned;
>> In the flame
> Twists and dies your murderer – Alapaha!

> Below – below,
> Right on the ground I lay listening
>> Here in the valley,
> And I heard your voice in the grave
>> Below – below,
> Your soft, soft laments;
>> And they called,
> Urging me to revenge – See, I obeyed.

> Out of the embers
> Shrill and loud sound his cries of woe,
>> Alapaha,
> Howling he tears at his fetters,
>> But in vain;

Weaker and weaker grow his ravings,
    And finished,
At last my vengeance! – at last! at last!

Chapter 39
Coda.

"So you've been in love with the girl all the while, Brown, and haven't said a word to me about it?" old Roberts asked the latter, as he held the young man's hand firmly in his.

Brown pressed it in silence; then he replied warmly:

"What would it have helped, sir? I had come too late and couldn't complain."

"And that scoundrel had almost –"

"He has been punished," Brown broke in as he spoke. "But now tell me honestly and frankly, will you entrust your daughter's happiness to me?"

"Yes – but hail and lightning," the old man said with a laugh of real surprise – "you ask me that as if I had a word to say at all about the whole business. Did I, in Rowson's case –"

"Roberts," the mother interrupted him pleadingly.

"But the girl," the latter cried, shaking his head – "she's the main person in this case, in any event."

"Father," begged Marion, who until this point had buried her delicate head in her mother's bosom, and now threw herself lovingly around the old man's neck.

"Ah!" said the latter, half laughing, half amazed – "so *that's* how things stand? Well, when the game rears up right away, the hunter has an easy chase. Besides –" he cried, shaking his finger at Brown while he kissed his darling child's forehead – "it seems to me that today isn't the first time the gentleman's been on the trail."

"And the mother?" asked Brown, leading the fair maiden over to her.

"Take her, sir," said the old woman, trembling – "she seems to be sweet on you, and I – I've sadly lost the right to make a choice for her."

"Mother," Marion pleaded, "don't talk so; you thought that you were only looking out for my happiness."

"Yes, I thought so, child; the Almighty is my witness. I believed it with a firm, heartfelt conviction; but the Lord alone knows the hearts of men; we poor mortals are weak and blind."

"Thanks – thanks – my deepest thanks, good people," cried Brown, as he clasped the lovely maiden fondly to his heart. "I hope that you shall never regret having entrusted your only child to me."

"And the boy doesn't ask me about it at all," then said Harper, who with moist eyes stepped forward and pressed his nephew to his heart – "you capital scamp – he doesn't act as if he had an uncle at all."

"I know your kindness, dear uncle," cried the young man, embracing him, "and I hope that a joyful, happy life will now blossom for you too."

"Yes," said Harper, as he passed his coat sleeve rapidly over his eyes, released his nephew, and put his hand on the head of his future niece: "it was inevitable that *this* life should one day end. Anyway, I couldn't have stood it any longer; Bahrens here and I are planning to set out on some ramblings within the month."

"Where to?" asked Madame Roberts, astonished.

"Where to?" said Harper – "to nowhere, to stay here, and to marry. Now the young fellow's grinning again, as if I were too old to marry. Listen, lad –"

"Here come riders!" cried Bahrens, pointing in the direction of the river, and immediately thereafter Stevenson, Cook, and Curtis burst into the clearing that wrapped around the farm.

Stevenson warmly greeted the women, whom he knew as old friends and neighbors, but shook his head and laughed when Mrs. Roberts reproached him for not having brought his wife and daughters to visit her. She had not, as she said, seen them in such a long time and so wanted to talk with them again at last.

"We can ride up there tomorrow," said Roberts.

"That's not necessary!" Stevenson cried in response, "you'll see us all you want, and get tired of us."

"How's that? You're staying here?" Roberts asked quickly.

"I've bought Atkins' farm," said the old Tennessean. "I like this region – the poor devil wanted to leave, and – so I made a deal with him."

"But you can hardly have yet examined the place, since that evening –"
"That's not really necessary," Stevenson said with a smile. "If it doesn't suit me, well, Crawford County won't run away from me. But if it's as Mr. Curtis and Mr. Cook here describe it, then I won't need to move again. I like the neighbors as well, since the pack has now been cleaned up a bit, and I'm beginning to see that the Fourche La Fave is not at all as bad as people make out."

"Well done, Stevenson, well done!" cried Roberts, shaking both his hands with great delight. "This is a lucky day. Hell and – well, all right – the dev – oh – foxes and wolves – listen, old woman, today you must allow me to curse for once, or it won't come out as sincerely as I mean it. But I'll be damned if

I know a time when I've been so pleased. Children – where's Ellen then? that noble girl can't miss –"

"In the house," said Brown.

"Alone in the house? Ay, why doesn't she come with us then? From now on she belongs to the family."

"As for her being *alone*," Brown answered him, laughing, "I believe that Mr. Wilson has taken care of that."

"Ah ha!" said Roberts – "so that's where the turkey hides? Well, come then, children, since she wants to know nothing of us, we must seek *her* out. But you are all my guests, and Stevenson, by jingo – where's your son, then?"

"I've sent him to the women, to calm them down," the old man said.

"Well done; so Stevenson must bring his family down here tomorrow as well; we'll make up a camp here, and next week – or as soon as it suits the young people – since they really have the principal say in the matter, after all – or at least they'll undertake what – if a person in the light of day –"

"Examines it, is perfectly right," Harper interrupted him, laughing – "so we'll have a wedding, and after that," he continued with a humorous glance aside at Brown, "a certain young man will leave his old uncle sitting here alone high and dry, climb on a chestnut horse acquired especially for this purpose, and ride to –"

"Little Rock – my little uncle," Brown inserted, extending his hand across to him – "there in order to buy the land on the Fourche La Fave where he and his young wife will live with this same old uncle from now on."

"And won't the governor be angry with you Regulators who have broken his laws?" Marion shyly asked her beloved, as she nestled tighter and closer to his chest.

"He might," the young man said with a smile, brushing the forehead of the lovely maiden with a soft kiss. "We have defended our rights and destroyed the brood that crawled, swollen with poison, through these stately woods. It was precisely his helplessness that made these criminals think that, even if discovered, they could in fact commit atrocity after atrocity unpunished. But our band of Regulators showed them the power that the simple farmer is capable of exercising the minute necessity and his own safety demand it. The danger is passed, and gladly will we once more exchange the executioner's sword for the peaceful field tools of the farmer."

* * *

The rest is soon told.

As for Wilson and Ellen, this time old Roberts had, as an old Arkansas saying has it, by no means "barked up the wrong tree."[1] That same week a justice of the peace who lived not far away placed both couples' hands in one another, and while Brown rode to Little Rock to look after the purchase of his land, Wilson wrote to his old mother in Memphis to invite her to join him, so that she could spend her final days by his fireside in peace and quiet.

By the next morning Atkins had left the Fourche La Fave, though he camped in the vicinity for a short while in order to conclude his business with Stevenson. But this occurred through the mediation of Curneales, since he could not resolve to associate again on friendly terms with a man by whose aid he had been delivered to punishment or abuse, even if both were deserved. With Wilson, however, he had another conversation, and Ellen also took leave of her foster parents before they left the state forever.

About Cotton, nothing further could be learned; an overturned canoe with a bullet hole in its side was found drifting below Harper's house; the only possible conjecture was that this was the same one in which the accomplices had tried to flee; but Cotton himself had disappeared without a trace, and since no one discovered any further tracks on the river bank, the belief soon won general currency that the fugitive, if not struck by one of the bullets fired at him, was nevertheless overturned with the boat, and, hindered in swimming by his clothes and perhaps some other baggage he had taken along, drowned. Similarly, little was learned about the mulatto, although the men who a few days afterward cut down Johnson's body and buried it claimed to have seen the shadow of his dark form on the edge of the cane brake that stretched from the bank of the Fourche La Fave back toward the hill.

The lawyer from Little Rock had, immediately following the conclusion of the meeting, thrown himself on his horse and raced off at a full gallop, though, as was later learned, not in the direction of Little Rock, where no one knew anyone named "Wharton."

The Indian, however, remained camped next to his wife's grave for nine days after the death of the Methodist, maintained a fire there, and nightly brought her his offering of food and drink. But on the morning of the tenth day, he walked, with blanket and rifle on his shoulder and ready for travel, into Harper's cabin, which, until their own house was erected, the young newlyweds occupied for the time being. There he gravely and silently extended a parting hand to his friend.

"And will the Feathered Arrow not end his days with his friends?" Brown asked him warmly; "Assowaum has no one who will cook for him and mend his moccasins. Will he share the roof of my cabin with me?"

"You are good!" said the Indian, as he nodded his head in a kindly manner; "your heart means the same as your words, but Assowaum must hunt. The white men have killed the game on the Fourche La Fave; the tracks of the deer have become scarce, and bears now come only as wanderers into the bottom lands of this valley. The herds of the whites have thinned out the cane thickets in the swamps, and in vain the bear looks around them for a bed. Assowaum is sick; buffalo meat will make him healthy. He moves to the west."

"Then at least don't go so far, and when you are tired of your wanderings, return to us; you have a home here."

"My brother is good – Assowaum will think of this."

"And Ellen? – have you already taken leave of her?" Brown asked him.

"Assowaum never forgets those who were good to him," said the Indian. "The young girl saved his life, but still more – she saved his vengeance. – My path leads past her house – Good bye!"

Once more the chief shook his white friend's hand warmly and heartily – likewise that of his young bride – once more he waved back a final farewell, and the next moment the thick foliage of the bushes closed behind him as, springing over the fence, he vanished into the woods, into the green, blossoming, fragrant woods.

THE END

Note

1. The expression is not limited to Arkansas, but this appears to be one of its earliest uses. It was first recorded in James Kirk Paulding, *Westward, Ho!* (1832).

Selected Bibliography

Bukey, Evan Burr. "Friedrich Gerstaecker in Arkansas." *The Arkansas Historical Quarterly* 31, no. 1 (Spring 1972): 1–14.

Cochran, Robert. "The Gentlemen and the Deerslayer: Contrasting Portraits of Pioneer Arkansas." *The Arkansas Historical Quarterly* 53, no. 1 (Spring 2014): 31–41.

Condray, Kathleen. "The *Kerl* in the Wild West: Friedrich Gerstäcker's *Die Regulatoren in Arkansas* and Friedrich Schiller's *Die Räuber.*" *The Arkansas Historical Quarterly* 53, no. 1 (Spring 2014): 69–77.

Condray, Kathleen and Patrick Williams, eds. "The Legacy of Friedrich Gerstäcker: Arkansas and the Wild West." Special issue, *The Arkansas Historical Quarterly* 83, no. 1 (Spring 2014).

Evans, Clarence. "Friedrich Gerstäcker, Social Chronicler of the Arkansas Frontier." *The Arkansas Historical Quarterly* 6 (Winter 1947): 440–49.

———. *Beiträge zur Friedrich-Gerstäcker-Forschung,* 2 ("Ein kulturelles Band zwischen dem Deutschland des 19. Jahrhunderts und den Arkansas Ozarks"; "Slowtrap vom Fourche la Face"; "Gerstäcker und die Konwells vom White-River-Tal"). Braunschweig: Friedrich-Gerstäcker-Gesellschaft, 1982.

Fletcher, John Gould. *Arkansas.* 1947. Fayetteville, AR: The University of Arkansas Press, 1989.

Gerstäcker, Friedrich. *Australia: A German Traveller in the Age of Gold.* Edited by Peter Monteath and translated by Peter Monteath et al. Mile End, South Australia: Wakefield Press, 2016.

———. *Die Flußpiraten des Mississippi,* 4th ed., 3 vols. Leipzig: Costenoble, 1862.

———. *Gerstäcker's Louisiana: Fiction and Travel Sketches from Antebellum Times through Reconstruction.* Edited and translated by Irene S. Di Maio. Baton Rouge: Louisiana State University Press, 2006.

———. "Geschichte eines Ruhelosen." *Die Gartenlaube* 16 (1870): 244–247.

———. *Heimliche und unheimliche Geschichten.* Munich: Borowsky, 1980.

———. *In the Arkansas Backwoods: Tales and Sketches by Friedrich Gerstäcker.* Edited by James William Miller. Columbia, MO: University of Missouri Press, 1991.

———. *Die Regulatoren in Arkansas: Aus dem Waldleben Amerikas—erste Abteilung.* Edited by Thomas Ostwald und Wolfgang Hochbruck. Braunschweig: Friedrich-Gerstäcker-Gesellschaft, 2004.

———. *Wild Sports: Rambling and Hunting Trips through the United States of America.* Foreword by Robert Wegner. Mechanicsburg, PA: Stackpole Books, 2004.

Graf, Andreas. *Abenteuer und Geheimnis: Die Romane Balduin Möllhausens.* Freiburg: Rombach, 1993.

Hochbruck, Wolfgang. "Leatherstockings and River Pirates: The Adventure Novels of Friedrich Gerstäcker." *The Arkansas Historical Quarterly* 53, no. 1 (Spring 2014): 42–55.

———. "'Re-cognition' of the Borderlines of German-American Authorship: The Case of Friedrich Gerstäcker." *Comparative American Studies* 4, no. 3 (2006): 269–84.

Möllhausen, Balduin. *Geschichten aus dem Wilden Westen.* Edited by Andreas Graf. Munich: dtv, 1995.

Ostwald, Thomas. *Friedrich Gerstäcker. Leben und Werk: Biographie eines Ruhelosen.* Braunschweig: Friedrich-Gerstäcker-Gesellschaft, 2007.

Prahl, Augustus J. "Friedrich Gerstaecker, the Frontier Novelist." *The Arkansas Historical Quarterly* 14, no. 1 (Spring 1955): 43–50.

Rupp, Caroline S., with additions by Wolfgang Hochbruck. "Publications in the United States of America / Veröffentlichungen von Friedrich Gerstäcker-Texten in den USA." Special issue, *Mitteilungen der Friedrich-Gerstäcker-Gesellschaft* 29 (October 2006).

Sammons, Jeffrey L. *Ideology, Mimesis, Fantasy: Charles Sealsfield, Friedrich Gerstäcker, Karl May, and Other German Novelists of America.* Chapel Hill: University of North Carolina Press, 1998.

Smith, Kimberly G. and Michael Lehmann. "Friedrich Gerstäcker's Natural History Observations in Arkansas, 1838–1842." *The Arkansas Historical Quarterly* 53, no. 1 (Spring 2014): 17–30.

Stäge, David and Thomas Ostwald. *Vergleichslesung "Regulatoren in Arkansas." Beiträge zur Friedrich-Gerstäcker-Forschung,* 8. Braunschweig: Friedrich-Gerstäcker-Gesellschaft, 2001.

Steinbrink, Bernd. *Abenteuerliteratur des 19. Jahrhunderts: Studien zu einer vernachlässigten Gattung.* Tübingen: Niemeyer, 1983.